M

So

W

"Marksman."   Copyright © 1940 by
    published in *Clues*, September 1940.

"They'd Die for Linda." Copyright © 1946 by Street & Smith Publications, Inc.
    First published in *S&S Detective Story Magazine*, September 1946.

"Tin–Pan Alibi." Copyright © 1946 by ~~Popular Publications, Inc. First published in~~
    Dime Detective, November 1946.

"Creature of Habit."   Copyright ©
    published in *Fifteen Mystery Stories*

"Dead End for Delia." Copyright ©
    published in *Black Mask*, Novembe

"Conspiracy." Copyright © 1957 by
    Alfred Hitchcock's Mystery Magazi

"The Unholy Three." Copyright © 19
    published in *Manhunt*, May 1956.

"Deadly Beloved." Copyright © 195
    published in *Manhunt*, October 195

"Death of a Big Wheel." Copyright ©
    published in *Manhunt*, April 1957.

"Don't Crowd Your Luck." Copyright
    published in *Ellery Queen's Myster*

"No Client of Mine."   Copyright ©
    published in *Mercury Mystery Mag*

"Stolen Star." Copyright © 1957 by Fl
    in *Manhunt*, November 1957.

DATE DUE

DEMCO, INC. 38-2931

Marksman and Other Stories

Marksman and Other Stories by William Campbell Gault is set in 10-point Times New Roman font and printed on 60 pound natural shade opaque acid-free paper. The cover illustration is by Tom Roberts and the Lost Classics design is by Deborah Miller. *Marksman and Other Stories* was published in March 2003 by Crippen & Landru, Publishers, Norfolk, Virginia.

Marksman and Other Stories

CRIPPEN & LANDRU LOST CLASSICS

Crippen & Landru is proud to publish this series of new short story collections by great authors of the past who specialized in traditional mysteries. All first editions, each book collects stories from crumbling pulp, digest, and slick magazines, and from collectors and the estates of the authors. Each is published in cloth and trade softcover.

The following books are in print:

Peter Godfrey, *The Newtonian Egg and Other Cases of Rolf le Roux*, introduction by Ronald Godfrey
Craig Rice, *Murder, Mystery and Malone*, edited by Jeffrey A. Marks
Charles B. Child, *The Sleuth of Baghdad: The Inspector Chafik Stories*
Stuart Palmer, *Hildegarde Withers: Uncollected Riddles*, introduction by Mrs. Stuart Palmer
Christianna Brand, *The Spotted Cat and Other Mysteries from the Casebook of Inspector Cockrill*, edited by Tony Medawar

The following are in preparation:

Gerald Kersh, *Karmesin: The World's Greatest Crook — Or Most Outrageous Liar*, edited by Paul Duncan
Joseph Commings, *Banner Deadlines*, edited by Robert Adey
Margaret Millar, *The Couple Next Door: Collected Short Mysteries*, edited by Tom Nolan
William L. DeAndrea, *Murder — All Kinds*, introduction by Jane Haddam
C. Daly King, *The Complete Mr. Tarrant*, introduction by Edward D. Hoch
T.S. Stribling, *Dr. Poggioli: Detective*, introduction by Arthur Vidro
Philip S. Warne, *Who Was Guilty?: Three Dime Novels*, edited by Marlena Bremseth
Helen McCloy, *The Pleasant Assassin and Other Cases of Basil Willing*, introduction by B. A. Pike
Rafael Sabatini, *The Evidence of the Sword*, edited by Jesse Knight
Gladys Mitchell, {*Untitled Short Story Collection*}, introduction by Nicholas Fuller

Marksman and Other Stories

By William Campbell Gault

Edited and with an introduction by Bill Pronzini

Crippen & Landru Publishers
Norfolk, Virginia
2002

ISBN (cloth edition): 1–885941–92–7

ISBN (trade edition): 1–885941–93–5

FIRST EDITION

Crippen & Landru Publishers
P.O. Box 9315
Norfolk, VA 23505
USA

www.crippenlandru.com
CrippenL@pilot.infi.net
CrippenLandru@hotmail.com

Contents

Introduction

William Campbell Gault was a writer of the old school, a consummate professional throughout a distinguished career that spanned more than half a century. From 1936 to 1995 he published scores of novels, both mysteries and juvenile sports fiction, and hundreds of short stories, and counted among his awards an Edgar from the Mystery Writers of America and the Life Achievement Award from the Private Eye Writers of America. Noted author and critic Anthony Boucher said of him: "(He is) a fresh voice — a writer who sounds like nobody else, who has ideas of his own and his own way of uttering them." Another of his peers, Dorothy B. Hughes, stated that he "writes with passion, beauty, and with an ineffable sadness which has been previously been found only in Raymond Chandler."

He was in his mid–20s when he entered a story called "Inadequate" in a Milwaukee *Journal–McClure* Newspaper Syndicate short story contest. The judges found it to be anything but inadequate, awarding it the $50 first prize. Spurred on by this success, he wrote and placed several more stories with the McClure Syndicate, then in 1937 entered the wide–open pulp field with the sale of a drag–racing story, "Hell Driver's Partnership," to *Ace Sports*. Over the next fifteen years he was a prolific provider of mystery, detection, sports, both light and racy romance, and science fiction to such pulps as *10–Story Detective* (where his first criminous story, "Crime Collection," appeared in January of 1940), *Detective Fiction Weekly, The Shadow, Clues, All–American Football, Strange Detective Mysteries, Adventure, Dime Mystery, Dime Detective, Doc Savage, Argosy, Detective Tales, Five Novels Monthly*, and *Thrilling Wonder* and to such "slick" and specialty magazines as *The Saturday Evening Post, Grit*, and *McClure's*. In the late forties he was featured on the covers of the king of the detective magazines, *Black Mask*, in whose pages he published nine stories, five of them featuring an offbeat, Duesenberg–driving private detective named Mortimer Jones.

When the pulp markets collapsed in the early fifties, Gault turned his hand to book–length works. He published the first of his 33 novels for young readers, *Thunder Road*, in 1952, a work which remained in print for more than three decades. Appearing that same year was his first mystery, *Don't Cry for Me*, one of the seminal crime novels of its time.

Prior to *Don't Cry for Me*, the emphasis in mystery fiction was on the whodunit/whydunit aspects. Gault's novel broke new ground in that its whodunit elements are subordinate to the personal lives of its major characters and to a razor–sharp depiction of the socioeconomic aspects of its era — an accepted and widely practiced approach utilized by many of today's best writers in the field. His fellow crime novelist, Fredric Brown, said of the novel: "[It] is not only a beautiful chunk of story but, refreshingly, it's about people instead of characters, people so real and vivid that you'll think you know them personally. Even more important, this boy Gault can *write*, never badly and sometimes like an angel." The Mystery Writers of America agreed, voting *Don't Cry for Me* a Best First Novel Edgar.

Gault's subsequent mysteries are likewise novels of character and social commentary, whether featuring average individuals or professional detectives as protagonists. Many have unusual and/or sports backgrounds, in particular his non–series works. *The Bloody Bokhara* (1952) deals with the selling of valuable Oriental rugs and carpets in his native Milwaukee; *Blood on the Boards* (1953) has a little–theater setting in the Los Angeles area; *The Canvas Coffin* (1953) concerns the fight game and is narrated by a middleweight champion boxer; *Fair Prey* (1956, as by Will Duke) has a golfing background; *Death Out of Focus* (1959) is about Hollywood filmmakers and script writers, told from an insider's point of the view. An entirely different and powerful take on the Hollywood grist mill is the subject matter of his only mainstream novel, *Man Alone*, written in 1957 but not published until shortly before his death in 1995.

The bulk of Gault's 31 criminous novels — and many of his short stories — showcase series detectives. One of the first was Mortimer Jones, in the pages of *Black Mask*; another pulp creation, Honolulu private eye Sandy McKane, debuted in *Thrilling Detective* in 1947. Italian P.I. Joe Puma, who operates out of Los Angeles, was created for the paperback original market in the fifties, first as the narrator of a pseudonymous novel, *Shakedown* (1953, as by Roney Scott), and then of several books published under Gault's own name between 1958 and 1961, notably *Night Lady* and *The Hundred–Dollar Girl*. His last and most successful fictional detective was Brock "The Rock" Callahan, an ex–L.A. Rams lineman turned private eye, who first appeared in *Ring Around Rosa* in 1955. Callahan, along with his lady friend, interior decorator Jan Bonnet, did duty in six novels over the next eight years. In a rave review of *Day of the Ram* (1956), *The New York Times* called Callahan "surely one of the major private detectives created in American fiction since Chandler's Phillip Marlowe."

After the publication of *Dead Hero* in 1963, Gault abandoned detective fiction to concentrate on the more lucrative juvenile market. It was nearly twenty years before he returned to the mystery field; and when he did return, it was exclusively with stories of an older, wiser, married (to Jan Bonnet), inheritance–wealthy, and semi–retired Brock Callahan. The new series of Callahan books began with *The Bad Samaritan* (1982); six others followed, culminating with *Dead Pigeon* in 1992. In *The Cana Diversion* (1982) Gault also brought back Joe Puma — *dead*. The novel's central premise is Puma's murder and Callahan's search for the killer, a tour de force that earned a Private Eye Writers of America Shamus for Best Paperback Original.

The hallmarks of Bill Gault's fiction are finely tuned dialogue, wry humor, sharp social observation, a vivid evocation of both upper class and bottom–feeder lifestyles, and most importantly, the portrayal of people, in Fredric Brown's words, so real and vivid that you'll think you know them personally. These virtues are abundant in the dozen stories that follow, making them some of the best of the hundreds that carried his byline.

The first six are non–series tales, five of which first appeared in pulp magazines, the sixth from *Alfred Hitchcock's Mystery Magazine.* Each is quite different and demonstrates the range of Gault's interests and skills. "Marksman" is a fine character study about justifiable homicide, and the first criminous story he wrote and the second to be published, several months after "Crime Collection" in 1940. "They'd Die for Linda," an eternal triangle tale with a twist, makes effective use of the difficult storytelling device of multiple first–person narration. "Tin–Pan Alibi" has a swing music and gambling background and an appealing gambler protagonist trying to save his clarinetist brother from a murder charge. One of only a handful of Gault short–shorts, "Creature of Habit" packs a mordant wallop into less than 1500 words. "Dead End for Delia," arguably the best of his nine *Black Mask* appearances, was the basis for an episode of a cable–TV series of hardboiled short films in the early nineties. "Conspiracy," a deceptively simple tale of bank robbers, stolen money, and two summer–idle kids, shows his unique ability to portray young people with understanding and insight.

The remaining six entries are detective stories featuring Joe Puma, all published in 1956 and 1957 in *Manhunt, Ellery Queen's Mystery Magazine,* and *Mercury Mystery Magazine,* and representing the entire Puma short–story canon. Curiously, although Gault's primary fictional sleuth was Brock Callahan, he did not write a Callahan short until late in his career, preferring to utilize the harder–edged but nonetheless compassionate and likable Puma for his magazine fiction. The mean streets of Southern California, the playgrounds and slaygrounds of the rich, the Hollywood film industry, are the stuff of these fast–paced, colorful yarns; and their plots and elements of detection lift them well above the average private eye yarn of the period. Particularly good are "The Unholy Three," in which Puma is "hired" by an eleven–year–boy to investigate a "no–good guy" his bank teller sister is dating; "Don't Crowd Your Luck," a complex case which begins with Puma agreeing to act as bodyguard to a man whose life is being threatened after his recent marriage to a woman allegedly worth $82,000,000; and "Stolen Star," about the strange kid–napping of a young starlet which may or may not be a publicity stunt.

Joe Puma self–effacingly describes himself as "a plain man" and "a straight guy," terms that for my money include honesty, integrity, sincerity, generosity, and humanity. By that standard Bill Gault, in addition to being a fine writer, was likewise a plain man and a straight guy. It was my privilege and pleasure to be his friend during the last fourteen years of his life, and to have had the opportunity to compile this long overdue collection of his short fiction.

Bill Pronzini
Petaluma, California
July 2002

Non-Series Tales

Marksman

I am very ordinary. I am of medium height, medium income, average intelligence — strictly middle class. In fact, I am a little less than ordinary because I lack physical courage.

Still, I murdered a man! My neighbors all know it. The whole country knows it. And when my eighteen–month–old son grows up, he will hear about it. And that hurts more than all the rest. But I couldn't help it. I had to —

I was sitting in my living room. I was reading about the Finns' gallant stand against the Russians and feeling the admiration that weak men feel for the brave. I admired them particularly for the beautiful way they were handling their rifles. I could appreciate that, because in this one way I am a little above the ordinary. I am president of the local rifle club, and last year I won the Southern States Champion–ship.

I was sitting there alone because Alice had gone out to her bridge club and I had to stay home with Buster. There were just the two of us in the house. Buster was in the back bedroom, asleep in his crib. I was in the living room reading about the Finns and I began to feel nervous.

I began to feel nervous because I am afraid of the dark, and if you think that's funny in a grown man, let me correct you. It's sad and damnable and maddening; but it's not funny — not at all.

I put the paper down. It was a gloomy night outside, and the light from the street lamp was haloed in a late spring fog. It was a hell of a night for a man afraid of the dark to be home alone.

I decided to put Buster into the big bed and climb in with him. I am just ordinary enough to enjoy that. I turned out the lights in the living room and was halfway to the bedroom when the phone rang.

I had a premonition as I picked up the receiver. Or perhaps I was just scared. Perhaps, if it had been Alice, I would have had the same chilled feeling. But it wasn't Alice. It was a man's voice, low, muffled.

He said: "It's important that I see you tonight, Mr. Johnson. Where can you meet me?"

I hesitated. "Who is this?"

"It's about the Reform League," he said. "I can't give you my name over the phone."

I knew him for a phony then. Because if he could say "Reform League" over a phone, he could give his name. There was nothing secret about that. All of us were listed on the league stationery.

My heart began to hammer and I fought to keep my voice calm. I said: "You can see me at my store in the morning."

"No!" the voice said. "I'll be over in about ten minutes."

I started to object but the line was dead.

I was scared. I went into the baby's room and closed the window. I latched it. I looked into his closet. Then I watched him for a second, and I was close to tears. He was lying flat on his back, his hands above his head. He was smiling faintly. I turned off the light and looked out the window into the back yard.

But all I could see was mist and shadow.

From the shelf in my closet, I took out the Camp Perry model Colt that Alice had given me for Christmas. It had a long barrel, but the pockets in my corduroy house jacket were ample. I turned on the porch light and sat down to wait.

This Reform League was the latest attempt to clean up our town. And it wasn't having any more success than its predecessors, because whoever controlled the graft in this rotten little metropolis was in absolute control.

The police dragged in hoodlum after hoodlum and turned on the heat. They even pulled in one poor snowbird and kept him off the stuff for a week. He was about ready for the asylum then, but it did no good. Nobody would break.

All the law could do was sentence them; squealing would mean certain suicide.

I had been made an honorary member when I won the Southern States and had promptly forgotten all about it. But evidently somebody else hadn't.

I shivered a little and looked out the window. I hoped against hope that Alice wouldn't come home early. Then, as I fingered the Colt in my pocket, the doorbell rang.

I could feel the hair on my neck bristle, and my hand on the door knob shook. The man standing on the porch was about my height, but broad.

I said: "Come in."

He didn't say a word as he walked into the living room. He was foreign–looking, with a bluish cast to his beard stubble, and dark, murky eyes. He sat down on the room's biggest chair and tensed on its edge.

He didn't give me a chance to open my mouth. He said: "You're a good shot with a rifle? An expert?"

I nodded.

"We've got a job for you — to kill a man!"

I was plenty scared. But I took out the Colt. I said: "What's to prevent me from doing that right now?"

I was the only frightened person in that room. He said: "Put it away. You could kill me all right. But your wife — and the kid —" He shrugged. "The boss never makes a mistake. You'd better just sit and listen."

I thought of Alice and Buster. I sat down shakily.

He said: "Bruce Barnum is going to give a surprise talk at the band concert in the city park. He's got some names to name and dirt to spill. You will be in the loft of that garage across the street. You will kill him from the window with a rifle. The boss thinks it should put an end to all this reform stuff. The boss is getting annoyed with all these reform movements that keep popping up."

Bruce Barnum was head of the league. He was fearless and a bachelor. That's why they'd picked him for the job. And he was my friend. I told Bluebeard that.

He shrugged again. "Even if I felt sorry for you, it wouldn't make any difference. I work under orders."

I said slowly: "There's quite a bit of money represented on the league board. It would be worth all we could raise to learn the name of the boss."

He smiled faintly. "I'm one of the few guys who know that. And there isn't enough money in the world to buy my life." He paused. "We've tried to get Bar– num a couple of times. But he's pretty well guarded. That's why we have to do it from a distance. And you just happen to be the unlucky guy."

"And if I refuse?"

For the third time he shrugged. "Maybe you, maybe your wife or the kid —"

I almost went for the Colt again. But it would do no good. As he said, he was only working under orders.

As he rose to go, he said casually: "Don't look so sick. Murder's a little tough the first time. But you get used to it." His eyes fell on the paper. "They're sure getting used to it in Russia."

The whole thing was like something out of a gangster movie, one of those wild B pictures. But this was no movie. This was happening to me, George Johnson, citizen. I tried to get a grip on myself, reason sanely. But my mind was numb.

At the door, Bluebeard said: "We'll get in touch with you again, probably tomorrow."

I only nodded.

I went back to the living room and sat down again. I was still sitting there, staring dumbly at nothing, when Alice and Fred Lock came in.

Alice said: "Why, George Fraidy–Cat Johnson! Don't tell me you saw another ghost?"

I tried to smile. Fred Lock was looking at me curiously.

Alice sensed, then, that this was something more than my usual home–alone nervousness. "What happened?" she asked.

I hesitated. It was Fred who had nominated me for the league. If I told anyone, I could tell him. But I shook my head. "Nothing happened," I said. "I don't feel so well."

Fred left then, and Alice said: "You're not jealous, are you, George? I mean — I know he's been around a lot lately, but —"

That was almost funny. Alice and Fred had been practically engaged all through college. Then Fred went to law school, and I stepped in. Fred just couldn't keep away from her, now, and I wouldn't have liked that if I hadn't trusted Alice a hundred percent.

"I'm not jealous," I told her. "I'm a little fagged out. There's been a lot of trouble at the store lately, spring inventory and all." I knew then that I'd never be able to tell her.

I remembered Bluebeard's comment, and I tried to tell myself that mass murder was going on in Europe; that I had to do this for my family. But I couldn't. I'd never even been able to go hunting, and, now, I was expected to kill a man.

I wasn't worth anything at the store next morning. I thought of taking the family out of town. But I would probably be trailed, and I didn't have the money to reestablish myself in another town.

There was a luncheon meeting of the league at noon. I had to stay active to keep from going crazy so I attended.

When Bruce Barnum got up to speak, I kept my eyes averted. I kept seeing a bullet hole in his high forehead, blood in the grayish–black of his hair. Nausea stirred in me. Fred Lock was sitting next to me, and he whispered: "What's the matter, George? You still sick?"

I nodded.

Barnum was saying: "I want you all to understand that the police are one hundred percent behind us. There have been rumors — and one of the papers has hinted — that a corrupt police department is partly responsible for this town's criminal record. I have investigated this thoroughly for the past month and have proved to myself that the rumor has no basis in fact. I wish you would give this information all the publicity within your power. I know and —"

I couldn't listen any more. I mumbled something to Fred about explaining to the others; then I slipped out the door.

But, outside, there was no place to go. I could have gone back to the store; but it's a sporting–goods store, and I feature a complete line of rifles. I didn't want to look at any rifles this afternoon. I got into my car and headed for the country.

It was beautiful. The mist of the evening before had brought out all the sleepy beauty of our southern spring. The sun was hot, but the sun could never get too hot for me. I love it too well. Which is just another way of saying I hate the dark.

I think, if Bluebeard had approached me in the daytime, I would have shot him.

My mind went back to the luncheon. I remembered Barnum's words regarding the police department. Perhaps — just perhaps — the police had uncovered something new. I turned the car back toward town.

My association with the league gave me a few privileges, and I had known the chief of police since boyhood. He shook his head at my question.

"Nothing new, George. It's the same old story, and it will continue to be the same story until we get the headman." He shook his bushy head hopelessly. "Terror rules this gang. If we could get the boss, the organization would dissolve. I know that as well as I know my name. I'm willing to admit that we've hit a new low in the viciousness of our third degrees; but not a man will break. They're scum, every last one of them, but their fear of the boss is greater than their fear of us."

I knew that too well. Because here I was, three feet from the law, and I was no criminal. Still, I couldn't say what I wanted to say. I couldn't tell an old friend about Bluebeard. I couldn't go to the law which I was pledged to uphold. It was like living under a dictator — a criminal dictator! It wasn't American.

Oh, I cursed myself silently. And I was thoroughly ashamed of my yellow streak. But I didn't say anything. That, really, is what is important.

I left, and again I had no place to go.

Then I remembered I had to go one place. Fred Lock had borrowed my Varminter a few weeks ago for a local meet. It was the gun I intended to use. I drove over to the boulevard.

There was a black sedan in the drive. If it was Fred's, it was a new one. But it wasn't Fred's. A little man in a loud suit was sitting in Fred's study when the butler ushered me in.

Fred was saying: "And, you can tell your boss that I have no price. You can tell him that it's only a matter of weeks, now, before we bust his rotten ring wide open. Now, get out of here!"

The little fellow growled something, shot me a scornful glance and walked out.

Fred was smiling grimly. "One of the big boy's stooges trying to buy me off. I'd have thrown him in jail if I thought it would do any good."

I said something about his courage, and he shook his head. "It's not courage. I have all the money I need and enough love for my home town to fight for it."

I asked for my gun, and he lifted it from the rack in one corner of the room.

"It's a beauty, George. If you ever want to sell it —"

After I used it, I would be glad to give it away. But I didn't tell Fred that.

It was late enough now to go home. And I dreaded it because the more I saw of Alice and Buster now, the more I would miss them later. For I knew, despite my weakness, that I could never again face them unless I confessed. And that would mean a life sentence, at least.

Buster was in one of his playful moods. For a half–hour I tried to share that mood; tried to hide the sickness and the fear within me. But it was hopeless. I went down into the basement to load some cartridges. As I passed through the kitchen, Alice looked at me curiously. But she said nothing.

I have all the paraphernalia for making my own cartridges, including a mold of my own design. It would be possible for me to make a bullet which would hit Bruce Barnum between the eyes and still not kill him.

For a moment I toyed with the idea. It would be possible, but the results wouldn't be a certainty. And if Bluebeard's boss should suspect — I shivered.

I heard Buster's feet on the floor above; heard Alice moving about the kitchen. I was a weak man, but I could commit murder for them.

I compromised then. Two of the cartridges carried the regular load; the third I loaded lightly.

I put the gun in a machine rest and fired it with the light load. Then I examined the pine board I had used as a target. If I were to use a load that light, I would have to compensate for the comparatively short distance from the garage loft to the bandstand. And Bruce Barnum would be blind for life, even if I didn't kill him!

I made another of the light cartridges before Alice called me to dinner. I would take it along, tomorrow night, and perhaps I would have the nerve to use it.

Bluebeard called at ten o'clock. "Tomorrow night's the band concert," he said. "I'll pick you up in front of your store at eight."

I mumbled something and hung up.

Back in the living room, Alice put down her paper. She said: "I want to know what's wrong, George." Her blue eyes were filled with worry. "Don't tell me its business. And it's not your health. It's something a lot more important than either — and I want to help."

I was silent for seconds. Finally, I said: "You'll know by Saturday. It's about the league and I'm pledged to secrecy. But I promise you'll have all the details by Saturday."

Quietly, she asked: "Is it dangerous, George?"

I nodded. "It's dangerous, honey. But I have to go through with it." I looked at her squarely. "Remember, honey, that whatever I do, I do for you and Buster. I'm not the cinema type, but you can believe that no one could love you more than I do."

She smiled then, and there was more than love in that smile. There was admiration, and that was something I didn't deserve. I kissed her humbly.

That night was sleepless of course. And I will never remember that next day. I was going through the mechanics of my regular routine. But behind the front, I was a jumbled mass of nerves, and I knew that without some form of opiate, I would be a poor marksman that night. All the long day I fought myself, and by six o'clock I had regained some semblance of normalcy.

I had brought my rifle down in the morning; so I didn't need to go home for dinner. I decided to eat at a restaurant, and then come back to the store to meet Bluebeard.

I called Alice.

"This business," she asked hesitantly, "Is it coming off tonight?"

"It is," I said.

The line was quiet a moment. Then: "You took your rifle this morning, George — that new one."

"I did," I said.

Her voice was almost a whisper, now. "I'll wait up for you, George. And — I'll pray."

I was physically sick for the next fifteen minutes. I decided not to eat. I locked the store and turned out the lights. And for the next two hours, I walked the streets.

I don't know what streets. I walked and cursed. I cursed myself and the criminal boss. I even cursed Barnum for starting the league. But, mostly, I cursed myself.

I was in front of the store at eight o'clock. And a big black sedan was waiting. The front door was open. Bluebeard was behind the wheel. I got my gun and came out again.

Without a word I climbed in. Bluebeard just nodded; then he swung the big car away from the curb and up toward the city park. The park was nearly filled when we pulled into the alley alongside the garage. The huge bandstand was brilliantly lighted; the shell behind it looking like an inverted sea shell, magnified thousands of times.

Bluebeard said: "You've got a good white background there, and the lights in the garage will do."

I said nothing.

Only one man was in the lower part of the garage. He watched us as we silently climbed the stairs to the loft. He may have been an accomplice or he may have been another me. I didn't know, and I didn't care.

The loft smelled of oil and rubber and dust. At one end, the window was open toward the park. The light was all right, and it was an easy shot. And my nervousness was gone. I was an inanimate piece of flesh at the moment. A murderer!

There were three men on the bandstand, three men in evening clothes. Their black suits stood out against the shell of the rostrum. The middle man was Barnum.

The man on the left, the man who was rising to speak, was Fred Lock. He said over the public address system: "We have a surprise for you tonight —"

I didn't listen; Bluebeard was talking. "We thought you might try to pull a double cross; so I brought along a cartridge that we know will do the trick. I'll take those you have in your pocket."

I handed him the three I had brought along. He took a stand against the opposite wall. The muzzle of his automatic was on me and it didn't waver a bit.

I broke open the breech. From force of habit, I weighed the cartridge in my hand; glanced at it. For a second my heart stopped beating.

That mark on the rim! Was it — It was, beyond a doubt. And the bullet had been cast in my own mold. The taper was unmistakable, and so was that mark that had been made when my tool slipped — the J–shaped mark that wouldn't be duplicated in a million shells.

It was one of the cartridges I had given Fred Lock!

All the incidents of the past turbulent days came to my mind. The car in Fred's drive, the same that had carried me tonight. I had caught him unawares, and he had covered his windy speech to the little fellow. And tonight's talk was to be a secret among the members of the league. Yet, Bluebeard had known the night he first came to call. And I remembered that Fred had been a poor credit risk two years ago; while today he was wealthy. And he had always coveted Alice. He would want me out of the way!

I snapped the gun shut and laid it on the sill. I wasn't afraid. I wasn't nervous. I was something far worse than that. I was filled with hate!

I knelt behind the rifle, my hands steady. I caught Fred's forehead in the 'scope. I pulled the trigger gently.

It was an easy shot.

It wasn't courage that filled me when I turned to Bluebeard. I was beyond courage. I wasn't even fully conscious.

"I missed Barnum," I said.

His face was stoical as he crossed the room toward me. He had the automatic jammed in my ribs as he looked out the window. The people were streaming onto the stand, but he saw what he wanted to see.

Then he turned to me, and still I felt no fear.

"Maybe," he said softly, "you didn't miss. You'd better git; nobody's coming this way, yet."

I said: "You mean you're not going to —"

"Nobody wants to kill," he said. "Not even me, unless there's money in it. And who'd pay me, now?" He threw the automatic behind a pile of tires and clomped down the stairs, out of my sight and out of my life —

I was cleared of course. Especially after a police search of Lock's papers. And our town is clean. But I killed a man! And it doesn't help to know I had to. My guns are sold, my beautiful guns. And fishing isn't in it with target shooting.

But I suppose I'll learn to like it after a while.

They'd Die for Linda

From the viewpoint of Lester Coles:

The thought that Linda might be linked with the death of George Course never for a moment occurred to me. There was nothing in the newspaper account of his death to indicate it. There was nothing in the newspaper account of his death to indicate, for that matter, anything but accidental death. Detective Ryan seemed to have other ideas.

He was a slim, virile man of medium height, dressed in clothes of undoubted quality but very little originality. He stood in the center of my living room, looking faintly bewildered.

I smiled. "Don't you like it?"

His eyes were deeply blue and inquisitive, alive. "Lester Coles," he said. "The name is familiar. There's another word that should go with it. Lester Coles —"

"A Lester Coles Interior?"

"That's it." He smiled, very disarmingly. "I should have realized as soon as I saw this room."

It was a blend of *directoire* and modern, and rather ordinary, I thought. But the height of the windows almost forced that treatment.

I said, "Perhaps it isn't masculine enough for a man's apartment."

He shrugged slightly. "Perhaps it's just a little advanced for me."

"Something in a mohair frieze, sir?" I thought. Something in a three–piece suite for a hundred fifty dollars. Which was just malice, of course.

I said, "I'm sure you didn't come to see the apartment." I indicated a chair.

He sat forward on its edge and studied me. He answered, "No, I didn't." He paused. "You knew George Course?"

"I've met him."

"He was in love with your sister?"

The frontal attack. Boldness and surprise the motif, dropping a question like that into the calm. Police procedure, undoubtedly, out of the manual.

"My sister is married," I said stiffly.

"Your sister is beautiful," he pointed out.

"And civilized," I added. "George Course may or may not have been in love with her. Any man who met her would be a little in love with her. Any man with any sensitivity at all would recognize her innate fastidiousness. My sister is a lady in the true sense of that overworked word."

"You're twins, aren't you?"

I nodded. "Linda and Lester. Rather middle–class, don't you think?"

He looked puzzled.

"The alliteration," I explained.

Then he said, "Oh." He was looking thoughtful, perhaps planning another line of attack.

I went on, "According to the papers, George Course's death was accidental. Was there some thought of suicide that brings you here?"

"Because he loved your sister, who is married?"

"Well, I suppose that could —"

"No," he broke in. "No, it wasn't suicide. It was murder."

There was no sound in the room no motion but the beating of my heart. I said, "You think Linda —"

He shook his head. "It's too early to think anything, yet. I need to get what information I can before I permit myself to think." He ran a finger around the crown of his hat, which was on the floor. Then he looked up at me. "I wanted to get your impression of George Course, all you know and think about him."

"Most of what I know is hearsay," I said. "I understand he was one of those animals who become human through the skill of a tailor. I've heard he was extremely wealthy, and completely vulgar."

Ryan's voice was on a dead monotone. "You didn't like him, I take it."

I met the stare of those blue eyes. "If I thought Linda would have anything to do with him, I would have killed him. But you're not interested in what would have happened. The purely technical fact remains that I didn't kill him." I paused. "Nor did Linda."

He looked down at his hat again, and went through the routine of running a forefinger around its crown. An annoying habit, I thought.

He looked up again. "How about Barbara?"

Barbara is my other sister, my younger sister. "What about her?" I asked.

"She knew Course, more intimately, perhaps, than her sister."

"Yes, I believe it was through Barbara that Linda met Course."

"You didn't worry so much about her?"

This Ryan was no fool; this Ryan was no customer for a mohair frieze suite, either, I was beginning to suspect. I said, "Perhaps I'm not quite normal in that regard. Linda has always been a special concern of mine. We were both very young when dad died, and I promised him that I would watch over Linda."

"And Barbara?"

"Has been completely capable of taking care of herself since she was three."

He looked down at his hat again, and over at the tall windows. I heard the sound of an elevator door closing in the hall, outside, and from somewhere the whir of a vacuum cleaner. I experienced that psychic feeling, that sense of communication with Linda for a brief, hazy moment.

He looked at me and asked, "Where were you yesterday, between two and four in the afternoon?"

"At my office, my studio. I have a study there, and I spent the entire afternoon working over some plans."

"Alone?"

"I was alone in my study. Miss Riordan, my assistant, was in the outer studio, and she can substantiate my statement."

"There's only one door?"

"Only one."

"And she was in view of that at all times?"

"She couldn't be anything else. It's a small studio."

Was it disappointment I saw on his face? He picked up his hat and rose. He looked around the room. He said, "I'm beginning to get used to this place. I kind of like it."

A new approach, flattery. I was supposed to bubble over with gratitude now and become talkative. But not where Linda was concerned. No harm must ever come to her.

I walked with him to the door. Before he left, he said, "You understand that everybody is a suspect to me. There's nothing personal in this questioning."

"I understand," I told him.

He left.

I saw the mahogany bed again, and dad's thin, tired face. I saw all the shadows in that ugly bed room, and heard dad's whispering voice, "Keep Linda straight, Les. Keep her always true and fine."

That was five days after my mother got her divorce from dad and married Gerald Gifford. That was the night dad died. Mother had had three husbands since.

I realized, for the first time, why I always had avoided mahogany. It was something a psychiatrist probably could have told me long before this.

I phoned Linda. I asked her, "Were you thinking of me about five minutes ago?"

"I was."

It wasn't the first time that had happened. I said, "Why?"

"I wondered if that Tommy Ryan was bothering you."

"He was. You call him Tommy?"

"Oh, he's a friend of Greg's. You know Greg."

Greg was Gregory Shaw, and Linda's husband. He wrote detective stories, but was otherwise more or less normal. I admired him.

I asked, "What does Greg think of all this?"

There was a silence I didn't like. Then, "I wish I knew."

My hand tightened on the phone. "Linda, he doesn't think you —" I couldn't finish that.

"I don't know," she said. "He'd better not, or I'll tear up all his reference books and smash his typewriter and charge a platinum mink coat to his account."

Then we both laughed. I told her, "I think I'll drop over for lunch."

"Why not?" she agreed. "We can gang up on Greg and make him unhappy. We'll make him suffer. We'll make him listen to our plots."

"I've a good one," I told her. "It came to me last night, in the dark, and he could sell it without the least bit of trouble."

"At noon," she said.

"At noon."

I went down to the studio first. Miss Riordan said, "There was a Mr. Ryan to see you, this morning. I told him you were at home."

"I saw him there. Did he ask you any questions?"

She looked worried. She has a thin face, and she always looked a little worried, but this was more than usual. She said, "He wanted to know where you were between two and four yesterday afternoon. I told him you were in your study."

"That's all?"

"That's all." She hesitated. "Lester, you're in some sort of trouble, aren't you?"

"Some," I admitted. "Mr. Ryan is a detective. He suspects I might be a murderer."

She gasped. "You're joking, Lester!"

Her thin face was white, her sharp eyes staring.

"No," I answered, "I'm not joking." Then, "I'm going to my sister's for lunch, if anything important comes up."

She was still staring.

I said, "All of us are potential murderers, Jane. Or didn't you know that?"

She shook her head slowly. She was still staring when I left.

Linda likes Chippendale. I don't, but she does, and her apartment reflects that. I didn't have my heart in it, and I failed her miserably. But she adores it.

She was waiting for me in the doorway, when I got out of the elevator. She said, "Greg doesn't think one murder is enough."

II.

From the viewpoint of Gregory Shaw:

"I think one murder is enough," I said, "but my readers won't. I don't write for myself, darling. I write, or I hope I write, what the readers want to read. That's why we can have our apartment done in the expensive fashion of Lester Coles."

Les added, "With Mr. Coles' advice gratis, of course, and really against his better judgment."

Linda sighed. "Are we going to start that all over again?"

"I'm not," Les said. "I really came to give Greg a plot."

"No," I pleaded, "not now. I'm right in the middle of something, and it would confuse me. Please, Les, not now."

He was smiling that semi–sadistic smile of his. He said, "It's a locked room, fifty stories up. The only possible means of entry an open window, but fifty stories up. A man murdered, and not by his own hand. Now, mull that over."

I ignored it. I said, "We've got onion soup for lunch."

"With croutons and Parmesan cheese," Linda added.

"Made by the cunning hand of Martha," I supplied.

Martha is our maid of all work. She weighs two hundred and twelve pounds and is the best cook in the world.

I thought Les looked worried. I thought he was studying Linda carefully, thoughtfully. But I'm always looking for things like that because of my business.

Fifty stories high, and no entry except an open window. There were only two possibilities, of course. I said, "Either the killer had a helicopter or balloon or he came down from the roof with a rope."

Les shook his head. "No mechanical gadgets."

They preceded me into the dining room. I studied the slim arrogance of Linda's figure from that angle and the long loveliness of her legs.

Even after three years of married life, I can enjoy that.

Linda has wheat–colored hair, direct gray eyes and a disposition even I can't ruffle. And I can be very nasty at times. Like when I'm working, and get stuck, or when I put my heart and soul on paper, and some editor thinks it smells.

I wondered why Linda had refused to tell Tommy Ryan where she was from two to four the previous afternoon. She had said she was shopping, but Linda never shops for two hours without buying something. Never until yesterday, at any rate. She's no window shopper.

We were enjoying the soup, now. Les said, "This George Course business is nasty, isn't it?" He was watching Linda.

Linda's eyes were on her soup. "Even alive, George Course was nasty," she returned,

A pause, and then Les again, and I thought his voice was strained. "You ... ah ... seem to speak from some personal knowledge."

Linda looked up to meet her brother's gaze. "I knew him. You couldn't know him five minutes without knowing what he was. No woman could, at any rate."

I asked, "What did Ryan have to say to you, Les?"

He shrugged. "Where was I from two to four and did I like George Course and why didn't I worry about Barbara as I worried about Linda?"

Linda looked startled. "What do you suppose he meant by that?"

"By which?" I asked.

"About why Les doesn't worry about Barbara."

"Because he doesn't," I said, "and any outsider can tell it in a minute. Les worries about you and you worry about Barbara and Barbara worries about humanity."

"Oh," Linda said.

"And now," I went on, "in the privacy of our little family circle, perhaps you can tell us why you lied to Tommy Ryan."

Linda looked at Les, not at me. She answered, "I didn't lie."

"For three years," I said, "I've known you intimately. For three years, every single time you went shopping, you bought something, if only a little inexpensive forty dollar hat. It is an impossibility for you to go shopping without buying something."

"I didn't lie," she repeated.

"You didn't claim to go to any of the small shops," I pointed out. "If you had, it could be more easily checked. You said you went to the department stores where you wouldn't be recognized. Even if it's true, it doesn't sound true. And I'm sure it didn't sound true to Tommy Ryan. He's not dumb."

Les said, "You don't think she had anything to do with it, do you, Greg?"

His voice was cold, and when I looked into his eyes, I realized he must have misunderstood my questioning. I answered quietly, "I don't think she killed George Course and I don't think she was ever untrue to me. That's as far as my beliefs go, at present."

He looked relieved. He smiled. "No helicopter," he said, "and no rope."

"Oh, all right," I said. "I give up."

"A midget," he explained. "This man had incurred the wrath of a midget, and the midget had a friend who was an eagle, and the eagle just flew him up there, and waited until he'd —"

"Please," I begged. "No more."

Linda was smiling, too, now. "I think it's fine," she said. "You're just being difficult because you didn't think of it yourself."

"Can't we be sensible?" I asked. "It seems as though we're involved in a murder for some reason. I don't think it's any time for humor, even poor humor."

"I think it's just a routine of the police," Les put in. "The papers claimed it was an accident, that it happened while he was cleaning his gun."

"The gun was in his left hand," I said, "and he was right–handed. A paraffin test indicates he didn't fire the gun."

"You told me once," Linda reminded him, "that a paraffin test is not infallible."

"Not in a new gun. In one as old as this, it's very close to infallible."

"Which means," Les said, "that he didn't commit suicide. Not with his left hand."

"And he had no cleaning rags out," I pointed out, "nor had the gun been licensed in his name. It was the kind of gun you can pick up in any pawn shop."

They were both looking at me curiously.

"The killer," I said, "obviously tried to make it look like suicide. Putting the gun in the left hand would be a natural mistake, in the excitement, and facing the body."

Neither of them said anything.

I began, "Well —"

"We're listening," Linda said. "We wouldn't think of interrupting an author."

"And an expert," Les added.

"You two are very bright," I said sourly. "You should go on the stage. Linda and Lester — Two Bright Jesters, Humor At All Times."

"I can dance," Les said.

"And I could sing." This from Linda.

"I love you both," I told them, "and I hope neither one of you winds up in the electric chair. Now, if you'll excuse me, I'll get back to work."

I went back to the little room I laughingly refer to as a study, and tried to work another murder into the current opus. But nothing came, nothing worth considering. I kept thinking about Linda, wondering why I thought she was lying, when I had absolutely no proof. It's possible to go shopping without buying anything. It's possible to do all your shopping, without buying, in large department stores. But not for Linda, damn it, not for Linda!

Les stuck his head in the doorway a little later, and said he would be breezing off, and I went to the door with him. When I came back, Linda was sitting on the love seat in the sun room, her legs curled up under her. She was smoking. She didn't even notice me go by.

I went back to the typewriter, and turned out one very badly worded page. I tore it up. I lighted a cigarette, and went out to the kitchen to see if there was any coffee.

Martha said there was none, and she sniffed. She thinks my constant coffee drinking is an affectation. I have explained to her patiently, many times, the benefits of caffeine to creative endeavor, to no avail.

I said, "Please make some," and left the kitchen on her second sniff.

I had torn up a second page when I looked up to see Linda in the doorway. She came over to kiss me on the forehead. She had my chin in her two hands, and she lifted up my head to meet her gaze.

"What makes you think I was lying?" she asked me.

"I don't know. I guess I just sensed it."

"You're getting like Les, now. He thinks he's psychic."

"Maybe he is," I said.

Her gray eyes widened. "Is there such a thing?"

"There could be. There are a lot of stupid people who believe both ways, and a lot of intelligent people. I'm not competent to judge. I don't ridicule anything I don't understand."

"Well," she said, "I was lying."

I pulled her down on my lap. "Tell me about it."

"At two thirty I was in George Course's apartment. He was alive, then."

Sickness welled in me, and my shock must have been apparent to Linda. For she stiffened in my arms.

She said, "Greg, you don't think — Lord, no!" She buried her face in my shoulder.

"Steady," I told her. "I didn't think anything I shouldn't." Which was a lie.

"Greg, you're so stupid sometimes. I think you've even entertained, the idea that that horrible, vulgar creature had some charms for me."

"No, but why —"

"You poor, blind dear. Barbara, of course."

"You mean, Course and Barbara were —"

"They weren't anything, yet. But George was wild about her, and you know what a bleeding heart she is for anyone she thinks might be misunderstood. Oh, Greg, she's such a sentimental idiot."

"Isn't … wasn't Course married?"

"Yes, but he didn't live with his wife. And she is a complete shrew, so George did get a lot of sympathy there. I could just see Barbara seeking out the hidden goodness in his character, and marrying him to reform him, if his wife would divorce him. And if his wife wouldn't divorce him — well, don't you see?"

I smiled. I said, "You went to him to plead for your sister? Is that the pitch?"

She grinned ruefully. "I suppose it was a little melodramatic. But it does make sense, doesn't it, honey?"

"Only to you," I answered. "Look, Barbara is no fool. She seems to have a Florence Nightingale complex, but that's something to be admired, not scoffed at. It's a sublimation, perhaps. She's a vital, loving and lovable girl, and she will some day make some man a loving and lovable wife. She could no more be fooled by this Course than you were. There is even less chance in her case, perhaps."

"Ouch," she said.

I kissed her. "It's not meant as a reflection on you. But she deals with all kinds of people all day long, and your life has been fairly sheltered."

"By Les?"

"By Les, and later by your unreasonable but too much in love husband."

"That's a clue." She considered me gravely. "You could have followed me, out of jealousy. You could have gone in and killed him, and fixed it to look like suicide, and —"

I interrupted her. "No, I couldn't. I couldn't have bungled it as badly as this was bungled. And I'll let you in on a secret. The way to commit a murder is to make it look like an accident. Thousands of murders have been covered this way. It's the safest and the best."

"I'll remember that," she said, "next time." She stroked my hair absently. "Are we going to tell Detective Ryan what I told you?"

"I think so. I think it's best."

"But you're not certain."

"No," I answered. "I'm not certain."

She climbed off my lap. "Remember, you told me never to bother you during working hours."

"I can't work today. Nothing comes."

"Work, hack!" she ordered. "Linda needs a new mink."

But I didn't work. I had stopped thinking about Linda, but I was thinking about Barbara. Barbara is shorter than Linda, but her figure is not one heartbeat less appealing. Barbara is sleek as a black kitten, dark and with warm brown eyes that love all the world.

Barbara could no more commit murder than ... than — Well, I guess anyone could commit murder. Practically anyone. But not Barbara, damn it, not Barbara!

Martha came with my coffee and set it down without a sniff, and I thanked her.

There was no reason I could think of why all Tommy Ryan's suspicions should be directed at us. And perhaps Les had been right in assuming it was just a routine investigation. At any rate, none of them acted guilty.

But, of course, I hadn't seen Barbara since the murder. She lived with us, but I had been out of the house most of yesterday, and she had gone down to the mission before I was up this morning.

Tonight, Linda and I were going out for dinner, and there was an off chance Barbara might not get home before we left. But I wanted to see her. I wanted her reaction.

I wanted her reaction, my conscience told me, to judge whether Linda had been lying.

III

From the viewpoint of Barbara Coles:
There was a fat man breathing down my neck. There was a thin man breathing close enough to my nose for me to detect the odor of garlic. Somebody else stepped on my foot. I was annoyed.

"Easy, Miss Nightingale Coles," I told myself. "These are the people. These are those you serve in your noble way, in your humble way. Don't ever get annoyed with these, your public."

But it was too darned late for the bus to be as crowded as it was. It just didn't make sense. And I'm no Florence Nightingale, either. That's just Greg's name for me. And I'm no bleeding heart, either, as Linda claims.

Tonight, both of them would be out to dinner and Martha would be at a movie. Tonight, I would just loaf. A nice hot shower and a cold one, and maybe scrambled eggs, and then a story or two, and early to bed.

Only, it was too nice a night to go to bed early. I realized that as soon as I got off the bus. Spring was finally here, and the air was warm, and the moon overhead was a musical comedy moon. Trees were budding, winter was gone, and Barbara would curl up with a magazine and read about love.

Well, what else was there?

I walked along Ardmore slowly, turned at Pointer Drive and down the drive slowly to the apartment. There was a coupé parked in front, I saw, and a man sitting in it, but it had no significance for me at the time.

There were no lights in the apartment, I saw, but I hadn't expected any.

I walked slowly through the court and into the lobby. The self–service elevator was down on the main floor, and I went up in that.

It wasn't three minutes after I turned on the light in the living room that the door chime sounded.

I remembered the man in the coupé, and realized he could have been waiting there for the light to go on. There was no reason for me to feel uneasy, but I was. I hesitated for seconds, in indecision.

Then I went to the door.

He was a well–dressed, slim man, fairly tall, with the bluest eyes I ever had seen. He said, "Detective Ryan — homicide," and displayed a badge.

I must have known at that moment what had happened. But it didn't register. I said, "I don't understand."

"About George Course," he said. "Greg told me you'd be home soon, and I waited outside."

"George Course?" I asked blankly.

"Was murdered. Don't you read the papers?"

I put a hand on the wall near the door, and my voice was only a whisper. "No, I didn't, not yesterday or today. Murdered, you say!" The darkness seemed to be creeping through my mind.

Jack Hunter and Teddy Agell, and now George Course. But Jack and Teddy hadn't been murdered. I mustn't let myself think anything like that, not about Linda.

The detective's voice, like a voice coming from far off, "Are you all right, Miss Coles? I'm sorry if I've been blunt. I thought, of course, you knew."

"Come in," I said. "It ... it's just the coincidence. Back in Booneville —" And I stopped. No, not that, not to a detective.

"Back in Booneville?" he prompted me.

"Nothing," I said. I led the way to the living room. "I meant, I wish we had stayed back in Booneville. I've never liked the city."

Which was a poor lie, and those bright–blue eyes weren't fooled for a second. He said quietly, "You mentioned coincidence."

He didn't look like a detective, I thought. But then, I had no idea what detectives looked like, except from Greg's stories or from the movies. But he looked nice. Not gruff, and not smoking a cigar and not fat.

"You mentioned coincidence," he repeated.

"I meant the coincidence of your being here just when I got home. I was startled, you see, and —"

"You loved George Course?"

My surprise must have shown on my face. "Me? Why, no, of —"

"Linda, then?"

"No, no, not Linda. He was my friend. He was wild about me, but —"

"It doesn't help to lie," he said.

I tried to put some indignation in my tone. "Well, really —"

He smiled. "Miss Coles, I'm not here to accuse you of murder, or to threaten you. But a murder's been committed and I'm out for what truth is available. You're not helping any."

When he smiled, I saw the dimple, and his blue eyes seemed to light up, but he wasn't fooling me. He was still a detective.

"If I could help, I would," I told him. "It's been a bad day. I'm nervous and I'm hungry and I'm upset about this business. Would you like to question me while I eat?"

"I'll wait," he said. "Or better still, I'll go out for a while, and come back after you're through."

I looked at him suspiciously.

"You'll go out to eat, you mean?"

"Well, no, I —"

"It doesn't help to lie," I said. He laughed, and the blue eyes laughed with him, and I thought there could be no malice in this man. I felt better. "You could eat right here, with, me. If you don't mind scrambled eggs and rolls and maybe some bacon, and whatever else there is."

"It doesn't seem quite right," he demurred.

"Nonsense," I said. "You're a friend of Greg's, aren't you, and Linda's?"

He nodded. "Of Greg's, at any rate."

"Well, then, sit down and make yourself comfortable, while I scramble some eggs."

He sat down.

There was, besides eggs, some onion soup left over from lunch, some bacon, and plenty of rolls, including rye.

We ate in the breakfast nook. He didn't have much to say, at first, except to praise the onion soup.

Then, over the coffee, he said, "Tell me about Booneville. And the coin–cidence."

I had a cigarette, and he flicked a lighter and lighted it for me. "No," I told him. I felt cold and strangely lonely.

"It's bothered you, hasn't it? It's bothered you before this."

That startled me, and I wondered how he'd guessed it. "No," I said.

He was quiet, then, for a moment. He was studying the tip of his cigarette. He said, "You're being very stupid."

I didn't answer.

His voice went on, "I wonder how many innocent people have suffered because some witness or some person concerned in a murder case concealed information? They get mistaken ideas about protecting someone they love, and louse up the case. Later, somebody else dies, and the person who could have revealed that information is just as guilty as the murderer."

"I've no important information, nothing definite," I protested.

"Why don't you let me decide if it's important? I could go up to Booneville, I suppose, and dig it out. But then, if it wasn't important, others might begin to suspect something, something that might not be true."

I said nothing.

"You all lived in Booneville? That's your home town?"

I nodded. "Up until five years ago."

He smiled again. It was a smile that relieved all the tension in his face and made him someone else. "Won't you tell me?"

It had been on my conscience a long time. I had lived with it, for years, and only lately had my suspicions dulled. I said, "It's probably silly. But there was this Jack Hunter, this lout, this completely foul person. We were in high school and he had a crush on Linda. And Linda is susceptible to the type, for some reason. But Hunter died. He drowned. It was an accident."

He was crushing out his cigarette in an ash tray. I couldn't see his eyes. "Go on," he said.

"Then Teddy Agell. Linda was in college then, but home for vacation. And Teddy was about the same as Jack, though perhaps more suave. And he died. He had an old ramshackle flivver and it must have got out of control. He went over a cliff, on a road through the mountains there, and they called it an accident."

He said gravely, "And now there's George Course, about the same type. Course's death was no accident."

He was looking at me. I had a solid intuition that we were thinking the same thing. I was lonely again, and frightened.

"Course wasn't in love with you, then?"

"Maybe, at first. I didn't want any part of him. No one but I knew he was in love with Linda."

"Someone might have thought he was."

He had almost said it then. I heard my own voice saying, "Maybe."

"I thought he was in love with you. I went over to the mission today. Did you know that?"

I shook my head.

"I saw you there, and I decided to wait, to question you after I had questioned the others."

"Why?"

"I don't know. Except that you looked so ... so right and good." He paused. "And pretty, probably. I guess we're all vulnerable to that."

He still wasn't saying what we were both thinking. I asked, "Have you any ideas on this ... this death, now?"

He didn't answer. He said, "I think I'd better be running along."

"Couldn't you — Is it necessary that you go right away?"

"No." He looked at me quizzically. "Why?"

"I'm frightened. Linda and Greg should be home pretty soon, and I wish —"

"I'll stay," he said. "But there's no reason to be frightened."

I searched my mind. I told him, "It's all so ... so unnatural."

"Let's not think about it," he said. "Let's get at the dishes."

Martha would do them, I knew, but it was something to keep me occupied. I wanted to be occupied now. I didn't want to think any more than I had to.

He asked, "Your mother still alive?"

I nodded. "She's in Paris, with her fourth husband. We don't hear much from her."

"You all worshiped your dad?"

I nodded. "He got a pretty rotten deal, I guess. Mother was — well, susceptible to heels."

We were still in the kitchen when Linda and Greg came home.

Linda looked at Ryan doubtfully, but Greg was watching me. And he seemed to be relieved at what he saw, for some reason. He asked, "What is this copper doing in our kitchen?"

"Investigating my love life," I answered.

Greg said, "Tommy, would you come to my study for a minute? There's something I want to tell you."

Linda seemed to turn pale, and she looked beseechingly at Greg as the two men left the kitchen.

She went out into the dining room. I tried to stop thinking what I was thinking. It was crazy. It was horrible and frightening. I went out and into the living room, and saw her standing near the door of Greg's study, as I passed through.

I turned on the radio, and turned it off. I tried to read a magazine, but the words were meaningless. A little later, Greg, Linda and Tommy came into the room.

"Thanks for the supper," Tommy said, and he turned on that smile.

My answering smile must have been ghastly.

He picked up his hat. "I'm sorry things have to be as they are. It's —" He shrugged.

I went with him to the door. Linda was turning out the lights in the dining room, now. In a little while, all the lights would be out and the apartment would be dark.

"Good night," he said.

"Good night," I answered.

"Try not to think of it." His voice sounded worried.

I nodded, and closed the door.

IV

From the viewpoint of Tommy Ryan:

It was clear enough now. All but the alibi. It wasn't something you could take into court. There was no confession. I could even be wrong. But I didn't think so. And neither did she.

That girl, that poor kitten. The golden twins and that poor outsider. But I liked her type of beauty more than Linda's. I liked her more than was comfortable. I put my mind from that.

Well, it was a two–story place, this spot I was going to next. And it was old, and I could force it easily enough, I supposed. Unless the door was better than the doors usually are in those places.

Outside, there was a threat of rain in the air. Clouds, moving in from the east, were obscuring the moon. The breeze was moist.

I drove down the drive to Ardmore and down Ardmore to Lincoln, and followed the bus route downtown. It was about a five–mile drive and I was thinking of Barbara Coles all the way.

This place had been a home, when the city was younger. A narrow, tall, expensive home. There were no lights on. The front door had a cylinder lock, a good one.

I went down three steps and around to the side. As I was contemplating one of the windows there, the first drops of rain began to fall. Thunder rumbled in from the east.

I jumped, got a grip on the window's stone ledge, and hoisted myself up. Kneeling there, on that broad ledge, I ran my fingers up to the top of the bottom window, and shoved. It moved. I felt at the window's lower edge and there was a gap. I shoved the lower half far enough up to let me slide in.

I went right through the big room to the small room in the back. I lighted a match here, found the light switch and flicked it.

The entire place was paneled. Which made my hunch right. But all the panels sounded solid, which made my hunch wrong.

There was another door here.

It opened on steps, steps going down. I went down them, into the musty emptiness of the cellar. Nothing here but some screens. And some windows which were barred and narrow. Not here, then.

Outside, thunder crackled, and I could hear the rising rush of the wind. If not here, where?

I went up the steps slowly.

I don't know why I looked up when I came to the head of the stairs. But I did. And I saw this trapdoor with the ring in it.

I reached up, pulled the ring, and a wooden staircase came slowly down — a staircase leading to the second floor. I went up these stairs.

There was a hall up here, leading to two doors at the back. Both of these doors led to bedrooms. But there must have been another staircase, at one time. This one I had come up was a temporary one, put in when the building was converted to business use.

There were no lights up here, and I was running out of matches. I went down the hall to the front, and here was the old staircase, the bottom of it walled in. To make that big room, downstairs, probably.

Right near the bottom, there was a landing, where the stairs turned, and a stained–glass window illuminated this landing. It wasn't locked. I opened it, and looked out.

Darkness out there, and the dim outlines of what could be a high stone fence. It looked like a courtyard.

Lightning flashed. I saw it was a courtyard, and this window was low enough to permit entrance and exit. Not visible from the street or the alley because of the wall around the yard.

I had no matches left and very little fuel in my lighter. But I found my way back, in the dark, and down the swinging steps. I closed the window I had entered through, and went out the front door.

Rain was pelting down as I made a dash for the coupé.

Well, he'd taken a chance, at that. If anything important came up, and he'd been missing — But he'd taken chances before, even in high school. Maybe he was beginning to like it. He hadn't had too much motivation, this last time.

I drove out toward the park, the windshield wipers clicking, and the tires singing a little on the wet asphalt. I thought about Barbara, and then called myself some derogatory names. It doesn't happen, except in the movies. Not the first time, *bang*, like that! I'd been keyed up, that's all.

Tomorrow would do just as well. There was no hurry, now.

Only here I was, for some reason, in front of his apartment.

Twenty stories up, there were some lights on in the high windows and they looked as if they could be his lights. It wasn't very late. I turned off the motor and listened to the storm. I used what little fuel I had left in lighting a cigarette.

Three puffs, and I threw it away. I shoved open the car door and made a dash for the apartment.

There was still an attendant on duty in one of the elevators.

"Twenty," I said.

"That would be the top," he said, just by way of making conversation.

We went up with no further dialogue.

The mask went on his face as soon as he opened the door. The supercilious, superior look went on. I looked into his eyes, and confirmed what I already knew.

He asked, "Are you here to heckle me again?"

I nodded.

"Come in and track up my rugs."

I went in, tracking up his rugs. In the living room, I didn't sit down, but he did. I said, "I've just been to your studio. I found that staircase and the window."

"You would, of course, eventually. It doesn't prove anything."

"We got an answer to our telegram to Booneville," I lied. "We learned about Hunter and Agell."

No sound came from him. His face got chalky, and his eyes seemed to be burning. His chest rose and fell, as he stared at me.

"Accidents," he said finally.

I went over to the high windows, and looked down. The lights of cars down there looked like fire flies.

I turned. "Maybe. But not Course. Course was murdered."

"Well, what about it?"

"Mrs. Shaw has confessed that she was there at two thirty. I don't know. She'd make a better case."

"No," he said hoarsely, "not Linda! You're lying."

I went back to stand closer to him. "I'm not lying. That's the truth. She told Greg and Greg told me."

"Damn you!" he said, and some other things.

Then he went limp in the chair, and his eyes closed. His voice was a whisper. "Sit down."

I sat down. I put my hat on the floor and ran a finger around its wet crown. A silly habit.

The whisper, "Don't you hate evil?"

"Evil, yes. But not the people who do it. I can't hate people."

"You know the kind of men who carry postcards, those foul, degrading postcards?"

"Hm–m–m."

Lightning flashed, close by, and the thunder crashed. I thought the building trembled.

"Jack Hunter was one of those."

"He was a boy," I said, "a high school kid."

"He was old enough to be rotten. And so was Teddy Agell. After Hunter, the rest came easy. Maybe — oh, Lord, no —"

"Maybe," I said.

"They looked like accidents, but Course was clumsy —"

"Right."

"That … that scene in dad's bedroom, with dad dying. I keep thinking of that. I was young, and —"

I looked at the floor.

"I could have gone to a psychiatrist, I know, but their damned digging, their damned questioning —"

I said quietly, "The strange thing was, I thought Course was in love with Barbara. When I told you he was in love with your sister, this morning, you immediately thought of Linda."

He was staring at me and a strangled sound came from him. Then, "He was after Linda. Barbara first, maybe, but —" His voice dropped off to a mutter.

I had a sudden feeling that he wasn't as relaxed, as limp as he meant to appear. I felt the reassuring bulk of my .38 under my arm but it wasn't for myself I feared.

Rain lashed the tall windows and then from my left, came the grandfather of all thunder peals. Involuntarily, I looked that way, away from the windows.

The next sound I heard was the crash of glass, and when I looked back, there was a hole in the big window, and I was alone in the room. I went over, to look down.

In the road, twenty stories below, the lights of a car stopped at a blob on the pavement.

The papers, next day, revealed that the death of George Course had been determined as accidental by the police, as was the death of Lester Coles, renowned interior decorator. The name of Detective Tommy Ryan appeared in neither of these accounts.

A fruit dealer over on Sixth stabbed a neighbor the next day, and I was busy with that for a few days. I don't think I thought about Barbara more than once an hour during that time.

Tuesday, Greg Shaw dropped in to see me. He looked uncomfortable.

"I suppose you all hate me," I said.

He shook his head. "Linda doesn't even suspect. I don't know about Barbara. Anyway, she — well, you play bridge, Tommy?"

I thought that over. Then I answered. "Sure."

"There's just the three of us," he said, "and we thought you'd like to make it a fourth. On Wednesday nights."

"Fine," I said. "Fine"

He left, then, and I went out to get a book on bridge.

Tin–Pan Alibi

I'd had a bad night. Not only because of the three grand I'd lost, or the hands I lost it on. I'd lost that much, and more, before. But this night, nothing worked. This night, I knew, began one of those slumps all gamblers get. Maybe this would be the big one, the final one. Maybe, after this one, I'd be penny–ante Paul, trying to make a nickel here and there the easiest way possible. It's the first time that thought ever lived with me, though it had lived with others, I know.

Confidence — that's one thing a gambler can't lose. Or anyone else who doesn't want to play it the safe way, the weary way. That's what I'd lost that night, along with the three grand.

It was around four in the morning, a misty miserable morning, and these thoughts were with me as the cab swung around the corner and stopped in front of the apartment.

When I stepped out, I saw the light, and wondered at it. It was on the third floor, in front. That's my apartment. I hadn't left it on, I was sure. And nobody knows where I live — keeping my address secret is the only protection I have against moochers twenty–four hours a day. Nobody knows except Joe.

Joe's my brother. He's all right. He's about the best clarinet this side of Goodman. He looks a little like Tyrone Power, and that doesn't hurt him with the ladies. He could maybe be a little more choosy about *which* ladies, but … Oh, Joe's all right. He's my brother.

I paid the cabbie and went slowly up the steps to the front door, and slowly up the three steps inside the front door to the second floor. I was fitting my key in this when the buzzer told me the door was unlocked.

That would be Joe, saving me time. He had a key, and he was up there, waiting for me at four in the morning. It would be trouble again. It would be some husband again. It would be my shoulder he'd want to cry on, again.

I wasn't in the mood, tonight, not my Dorothy Dix mood. But he's Joe — he's my brother.

When the cage ground to a stop at the third floor, he was waiting for me. He said: "Paul — thank God you're home, finally."

This was no jealous husband deal. This was no touch. His face was white and sick–looking. He was keyed–up, and his voice was almost a falsetto.

"They're after me," he said hoarsely. "I had to come here, Paul. It was the only place I —"

"Who's after you?" I said.

"The police," he said.

There was a silence. I remember thinking: *It's a good thing Ma isn't alive, to hear this.* I remember thinking: *It had to come, the way he was going. The clarinet isn't enough for him. It's enough for Shaw and Goodman, but not Joe. He's got to have the rest of it, too. The liquor and the women — maybe more.*

"The police?" I repeated, like some jerk in a soap box opera. "Why, Joe?"

"Murder," he said.

It's an ugly word. It hung there in the air, haunting us, not going away, vibrating there in the quiet, damp air. I couldn't take my eyes away from his. I couldn't stop staring at him, as though he was someone, something, I'd never seen before. Murder, murder, murder …

He said shrilly: "Don't look at me like that, Paul. God, you don't think I — Paul, you —"

Innocent, I thought. I can tell, with Joe. Relief washed through me, leaving me limp. "Keep your voice down," I said. "Let's get into the apartment."

He followed me in. The place was foul with cigarette smoke, and all the windows were closed. I opened a few, and turned down the floor lamp to its lowest filament. "Sit down," I told him, "and give it to me straight."

I got it. Not straight, but with side excursions into how bad it looked for him, and why they were trying to find him, and what a case it would make.

This was it: Rex Andrews was dead. Rex Andrews, the self–named Sovereign Of The Saxophone, leader of a popular if schmaltzy gang of waltz–worriers, a wealthy man married to a wealthy woman. The woman's name was Corinne, and it had been Corinne Belfast before it was Corinne Andrews. Her dad was Tom Belfast, and I'd been playing poker with him tonight.

I asked: "What was she to you, Joe?"

He lit a cigarette. He was looking down at the rug. "A hell of a lot less than I was to her. Paul, believe me, I never encouraged her. I kidded her along, sure, but it wasn't anything serious."

"Not to you, maybe," I said.

He didn't answer.

Joe had had words with Rex, the night before this one, in the bar of the club Joe played at. Enough people had heard that. Joe had gone up to see Corinne this very night, earlier, before he was due at the club.

"I just stopped in for a talk," he told me dully. "I wanted to break it off. She didn't mean enough to me, not nearly enough to get Rex riled up. I told her that, as tactfully as I could." He shook his head. "I was telling her that when Rex walked in. I thought he was having a rehearsal, or I'd never been there."

"That's when she left?"

He nodded. "Rex told her to get the hell out — he wanted to talk to me alone. I thought he was going to slug me; but he didn't. He was always a phony. He didn't even seem very rough, once she left. He said it looked bad, and I should lay off. I told him that's just what I had in mind."

I said: "He bawls you out, twice, in front of people. When you're alone, he changes his tune. That spell anything to you?"

"Just that he's a blow–off."

"Well, go on."

"We went to work after that. He quits a little earlier than I do — he's working at Danceland. He goes home, and his wife isn't back yet. She's over at the club, listening to me. He phoned her from a drugstore, had her paged at the club. He said he wouldn't be home any more that night. He was walking out."

Again, Joe shook his head.

"Corinne talked me into taking her along to Shorty's, for a little jamming, after I was through at the club. I got the word there."

"From Shorty?"

"From Shorty. He said he'd heard Rex Andrews had been clubbed to death, and the law was looking for me. He told me if I wasn't clean, I'd better get. He didn't want any cops in his place."

"And you got? You as much as told him you weren't clean?"

"I didn't know what to do. I left Corinne there, and came here."

"Why? She was with you, all the time. She's your alibi."

He was studying his hands. He wasn't looking at me. "One thing I didn't tell you. On the way to Shorty's, we stopped at her place. She had a platinum cigarette case of mine she wanted to return." Now he looked up to meet my gaze. "She said she wouldn't go up — scared I might duck out, if she did. She gave me her key, and I went up and got it."

Sure, that's Joe. The original fall guy. I asked: "How long did that take?"

"Couple minutes. Maybe five."

"Nobody was there?"

"Nobody. Anyway, I didn't see anybody."

"Wasn't that kind of dumb? What if Rex had been there?"

"He didn't scare me." He looked down at the carpet again. "I hoped he was. I didn't want her along, anyway."

"Where'd they find Rex?" I asked him.

He shrugged. "I don't know. Shorty didn't say, and I didn't wait to find out."

Unless Rex had been killed at home, Joe was in the clear. And Rex had said he was walking out. There were any number of places Rex could have been killed. Yet, Joe had come here to hide ...

I asked quietly: "Are you *sure* there was no one at the apartment when you went up to get the cigarette case?"

He shook his head. "I didn't see anyone. I suppose I'm *reasonably* sure. I didn't search the joint."

"Then why did you come here?" I asked.

He looked puzzled.

"If Rex wasn't killed at home," I pointed out, "you're safe. Corinne will be your alibi. You didn't have to run."

He looked at me, and away. He said in a thoughtful voice: "I guess I always come running to you when I'm in trouble. I always have, haven't I, Paul?"

"That's right," I said, "and I'm not kicking on that. But I think this is *one* time you shouldn't have run *anywhere*."

He took a deep breath. He ran his hand over his face in a weary gesture, and said nothing.

I said: "Nobody can prove you're hiding. You came to see me. You don't know anything. Understand that? You just came here to visit me."

He nodded wordlessly.

"You'd better hit the hay now," I told him. "I'm going to make myself a cup of coffee. The morning papers will be out with it soon. I want to see where Rex was killed."

He tried a smile, but it was a sad attempt. He said: "Paul, if I get clear on this, you won't have to worry about me ever again. That's a promise."

"Sure," I said. "But hit the hay, now."

Despite the coffee, I felt like hell. My eyes kept closing on me, and there was the gummy taste of too many cigarettes lingering in my mouth. I brushed my teeth, but that didn't do much good.

I thought: *It won't help the kid any, being my brother.* I'd never had any trouble with the law — I gamble with people who can afford to lose. But they know me, down at headquarters and they don't love me. The kid would get no breaks, I was sure of that.

About five, I went out to the stand on the transfer corner. The old gent there was just unwrapping a fresh bundle of morning papers, and I got the top one, still warm.

There was a picture of Rex on the front page. There was a headline: BAND LEADER SLAIN.

I glanced at it, folded the paper, and tucked it under my arm. I didn't want the old gent to think I was too interested. I should have known better.

"Mr. Cornell," he called after me, and I turned. He had a paper in his hand. "Ain't this your brother Joe?" he asked me.

I tried to look surprised. I took my own paper out from under my arm and unfolded it. Joe's picture was on the lower half of the page, under the fold, and I'd missed it.

MUSICIAN SOUGHT was the title under that.

I nodded. "It is," I said. "I've been looking for him all night."

He shook his shaggy head. "That's sure tough, Mr. Cornell. I sure hope every-thing turns out all right."

"It will," I said. But I didn't believe it. Not the way my luck had been running lately.

I read the rest of the account after I got back to the apartment. The first thing I learned was that Rex had been killed in his own home. At least, he'd been found dead there. So Joe wasn't in the clear, not completely. Though, the paper stated, Rex Andrews' wife, Corinne, claimed that Joe had been with her continuously from the time Rex had phoned her until they had parted at Shorty's.

There was no mention of the trip up for the cigarette case.

I wondered if Joe would be safe here. The man at the newsstand knew who I was — he saw me every day. But he didn't know where I lived, excepting that it was in the neighborhood. I decided to let Joe sleep. I decided to try and get a little sleep myself.

Nobody knows where I live, I told myself, nobody but Joe.

I'd been tossing on my bed for an hour when the doorbell rang. The third time it rang, I slipped into a robe and went to the door.

I knew the man standing there. He was a Detective Sergeant Manning Keller, of Homicide. Nobody knows where I live. Not much.

"Paul Cornell?" he asked.

I nodded.

He flashed a badge, and told me who he was. He's not a tall man, nor heavy. But he's sharp and hard and overlooks nothing. He said, "I'm looking for your brother."

"So am I," I told him.

His dark blue eyes took in the robe. "In that?"

"I went to bed about ten minutes ago," I told him. "As soon as you leave, I'm going back to bed. Was there anything else?"

He seemed bored. "As long as I'm looking I thought I'd look here, too. If you don't mind?"

"Not if you've got a warrant," I told him.

"I haven't," he said. "I could get one pretty quick, though. If your brother isn't here there'd be no reason why I couldn't look around, would there?"

"There might be somebody else here," I said, trying to look Latin. "I think you'd better get the warrant."

He snapped his jaws once or twice, considering this. His eyes moved around my face and then came back to meet mine. "There's no reason," he said quietly, "for you to play it cute. If there's a babe in there, I can ignore her. All I'm looking for is your brother."

"And the only way to look for him would be to get a warrant," I said. I started to close the door, but his foot was there, suddenly. And there was a gun in his hand.

"I'm coming in," he said. "You can sue me later, if you want, but I'm coming in now." A forceful and direct man. He came in.

He took one glance around the living room and then headed for the rear, toward the kitchenette. I heard him open the bedroom closet in there, and then he was back in the hall. He paused, there, in front of the small bedroom door. I held my breath.

He opened it and went in.

No sound. I heard the door to the closet in there creak, but that was all. I waited. It couldn't have been long, but it seemed an hour. When he came out, he had a piece of paper in his hand. He said: "You've read this, I suppose?" and handed it to me.

It was from Joe. I read:

I'm blowing, Paul. There's no reason you should get mixed up in all my messes. Don't worry about me. I'll get in touch with you later.

I looked up to meet Keller's hard stare. "No," I said, "I hadn't read it."

"You told me you were looking for him. You thought he was there, didn't you? When'd he leave?"

I paused, and he raised a hand. "Don't bother to lie. The bed's not made. I know he must have slept here."

I said: "He must have left when I went out to get a paper."

"He was here all night?"

"He was here when I came home. That was four o'clock." I met his stare levelly. "I know it doesn't make any difference to the law, but the kid's innocent. He's clear of that Andrews deal."

"Sure," he said. "They're all clear. They always are." He was walking toward my bedroom.

I heard him walking around in there, and he went into the bathroom. When he returned to the living room, he moved directly toward the door. There he said: "When he gets in touch with you, you let us know. You let us know right away."

"Naturally," I said. "He's only my brother. I'd help you railroad him to the chair."

His glance moved up and down my frame. "There some special reason you don't like the law, Mr. Cornell? You've been pretty lucky, I'd say, for a gambler."

"That's what we live on," I said. "Luck."

He nodded shortly. "Let's hope it doesn't run out." The door closed quietly behind him.

I went to the window. I saw him leave the building, glance across the street, and step into a department car at the curb. Across the street, there was another car, and a man sitting in the front seat. That's where Keller had glanced. They were wasting their time. I felt sure Joe wouldn't come back here, not this time.

One of the best clarinets in the world, Joe is. A rabbit's morals, where women are concerned, and a fast lad with a dollar. But Joe's all right. They wouldn't rail- road him — not while I was alive.

I wondered where he'd gone.

I was still tired, but I knew sleep would be impossible. I went into the bathroom and took a cold shower. Then I dressed and went out.

The man in the car on the other side of the street didn't seem to notice me. He overdid it — he didn't look my way at all, though any man just sitting in a car would notice any moving object.

I walked down to the corner and turned. I stopped then, and walked back. He was getting out of the car. When he saw me standing there, he pretended to be examining a tire.

There was an off chance Joe might try and contact me on the street. I didn't want any company if that happened. I walked east, to the chain drug store three blocks up.

From a phone booth in there, I called Tom Belfast.

It was Tom who answered the phone. After I'd identified myself, I asked: "Would it be possible for me to see Corinne this morning, Tom?"

There was a silence. Then: "Why, Paul?"

"I want to know about Joe," I explained. "I want her story, Tom, if she feels like talking about it."

"I know the story," he said, and there was another silence. "Including the part about the cigarette case."

"I didn't read about that in the paper," I said. "Don't the police know it?"

"Neither Corinne nor I told them," he said. "And I'd — rather you didn't bother her this morning, Paul."

I could understand that. I said: "Joe's in the clear. I'm sure of that. Joe's no murderer."

"Killing Rex Andrews shouldn't be classed as murder," Tom said.

The line went dead.

I had some bacon and eggs at the lunch counter, along with three cups of coffee.

When I went outside again, the sun had driven away all the morning's mist, and the air was dry and light. My friend was parked about two cars back from the drug store entrance.

He was a bulky man, with a round, placid face. Something glimmered in my memory. Then he was grinning at me.

I knew him. Years and years ago we'd sat in many a two–bit limit game together. His name was Porky Wrede. I walked over to the car, and stuck my head in through the open window.

I said: "You could do better than this, Porky. This is a hell of a job for a grown man."

He chuckled. "I stayed in the minor leagues, Paul. I always figured poker should be your business." He reached over to open the door. "Going some place I can take you?"

"I don't want to get you in trouble," I said. "Keller might not like this."

"To hell with Keller," he said. "My uncle's the mayor's best friend." I climbed in.

"Besides," he added, "your brother's got an air–tight alibi. Even Keller would have a job breaking that."

I said carefully: "You call that air–tight? The two of them are together. I should think the first thing the cops would suspect would be that Joe got rid of an unwanted husband."

The big head shook slowly from side to side. "No. Your brother didn't want any part of that Andrews doll. His girl is *way* out of that class." His eyes were reminiscent. "What a dame!"

This was news to me. "What's her name?" I asked.

He looked at me in surprise. "You mean you never met her? You never met Linda Travis?"

I'd heard of her. She was the surprise star of last season's surprisingly successful drama *Winter Roots*. She was beautiful and talented and often in print. I'd heard of her, but never in connection with Joe.

"You should read the gossip columnists," Wrede said. "You must be about the only guy in town that doesn't know they're just about engaged."

"I don't see Joe much," I explained. *Only when he's in trouble*, I thought, but didn't say.

Wrede said musingly: "I'll bet that's where the kid will head. If Keller had any sense, he'd be covering her, instead of you."

Keller had sense, I was sure. Keller would have thought of that angle. I said: "Where does she live?"

"The Warkshire — seventh floor. Shares an apartment with some big shot's secretary over there. Very cozy."

"How'd you like to run me over there?" I asked him.

He shrugged. "Why not? I can watch you just as well this way."

The Warkshire was a tall, glazed brick building near Bay Park. Wrede stopped the car directly in front of the entrance, despite the 'No parking' sign there. "I'll wait," he said. Then, as I was closing the door; "There's nothing here, you understand, but you won't be wasting your time."

I smiled at him. "This I want to see," I told him.

There was a lobby in the building, and a desk clerk. The desk clerk looked at me with some coolness when I asked the number of Miss Travis' apartment.

"If you'll give me your name," he informed me, "I'll see if Miss Travis is in."

I gave him my name. I added: "Tell her I'm Joe's brother."

His eyebrows went up at that, and he may have looked a little frightened. He evidently had read the morning papers.

Miss Travis would see me. I could feel the clerk's eyes on me all the way to the elevator.

She was waiting there, in the doorway of her apartment, when I got out at the seventh floor. I'd had some words ready, an opening speech, but I forgot it.

She wore a white terrycloth robe. She had black hair, black as jet, and eyes like the Pacific on a clear day. She was slim, but not in any place she shouldn't be. Her hair was piled up in back, as though she was about ready for a shower.

If what Wrede said was true, Joe was doing very well. Something like envy, only stronger, moved through me. Something like jealousy.

She smiled, and held out her hand. "Joe's often spoken of you," she said softly. Her voice was low and pleasant.

I said something I've forgotten now, and we went in together. There, I said: "I wondered if you'd heard from him."

She shook her head, and looked at me strangely. "You think that he might —"

I shrugged. "If — I mean — you're —" I stopped. "Joe's never mentioned your name to me. But if he feels about you as I've been led to believe he does, he'll probably contact you, today."

Again she looked at me strangely. "We're nothing more than friends," she said. "What did you mean?"

"I thought — I'd been told you were practically engaged."

"No," she said, and smiled. "No, though we have seen a lot of each other. It's —" She frowned, faintly. "Maybe it's the clarinet. Or maybe it's just that he's such a — a tonic. He's a lot of fun, Joe is." Then, more gravely: "Do you think it's true the police want him for that — for what happened? They can't really believe that about him, can they?"

"They're not very sentimental," I told her. "They can believe anything the facts might fit."

There was a chair here, near a cigarette table, and I sat in it. There was an ash tray on the cigarette table, filled with half smoked cigarettes. Some of the cigarettes were tipped with lip rouge, and some were tipped with cork. The ones that were tipped with cork were Admirals.

That's what Joe smoked.

My eyes went from the ash tray to meet the gaze of those ocean–blue eyes. She was suddenly tense.

"If he isn't here now," I asked, "when was he here?"

"Not today, nor yesterday," she answered evenly. "We're lousy housekeepers here."

The rest of the apartment didn't look it. I thought: *They're only friends, but she covers for him. Joe always had all the luck.*

She was still watching me quietly, fearfully.

I said: "He's my brother. I have faith in him. You don't have to lie to me."

"I'm not lying," she said, and her voice was tight. She was chewing her lower lip now. "I — please — it's not that I want to seem unfeeling — but —" She paused. "But I can't afford any unpleasant publicity." Her chin was up now, and she was honestly speaking her mind. "I can't afford to mess up my career with a murder. I'm not that well established."

Maybe Joe wasn't so lucky. Maybe this is why she had claimed no more than friendship.

I said: "I'd always heard that any kind of publicity was good publicity for an actress. Or an actor. The public's morals aren't what they were."

"I'm not taking any chances," she said. "Joe isn't that important to me."

That was plain enough, that made sense. The rest had been part of her art.

"I understand," I said, and rose. "I don't suppose there's anything more?"

She shook her dark head. "Nothing."

I couldn't hate her nor pity her. It was her scene and I was just a minor member of the cast. I felt sorry for Joe. If he won her, or if he didn't, Joe would have something to regret.

She walked with me to the door. I said: "You're very young, Miss Travis."

"I'm not as young as you might think," she told me. She smiled. "Nor as hard." The door closed.

I went thoughtfully down the hall to the elevator, and down in the elevator to the street level. Wrede still waited outside. The sun was behind a cloud, and the mugginess was coming back.

Wrede was smirking. "Well?"

"Quite a girl," I said.

He nodded his big head. He asked: "Where now?"

"That Corinne Andrews — I suppose she's staying with her father?"

Wrede nodded.

"You know where he lives?"

"Tom Belfast? Keller and I spent an hour there."

"Let's go over there," I suggested.

Wrede kicked the car into life, and headed out into the traffic stream.

"You can never tell about an actress, can you?" I asked him.

He was still smirking. "She slap you, Paul?"

"Figuratively," I said, "only figuratively."

It was going to be a hell of a day. All of yesterday's sullen mistiness was back. I felt clammy and uncomfortable.

Wrede said: "According to Doc Sternig, that Andrews guy was dragged around. The back of his jacket was covered with lint, and so was the back of his head. That spell anything to you, Paul?"

"Somebody was a poor housekeeper," I suggested. *Linda Travis had claimed to be one,* I remembered.

"Sure," Wrede said. "But why drag the guy around? Unless he wasn't killed there?"

"I'm no detective," I said pointedly. "I'm just a guy whose brother happens to be in a jam."

"Sure," Wrede said again. "I suppose they'll find out some more at the lab about the lint. And Keller — nobody fools that guy for long."

"With eighteen unsolved murders for the year, so far," I said, "somebody's being fooled."

"You read the *Post*," Wrede said. "The *Post* is sour on us."

We had no further conversation on the trip to Belfast's.

I went in alone. Tom Belfast came to the door. He's a short man, with a lined face and gray–black hair. His eyes are as black as his hair once was. They weren't friendly this morning.

He came out onto the porch of his fine colonial home, closing the front door firmly behind him. He said: "If you've come to see Corinne, Paul, you can leave. She's not seeing anyone this morning."

"I can understand how you feel about it, Tom," I said, "but try to see my side of it, too. Joe means a lot to me, as much as Corinne does to you."

He said nothing for a moment. His black eyes were directed toward the floor of the porch. They came up to meet mine. "We're going to tell the police about the cigarette case," he said quietly.

"That was your idea," I guessed aloud, "not Corinne's."

"It was my idea," he admitted. "She's got to protect herself." He paused. "No matter who gets hurt."

I nodded, studying him. I said: "I've an I.O.U. of yours, Tom, for five thousand dollars. I've been carrying it a long time. Too long."

There was a hardness in his face now, in the black eyes. "You trying to black–mail me, Paul?"

I shook my head. "I'm trying to collect."

His voice was even. "I haven't got it, not handy. My luck's been as bad as yours, lately."

"That's right," I said. "But Corinne will inherit a bundle now. The cops will be glad to know about your financial condition."

His eyes were more than hard now. There was a rasp to his voice. He called me a name. He asked: "What the hell are you suggesting? You were with me all last night. I wasn't out for more than five minutes. Then I just went to the washroom."

"It makes a good story," I admitted. "Could I see Corinne now?"

He hesitated. Beneath his obvious rage, there was something else. It could have been fear.

"What do you want to talk about?" he asked me.

"About my brother," I told him. "He's missing and there are some things I want to know. If I knew where he was, I'd ask him. But he's not around."

He still hesitated. Then, finally, he said: "Come on in."

We went into the dim coolness of the house, into a long, fairly wide living room. The shades were drawn in here, the air cool and damp. It was an off–white room, tastefully furnished.

The girl who sat in the huge chair near the fireplace seemed to be in a trance. Her face was as white as the woodwork, her hands clenched on the arms of the chair.

I said: "I'm Joe's brother."

Her large violet eyes swiveled to meet mine. Her body didn't move, she didn't relax her grip on the chair–arms.

Tom said quietly: "It's all right, Corinne. He's just worried about Joe."

She had a slight but well–built body and lovely legs. She had a mass of soft, auburn hair. Her voice was tight. "What do you want?"

"I want to know when Rex came home, and what time he called you. I want to know what time Joe went up for the cigarette case."

"I wasn't there when Rex came home. I suppose it was right after midnight. Danceland closes at midnight. He phoned me a half hour after that. Joe went up to get the cigarette case about one–thirty, I think."

All this in a level voice — in a *rehearsed* voice?

"Did Joe see Rex when he went up there?"

Her eyes avoided mine. "If he did — he didn't tell me."

"That means he didn't," I said.

Tom Belfast said: "The police will decide that. You got all the answers you want, now?"

"I've got all I'll probably get," I answered. "I can't see why you're trying to frame Joe, though, Tom."

There was some sound from Corinne, half gasp, half sob. She said hoarsely: "What are you talking about?"

"Your father's going to tell the police about the cigarette case," I told her.

She was leaning forward now, staring at her father. "No," she said sharply. "Dad — you won't do that. Understand? You won't tell them about that."

His face was grave. He didn't look at her. "I'll do what's best for you," he said quietly. "I'll withhold nothing from the police."

She seemed to have forgotten me, now. Her slight body was bent forward, as though she were going to leap at her father.

I waited, but nobody said a word. She wanted to protect Joe. She must love him. She must love him more than that Linda did.

Outside, I could hear an automobile horn. In the room, nobody said a word.

Then Tom was looking at me. "Is that all you want? Don't you think you've disturbed her enough?"

I didn't answer him. I continued to watch Corinne, waiting for her to say more. But she evidently had no more to say.

I said: "If Joe should get in touch with you, let me know. And tell him I want to see him, I've got to see him."

She was still sitting in the big chair, staring at nothing, when Tom walked to the door with me. We parted without another word.

Wrede was smoking a vile–smelling cigar when I got back to the car. "Well?" he said.

"It's hard to tell about people, isn't it?" I asked him.

"What people?" he asked, reasonably enough.

"That Linda Travis, for example," I pointed out. "I'd figure her for an all–right gal. But all she wants is a career. And Tom Belfast I'd always known as a genial sort of guy. He isn't now. Joe always brought his troubles to me. When he's really in trouble, he ducks out, and goes it alone. That Corinne could be the most loyal one of the lot, and nobody seems to think much about her."

"It's too warm for that kind of talk," Wrede said. "Where can we get a beer around here?"

"At the Whist Club," I answered. "It's only a little ways from here."

It was more than that. It was a good mile. But I wanted to go there.

Wrede said: "They still running that game up on the second floor?"

"Could be," I said. I didn't tell him that that's where I'd been the night before.

It was a plain, two–story building of dark–red brick. The first floor was a combination bar and restaurant, with a room in the back for bridge players.

The second floor held the big games, not open to the general public. I left Wrede at the bar, while I went up to the second floor.

The room we had used was in the front of the building, the second floor washroom was in the back. In the hallway, leading between the rooms, there was a pay phone.

We were at least a mile from the Belfast home, and farther than that from the Andrews apartment. No, it couldn't be, not in five minutes, not in the length of time a man could go to the washroom.

Which left only Joe, but Joe's no murderer. Wrede was on his second glass of beer when I came downstairs again. His stogie, half smoked, was in an ash tray on the bar.

He gulped down the rest of his beer. His face, I saw, when he looked at me, was beaded with perspiration. "You're cute," he said. "You and Belfast were both here last night, weren't you?"

"If Tom told you that, it's true," I said.

"He told us that. There's some things you're not telling us, though, huh, Paul?"

"I'm telling you all I know."

His gaze moved around my face. "O.K. Where now?"

"The Ebony Club," I said. That's where Joe had played.

"O.K.," he said. "But I sure hope Keller doesn't find out about this. He'll raise hell."

"Don't forget," I reminded him, "that your uncle is the mayor's best friend."

They didn't know much, over at the Ebony Club. They didn't seem to want to know much. The bartender, who'd had Corinne paged for the phone call, didn't remember exactly when the call had come through. Around one o'clock.

He didn't know when Corinne had come in. He didn't remember who had called her. "They don't usually give their name," he explained.

Joe had left at what time?

He shrugged. "One–thirty, maybe. I don't remember."

The manager remembered even less. He kept telling me about all the trouble he had trying to get another clarinet.

"Try Shaw," I told him. "He or Goodman are all that can come close to Joe."

He had no answer to that.

Wrede didn't say "Well?" this time. But he looked at me inquiringly when I came back to the car.

"Nothing," I said. "None of them know anything, except how to run a night spot. You want to take me home?"

"Why not?" he said, and started the motor. His eyes were on the street. "I'll drop down to the station first, to make a report. You can wait on the corner." His voice was casual — too casual.

I got that feeling then. It's something I can't explain — it's something I've had before, a premonition. I play them, when I get them, and I make money when I play them. I wasn't playing for money, now.

I said: "O.K., I'll wait on the corner."

If Keller had put him on to me as a tail, if he was supposed to stick to me, how could he explain his presence at the station? How could he explain leaving me? That much was ordinary logic — the rest of it was that funny hunch.

He dropped me on the corner, and pulled away.

I didn't wait on the corner. Only until I saw his broad beam disappear into the wide doorway of the station house. Then I was moving swiftly after him.

There was the clatter of typewriters and the voice of an assistant D.A., giving somebody hell. There was a plainclothesman reading a newspaper on a bench, and some uniformed officers passing the time of day in a corner.

There was Porky Wrede's wide behind, disappearing around the bend in the corridor that led to Homicide. I followed, trying to look as though I had business here.

I made the corner just as he disappeared into one of the offices lining it. Fortunately for me, he didn't close the door.

I stopped outside the door, leaned against the wall, and pretended to be waiting for something or somebody.

I heard their voices clearly.

Wrede was saying: "… took him every place he wanted to go, just like you said. He fell for it. But he didn't come through with a damned thing."

And Keller's voice: "That's that, then. We can't keep your wife out of this forever. The papers are bound to find out she'd been dating this Andrews. Where the hell are we going to be then?"

"Just give me a little more time, that's all. Look, Keller, my wife and I — well, I mean she realizes now that —"

I stepped into the doorway.

Wrede's jaw seemed to drop a foot when he saw me. There was no change of expression on Keller's face. He said: "Where the hell did you come from?"

"From the hall," I told him, "where I was listening in. You won't need to worry about the papers, Wrede. I'll tip them off myself."

Wrede said worriedly: "Listen, Paul, I didn't —"

"You didn't frame Joe," I finished for him. "Not yet, you didn't. But you and your buddy were sure trying. The *Post* will love to hear about this."

Keller didn't look worried. Wrede seemed to be doing all of that. Keller said: "We're not trying to frame anybody, Cornell. I'd be a pretty sad louse, if I couldn't keep an innocent woman's name out of a mess like this."

"You've done all right up to now," I agreed. "You didn't seem to worry about my brother's name."

Keller looked down at his desk top, and up again. "If he's so innocent," he said quietly, "why did he run away?"

"Maybe he knows how you operate," I answered.

That reached him. His sharp face grew grim, and color mounted in his cheeks. He half rose and then seated himself again, fighting for control. His voice was almost a whisper. "That wasn't necessary, Cornell."

"Maybe not," I said. "But neither was the act you and Wrede put on. If my brother's guilty of murder, I'd turn him in myself. You can believe that, or not. I'd lie to protect him, if I thought he was innocent, just like Wrede would lie to protect his wife. But I don't think even Wrede would cover for a murderer. I hope he wouldn't."

Wrede said nothing. Keller said nothing.

"You come busting into my place," I went on, "with a gun in your hand, instead of a warrant. You were in a big hurry to find a fall guy, weren't you?"

"I'm not out to railroad anybody," Keller said. "You got a better suspect?"

"Only Wrede," I said.

Wrede shook his broad head. Keller said: "Wrede's covered, all the way. I checked his alibi personally. I wouldn't cover for anybody, either, Cornell. Not even another cop."

I believed him. We'd never be lodge–mates, but I had respect for Keller, after a fashion. "I've got another suspect, too," I said, "but it's just a hunch. It's nothing I'd want to bother you Einsteins with."

"Somebody we know?" Keller asked.

"Somebody you interviewed," I said, and started toward the door. "If it's all right with you, I'll go now."

Keller's smile was cool. "You won't mind if Wrede follows you?"

"He can take me, for all I care," I said.

Wrede looked at Keller, and Keller nodded. Wrede said: "C'mon, Paul, we'll work together. No hard feelings, huh?" He was holding out his hand. It was a big, damp and fleshy hand, engulfing mine.

It's easy to be wrong about people, I thought, about all of them, including Wrede. I could have been wrong about Linda Travis.

I asked Wrede to drive me back there. He told me something about his wife, on the way back. She was younger than he was, and still thought it all right to go to Danceland occasionally, even though Wrede was too busy to accompany her usually. That's where she'd met Rex Andrews.

"Nothing wrong with it," Wrede told me. "I know there was nothing wrong. She's just kind of young, yet." He sounded like a man who was trying very hard to convince himself.

I said nothing, only half hearing him.

Linda didn't open the door, this time. It was another girl, probably the secretary Wrede had talked about. I asked if Linda was home.

She hesitated.

I said: "I've got to see her. Please go and tell her."

She was a tall slim girl, with horn–rimmed glasses. Her smooth forehead wrinkled in doubt.

A voice behind her said: "Let him in, Carol. It's all right."

I came in.

Linda Travis wasn't wearing the terry cloth robe now. She had on a light blue linen one–piece dress which was very economically cut, back and front. Her legs were bare, and she was wearing platform shoes.

She was smiling.

"You're all right," I told her. "You put on a good act, but you're aces, just the same. Trot him out."

The surprise she feigned could have fooled anyone. "Trot who out? Or is it 'whom'?"

"It's my brother," I said, "remember? He's here. You're his girl, all right. You'd cover for him."

She shook her head. "Joe can take care of himself, Mr. Cornell. He's a big boy now."

"I want to talk to him," I said. "I've got to talk to him. He's playing it dumb. He's being gallant. He's putting his neck in a noose."

She was rigid, now, her eyes startled. "What *are* you saying?"

Then he was standing there, in the doorway that led from the hall. "What's the matter, Paul?" he asked me.

I said nothing, admiring his looks for a moment. He had never looked better, or more like a man. "I want to know about Corinne," I told him.

"What's there to know?"

"What time she came to the club, and who phoned her, and if you saw anything when you went up for that cigarette case."

"I've told you all I know," he said.

"Maybe," I agreed, "but not what you suspect. She was nervous when she came to the club, wasn't she? Something was bothering her?"

His silence was assent, I knew.

"You guessed, as soon as you heard about Rex, that she knew who had done it, that it had been on her mind all night?"

He said: "She's an emotional girl. She's been upset before."

"But not like last night, maybe?"

"She was pretty bad," he agreed. "But if Rex phoned her —"

"*If*," I said. "Or if anybody else phoned her, she could pretend it was Rex, and then stick with you, all the time, like a leech. A fine alibi, that."

His eyes closed a moment. "You think —"

"Why not? She might have sent you up for the cigarette case as a further alibi, as proof that Rex wasn't in the apartment then, or maybe to frame you. You see, he was dragged into another room after he was killed. Out where you wouldn't see him, so the police would suspect you."

He shook his head dazedly. "I don't get it."

I said: "If you went up there, and he was in plain sight wouldn't you phone the police?"

He nodded.

"All right," I went on. "That would just about clear you. And if you didn't go up there, you'd be in the clear, too, because you were working at the time he was killed, and you were at that jam session long after that. She had to get you up there."

"Not Corinne," he said, and shook his head. "She's nothing to me, Paul, believe it. And she had been fighting with Rex for a month. But she wouldn't try to frame me."

"She doesn't want to, now," I admitted. "She's had a change of heart. But after she'd clubbed him to death, it seemed like a good idea. She just hasn't got the stamina to stick with it."

Joe looked pale. Linda went over to stand next to him. They made a fine looking picture. "Why would she kill him?" Joe asked softly.

"Because he was cheating on her, right and left. Because he was browbeating her. Because a human being can take just so much of that kind of a slob, and then they go crazy."

Joe said quietly: "She didn't come into the club until twelve–thirty. I noticed that." His hand was around Linda's, now.

I left them, standing like that. I envied them, especially him.

It really wasn't any of my business. Excepting that Joe was still involved, as long as the police had nobody better. Back at the car, Wrede was looking impatient. "Anything new there?" he asked me.

"Nothing much," I lied. And I told him what I had told Joe and Linda.

"It makes sense," he agreed. "You want to go over and see?"

I told him what I wanted, and how I wanted it.

He took me about a block from there, and I walked the rest of the way.

The shades were still down in the living room, though there was still no sun. Tom came to the door.

"What now?" he wanted to know.

"It would be better," I told him, "if Corinne would confess. It makes it look less — brutal, that way."

"You gone crazy?" he asked me.

"It's practically sewed up," I lied. "They found out when it happened, and they know Corinne was home then."

His face was like marble, marble with two pieces of jet for eyes. "Come in," he said.

I went in. Corinne was still sitting in the same chair, though she seemed a shade more relaxed. Her eyes were droopy, as though she'd had a sedative.

I wondered if Tom had noticed that I had unlocked the night latch as I came in.

"All right," he said, "now tell me what you were talking about."

"You know," I told him. "You phoned her at the club, from that pay phone in the hall of the Whist Club, didn't you?"

"Sure I called her. I wanted to find out how she was."

"Why?"

His eyes met mine squarely. "Because she'd had trouble with Rex. I wanted to know if he was abusing her."

"You didn't tell the police about that. You let them think it was Rex who had called."

"Dad —" The voice was incredibly weary, and she was keeping her eyes open only by an exceptional display of will. "Dad — why should we hide, and lie? Remember what I almost — did to Joe, what — Please, Dad —" The eyes closed, flickered open again weakly.

Tom Belfast expelled his breath, and looked at me. "It's nothing to you, is it, Paul? There's no personal reason you'd want my girl to suffer for killing a man who had it coming as badly as he did? She killed him, sure, but —"

From the doorway, Wrede said: "That's all I wanted to hear."

The look Tom gave me should have shriveled my soul. Only I remembered he'd been trying to frame Joe. And Joe's my brother.

Corinne beat the first degree charge. She beat them all — on a plea of temporary insanity — and she brought enough witnesses into court to prove Rex was the boy who could drive a girl to that. Wrede's wife never got into it, though a lot of other wives did.

Joe's different, now that he and Linda are married. But then, Joe was always all right especially on the clarinet. They're going to name the first boy Paul.

Creature of Habit

Without the Friday nights he might have gone on and on. He had his own world, after office hours, his printed world, and adversity troubled him very little.

But always on Friday nights Bertha would be waiting in front of Bloom's, her two hundred and seventeen pounds outlined by the white store behind her. She'd be smiling. She was always smiling.

What the hell was so funny?

Two hundred and seventeen pounds, an even hundred more than Fred weighed, and her hand would be out and he'd put the week's wages in that, and she'd shove it into her tiny purse.

When they were first married Bertha had been young, shapely and romantic. Now she was still romantic and the Friday evenings were a must. In the interests of peace. Not that she'd scream, but she'd pout. A two–hundred–and–seventeen–pound pout is a horrible sight, and Fred avoided it by meeting her in front of Bloom's at 5:08 each Friday evening.

At the long counter in Bloom's Bertha would have a Double Banana Royale. Fred would have a sandwich and coffee.

Then the movie. Very few movies interested Fred; none failed to enchant Bertha. She held his hand all through the double feature. He loathed its damp capaciousness; he loathed Bertha.

One hundred and seventeen pounds and two hundred and seventeen pounds. People would turn as they walked by, would smile at them. Fred was sensitive, being the lighter one. Bertha? Who knows?

The street is so busy in front of Bloom's. There are so many people. Some are men, tall and superior. Some are women, beautiful and young. Smiling at Fred and Bertha.

Funny?

One of Fred's favorite writers was the minor–league philosopher, Ramsay Elleson. In one of the thin books Ramsay published — infrequently and at his own expense — Ramsay got going on Hell.

Eternity, itself, Ramsay claimed, was Hell, though it would be a personal matter. For the author, Hell would be an eternal box seat at an eternal football game, Ramsay being an intellectual (self–proclaimed). For football fans Hell would be an eternity in the library of Ramsay Elleson. And so on.

Fred gave the matter some thought and his personal view of Hell would be an eternity with Bertha. Eternity is only a word; he'd actually gone through most of it already. Twenty–two years of Friday nights. Twenty–two years of the Hollywood product for a man who could enjoy the profundity of Ramsay Elleson. Only a little less than twenty–two years of — avoirdupois.

Eternity can end. It can be brought violently to a stop. With determination and fortitude and something heavy to swing, a man can establish a better destiny than an eternity with Bertha.

Fred had this thought on a Wednesday night, while working out a cryptogram. He looked over at Bertha, monumental and placid under a reading lamp, and waited for the thought to go away.

The thought didn't go away.

He slept with it. He carried it, along with his lunch, to work the next day. The figures in his ledgers seemed to dance and form strange shapes, leering at him. He left early, his head aching.

At home, Bertha said, "Honey, you're sick …"

"What makes you think I'm sick?"

"You're home early. And you look sick, Honey."

"I'm not sick. I'm just a little tired. I didn't sleep very well last night." He rubbed the back of his neck with a trembling hand. "I'm going down to look at the furnace."

It was July.

She stared at him.

He said irritably, "Well, I can look at it, can't I? Damn it!"

She said soothingly, "Of course you can. I'll make some tea. I'll have it ready for you."

The floor in the cellar was dirt. It was a cheap house. He paid more rent for it than it was worth. But the floor was dirt, which suited his present purpose.

After a little while, she called, "Honey, the tea is ready."

He didn't answer.

"Fred?"

He didn't answer.

"Fred — answer me!"

He didn't answer, and she started down the stairs …

It was a restless, fretful night. Well, it was done; nothing could change that. He'd grown weary, digging, and had covered her very skimpily. But he could finish that tonight. He could use the time they usually wasted in the movie.

He ate his breakfast at a coffee shop near the office. He spent the day rereading meaningless figures. Ahead of him stretched a Bertha–less Elysium; to hell with figures, today.

Then, around five, one figure jumped to the front of his consciousness and burned a hole in his brain. It was the figure on his desk calendar.

Today was the 21st of July.

Today was the day the gas man read the meter in the cellar, using the duplicate key Bertha thoughtfully left for him under the reardoor mat.

Fred stood up, his stomach filled with flying birds. He stood up and saw the men talking to Mr. Pritchard at the front of the office. One was obviously a detective. The other was a blue–uniformed patrolman.

Mr. Pritchard was indicating Fred now, and both officers started his way.

Their faces were grave, watchful and ominous.

Fred didn't wait for his hat. There was a door at the rear, and old wooden steps going down to the alley. Fred bolted.

He saw the startled faces of the other employees and heard the shouted, "Stop, in the name of the law! Stop that man!"

Now Fred was through the door and going down the steps. From the head of the steps, as he was halfway down, he heard the "Stop!" again. He heard the single, deafening shot.

One shot — that missed. He was in the alley, and running. He came out of the alley on Eighth and turned north. He was still running, and no more commands reached his ears.

Eight to Grand and down Grand.

And then, suddenly, he stopped without the command. Stopped to stare, stopped to realize that single shot *hadn't* missed.

For there, outlined against the front of Bloom's, Bertha was waiting. Smiling, holding her purse, but her hand wasn't out for his wages.

What need was there for money — where they were?

Dead–End for Delia

The only light in the alley came from the high, open windows of the faded dancehall bordering its east length. From these same windows the clean melody of a tenor sax cut through the murky air of the alley. There was nothing else around that was clean.

The warehouse running the west border of the alley was of grimy red brick, the alley itself littered with paper and trash, cans and bottles. It was a dead–end alley, no longer used.

The beat officer was at its mouth, keeping the small crowd back, and now the police ambulance came from the west, its siren dying in a slow wail.

The beat officer said, "Better swing out and back in. Sergeant Kelley with you?"

"No. Why?" The driver was frowning.

"It's his wife," the beat officer said. "She really got worked over."

"Dead?"

"Just died, two minutes ago. How she lived that long is a wonder."

The driver shook his head, and swung out to back into the mouth of the alley.

From the west again, a red light swung back and forth, and the scream of a high speed siren pierced the night. The prowl car was making time. It cut over to the wrong side of the street and skidded for fifteen feet before stopping at the curb.

The man opposite the driver had the door open before the car came to rest, and he was approaching the beat patrolman while the driver killed the motor.

"Barnes? I'm Kelley. My wife —?"

"Dead, Sergeant. Two minutes ago."

Sergeant Kelley was a tall man with a thin, lined face and dark brown eyes. He stood there a moment, saying nothing, thinking of Delia, only half hearing the trumpet that was now taking a ride at Dreamland, the Home of Name Bands.

Delia, who was only twenty–three to his thirty–seven, Delia who loved to dance, Delia of the fair hair and sharp tongue — was now dead. And that was her dirge, that trumpet taking a ride.

He shook his head and felt the trembling start in his hands. He took a step toward the other end of the alley, and the patrolman put a hand on his arm.

"Sergeant, I wouldn't. It's nothing to see. Unless you're a Homicide man, it's nothing you'd — Sergeant, don't."

Sergeant Kelley shook off the hand and continued down the alley.

Dick Callender of Homicide was talking to the M.E. He turned at the sound of Kelley's footsteps.

Dick said, "It's nothing to see, Pat." Pat Kelley didn't answer him. There was enough light from the dance hall for him to see the bloody face of his wife and the matted hair above it. He hadn't seen her for four months.

Then he looked at Callender. "She say anything, Dick?"

"Just — *Tell Pat I'm sorry. Tell Pat Lois will know.* Make sense to you; the second sentence, I mean?"

"None," Pat lied. The band was playing a waltz, now.

Callender said, "We'll give it a lot of time. Homicide will shoot the works on this one."

Pat looked at him and used his title, now. "I want a transfer, Lieutenant. To Homicide." His voice was very quiet. "You can fix it."

A piece of dirty newspaper fluttered by, stirred by the night breeze. The white–coated men were laying the stretcher alongside the body.

Callender said, "We've got a lot of good men in Homicide, Pat." He didn't say, *And we want our suspects brought in alive.*

But Pat could guess he was thinking it. He said, "She left me, four months ago. I'm not going to go crazy on it, but I'd like the transfer."

"We'll see, Pat." The lieutenant put a hand on his shoulder. "Come on. I'll ride back to headquarters with you."

They went in the lieutenant's wagon. About halfway there, Pat said, "It could have been one of those — pick–up deals, some mugg out of nowhere who'll go back to where he came from." Shame burned in him, but he had to get the words out.

Callender didn't look at him. "I've got Adams and Prokowski checking the dancehall. They're hard workers, good men."

Pat said nothing.

Callender went on, quietly, "There must be some angle you've got on it. Your wife must have thought you knew this — this Lois, or she wouldn't have mentioned it. She didn't have enough words left to waste any of them on some trivial matter."

"My wife knew a lot of people I didn't," Pat said. "My statement will include everything I know, Lieutenant. Have her sent to the Boone Mortuary on Seventh Street, will you? I'll talk to her mother tonight."

"She — was living with her mother, Pat?"

"No. I don't know where she's been living these past four months. But it wasn't with her mother. I wish to God it had been, now."

They made the rest of the trip in silence.

It was a little before midnight when Sergeant Pat Kelley of the pawn shop and hotel detail, climbed the worn stairs of the four–story building on Vine. The place was quiet; these were working people and they got to bed early.

Mrs. Revolt lived on the third floor, in two rooms overlooking the littered back yard and the parking lot beyond. Pat knocked and waited.

There was the sound of a turning key, and then Mrs. Revolt opened the door. Her lined, weary face was composed, but her eyes quickened in sudden alarm at the sight of Pat.

"Pat, what is it?"

"I'd better come in," he said. "It's Delia, Mrs. Revolt. Something's happened ..."

She pulled her wrapper tightly around her, as though to stiffen her body against his words. "Come in, come in. But what —? Pat, she's not — it's not —"

He came into the dimly lighted room with the rumpled studio couch, the gate–leg table with the brass lamp, the worn wicker chairs, the faded, dull brown rug. In this room, Delia Revolt had grown from an infant to the beauty of the block. In this room, Papa Revolt had died, and Pat had courted the Revolt miracle.

"Sit down, Mrs. Revolt," Pat said now.

She sat down in the wicker rocker. "She's dead, I know. She's dead. My Delia, oh Lord, she's dead." She rocked, then, back and forth, her eyes closed, her lips moving, no decipherable words coming out.

Pat sat on the wicker lounge. "She was found in an — she was found near the Dreamland dancehall. She's dead. There'll be detectives coming to see you; other detectives, Mrs. Revolt."

Her eyes opened, and she stopped rocking. "Murdered — Delia? It wasn't an accident? Murdered — Delia?"

He nodded. Her eyes closed again, and a strangled sound came from her tight throat, and she toppled sideways in the chair.

Pat got to her before she hit the floor. He put her on the studio couch, and was waiting with a glass of water when her eyes opened again.

Her voice was a whisper. "How did it happen?"

"She was hit with something blunt, concussion. Nobody knows anything else. But there's something I wanted you to know."

Fear in her eyes, now. She said nothing.

"Before she died, Delia mentioned a name. It was Lois. I told the officer in charge the name meant nothing to me. I told him I didn't know any Lois."

The frightened eyes moved around Pat's face. "Why did you say that?"

"Because they're going after this one. She's a cop's wife and they won't be pulling any punches. This man in charge, Callender, can be awful rough. I'd rather talk to Lois, myself."

"But why should they bother Lois?"

"Delia mentioned the name, before she died. They're not going to overlook anything and they're not going to be polite."

"All right, Pat. I had a feeling, when you knocked, something had happened. I've had a feeling about Delia, for years. You can go now; I'll be all right. I'll want to be alone."

She was under control, now, this woman who'd met many a tragedy, who'd just met her biggest one. The fortitude born of the countless minor tragedies was carrying her through this one.

Pat went from there to Sycamore. He was off duty, and driving his own car. On Sycamore, near Seventh, he parked in front of an old, red brick apartment building.

In the small lobby, he pressed the button next to the card which read: *Miss Lois Weldon.*

Her voice sounded metallic through the wall speaker. "Who's there?"

"It's Pat, Lois. Something has happened."

He was at the door when it buzzed. She was waiting in her lighted doorway when he got off the self–service elevator on the fourth floor. She was wearing a maroon flannel robe piped in white, and no make–up. Her dark, soft hair was piled high on her head.

Her voice was quiet. "What's happened?"

"Delia's been murdered."

She flinched and put one hand on the door frame for support. "Pat, when — how —?"

"Tonight. In the alley next to the Dreamland ballroom. Slugged to death. She didn't die right away. She mentioned your name before she died."

"My name? Come in, Pat." Her voice was shaky.

There wasn't much that could be done about the apartment's arrangement, but color and taste had done their best with its appearance. Pat sat on a love seat, near the pseudo–fireplace.

Lois stood. "Now, what did she say?"

Pat frowned. "She said, 'Tell Pat I'm sorry. Tell Pat Lois will know.' She told that to Lieutenant Callender of Homicide, before she died. He asked me who Lois was, and I told him I didn't know."

"Why?"

"I was trying to protect you. It might have been dumb. But they're going to be rough in this case."

She sat down in a chair close by, staring at him. "I saw Delia two days ago, Thursday afternoon. She told me then that she was sorry she'd left you. Could it have been that, Pat?"

"It could have been. Yes, that's probably what she meant. What else did she tell you?"

"N — nothing. She was very vague. She'd — been drinking, Pat."

"Drinking? That's a new one for her. Was she working?"

"I didn't get that impression. She didn't tell me where she was living, either. Do you know?"

Pat shook his head, staring at the floor. The three of them had grown up in the same block on Vine, though they weren't of an age. Delia had been twenty–three, and Lois was — let's see, she was thirty and the fairly well paid secretary to a vice president of a text publishing firm. When Pat was twenty–two and freshly in uniform, he'd been Lois' hero, who'd been fifteen. At thirty–three, in another kind of uniform, U.S. Army, he'd been Delia's hero, and she'd been nineteen.

At the moment, he was an old man, and nobody's hero.

Lois said, "I guess you need a drink." She rose. "Don't try to think tonight, Pat. It won't be any good."

"I was without her for four months," he said, mostly to himself. "I got through that. I don't know about this. I don't seem to have any feelings at all. It's like I'm dead."

Her back was to him. "I know. That the way I felt four years ago." She poured a stiff jolt of rye in the bottom of a tumbler.

"Four years ago?" he was only half listening.

"When you married her." She had no expression on her face as she walked over to him. Her hand was steady, holding out the drink.

He looked up to meet her gaze. "Lois, what are you —?"

"I just wanted you to know," she said, "and now I'm glad you didn't tell that Officer you knew me. That's a gesture I can hang on to. It will warm me, this winter."

"Lois —" he protested.

"Drink your drink," she said quietly. "Bottoms up."

He stared at her, and at the glass. He lifted it high and drained it. He could feel its warmth, and then he started to tremble.

"You're one of those black Irishmen," Lois said softly, "who can go all to hell over something like this. And wind up in the gutter. Or examine yourself a little better and decide she was a girl headed for doom from the day of her birth and all you really loved was her beauty."

"Stop talking, Lois. You're all worked up. I'd kill anybody else who talked like that, but I know you loved her, too?"

"Who didn't love her? She was the most beautiful thing alive. But she was a kid, and she'd never be anything else. Even now you can see that, can't you?"

Pat stared at his empty glass, and rose.

"Thanks for the drink," he said, and walked to the door. There he paused, faced her. "It was probably a silly gesture, covering you. There'll be a million people who can tell them who Lois is. I'm sorry I got you up."

"Pat," she said, but he was through the door.

He caught a glimpse of her as he stepped into the elevator. She was like a statue, both hands on the door frame, watching him wordlessly.

The Chief called him in, next morning. He was a big man and a blunt one. He said, "Callender tells me you want a transfer to Homicide for the time being."

Pat nodded. "Yes, sir."

"How is it you didn't tell Callender about this Lois Weldon last night? A half dozen people have told him about her since."

"I wasn't thinking last night, sir."

The Chief nodded. "You're too close to it, Sergeant. For anybody else, that would be withholding evidence. I'm overlooking it. But I'm denying your request for a temporary transfer to Homicide."

Pat stared at him, saying nothing.

The Chief stared back at him. "You'll want a few days leave."

"Maybe more." He omitted the "sir."

The Chief frowned and looked at his desk top. His eyes came up, again. "I don't like to hammer at you at a time like this. But why *more?* Were you planning to work on this outside of the department?"

Pat nodded.

"If I gave you a direct order not to, that would be insubordination, Sergeant."

Pat said nothing.

The Chief said, "Those are my orders."

Pat took out his wallet and unpinned the badge. He laid it on the Chief's desk. "This isn't easy, sir, after fifteen years." He stood up, momentarily realizing what a damn fool speech that had been.

"You're being dramatic," the Chief evenly. "The thing that makes a good officer is impartiality. Last night you tried to cover a friend. In your present mood, you might go gunning on a half–baked lead and do a lot of damage. This department isn't run that way. But it's your decision, Sergeant." He picked up the badge.

Pat started for the door, and the Chief's voice stopped him. "It would be smart to stay out of Lieutenant Callender's way."

Pat went out without answering. He stood there, in the main hall of Head–quarters, feeling like a stranger for the first time in fifteen years. It was then he remembered Lois saying, *You're one of those black Irishmen who can go all to hell …*

He wasn't that complicated, whether she knew it or not. His wife had been killed and it was a personal business with him. His job for fifteen years had been to protect the soft from violence and fraud and chicanery, and this time it was closer to home. Only a fool would expect him to continue checking pawn shops; he hadn't thought the Chief was a fool. But then, it wasn't the Chief's wife.

Detective Prokowski came along the hall and stopped at the sight of Pat.

—Pat asked, "What did you find out at Dreamland last night, Steve?"

Prokowski licked his lower lip, frowning.

"Orders, Steve?" Pat asked quietly. "From the lieutenant?"

Prokowski didn't answer that. "Did your transfer go through?"

"No. I've left the force. Don't you want to talk about Dreamland? I won't remind you how long we've known each other."

"Keep your voice down," Prokowski said. "I'll see you at Irv's, at one–thirty."

"Sure. Thanks, Steve."

Irv's wasn't a cops' hangout; Prokowski was a Middle Westerner, originally, and a perfectionist regarding the proper temperature of draught beer. Irv had it at the proper temperature.

It was a hot day, for fall, and the beer was cool enough to sweat the glass without being cold enough to chill the stomach. Pat drank a couple of glasses, waiting for Steve.

Steve came in at a quarter to two and Irv had a glass waiting for him by the time he reached the bar.

He was a big man, Steve Prokowski, and sweating like a college crew man right now. "Nothing," he said wearily. "Lots of guys danced with her. Nothing there. Shoe clerks and CPA's and punk kids. There was a guy they called Helgy. That name mean anything to you, Pat?"

Pat lied with a shake of the head. "This Helgy something special?"

"Danced with her a lot. Took her home. Brought her a couple of times. The way it is, I guess, if you really like to dance there's only one place to do it where you've got the room and the right music. That's a place like Dreamland.

"I mean you can't catalogue a guy because he goes to a public dancehall, any more than you can catalogue people because you saw them in Grand Central Station. All kinds of people like to dance. This Helgy drove a smooth car, a convertible. That's nightclub stuff, right? But he liked to dance, and the story is, he really could."

Steve finished his beer and Irv brought another. Steve said casually, "Now, what do you know, Pat?"

"I'm out of a job. I don't know anything beyond that. The Chief acted on Callender's recommendation, I suppose?"

"I don't know. The lieutenant doesn't always confide in me. What can you do alone, Pat?"

"It wasn't my idea to work alone." Pat climbed off his stool and put a dollar on the bar. "Out of that, Irv, all of them." He put a hand on Steve's shoulder. "Thanks for coming in."

"You're welcome. Thanks for the beer. I still work for the department, remember, Pat."

"I didn't forget it for a minute."

He could feel Steve's eyes on him in the mirror as he walked out.

Once at breakfast, Delia had been reading the paper and she'd said, "Well, imagine that!"

"I'll try," he'd said. "Imagine what?"

"This boy I used to dance with at Dreamland, this Joe Helgeson. He's a composer, it says here. He likes to dance, and always has, and he knows very little about music, but he's composed. And he must be rich. Helgy, we always called him."

"You should have married him," Pat told her, "so you could have your breakfast in bed."

"There's always time," she told him. "But right now I'm happy with you."

After that, Pat had been conscious of the name. He saw it on sheet music, and it disturbed him. He heard Delia talk to friends about the composer she knew, Helgy, as though that was her world.

He swung his coupe away from the curb and headed toward the Drive. He knew the building; Delia had pointed it out to him once.

It was about eleven stories high with terrace apartments overlooking the bay. Helgy had one of the terrace apartments.

There was a clerk in the quiet lobby, too, and his glance said Pat should have used the service entrance.

Pat said, "Would you phone Mr. Helgeson and tell him Delia Kelley's husband would like very much to talk to him?"

The clerk studied him for a moment before picking up the phone.

He looked surprised when he said, "Mr. Helgeson will see you, sir."

The elevator went up quickly and quietly, and Pat stepped out onto the lush, sculptured carpeting of the top floor. There was a man waiting for him there, a thin man with blond hair in a crew cut, and alert blue eyes.

"Sergeant Kelley?"

Pat nodded.

"I've — been reading the papers. It's — I really don't know what to say, Sergeant."

"I don't either," Pat said, "except to ask you what you might know about it."

They were walking along the hall, now. They came to the entry hall of the apartment, and Helgeson closed the door behind them. There he faced Pat honestly.

"I've seen her a few times, Sergeant, since she — she left you. There was nothing, well, nothing wrong about it."

"That part doesn't matter," Pat said. "I'm not looking for the men who flirted with her. I'm looking for the man who killed her."

They went into a low, long living room with a beamed ceiling, with floor–length windows facing on the terrace. Helgeson sat in a chair near the huge, bleached mahogany piano.

"I can't help you with that," he said. "I danced with her, at Dreamland. I don't know what attraction the place had for me, except it was the only magic I knew as a kid. I never probed myself for any reasons. She was — a wonderful dancer. I didn't think of her beyond that. That sounds phony, I know, but —" His voice died.

"I'm surprised the Homicide section hasn't sent a man to see you, or have they? You said you'd been reading about it."

"Homicide? No. Why should they?"

"You're pretty well known, and they have your nickname."

"I'm not known down there, not generally. Not as the composer. I'm just another punk, just Helgy, down there. A rather aging punk." He stared at Pat. "But if you know, they know."

Pat shook his head. "I've left the force. I asked to be assigned to this case and was refused."

"Oh." Helgeson rubbed his forehead frowningly. "She told me, when she phoned to break a date yesterday, that she was going back to you. I thought —"

"Yesterday?" Pat interrupted. "She told you that, yesterday?"

Helgeson nodded, studying Pat quietly.

Pat could see the pulse in his wrist and he had a passing moment of giddiness. "Where was she living?"

"The Empire Court, over on Hudson."

"Working, was she?"

"I don't think so. She never mentioned it, if she was. She was kind of reticent about all that."

Pat looked at Helgeson levelly. "Was she — living alone?"

Helgeson took a deep breath. "I don't know. I never went in, over there. She was always ready when I called for her." He seemed pale and his voice was unsteady.

Pat felt resentment moving through him, but he couldn't hate them all. Everybody had loved Delia.

He said quietly, "There's nothing you know? She must have mentioned some names, or what she was doing. What the hell did you talk about?"

"We didn't talk much. We danced, that's all. Sergeant, believe me, if I could help I would." His voice was ragged. "If you knew how much I — wanted to help." He shook his head. "There isn't anything I know, not a damned thing."

"All right. I can believe that. If there's anything you hear, or happen to remember, anything at all, phone me." He gave him the number.

He went from there to the Empire Court, on Hudson. It was a fairly modern, U–shaped building of gray stone, set back on a deep lot. There was a department car among the cars at the curb.

The name in the lobby read: *Delia Revolt.* Pat pressed the button and the door buzzed.

It was on the second floor and he walked up. There were some technical men dusting for prints, and there was Lieutenant Callender, his back to the doorway, standing in the middle of the living room.

He turned and saw Pat. His face showed nothing.

"Anything?" Pat asked him.

"Look, Pat, for the love of —"

"You look," Pat said. "She was my wife. You got a wife, Lieutenant?"

"I'm married to my second, now." He shook his big head and ran a hand through his hair. "The Chief said you'd resigned."

"That's right."

"You've been a cop for fifteen years. You're acting like a rookie."

"I've only been a husband for four years, Lieutenant. I'm not getting in your way."

"We'll probably get a million prints, all but the right ones. We found a dressing robe we're checking, and some pajamas. The lieutenant's eyes looked away. "I'll talk to the Chief, Pat. I'll see that you get your job back."

"I don't want it back — yet. Thanks, anyway, Lieutenant." He kept seeing Delia in the room and somebody else, some formless, faceless somebody, and the giddiness came again and he knew he wouldn't have the stomach to look in any of the other rooms.

He turned his back on the lieutenant and went down the steps to the lobby and out into the hot, bright day. They were right about it, of course. A cop shouldn't be on a family case any more than a surgeon should. Emotion was no asset in this business.

He sat in the car for minutes, trying to get back to reality, trying to forget that cozy apartment and the lieutenant's words. The brightness of the day seemed to put a sharp outline on things, to give them a sense of unreality, like a lighted stage setting.

He heard last night's trumpet again, and started the motor.

The alley was bright, now, but no cleaner. The voices of the freight handlers on the street side of the warehouse were drowned by the racket of the huge trucks bumping past. He walked to the alley's dead end and saw, for the first time, the door that led from the dance hall, a fire exit.

It was open, now, and he could see some men in there, sprinkling the floor with some granulated stuff. There was the sound of a huge rotary brush polisher, but it was outside his line of vision.

He went in through the open door, along a wide hall that flanked the west edge of the bandstand. The men looked at him curiously as he stood there, imagining what it must have been last night. He could almost hear the music and see the dim lights and the crowded floor.

Along this edge, the floor was raised and there were seats up here, for the speculative males, looking over the field, discussing the old favorites and the new finds, wondering what happened to this transient queen and that one. Some had married and not retired.

One of the workers called over, "Looking for the boss, mister?"

"That's right."

"Won't be in this afternoon. The joint's been full of cops and he went out to get some fresh air."

"Okay." Pat turned and went out.

It was nearly five, now. He turned the car in a U–turn and headed for Borden. He parked on a lot near Borden and Sixth, and walked the two blocks to Curtes–Husted, Publishers.

Lois was busily typing when he opened the door to the outer office. She looked up at his entrance, and her face seemed to come alive, suddenly.

"Pat!" She got up and came over to the railing.

"I was pretty rough, last night. I thought a drink and dinner might take us back to where we were. Part way, anyway."

"It will, it will. Oh, Pat, if you knew what last night —" She put a hand on his on top of the railing.

The door to Pat's right opened, and a man stood there. He had a masculine, virile face and iron–gray hair. He said, "You can go any time, Lois. I guess Mr. Curtes won't be back."

"Thank you, Mr. Husted," she said. "I'll be going in a minute."

He smiled, and closed the door.

"My boss, the VP," she whispered. "Isn't he handsome?"

"I suppose." Pat could feel her hand trembling.

She said quietly, "You're better, aren't you. You're coming out of it."

"I'm better," he said. "This whole case is one blind alley."

"Delia knew a lot of men — of people. I'll be with you in a minute."

They went to the *Lamp Post*, an unpretentious restaurant nearby.

They had a martini each, and Lois told him. "Their spare ribs are the best in town."

He ordered the spare ribs.

She seemed animated. She said, "It's going to be all right. It's going to take some time, and then you're going to be really happy, Pat. I'm going to see that you're happy."

He ordered another pair of drinks, and they finished those before the ribs came. They went from the *Lamp Post* to a spot on the west side, and Pat tried very hard to get drunk. But it didn't work; the alcohol didn't touch him.

They went back to Lois' place. He sat with her in the car in front of her apartment.

"Come up," she said. "I'll make some coffee."

He shook his head. "I know Husted was paying for that apartment Delia was living in. I've known it for two months, Lois. And you did, too, didn't you?"

Her silence was his answer.

"You probably thought Husted killed her, and yet you've told the police nothing. Delia probably told you yesterday or the day before that she was coming back to me. But you didn't tell me that. Was it yesterday you saw her?"

"The day before. I didn't want her to come back, Pat. And I didn't tell you about my boss because he's got a family, because he's a fundamentally decent man."

"You didn't want her to come back. Because of me?" Pat's voice was hoarse. "You poor damned fool, you don't know me, do you? No matter what she was, Lois, I'll be married to her the rest of my life. But you were the one who could have told me she was coming back. You could have saved her life."

"Pat —"

"Get out, Lois. Get out — quick!"

She scrambled out.

The liquor was getting to him a little, now. He finished the note, there on his dinette table, and then went to unlock the front door. Then he called headquarters, gave them the message, and went to pick up the note. He read:

Lieutenant Callender:

I wanted to work with Homicide because I thought it would be safer that way. I could see how close you boys were getting. But it doesn't matter now, because I've no desire to escape you. I killed my wife with a wrecking bar which you'll find in the luggage deck of my car. I couldn't stand the thought of her loving anyone else and I wasn't man enough to rid myself of her. The checking I've done today reveals to me I would probably have escaped detection. I make this confession of my own free will.

Sergeant Patrick Kelley.

He waited then, .38 in hand. He waited until he heard the wail of the siren, and a little longer. He waited until he heard the tires screeching outside.

Then he put the muzzle of his .38 to the soft roof of his mouth, and pulled the trigger.

Conspiracy

Johnny and I were trying to drown out a gopher when we first saw this car just tearing around the big bend above Nestor's corn field. Wow, that car was really going; you could hear the tires screech where we were standing and we must have been a half mile away.

Johnny put the tin can full of water he was pouring into the hole down next to him and stared at the car as though he was waiting for it to go over.

"Crazy, huh?" I said. "Man, he's moving."

Johnny nodded without looking at me. "I'll bet he won't make that next one; it's harder."

I didn't want to look, but I couldn't take my eyes away. There was a straight stretch after the big bend and then a little hill and right by our stand of timber, this side of the hill, there was a real sharp curve and a culvert. You couldn't see the turn from the other side of the hill, though there was a big sign up there warning everybody. Before they put the sign up, a lot of guys hadn't made that turn by our timber, most of them because they were drunk and coming back from a dance somewhere. It isn't a main road and we don't get any strangers driving it much.

From where we stood, on the bluff above the creek, we could see this speeding car coming to the hill now and he wasn't slowing none at all.

"He's not going to make it," Johnny whispered. "Watch this, Steve!"

The car came over the top of the hill and we heard the tires screeching again as the driver tried to swing it around the sharp turn. He was good, that guy. He almost made it.

And then the car was drifting toward the culvert and the front end of it crashed with a horrible clang and we saw it go up on its nose. It was like a slow motion picture, almost, as it went end for end down the bank of the creek and one door flew open and we saw a guy falling out and then we couldn't see the car any more.

We just stood there.

In a couple seconds, Johnny said, "The water's deep there. If there was anybody else in the car, they could drown, Steve."

"We'd better go over to Nestor's and call the sheriff," I said.

We don't have a phone. Pa says they're a waste of money. Ma wants one, but Pa says they're a waste of money.

"I guess we'd better," Johnny said, and then he pointed. "Hey, look!"

A man was climbing up over the bank. He had cotton army pants on and a light blue sweater and a gray cap. He was carrying a suitcase.

The way I figured right then, he was maybe a bum the guys in the car had picked up and he was getting out of there so he wouldn't be questioned by the sheriff. He was limping. I figured he'd head down the road toward us, but he didn't.

He went trotting and limping toward our little stand of timber that runs along the road.

"He's running away," Johnny said. "Why didn't he head for Nestor's, for a phone?"

"I don't know," I said.

"It's damned funny."

"Pa says you shouldn't swear, Johnny."

"To hell with Pa. It's damned funny."

"Maybe he's a bum, Johnny."

He turned to face me. "With that suitcase? That was heavy. Did you see the way it dragged him?"

I didn't say anything. I was watching the other end of the woods, the end that runs along the other road, the road to Saugus.

Johnny said, "We'd better get to Nestor's. I guess we're the only ones that saw it happen."

"Look," I said, and pointed at the far end of the woods.

The man in the army pants was coming out from there now, heading for the other road. And he wasn't carrying the suitcase.

Johnny looked at me and I looked at Johnny. I don't know what we were thinking as we looked at each other. And then we heard the siren and we could see the sheriff's car coming down the road from Ridgeland.

It was like we were in the balcony watching a play or something; the whole thing was spread out below us, the sheriff's car storming from where the other car had come and the man walking out of the woods without the suitcase and remembering that car we couldn't see down in the creek and the whole day so bright and peaceful around us. I got the shivers.

The sheriff knew about the sharp turn and his car slowed up before it came to the top of the rise. And from there, he must have seen the car in the creek, because he slowed more and pulled over on the side of the road and stopped.

And I could recognize him, him being so fat, but I wasn't sure who the other guy was that got out of the car on the other side.

Johnny said, "Let's go down there. C'mon, Steve, I'll race you down there."

Johnny's thirteen, a year older than me, and bigger, and he knows he'd beat all right. But I raced him anyway because I wanted to get down there to see what the sheriff had to say.

By the time we got there, the thinner man had gone down to the creek and come up again and I could see it was Jess Laurie, one of the deputies.

I was puffing like a steam engine and Johnny, too. Johnny took a couple of real deep breaths and asked, "What happened, Mr. Laurie?"

"Three men robbed the bank in Ridgeland," he said. "Did you boys see this car tip over?"

I nodded. Johnny looked at me and frowned. Then Johnny said, "We were just on the way to Nestor's, to phone you. Boy, was that car ever moving." He took another deep breath. "Is anybody in it, Mr. Laurie?"

Jess Laurie looked at him sharply. "Of course. You don't think the car got all the way out here by itself, do you? Why did you ask that? Did you see somebody walk away from the wreck?"

Johnny looked at me and I knew we were both thinking of the suitcase. Johnny looked real steady at Mr. Laurie and said, "Yes, sir, we did. We saw a man with a suitcase."

Jess looked over the bank and said, "Hey, Sheriff, we got a lead. Better come up; maybe we can still catch the third man."

Old, fat Sheriff Taggart came puffing up the bank. "I don't know as we ought to leave here until we get an ambulance out, Jess. One of those men looks like he's still alive."

I was watching Johnny and I could tell his mind was racing. Mine was, too.

Johnny didn't wait to be asked. He said, "We saw this man come up the bank and then a car came along, and the car stopped and this man with the suitcase got into it. It sure looked funny to me, the way that car came along."

Jess said quickly, "What kind of car?"

"It was a brand new Pontiac," Johnny said slowly. "It was dark green and it had white–wall tires and it went straight down the road toward Center City."

"How about the man with the suitcase? Could you see him?"

"Not his face," Johnny said. "He had blue pants on and a blue denim jacket and no hat. He was kind of fat and short."

I kept looking at Johnny as he lied. I couldn't look at Mr. Laurie or the Sheriff. Johnny can think fast and move fast; that's where he's got it all over me. And when he lies, he smiles, like he knows you're not believing him, but he doesn't care if you do or not.

Jess looked at the Sheriff and the Sheriff said, "I'll stay here for the ambulance. You take off."

"Alone, Tom?" Jess asked. "He's armed, you know."

The Sheriff said grouchy, "Okay, I'll go and you phone for the ambulance."

Jess said, "I'll go, I'll go —" He started for the car. He turned and said, "And don't forget to send out an all points for that Pontiac."

"Yes, Jess," Sheriff Taggart said, tired–like. "Of course, Jess." He went toward the Nestor's place as Jess Laurie drove off.

We were alone.

Johnny looked at me and said, "I'll race you to the woods. Why didn't you tell Jess Laurie I was lying, tattle–tale? How come you didn't tattle? You always do."

I didn't say anything.

"I'll race you to the woods," he said again.

I shook my head.

He laughed. "A little nickel–nurser like you and you won't even run for all that money? What's the matter, you worried?"

I nodded.

"What's there to worry about?" He laughed again. "We're just kids, Steve. Just a couple kids was drowning out a gopher and saw an accident. We didn't rob no bank."

"I'm worried about you," I said. "No patience, that's what's the matter with you. You got to run all the time. With the Sheriff there where he can see the woods, and the Nestors sure to be out here in a minute, you got to run for the money."

He laughed again. "You're not fooling me. Patience means you want me to wait for you. You want some of that money."

I nodded. "I want half."

He stared at me. "Maybe you want a poke in the yap, too, huh? Who did the lying? Who got the idea? Half, huh!"

I said patiently. "Just half, that's fair. Or I tell the Sheriff you lied to him. Decide right now, Johnny."

"I ought to poke you in the yap," he said. "I think I will. If you tell the Sheriff anything, you'll be sorry, Steve."

"Decide, Johnny. Half?"

He stared at me for what seemed a long time, but probably wasn't. "Okay. I guess there'll be enough." He patted my shoulder. "I guess there'll be *plenty*, huh, old Stevie–boy?"

That's Johnny for you. He can't stay sore. He can get so mad he'd darn near kill you and then be so sorry you want to cry for him. He's a crazy guy.

I said, "That man that left the suitcase ain't going to be back for awhile, you can bet. We got time, Johnny. We can at least wait until it's dark."

He nodded and smiled. "A green Pontiac with white–wall tires, that was pretty good, huh, Steve? Maybe we ought to buy one, huh? With a radio and a heater and four carburetors and —"

"Shut up," I said. "Here comes the Sheriff."

He winked at me. "Right. Patience. Old patient Steve, the nickel–nurser; this is the time to listen to him."

We could hear another siren now, probably the ambulance. And over the top of the rise a wrecker was coming from Chopko's garage in Ridgeland.

The Sheriff said, "This isn't going to be anything you boys should see. Run along and play now. That's what vacations are for."

"It won't bother me," Johnny said. "I watched Pa stick pigs, and this won't bother me. Steve better take off, though, huh, Sheriff?"

Sheriff Taggart waved at us with the back of his band. "Both of you take off right now. Scat!"

"Okay," Johnny said. "C'mon, Steve, let's go play in the woods."

I couldn't have said that. Johnny's got the guts to say anything. And he's a fast thinker. I would have to be careful and watch him or I'd never see any of that money.

We went over to the woods and climbed a tree, so they'd think we were playing. Johnny went up real high, where he knew I'd be scared to follow and he yoo–hooed like Tarzan and the men who were running the hoist line down to the car looked our way and one of them waved. The ambulance was turning around in Nestor's driveway, getting ready to back down to the culvert.

And then Johnny said, "They won't be watching us now, Steve. Let's go down and look around."

"Take your time," I said.

"C'mon, sissy," he said, "before I forget you're in for half."

We climbed down and started walking around in there, looking for hiding places that a man in a hurry might see. It was Johnny who found it, a hollowed out place under a ledge overhanging with Johnson Grass and weeds. We could just see the handle of the suitcase in there.

Johnny started to reach, and I said, "Not yet. We know it's there, but we don't know who's watching. Not yet. Patience, remember."

He looked at the handle of the suitcase and I could almost see him tremble. He said, "Tonight, as soon as it's dark."

"As soon as it's dark," I agreed.

We went back to where we'd been pouring water down the gopher holes. It was high up there and we could watch the woods and the car being pulled out of the creek. It was almost all the way up, now, full of mud and all bent out of shape.

From the corner of the barn, Pa and Ma were looking over at the wreck and then Pa called us.

Johnny said, "You go. Somebody's got to watch that woods."

"He's mad," I said. "We were supposed to hoe corn this afternoon. We'd better both go."

When we got to where they were standing, Pa said, "What happened over there at the turn?"

"Some bank robbers went into the ditch," I said, "but one of them got away."

Ma said, "You boys were supposed to work this afternoon. Your father promised you a penny a row for hoeing." She smiled at me. "That wouldn't mean much to Johnny, but I can't see you forgetting it, Steve."

Johnny said, "The Grange is offering ten cents each for gophers and we were going after them."

That was a lie, I knew, but I didn't say anything. I didn't want Johnny mad at me, not with that suitcase still in the woods.

Pa said, "Well, forget the gophers and get out into that corn. Both of you, *right now!*"

"Yes, sir," Johnny said, and winked at me. "C'mon, money–bags."

When we were where the folks couldn't hear us, I said, "You're too mouthy. Did you have to mention money?"

"I meant the ninety dollars you saved," Johnny said. "Any guy that can save ninety bucks on the green nickels Pa hands out is a real money man. I'll bet you'll be rich some day, Steve."

I nudged him. "We're rich already, maybe, Johnny. But let's be careful. Don't go sounding off all the time."

"*Right,*" he said, and picked up a hoe. "C'mon, I'll race you."

C'mon, c'mon, c'mon — that was all I ever heard from Johnny. And I followed him around like he was a general or something. I was dumb to follow him all the time, to take his dares and let him lead me around by the nose.

"I don't want to race," I said. "A penny a row — who needs it?"

He laughed. "Oh, Steve, that sure didn't sound like you. You're starting to think like a rich man now instead of a miser, huh? You got big ideas."

"Lay off," I said. "You've always got your big mouth on me. Lay off."

He stood there with the hoe in his hand, studying me. "What you all wound up about? The money? Boy, that's got you real nervous, ain't it?"

I looked right back at him. "Darn right. You know there could be thousands of dollars there? You know what that could mean when we grew up and invested it?"

"Grew up? You crazy? As soon as I get to high school this fall, I'll be in town where I can use that money. I ain't going to wait until I grow up."

"You start spending this fall, Johnny, and you'll wind up in jail. Remember, we're *stealing* that money."

He shook his head. "They stole it. We found it."

"It's not ours, either way. Jeez, Johnny, for the first time in your life, use your head."

He studied me a couple seconds more and then he started to hoe. "You sound like an old man," he said. "You sound like you're a million years old."

We paired off and worked down the rows. I kept thinking about the money, what a big lucky break it had been and how Johnny would probably ruin it. He just didn't have any sense at all. He talked fast and thought fast, but that's different than having sense. Why hadn't I been alone when that car went over the bank?

I wasn't working any harder now than I had been climbing that bank to get water for the gopher hole, but this was different; this wasn't doing what I wanted to do. I thought about Pa, who'd worked like this since he was my age, and Ma, who didn't have anything she wanted, not even a telephone. When I was their age, would I be living like they did? Would I work as early and late as there was sun to see by?

If Johnny started spending that money in town, we'd be in trouble. Worse than that, we'd lose the money. Of course, if Johnny hadn't lied to the Sheriff ...

Chopko's tow car had already hauled away the wreck, and nobody was standing down on the road any more. I looked over toward the woods and nobody was there, either. Maybe he'd come back for the money tonight. We had better get there the minute it got dark. Or maybe he'd been caught ...? Not if the police were looking for a fat, short man wearing a denim jacket.

Around five–thirty, we heard the bell clang up at the house, and both of us stopped right where we were, without finishing the row.

As we walked to the house, I said to Johnny, "We'd better get to the woods the second it gets dark."

He nodded.

"That guy might be back," I explained.

He nodded.

"You're sure quiet," I said. "You haven't said a word since we started hoeing."

"I don't want to be mouthy." He stopped walking. "Steve, does it bother you when I razz you? I didn't know it bothered you that much."

I smiled. "No. I guess I'm just nervous."

He put a hand on my shoulder. "Because remember we are brothers, Steve. I give you a rough time, huh?"

"It's okay," I said, and kept walking.

What was he planning now? What was he being so buddy–buddy about? That Johnny, he scared me.

While we were washing up, Pa said, "Those two crooks in the car are dead. But they didn't find the other one. And he's got the money." He shook his head. "Forty–eight thousand dollars!"

Johnny looked at me and at Pa. "Forty–eight thousand? Where'd you hear that?"

"Len Nestor heard it on his radio." Pa picked up a carrot and started to chew it. "Makes an honest man sick, don't it?"

Neither of us said anything. I started to tremble. Then Johnny laughed. "Gosh, a guy would have to hoe a lot of corn to earn forty–eight thousand dollars, huh, Pa?"

Ma laughed, but Pa didn't seem to think it was funny. Johnny is supposed to favor Ma and I'm supposed to be more like Pa. I don't know about that, but I know Ma favors Johnny. He's her pet. She thinks he's as funny as Red Skelton.

I guess Pa don't favor anybody, but he admits I'm more sensible. That don't mean he liked me any more.

While we were eating, I figured it in my head. Forty–eight thousand dollars at six percent came to two thousand, eight hundred and eighty dollars a year. Gosh, a guy wouldn't have to spend his principal, just rent it out. Half of that would be mine, and half would be one thousand, four hundred and forty dollars a year. That's a lot of corn at a penny a row.

After supper, Johnny said, "Steve, what do you say we do a little more hoeing before it gets dark? At least we could finish those rows."

Both Pa and Ma looked puzzled; that wasn't the kind of thing Johnny would say. But I knew he wanted to be sure we could get out of the house when it was dark. We could go right to the woods from the cornfield.

Pa said, "Well, our oldest is finally getting some money sense. I'm glad to see it."

Johnny smiled and said, "It's about time, Pa?" And then he winked at me.

Outside, as we walked back to the field, I said, "You're a funny guy; you ought to be on television, you're so funny. Keep talking funny and lose forty–eight thousand dollars."

He laughed. "We got out of the house, didn't we? You never thought of that. I had to think of it. And I had to lie to the Sheriff and if that guy comes back for the money, old sissy Steve will be so scared he'll run and get it for him."

"I suppose you wouldn't be afraid of no bank robber? Not much!"

"Not me," he said. "Wait'll we get the money; you'll see." He laughed. "I wonder if old Jess Laurie is still looking for that fat man in the Pontiac."

He had to keep reminding me about that, letting me know that if it hadn't been for his big mouth we wouldn't have no chance at the money at all. He thinks he's smart. And maybe he is, but he sure hasn't got any sense.

I never saw the sun go down so slow, or the rows look so long. I worried about Pa; he must think it was queer for Johnny to want to work after dinner. Pa would be in the barn now, milking the one cow we kept just for our own milk and butter. And he could see us from the barnyard. I kept hoeing away and so did Johnny.

Then we saw Pa go up to the house with the pail, and it was almost dark, and Johnny said, "Maybe we'd better not wait any longer, huh?"

"Let's go," I said. I was trembling again and my voice shook.

Johnny was smiling. "If it's still there, we'll bring it back to the barn and find a place to hide it."

"What do you mean, if it's still there? Where could it be?"

"Maybe the man came back when we weren't watching."

"Don't be crazy," I said. "It's there. It's got to be there." I started to run.

But Johnny passed me up before I'd gone twenty steps and we ran like fools down the slope to the culvert and over it into the woods.

"Wait," I hollered. "What's your hurry?"

But he kept running and laughing and I hated him for it and I tried to run faster, but my lungs were burning already and my legs were aching and tightening up.

And then Johnny stopped running and laughed louder. "Oh, Steve — take it easy. I scared you, huh? C'mon, brother, let's walk. We're partners."

I didn't say anything. I sucked in all the air I could and didn't look at him as we walked over to where the suitcase had been that afternoon.

Johnny put his hand in under the overhang and looked at me with his eyes wide. "It's gone!"

My stomach gave a lurch and I started to reach past him to feel around in there. But he pushed me back and laughed — and swung the suitcase out.

My stomach settled down then and I felt better than I had all day. Forty–eight thousand dollars in one package without even an hour of work.

Johnny said, "Once we find a place to put the money, we'll get rid of the suitcase, right?"

"Right," I said. "Let's take it to the tool shed; we can lock that door from the inside and there's a flashlight in there."

The tool shed was on the other end of the barn from the house and Pa had let Johnny and me use one end of it for a clubhouse.

Johnny said, "Remember that old hole we dug under the floor? That's big enough to hide this. We'd better not stay out tonight, though, Steve. Pa will wonder what we're doing."

"We can open it, at least," I said, "and look."

"Sure," he said.

The suitcase bumped against me as we walked along in the dark. "Is it heavy?" I asked.

"Plenty," he said. "But I can carry it."

We could see the lights in the house now, but no light in the barn. We walked up the back way, keeping the barn between us and the house.

"Pa's going to be looking for us soon," I said. "What'll we do?"

"Like you said, take it into the tool shed and lock the door."

"But he'll come down there for sure."

"The door will be locked. And we can hide this before we unlock it."

I was getting nervous again. Johnny was so crazy and careless. He didn't have any sense and any patience and he didn't realize how much more important it was to be sensible now. To Johnny, money was just something to spend.

We came to the tool shed, and I went ahead to open the door and find the flashlight. When he came in, I closed the door behind him and put the two–by–four across it to lock it.

Johnny put the suitcase down in the middle of the floor and I turned on the flashlight and he opened the suitcase.

Green, green, green … All the bills were stacked in hunks with a strip of brown paper around each hunk. Fives and tens and twenties. Johnny lifted one package out, and there were hundred dollar bills underneath.

"Man!" he said. "Oh, Steve!"

My stomach was fluttering and I was listening for a sound outside. "Let's hide it. Quick!" I said.

He didn't seem to hear me. "Look, how neat they stacked it. Man, they must have been cool guys, huh? Stacking this stuff so neat right in the bank full of people. Boy, if —"

"Hurry," I said. "Let's get it hid."

He looked up and smiled. "Scared, Steve? Your voice is shaking."

I stood there, glaring at him — and then came a knock at the door. And Pa said, "You boys in there? What's going on in there?"

I couldn't talk. The trembling went through me like a sickness and my mouth was brassy and I was glaring again at Johnny.

Johnny called out, "We're having a meeting of the club, Pa, a secret meeting. We'll be through in a couple minutes."

A silence, and then Pa said, "All right, all right. But you be up at the house in five minutes. I don't like you out in the dark like this."

"We'll be there, Pa," Johnny said, grinning at me.

Silence again, and then Johnny said, "Old gutless Steve. Man, you were green."

"You're crazy," I said, "absolutely crazy. You ought to be in a nuthouse."

He wasn't smiling any more. "I'm crazy? Who lied to the Sheriff? Who got us out of the house? Who stalled Pa? I'm crazy, all right, forty–eight thousand dollars crazy. What'd you do? You're a penny–a–rower, that's your speed."

"It's half mine," I said. "You promised it's half mine."

"I promised. And it is. But you'd better get some guts, Steve. This ain't corn–hoeing money."

"I've got guts, don't worry. You'll see. I got plenty of guts now."

We moved the old cream separator that we'd used when we had cows, and moved out the loose plank flooring under it, and put the suitcase full of money underneath, in the hole. Then we put the flooring back and put the separator on top of it.

"We'll think of a better place later," I said. "That ought to be good enough now."

He didn't say anything. I put the flashlight back and we unlocked the door and went out.

We walked to the house and he didn't say a word. What was he thinking about? Maybe he finally got some sense. Or maybe he was remembering I really didn't do anything to help get the money.

Len Nestor and his wife were in the kitchen when we got to the house, and they were talking to Ma and Pa about the robbery. They'd brought the *Ridgeland Courier* along; we don't get a newspaper. Pa says they're a waste of "good" money. What other kind of money is there?

Len Nestor was saying, "The men wore paper bags over their heads, with holes punched out to see through. Wilderson said it was some sight." Then he looked up and saw us. "Well, you boys made the paper, all right."

Johnny smiled. "No kidding? Could I see it, Mr. Nestor?"

Mr. Nestor handed Johnny the paper and we took it over to the table and he spread it out. We read how "two sharp–eyed youngsters at play in a field" had given Sheriff Taggart a "surprisingly complete description" of the robber who had escaped in the green Pontiac.

Johnny nudged me. "We're famous, Steve." And then he whispered real low, "Famous and rich."

I didn't say anything.

Pa said, "What's that, Johnny?"

Johnny looked up. "I said that we were famous, Pa."

"And then you whispered something. It sounded like cussing to me."

"I didn't cuss, Pa. Honest."

Ma said, "We're going to have coffee. Would you boys like some cocoa?"

"Not me," Johnny said. "I'm tired; I'm going to bed."

"Me, too," I said.

As we went up the steps, I heard Mr. Nestor say, "That Johnny, he's a funny one. I'll bet he'll be a comedian, that kid."

"I wish he'd get some sense," Pa said.

Johnny said to me, "Sense — like he's got. Lost all our cows and wound up with nothing."

"Pa didn't lose 'em," I said. "He just found out there wasn't enough money in dairy farming."

"Sure," Johnny said. "Oh, sure."

We went into our room and he went over to stand by the window, looking out at the barn. "We're in trouble, Steve."

"How?" I said.

He turned around to stare at me. "Think. That robber that got away, he can read, can't he? He's going to read that cock and bull story about the Pontiac, ain't he? And won't he know it's a lie and won't he wonder why we lied?"

I sat down on the bed. "Yeah. Oh, God!"

He smiled. "How are the old guts, now, Steve? I mean the new guts."

"Don't worry about me," I said. "What can he prove? What can he do?"

"I don't know," Johnny said. "Do you? You're the sensible one."

I didn't say anything.

"Well," Johnny said, "it don't do us any good to worry now. For all we know, the guy might be in China, right now. Maybe he's still running."

Because of that forty–eight thousand dollars that he'd hid for himself, I didn't think the guy would keep running and Johnny didn't either. A guy that's cool enough to stack that money so nice wasn't going to panic. Nobody had seen his face; he could come back any time.

Johnny opened the little drawer in the bureau to put away the junk in his pockets and then he put his hand in the drawer and took out the hunting knife he'd earned, selling salve.

He took it out of the scabbard and held it up. "I could give him this, right in the belly, huh, Steve?"

I didn't say anything. The knife was real bright and it sent reflections running around the room. Johnny touched the tip with one finger, and winked at me.

But he wasn't fooling me. When we used to trap, I had to open all the traps. Johnny couldn't handle a dead or wounded wild animal. A pig, now, that was different. Or a hen. But anything wild, Johnny was soft about.

"Put it away," I said. "You're talking foolish,"

"For a hundred thousand, I might," he said, and laughed. "But not for a crumby forty–eight thousand." He put the knife back into the scabbard. "I sure sold that salve. I bet I could sell anything."

He'd forgotten about the man already. If the man came, Johnny would think up some more lies, but he wasn't planning ahead. He never did.

If the man came, if the man came … When the man came. Oh, he'd come, all right …

Long after Johnny was asleep, I kept thinking about the man and hoping something would happen that would keep him from coming back.

In the morning, Pa had to go to town to see about a note at the bank and Johnny told Ma he thought we ought to clean up the barn. She thought that was a good idea, and mighty thoughtful.

The way Johnny explained it to me, he didn't want to be out in the corn if that man came back. He wanted to be around where he could keep an eye on him.

So we swept and dusted and washed windows and hosed down all the stanchions that weren't being used any more. And in the corner, where the old milk cans were stacked, Johnny got his idea.

"We could put that money in one of these and bury it," he said. "We could bury it someplace where nobody'd ever think of looking."

"When would we get the chance?" I said. "The folks are always here."

"Not always. They go away every once in awhile. To town, or over to see Uncle George."

"And we go along."

"Not next time."

"They'd wonder why we wanted to stay home."

He nodded. "You don't expect to keep that money in the suitcase, do you? The first rain, and the water seeps under that floor and it's ruined. We've got to keep it dry and safe."

I smiled. "I thought you were going to spend it when you went to school this fall."

"That was before," he said. "Before I knew how much there was. Forty–eight thousand, that makes it different."

"Even half, your half, makes it different."

He grinned at me and started to answer, and then stopped, looking past me.

I turned and looked out the barn door toward the road. A man was coming up the road. He was wearing cotton army pants and a blue sweater and he was limping. He carried a small bag.

That brassy taste was in my mouth again. I said, "The other man wore a cap, a gray cap. Remember?"

"Anybody can throw away a cap," Johnny said. "I'll bet you a dime he turns in here, Steve."

I didn't answer.

"I'll bet you twenty–four thousand dollars he turns in, Steve. C'mon, be a big gambler."

It sounded like he was talking through a tunnel. And the man got so big he seemed to hide everything behind, the trees and the road and the cornfield. I promised myself if he turned in or not, he'd never get a smell of that money. He wouldn't scare anything out of me.

He turned in. And went up the dirt driveway toward the house. I could see Ma in the back yard.

"C'mon, Steve," Johnny said. "Let's go and see what he wants."

"Maybe he'll go away," I said. "Ma's in the back yard and she might not hear him knock."

"He's not going away. C'mon, sissy."

I followed him out of the barn and out to the front yard. The man was on the porch, standing in front of the door.

Johnny said, "My Ma's in the back yard. What do you want?"

He was a kind of thin man, about as tall as Pa, with bushy black eyebrows and gray eyes that seemed to look right through Johnny and me. He said, "I want to talk to your Pa, boy. Run and get him or tell me where he is and I'll go there."

"He's in town," Johnny said. "He won't be back for awhile. What do you want?"

"I'll wait," he said.

"Stay here," Johnny told me, "and keep an eye on this bum, Steve. I'll get Ma."

"I'll get her," I said quickly, and I ran around the end of the house to the back yard.

Ma said, "What are you so pale about? Maybe he's just selling something, Steve. You don't have to get all excited." She put a hand on my forehead. "You're feverish, son."

"No," I said. "I've been working hard. The man looks like a bum, Ma."

She frowned and went around the side of the house and I followed. The man was off the porch now, standing on the grass near Johnny. Johnny was grinning and the man was smiling.

He said, "What is it you want, mister?"

"I'm looking for work," he said. "I need it bad, ma'm. I'd work for my keep, or I had another idea."

"What idea?"

"That timber, down on the turn, that's yours, isn't it?"

Ma nodded.

"It could stand some thinning," he said. "I figured I could cut it up the right size and we could sell it for firewood on shares."

"There's not much money in firewood," Ma said.

"If a fellow goes around to the right districts with a truck, ma'm, it's surprising the price you can get for fireplace wood."

Nobody said anything for a second. And then Ma said, "Well, you can wait until my husband comes home. Come into the kitchen and I'll fix you a couple of eggs."

"Thank you, ma'm," he said.

They went around to the kitchen door and Johnny and I stayed in front. Johnny was still grinning.

"What's so funny?" I asked him.

"That guy," Johnny said. "He's a cool one, huh? He told me I shouldn't call him a bum. He said he was proud to be a hobo, but he wasn't no bum."

"You call that funny? He's going to sleep in the tool shed. Laugh that one off."

He kept grinning. "Steve, the way you worry, a guy would think that was your money."

"It's half mine. And how about a bank robber sitting in the kitchen with Ma? Is that funny?"

"I guess not, Steve. Why don't you run right in and tell her he's a bank robber?"

I felt something bitter in my throat and it came up into my mouth. There was a red haze all around Johnny. He's so awful smart. He'd learn how smart he was if he ever tangled with that gimpy guy in the kitchen. I almost wished the money wasn't half mine, so I could be glad when Johnny got out–foxed.

"What's the matter with you," Johnny said. "You look like you've lost your mind."

I couldn't say anything.

"I wish I had a mirror," he said quietly. "You should see your eyes."

The haze grew around him and the house behind him began to tilt. I wavered on my feet, and he came over fast and put an arm around me. "Are you sick, Steve? What the hell's the matter?"

"I'm all right," I said. "Don't touch me."

Then I heard the pick–up rattling along the road and Johnny said, "Here comes Pa."

I took a deep breath and held it. I said, "Don't say anything about me being sick. We got to stay on our feet. And you've got to get some sense."

He moved a step away from me. "I'll tell you something. I worry more about you than I do about me. I worry about your guts."

Pa stopped the pick–up right next to us and cut the engine. He said, "What were you boys doing, wrestling? With all the work to be done around here?"

"We weren't wrestling, Pa," Johnny said. "I was just hugging my loving brother. You should see the barn, if you think we haven't been working."

"I'll do that right now," he said, and climbed out of the truck.

"There's a man in the kitchen wants to see you," I said, "A bum looking for easy work."

"I'll see him first," Pa said.

When he went through the front door, Johnny said, "That was all right, that crack about easy work. You're learning."

"Don't worry about me," I said.

"If he stays here," he said, "you know what we ought to do? We ought to go out tonight, after everybody's asleep, and get that money and bury it in one of those milk cans."

"That's risky," I said. "And Pa would miss the can."

"So? What's he going to do, dig up the whole hundred and sixty acres looking for it?"

"But if we get caught out late at night —"

"All right," he said. "You think of a better idea. I'm going into the kitchen and listen to that crook out–smart Pa."

I went back to the barn when Johnny went into the kitchen. One corner of it was clear and clean, the corner near a window, and there were some beams overhead.

I got a hammer and some nails and a couple of worn–out tarps. I got a ladder and hung the tarps to the beams, so that the corner was just like a room now, with the tarps making the walls.

I was just putting the ladder away again when Johnny came down to the barn. He looked at the tarps and shook his head. "Oh, boy, you're really giving it away."

"I don't get you, Johnny,"

"Look, the guy will figure the money's in the barn or the tool shed, right? So when you fix him up a place in the barn, what's he going to think?"

"Let him think. We'll get it out of the tool shed before he gets a chance to look in there. I didn't want him to sleep there tonight."

Johnny shrugged.

I asked, "Is he going to stay?"

Johnny nodded. "He's going to cut the timber on shares. You know what him and Pa were talking about?"

"The robbery?"

"That's right. He was talking to Pa, but he meant it for me to hear, about how he'd read we saw the man with the suitcase and what smart boys we must be to remember about the kind of car and all. Man, he put it on, all for me."

"And what'd you say?"

"I kept my mouth shut." Johnny rubbed the back of his neck. "And then Pa said, 'Do you really think there's any money in that timber?' And the guy looked *right at me* and said, 'There used to be. Maybe there still is.' I tell you, Steve, this guy's not scared of nothing."

"Forty–eight thousand dollars don't grow on trees, Johnny. That kind of money builds up a guy inside."

He looked past me, over at the woods, not saying anything.

I said, "Maybe tonight we'll bury it in a milk can? We ought to take one outside now, so we don't have to come in here where he's sleeping tonight."

"All right," he said. "You'll have to wake me tonight, though. I always sleep right through until morning."

So we took the can outside and then got a cot out from the tool shed and dusted it and set it up behind the tarps and even put some nails in the walls for him to hang his clothes on.

When Pa saw it all, he shook his head. He looked around the clean barn and the room I'd made and almost smiled. "And I didn't offer you a dime for all this work."

Johnny said, "You can offer it now, Pa, if you want."

He shook his head. "You boys aren't fooling me. You fixed this up so you wouldn't lose your secret meeting place."

Johnny laughed. "You're too smart for us, Pa. If we help the man with the timber, would he pay us, you think?"

"Maybe," Pa said. "I'll talk it over with him and maybe we can work something out. You got the key to the tool shed? I got to get those saws sharpened up."

"I'll get 'em, Pa," Johnny said. "Don't forget to tell him what good workers we are, huh?"

Johnny went to the tool shed and I went up to the house. I could see the man sitting on the front porch, smoking, so I went in through the kitchen door.

I wasn't scared any more; I just didn't want to talk to him.

Mom said, "Where have you been? Everybody's eaten but you."

"I was fixing a room for the man."

"For Frank?"

"If that's his name. I'm not hungry, Ma."

"Come here," she said. "Let me feel your head."

I came over and she put her hand on my forehead. She said, "It seems all right. But maybe you'd better take a little nap."

"Maybe," I said. "I'll try, anyway."

"You worked hard this morning," she said. "You're probably tired."

I nodded, and went up the steps to our bedroom. I wasn't tired. I just wanted to be alone, to think. I had to think this all out careful because there was more at stake than there probably ever would be in my life again. I'd bet there wasn't a farmer in the township that ever saw forty–eight thousand dollars in one hunk.

Pa had been paying me for chores for three years now, and I'd saved every penny of it and had ninety dollars, including Christmas money from Uncle George.

Johnny was right about me, in a way. He had more chance of protecting that money because he had more guts and was older and he had more gab. And he thought fast, when he had to.

I went over to the window and looked out and everything was green, the color of money. Johnny thought fast; I'd have to think careful. And once I decided what the surest way was to protect that money, I'd have to find the guts to go through with it.

I was lying on the bed when Johnny came up. He said, "We ought to get rid of the wrappers on that money. That shows it's the bank's money. With those gone, who could prove it?"

"I've been thinking of that," I said.

"What else you been thinking?"

"Everything. Like building up my guts."

He laughed and lay down on his bed. "Well, old Frank's down starting on the timber and Pa's working on the fence near the Saugus road and Ma's going over to Nestor's. Why don't we get rid of those brown wrappers as soon as she goes?"

"A good idea," I said. "And something else — why don't we spike down that tool shed floor until we get a chance to bury the money in the milk can?"

"You're thinking, Stevie boy," he said. "You're hitting on all eight."

Ma left in a couple minutes and we down to the tool shed. We took all the wrappers off and put them in a paper sack and put the money back and spiked the floor down good.

Johnny said, "We ought to burn these wrappers, but where?"

"Give 'em to me; I'll get rid of 'em," I said. "You keep a watch on Frank until I come back."

He smiled. "Brave Stevie boy."

When I came back, he said, "Why don't we go swimming, like fun–loving kids? I'll bet this new Steve would even dive off the bank, now."

"Any time," I said.

"Remember, Pa said he'd skin us if he caught us diving off that bluff."

"Pa can't see us from the Saugus Road," I said. "I'll bet you a dime I'll dive closer to the rock than you will."

"It's a bet," he said. "C'mon, I'll race you to the house for our trunks."

The bank was maybe twenty feet high and the water was deep enough below it, but there was this sharp rock near the middle that came almost to the surface. Pa said if we ever hit that, diving, it would split our head wide open and I guess he was right. But Johnny used to dive real close to it until Pa caught him one time. And then he said we couldn't dive from the bank at all.

Johnny beat me to the house and got into his trunks faster and went racing out ahead of me. But when I came down there, he was still standing on the bank.

"The bet's off," he said.

"All right, you owe me a dime."

"All right, I owe you a dime. You know why the bet's off?"

I shook my head.

"I was never worth forty–eight thousand dollars, before. I can't take chances with myself, now, huh, Stevie?"

"You're getting some sense," I said, "but you're only worth twenty–four thousand dollars."

He laughed. "I just said that to heckle you." He looked over toward the woods. "That Frank's sure working. I wonder how long he'll work before he gives up?"

"How long would you," I asked, "for forty–eight thousand dollars?"

Johnny didn't answer. He just stood there, looking at the woods. If it hadn't been Johnny, I would have said he looked scared. For the first time in my life, I felt bigger than Johnny.

Around four o'clock, we got tired of swimming and went up to the house for some milk. Then Johnny said he was going to take a nap. I put on some clothes and went over to where Pa was stringing new fence. I helped him out there until Ma rang the bell for supper.

Frank ate with us. He sat next to me and didn't talk much, except to Pa, about the timber. Johnny didn't talk at all and that was maybe a new record. After supper, Johnny went upstairs to read, he said.

Frank stretched and looked out through the kitchen window and said, "I've got a couple axes to sharpen. How much would you charge me to turn the grindstone, Steve?"

"Ten cents an axe," I said.

He looked at me sort of half smiling. "Make it a nickel."

"Ten cents," I said. "I don't need the money."

Pa laughed and Ma smiled. Frank said, "All right. You drive a hard bargain, Steve."

"He's got ninety dollars saved," Pa said. "Steve will never wind up on the poor farm."

Frank and I went out to the barn with a can of water to wet down the grindstone. He had a hand axe and the big double–edged axe with him and I should have been scared, but I wasn't, much.

He poured some of the water into the container that dripped on the stone, and said, "I've been thinking about those robbers. I read where they got away with forty–eight thousand dollars. If I had that kind of money, I know where I could double it in six months."

"Gee," I said, "it's too bad you don't have that kind of money, then."

He stood there with the hand axe in his hand, staring at me. "How old are you?"

"I'll be thirteen next month," I said.

He shook his head. "Well, I'll be —"

"You'd better not let Pa hear you swear," I butted in, "or you won't be cutting any more timber. Pa don't hold with swearing."

He took a deep breath. "I'd better be careful, then. I wouldn't want to get cheated out of all that money."

I didn't say anything.

"The money I'm going to make on the timber," he explained.

"Sure," I said. "What else? You want me to start turning now?"

"Any time," he said. He took another breath. "I'm a patient man."

"Me, too," I said, and started to turn the grind stone.

He sure knew how to sharpen an axe, that Frank. Slow and easy until he had the edge sharp as a razor. He wet some of his whiskers with spit and shaved 'em right off with that hand axe while I stood there.

Then he took the big axe and I started to turn again. He said, "We work pretty good together, Steve. I bet we could make out all right, working together."

"Maybe," I said. "Who knows?"

"I've kicked around a lot," he said. "I think I've learned how to turn a buck by now."

I didn't say anything.

"I wouldn't have to rob a bank, if I had a stake," he went on. "I'd know how to make it grow."

"Pa says it takes money to make money," I said.

"And he's right. The way things are these days, a guy with a nest egg could fix himself up for life,"

"Not a nest egg of ninety dollars," I said.

He smiled. "I guess not."

"If I knew a place to get more," I said, "you could tell me how to make it grow, I'll bet."

"You're dead right, kid. You think about it. A kid needs help when it comes to getting rich. I could show you lots of angles."

"I'll think about it," I said. "Maybe Johnny knows a place where we can get some money."

He nodded and kept working the big axe lightly over the turning stone. He looked awful pleased with himself, I'd say.

He gave me twenty cents when we were finished and I went up to the house. It was getting dark now. We don't have daylight saving time on the farm. We don't have much of anything on the farm.

I thought about those two guys that had been killed trying to get away from the robbery and Johnny's lie about the Pontiac and the way he was acting since we went swimming this afternoon. Johnny was losing his guts, maybe. It wasn't a big funny lie, any more, a wise guy's game. This Frank had changed it from a game.

In the kitchen Pa said, "Well, you've had a full day, haven't you?"

"Yes, sir," I said, "I sure have."

"Maybe you'd better hit the hay early."

"I'm going to," I said. "I'm going up now. Good night, Pa."

In our room, Johnny was reading an auto racing book. That's about the only kind he likes. He looked at me and asked, "What'd he say?"

"He said if he had a stake, he knew how to make a million."

"What'd you say?"

"I told him it was too bad he didn't have a stake, then."

Johnny stared at me for seconds. "Man, you've changed."

"You, too," I said.

"Don't worry about me."

"I'm not," I told him, "not any more."

He kept staring at me without talking. Then he looked back at the book. I laid down on the bed and thought.

In a little while he got up and took off his clothes and climbed under the covers. "Steve," he said, "I think I'm getting scared."

"Don't," I told him. "Don't think about it. Nobody can prove nothing on us, *nothing*, unless we get scared and blab."

After a few seconds, he said, "That's right. You're right. Well, they'll never get anything out of me, I promise you that."

I didn't answer him.

In a little while, he fell asleep and I went over to sit by the window and look out at the bright moonlight.

In the morning, I heard Ma in the kitchen and she sounded half crazy and then Pa came charging up the steps, and I closed my eyes. Johnny's bed is closest to the door and Pa shook Johnny until he woke up.

Then Pa said, "Run right over to Nestor's and tell them to call Sheriff Taggart. Tell them to send the Sheriff here right away, this second."

"What's the matter, Pa?" Johnny asked. "What happened?"

"Never mind what happened. Get some shoes and pants on and get over there right away. I got to stay with your Ma; she's half crazy, she's so scared."

Pa left and Johnny came over to shake me. "Steve, something's happened."

I sat up. "What?"

"I don't know. But I got to run to Nestor's to call the Sheriff. Steve, it must be about Frank. What could it be?"

"I don't know," I said. "Maybe one of his buddies came here and they had a fight. How do I know what happened?"

He put some pants on and a pair of shoes and went running out, without a shirt. I got up and dressed.

When I came down to the kitchen, Ma was sitting in the rocker, rocking and hanging on tight to the arms. "I had to call him," she said. "I had to call him for breakfast."

"Who, Ma?" I asked. "What happened?"

Pa came in from outside. "Never mind, boy," he said rough. "Your ma's had a shock. Better go out in the front and wait for the Sheriff. Tell him to go down to the barn."

I went out and stood on the front porch to wait for the Sheriff.

"Stabbed three times in the throat," Sheriff Taggart said, "and four times in the chest. And these money wrappers scattered all over the floor. How would you figure it, Jess?"

Jess Laurie just shrugged his shoulders. They were standing in the front yard, waiting for the Coroner from Center City. I was standing in the bushes at the side of the house. Pa and Ma were in the house with the Nestors and I didn't know where Johnny was.

"I'll tell you how I figure it," the Sheriff said. "I figure this was the guy that drove that Pontiac. And he swindled the money from that fat guy in the denim jacket and came back here to hide. Only the fat guy found him, that's what I figure."

"It don't make sense," Jess said, "for the guy to come here to hide. Why would he come here?"

"Use your head," Sheriff Taggart said. "Where would be the last place in the world the fat guy would look for him?"

I came out from the bushes. "Sheriff, I heard something funny last night."

"Funny?" He frowned at me. "What — what do you mean?"

"I woke up," I said, "and heard talking in the barn. And then I heard a big thump, and then a little later, I heard a car start, up the road aways. I went to the window, but I couldn't see any lights."

Jess Laurie stared at me. "You heard talking in the barn and didn't go out there? Why not?"

"I thought maybe it was Pa talking to Frank. I didn't know what time it was. And I thought maybe the car was neckers, you know."

"Was it your Pa's voice?" Jess asked.

"I couldn't make out the voices," I said. "I didn't think nothing of it until after what happened this morning."

"You didn't see the car?" Sheriff Taggart asked.

"No, sir. I just heard the starter and then it driving away."

"It was a bright night," Jess Laurie said.

Sheriff Taggart looked down the road. "Where's your window, Steve?"

I pointed to it.

"The car could've been around the bend," he said. "The guy could've come up to the barn without being in sight of the house. I'd bet ten dollars those weren't no neckers. I'd bet it was a green Pontiac parked down there."

"You mean the robbers, Sheriff?" I asked.

He looked at Jess. "Who else?"

"I'm scared, Sheriff," I said. "I don't want no robbers coming around here."

Sheriff Taggart smiled. "Don't worry, boy; they won't be around. They got no reason to come here any more."

"Is there anything else you heard or saw?" Jess Laurie asked me.

I shook my head. "No, sir, that's every bit of it."

Then the Coroner's car was coming up the road and they went out to wave him down and I went looking for Johnny. I could have told them I'd seen a green Pontiac, but if they ever found out the Pontiac had been a lie of Johnny's, I'd be in trouble. The way I'd told it, they couldn't ever prove what I'd said wasn't true.

In the back yard, Pa and Mr. Nestor were talking. Pa was saying, "I guess the other one came back for the money. Gosh, Len, could you kill a man for money?"

Mr. Nestor said, "All of us have done mean things for a lot less than forty–eight thousand. I guess murder's just another step up the ladder, John."

Pa said, "What are you doing out here, Steve? I told you to stay in the house."

"I'm looking for Johnny," I said.

"He's in the house. Get in there, now, until I tell you to come out."

I went into the house. Ma and Mrs. Nestor were in the front room. I went up the steps and there was Johnny on his bed. He was lying on his back, just staring at the ceiling.

He didn't look at me. "Where'd you put my knife? Where is it?"

"You crazy, Johnny? What would I do with your knife?"

"Don't be funny. Where is it, Steve?"

I sat down on the bed and looked at him. For the first time in my life, he didn't seem bigger to me. For the first time, he seemed like an equal, no more. I had proved myself.

I said, "Let's not talk about your silly old knife, Johnny. You can buy another one. Think of the money we've got."

He sat up. "What's happened to you? You've changed."

"Everybody changes," I said, "sooner or later, right?"

He took a deep breath. "I know you killed him, Steve. Because of the wrappers."

"What wrappers, Johnny?" I asked.

"The ones you were going to get rid of." His voice dropped. "The ones that were all over the floor in Frank's room."

I said, "Maybe the guy with the green Pontiac put them there. That's what the sheriff thinks."

He sat there staring at me and I stared right back. He laid down again, frowning at the ceiling.

"You told me I had no guts, Johnny," I reminded him. "I had to prove myself, you told me."

He closed his eyes. "You're crazy. It was too much money. It put you over the edge. You're crazy as a loon, Steve."

"No," I said. "Don't talk like that. Think of the money and don't talk like that."

He didn't answer. He opened his eyes again, but didn't look at me. I lay down on my bed.

His voice was almost a whisper. "It was the way you were heading. You were always money–crazy. This just brought it on faster."

"Everybody is," I said, "everybody with any sense."

"Not everybody," he said. "Not me."

"When you're old enough," I told him, "you can buy a big Cadillac. You can even buy a racing car. There won't be any smart crook looking for you, figuring a way to steal your money back."

"Shut up!" he said. "You're loony, I tell you."

"Be sensible, Johnny. *Think!* All right, I'll shut up."

Silence. I closed my eyes and I could hear the voices of Ma and Mrs. Nestor below and the Sheriff out in the front yard talking to somebody. I saw Frank's face smiling in his sleep, and I got sick to my stomach, but I fought it, and changed my mind from that to thinking of the money, all that money.

I said quietly, "I wonder how many guys Frank killed in *his* life." I licked my lips. "A dirty old bank robber like that."

Johnny didn't say anything.

"Maybe he had getting killed coming to him."

Johnny still didn't say anything.

I stretched and kept my eyes open, so I wouldn't see any more ugly pictures. I heard a couple of car engines start out in front and then I heard Pa coming up the stairs. Johnny sat up, as though he'd been waiting to tell Pa something.

Pa came in and said, "Your mother's going over to your Uncle George's and Aunt Jane's for a couple of days. I'm taking her over now. You boys afraid to stay here?"

I shook my head.

Johnny said, "I'll stay, too. How soon will you be back, Pa?"

"In a couple hours. Why?"

Johnny started to talk, stopped, and then said, "I just wondered." He lay back again, looking very thoughtful.

"Maybe you ought to get out of the house," Pa said. "Why don't you go swimming? It's hot today."

Johnny nodded. "Maybe I will."

"If you dive off that bluff," Pa said, "stay clear of that rock. I guess I can trust you to do that, can't I?"

Johnny nodded again. "Don't worry. I'll be careful, Pa."

Pa went out and we heard him talking to Ma. Ma never came in to say good–bye. I guess she was still in shock. I heard the pick–up rattle out onto the road and then it was suddenly so quiet I could hear Johnny breathe.

I said, "Why did you want to know when Pa was coming back? Were you going to tell him —? I mean, about the — knife and the wrappers?"

He didn't answer.

I got up and went to the window. "It started with *you*, remember," I said. "With that story about the Pontiac. That started the whole thing."

"I'm remembering that," he said.

I turned around to face him. "You did something. I did something. So now we got the money. I did something, didn't I? I thought you'd be — well, I thought —" I stopped. I wasn't going to tell him I wanted him to be proud of me.

He wasn't listening to me, anyhow. "Maybe," he said, "I haven't got the guts to tell the Sheriff I lied about that Pontiac, and maybe I have. That's what I've been thinking about."

"Now why would you do that? That would be foolish."

He didn't answer. I didn't know what he was thinking about; I hoped it was the money, that big bunch of money and what it would buy. I was actually wishing he'd get back to talking big–mouthed, like he did before.

After a couple seconds, I said, "You could give your half away, if you didn't want it. You could give it to the Salvation Army."

He didn't answer and he didn't look at me. I said, "I'm going swimming. I'm not going to argue with you if you don't at least argue back."

Still nothing from him.

I put on my trunks and a pair of shoes and went out without saying any more. I was worried about him. He was unpredictable. I went down to the bluff and stood there, looking at the rock. It looked big.

What would I gain by trying to prove myself twice in twenty–four hours? What could I gain, by seeing how close to the rock I could dive?

I was rich now; I had too much to lose. Getting myself killed now would be a big waste.

But it came to me in a strange way that when you've got a lot to lose, you have to be sure you're not gutless. I don't mean you got to be reckless, but you can't be gutless. Because there would be a lot of guys wanting to take that money away from me.

So I stood there, measuring the distance, and made the dive, as close to the rock as I had guts for. I skinned my hand, going down, rubbing it along the sharp edge of the rock.

I came up feeling sick again, but good, too, because I'd made the dive. I looked up and there was Johnny on the bluff above.

"That was close," he said.

I smiled and nodded.

Then he came down, in one of his beautiful, clean dives and it looked for sure like he was going to hit right on top of the rock. But at the last, he twisted away, and his body seemed to scrape as he hit the water.

He came up and I said, "Closer. You're a better diver."

"Let's go over to the bank," he said. "I want to talk to you."

We came up on the bank and we were right at the place where Frank had stacked the cordwood. He could sure handle an axe and saw, that Frank. I got a funny feeling thinking of him dead, and his firewood still stacked there, wood he'd cut only yesterday.

"You're shivering," Johnny said.

I didn't answer. I looked at my scraped hand. It wasn't bleeding any more.

He sat on the cordwood. His voice was very soft.

"What was it like? Was it hard to do? How did you get the guts?"

"It was — scary," I said. "After — well, after the first — cut, it was easier." I looked at him steady. "I could do it again — I think. He probably killed people, lots and lots of 'em, so —"

"Was it only the money, Steve? Is that why, or was there another reason, too? Was any of it my fault, the way I called you gutless and like that —?"

"The money mostly," I said. "Everything — but the money mostly."

"What do you mean — everything?"

"Oh, Pa grubbing and — well, Ma favoring you and the way you always looked down at me. You don't act like no brother, Johnny. You act like a big bully, most times."

He nodded. He kept nodding, like he was remembering a lot of things. Then he said, "You give that money to the Salvation Army or the Red Cross, and there'll never be a word out of me to Pa or Sheriff Taggart or anybody else in the whole world."

I stared at him. "How could I do that? Where would I tell 'em I got it?"

"I don't mean now. Later, I mean. You could just send it in a package with no return address. It would be easy."

I sat down and looked at the water. "And Pa keeps grubbing and Ma, too. And the whole thing was for nothing. Your lying and my — doing what I did, and nobody gets nothing out of it but the lousy Red Cross. It's not sensible, Johnny."

He sat there, frowning. I sat there looking at the water. It seemed like a long time before he said, "Well, maybe we could fix some way to let Ma and Pa get some of it. They sure can use it better than the Red Cross. And we owe them something."

"Sure," I said. "They could at least get a halfway decent car, right?"

He nodded, and I could see his eyes flash when I said *car*. *Racing car*, I figured he was thinking.

He sucked in the hot, bright air. "The money's safe, huh?"

"Oh, yeah," I said, "plenty safe."

He looked up at the bluff and over at the rock and down at the ground, everywhere but at me. "Maybe, we got some of that money coming, too, don't you think? It was like we did a service, getting it and all, you know."

"And we ought to by rights get paid for our time, that what you mean?"

"Yeah. Sure."

"You're the boss, Johnny," I said.

But I knew he wasn't, really. Not now.

And I think he knew it, too.

Then I said, like I was giving an order, "We won't take any more of that money than what's coming to us. But that's quite a bit, come to think of it."

Joe Puma Stories

The Unholy Three

I was trying to figure how to pay seven hundred and forty dollars worth of bills with three hundred and twelve dollars I had in the bank when he walked into the office. It was almost dinner time and I was hungry.

So maybe my voice was gruff. "What's your trouble, son?"

His face was thin, his eyes a deep blue and they considered me with some apprehension. He was about eleven years old. He said nothing.

"Get the wrong office?" I suggested.

He shook his head.

I tried to appear more genial. "You've been watching the private–eye shows on TV and you came in to see what a *real* one looks like, huh?"

He took a deep breath and shook his head again, hard. I matched his silence. I went back to evaluating which bills were most imminently disastrous. A minute of silence moved by.

Then he said, "It's my sister."

I looked up. "Oh —? Has something happened to her?"

He frowned. "Well — not yet."

"I see," I said, though I didn't. "How old is your sister?"

More hope in his glance now. "She's twenty–three. She's very pretty."

"And what's going to happen to her?"

"I don't know. But she's going with a guy, a no–good guy."

"What's your name?" I asked him.

"John, John Delavan. My sister calls me Johnny."

"Okay, Johnny, listen carefully. First of all, I generally get fifty dollars a day when I work. And second, I can't stop your sister from going with a no–good guy. And third, how do you know he is one?"

"I know all right. And about the money, I thought I could owe you. I've got a paper route. You could investigate the man, couldn't you? There's no law against that."

"If your sister asked me to, I could. What about your parents?"

His face was bleak. "There aren't any. There's just me and Eileen."

Silence for a few moments, and I asked, "Do you live in the neighborhood?"

He nodded. "In the Belvoir Apartments, over on Third. You don't want the business, is that it?"

His steady gaze met mine. "Johnny," I said softly, "I don't want to charge you fifty dollars a day for work I'm not authorized to perform. Don't you see my position?"

"I see it. Sitting, that's your position. To heck with you, Mr. Puma." He turned.

"Wait, Johnny," I said. "I'm trying to be honest with you."

He didn't turn back; he continued to walk and the door slammed behind him. The glass in the door rattled, the glass that held the lettering *Joseph Puma, Investigations.*

I sighed and wondered if Eileen's suitor was really a no–good guy or just a guy who didn't like the Giants.

For some reason, I took out a card and typed on it: Eileen and Johnny Delavan — Belvoir Apartments.

Then I looked at my watch, and there was still time ...

In The House Of Genial Lending, Max said, "How much this time?"

"Five hundred," I told him. "She's in good shape, Max. I just put on a new set of tubeless tires."

"And she'd bring six hundred in a quick sale," he said.

"That's more than I'm asking for. Of course, if you want to make it six hundred?

"Five," he said quickly. He sighed. "Joe, you're too bright a young man to waste your life in such a precarious profession. When are you going to get smart?"

"I'm doing better every month," I told him. "Last time I had to borrow seven hundred, remember?"

He shook his head sadly. "Bright fellow like you, it beats me ... Where's the pink slip?"

While he was getting the papers ready, I asked him, "Do you know the Delavans who live over in the Belvoir? There's an Eileen and a Johnny."

He looked thoughtful. "Eileen Delavan? There's a girl at the bank by that name. Beautiful girl. Her parents died a couple of years ago, I think, if that's the one."

"That could be the one," I said. "Do you mean the Security Bank?"

He nodded and continued to look thoughtful. "Now, let's see, I think her brother delivers my paper. About twelve, isn't he?"

"I guess you've got the family, all right." His glance was worried. "They're not in trouble, Joe?"

I chuckled. "I doubt it. Johnny doesn't like his sister's boy friend. He wanted me to investigate him."

Max didn't smile. "Who's the boy friend? Maybe I know him, too."

"I didn't ask."

Max shook his head again. "No wonder you're always borrowing money. Some detective." He held out a sheaf of papers. "Sign all three copies."

I signed all three copies and walked out a minute later with a check for five hundred dollars. I was rich again; I went over to Heinie's for some wiener–schnitzel.

Somebody had left a paper on the table. I read that the President was progressing satisfactorily after his heart attack and the Russians were trying to get Poland into the Security Council. Locally, the Mayor was worried about the increase in juvenile delinquency.

The vision of Johnny Delavan came to me and I turned to the sport pages. A no–good guy ... Probably because he could dance, or used slickum on his hair. Kids were too quick to judge their elders.

Reichoff, the beat cop, came in and looked around.

I called over, "Buy you a cup of coffee, Ben."

He came over and took the chair across from me. "Still eating, huh, Joe? That's pretty good, in your business."

"I make out," I told him. "I'm lining up some big accounts right now."

"Sure you are," he said tonelessly. "I saw you come out of Max's half an hour ago."

"Do you know the Delavans?" I asked him.

"Eileen and Johnny." He nodded. "Fine people. I wish all the kids in this neighborhood were like Johnny Delavan." He paused. "They're not in any kind of trouble, are they, Joe?"

I smiled. "No, Johnny came into my office about an hour ago. He wanted me to investigate his sister's boy friend."

"And who would that be?"

I shrugged. "I didn't ask the kid."

"I'll ask him," Ben said. "I'm surprised he didn't come to me in the first place."

I stared at him. "You're kidding. You wouldn't take a kid seriously about a thing like that?"

"I'm not busy," Ben said. "I'll ask him. You never know what a question might turn up, Joe." He yawned. "Thanks for the coffee, Joe. I've got to be getting along."

He smiled and went out, two hundred and twenty pounds of municipal guardian. It has been rumored about him that he is meddlesome and nosey, but a neighborhood cop is supposed to be.

I drank another cup of coffee and went out to face my evening. At thirty–one, without a wife, an evening is something to face when I've nothing to work on.

My kitchenette apartment held no lure for me and I had seen all the movies around. One early star winked down at me.

Well, what the hell, why not? I looked up Delavan in the phone book and found the one who lived in the Belvoir Apartments.

Luckily, Johnny answered the phone.

I said, "Joe Puma, Johnny. You never did tell me the name of that fellow you want investigated."

His voice was almost a whisper. "Are you going to work on it, Mr. Puma?"

"I thought I'd give it a free neighborhood routine investigation. Is your sister home? Is that why you're speaking so quietly?"

"That's right, Mr. Puma." His voice was even lower. "The man's name is Jean Magnus and he lives at the Stratford Hotel."

"What don't you like about him, Johnny? What makes you suspicious of him?"

A feminine voice in the background said, "Who are you talking to, Johnny?"

Johnny said, "Goodbye, Mr. Puma. See you tomorrow."

The feminine voice started again before the line went dead.

Well, I knew the houseman over at the Stratford. He'd tried a spell of private work, himself. I drove over there.

Lenny Donovan, the houseman, was in the small office behind the clerk's desk. He was reading a hunting and fishing magazine.

He looked up genially. "A little cribbage, Joe? Or is this a professional call?"

"Semi–professional," I told him. "I am working free for an eleven–year–old neighborhood client."

He smiled. "Young Delavan, maybe?"

I nodded and sat down. "How did you guess?"

Lenny yawned. "The kid was hanging around here evenings, hanging around the lobby with those big eyes and ears of his wide open. I ran him out."

"His sister's going with one of your guests."

"Oh —?" Lenny looked interested. "He wouldn't tell me why he was hanging around." He pulled at one ear. "Who's the guest?"

"A man named Jean Magnus."

Lenny reached forward to thumb through a card index box. "That would be — let's see — 324. Oh, yes, big Victor Mature type. Real charmer. I can't blame Johnny's sister. This boy's really got it."

"What's his line?"

"Promotion, investments, speculation. You know, Joe, a wheel."

"Self employed?"

Lenny frowned. "Aren't you getting a little nosey, Joe? This man's got one of the better suites."

"Is it all right if I go up and talk to him?"

Lenny's frown was deeper. "Because a kid doesn't like him? This isn't much of a job, but I'm happy in it. Let's get to the cribbage." He reached into a drawer and brought out a cribbage board.

I shook my head.

I stood up. "Mind if I sit in the lobby for a while?"

"I sure as hell do. You're really reaching for business, aren't you, Joe?"

"It's hard to find," I admitted. "Well, get some exercise; you look a little jowly."

"That's because I eat regular. Good night, Joe." He was chuckling as I left.

There really wasn't any reason for me to feel annoyed. I had made an ass of myself and Lenny had pointed it out. I continued to feel annoyed. I knew what Lenny was earning; 340 a month and his room. He didn't have to be so superior; I'd turned down the job.

I was going through the door to the street, immersed in my own self pity when I ran into a large hunk of man.

We both bounced and then he growled, "Why'n hell don't you look where you're going?"

The face was broad, and for a moment a flare of incomplete recognition flickered in my memory, then died.

"Sorry," I said, and tried to recapture the near–memory. "Haven't we met?"

"Head–on," he agreed, and went through the doorway.

Overhead, the star was lost. In front of me, traffic growled and smoked. All around me, the lights were beckoning to buy, drink, dance or see a movie. The Chev started with a whine, and I headed her toward the Belvoir.

In the lobby, I took the phone off the hook and pressed the buzzer for the Delavan apartment.

A feminine voice came metallically through the speaker, and I said, "Could I speak with Johnny?"

"He's at a Scout meeting. Who is this?"

"John Foster Dulles," I said, and replaced the phone.

From there, I went to the East Side Station. Buddy Loeske called Headquarters for me and they had nothing on a Jean Magnus. That ended my day; I went home.

It would have ended my involvement with the Delavan problem, except for two things that happened next day. For one thing, Johnny came to see me at noon.

"Sis is burning up," he told me. "When you phoned, I told her you were my route supervisor, but she didn't believe me. And then when you talked to her last night, she knew something fishy was going on."

"I don't blame her for burning. How did she ever meet this Magnus?"

"He came into the bank to rent a safety deposit box and she took care of him. What did you find out, Mr. Puma?"

"Nothing. Except that you'd been hanging around the Stratford lobby. And what did you find out, doing that?"

"I found out Magnus' name isn't Jean. One of his friends called him Nick, right there in the lobby."

"Oh? Anything else?"

He shook his head, his eyes intent on mine.

"Johnny," I said patiently, "what's your real beef with this Magnus? Don't you want your sister to get married? Is that it?"

"That's not it. He's no good. He's got a big lard bucket friend looks just like a crook. I saw him a lot of times when I was watching the hotel." Johnny took a deep breath. "And then there's a little ratty guy he knows, too."

"Crooks don't look like anything special," I told him gently. "You've been seeing too many movies, Johnny."

He gave me a look of complete scorn. "Okay. So I'm a dope. I've been earning money for two years, but I'm a dope. Okay. So–long —" He turned and went out.

The second thing that happened was that my phone rang, and it was the assistant manager at the Stratford. He wanted to know if I knew where Lenny Donovan was.

I told him I didn't and asked him why he thought I would.

"The clerk told me you came to see Mr. Donovan last night. He didn't show up for work this morning and I've exhausted every other source of possible information."

"Doesn't he stay there at the hotel?"

"He does. And his clothes are in the room, all except for those he was wearing last night."

"I've no idea where he is."

"Thank you, anyway. And incidentally, Mr. Puma, in the event Mr. Donovan hasn't an adequate excuse for his absence, would you be interested in the job here?"

He should have asked me *before* Max lent me the five hundred. I said with simple dignity, "I'm sorry. My living costs are too great for that."

I thought I heard him chuckle when I hung up. He knew I ate at Heinie's.

So Jean is called Nick and Donovan is missing. Not really important facts, and nobody was paying me. I went out for lunch.

I was halfway through the giant–sized bowl of clam chowder when the girl came in and walked over to Heinie. And then Heinie pointed at me, and she came my way.

Red hair and fine figure and dressed in nice, if modest, clothes. Under other circumstances, a girl it would be a pleasure to meet.

But now her eyes were blazing and the fine body seemed rigid. "Joseph Puma?" she asked me.

I stood up and nodded. "At your service, M'am."

"I don't want your service. Are you also John Foster Dulles, by any chance?"

I smiled. "Occasionally. I have a lot of disguises."

"I can imagine. Any of them would be better than the one you're wearing. And what gives you the right to establish a residence in my hair?"

"I didn't know I had," I said. "Just exactly what is your complaint, M'am? And your name?"

"My name," she said evenly, "is Eileen Delavan. Last night, an officer Ben Reichoff interrogated me. He said you had told him something that needed in–vestigating. And you were the one who talked to Johnny on the phone last night, weren't you?"

"No M'am. Are you having some kind of trouble, Miss Delavan?"

"Too much. And I'll thank you to stay out of my business. Is that clear?"

"That's clear enough. You're welcome. Believe me, Miss Delavan, you're badly confused, but I haven't the time nor the patience to quarrel publicly about it. Could you keep your voice down?"

She glared and glared and then uttered something between a snort and cough and turned and stalked out. The patrons in Heinie's were all smiling; it's a small place and her voice had unusual clarity.

I finished my clam chowder and went over to the Stratford.

Lenny was still missing, the assistant manager told me. That fact hadn't yet been reported to the police.

I asked, "Is Mr. Magnus still occupying Suite 324?"

He nodded. "What would that have to do with Mr. Donovan?"

"I'm not sure it has anything to do with that. Has Lenny been drinking at all?"

The man shook his head. "Not to my knowledge. Not enough to interfere with his duties, at any rate."

"And he left no message behind?"

"None." He paused. "What about this Mr. Magnus, Joe? Why did you ask about him?"

I shrugged. "I was talking to Lenny about him last night. There's a possibility Lenny went to see him and Magnus would then be the last man to have seen Lenny before he disappeared. But that's way out in left field. I haven't any substantial reason for thinking there's anything fishy about Mr. Magnus."

"What insubstantial reason would you have?"

"The dislike of an eleven or twelve–year–old boy, the brother of a girl Magnus is going with."

The manager looked at me queerly. Then he sighed.

"It's not quite that ridiculous," I protested.

He sighed once more. "We are certainly fortunate we didn't manage to secure your doubtful services, Fearless Fosdick. Well, drop in again, but not soon, please?"

"To hell with you," I said, and gave him my back.

Going through the lobby, I felt an urgent need for a drink. I turned right, into the bar. It was a dim and quiet bar. Two men with brief cases were on stools at the far end, quietly downing an after–lunch drink. In a corner booth, there were three men who interested me more.

One of them was the bulky man I'd bumped into going out of the lobby last night. The other was small, ratty looking. The third had a dark–haired, dark–eyed charm I could guess would appeal to some undiscerning women.

I thought their talking ebbed when I came within vision and I thought they examined me with interest. There wasn't any doubt in my mind that this was the unholy trinity Johnny had described.

The bartender came up with his smile and I ordered a bourbon and water. The two men with brief cases discussed the merits of term insurance. The three men in the booth directly behind me discussed nothing.

When the bartender brought my drink, I asked, "You haven't seen Lenny Donovan around this morning, have you?"

The bartender shook his head. "And he's usually in by this time."

"If you see him," I said, "you can tell him I got the information he asked me for."

The man nodded. "And your name?"

"Joe Puma. He knows me. My office is right over on Third Street." I paused. "I'm a private investigator."

Can a silence deepen? I thought the one behind me did.

The bartender wasn't aware of it if it existed. He said blandly, "I'll be sure to tell him and he's bound to come in. Lenny couldn't go a whole day without a drink."

"He didn't show up for work this morning," I said. "Maybe he's doing his drinking somewhere else. Well, I'll try a couple of his favorite haunts." I finished my drink. "I've got to find him."

In my office, I was looking busy when he came in. He had a rather worried smile on his dark face. "Are you — currently available?" he asked me.

I nodded, and indicated my customer's chair. "Sit down, Mr. —?"

"Magnus," he supplied. "Jean Magnus. I was in the bar over at the Stratford when I heard you ask about Leonard Donovan."

"Oh, yes. With a briefcase, weren't you?"

He shook his head, studying me. "I was in a booth right behind you. Maybe you didn't see me."

"I'll have to admit I didn't notice you, Mr. Mangus. What brings you here?"

"*Magnus*," he corrected me. "Mr. Donovan's disappearance is what brings me here. Do you know him very well?"

I shook my head. "Very slightly. Through the manager of the Stratford. Is he a friend of yours?"

Magnus smiled. "Hardly. He was married to my sister. He owes her some back alimony."

"Oh? And you followed him to the Stratford?"

Magnus shook his head. "It just happened that I ran into him there. I tried to reason with him. And now he's disappeared."

"Leaving his clothes behind."

Magnus frowned. "Are you sure? That isn't what the manager told me."

"It's what he told me, an hour ago. Did he tell you anything else?"

Magnus shook his head again.

"He just didn't mention it, either way. Well, that would indicate he's coming back, wouldn't it? So I suppose there'd be no point in my hiring you."

"To find Lenny? If he's an alimony dodger, you wouldn't need me. The police would be happy to look for him."

"I don't want to make trouble for Lenny. He's lacking in a sense of responsibility, but I think he's open to reason. Jail wouldn't be any solution for him or my sister."

I said nothing, studying the handsome, grave face in front of me.

Magnus took a deep breath. "I've an idea where Lenny is. But I don't think I should be the one to go out there and find out. Could I hire you for that?"

I nodded.

"It's a cottage at Elk Lake," he went on. "Do you know where Elk Lake is?"

I nodded again.

"A girl lives there — well, a woman, really. Around forty. Very attractive woman, and the reason Lenny left my sister. There's a fifty–fifty chance Lenny could be there."

"Her name?" I asked.

"Amalie Johnson, Mrs. Amalie Johnson. She's a widow. The cottage is a fieldstone place, about three houses off the main road on Elk Lane. Her name should be on the mailbox."

"I could check," I said. "And what would you want me to tell Lenny?"

"Tell him I can give him a better job than he has if he is willing to resume his alimony payments. Tell him to use his head for a change. I'll be waiting for his call."

"And wouldn't it be just as simple for you to tell him when he comes back to the hotel? Remember, his clothes are still there; he must be coming back."

Magnus looked at me thoughtfully. "Is business that good, Mr. Puma? Or don't you want *my* business?"

"I can always use the money," I told him. "But I get paid whether Lenny is there or not. That would be fifty dollars, and gas, for the trip."

He reached into his jacket pocket and brought out an alligator wallet. He put two twenties and a ten on my desk. "The gas you can bill me for later."

"Check," I said. "I should be back before midnight. You'll be at the hotel?"

He rose and smiled. "I'll be waiting."

Once out of town, I ran the Chev up to a steady sixty–five. Elk Lake was right off the highway and the directions Magnus had given me should be complete enough.

As I drove, I tried to remember where I had seen that heavy man before, the man I'd collided with.

The face was ringing a very dim bell in my memory and I had a vague feeling there had been a number under the face last time I'd seen it.

So Johnny's visit hadn't been completely fruitless. I was now earning fifty dollars because of my interest in Jean Magnus. Plus gas. The Chev doesn't use any oil.

Magnus could be as phoney as he sounded. And this could be a wild goose chase. I'd know, when the door opened at Elk Lake. If a woman answered the door, there'd be reason to believe his story.

If a woman didn't answer the door, I wouldn't be too badly off. Because my hand would be on my .38 in my jacket pocket.

At the turn–off, there was a small grocery store and boat–rental station and two unattended gasoline pumps. The first mailbox after that was weather–worn and in the gathering dusk I couldn't make out the name.

Three houses up from there, however, the name of Amalie Johnson was blackly clear on an aluminum–painted box. The flag was down.

The lawn was gray and the earth around the shrubs showed no signs of recent watering. It looked like a rented house to me, or the house of an uncaring owner. I touched the bell.

The sound of door chimes and footsteps, the rasp of a latch and an attractive, dark–haired woman looked at me wordlessly from the open doorway.

"Mrs. Johnson?" I asked. She nodded.

"I'm looking for a man named Leonard Donovan," I told her.

A few seconds more of silence and then she asked, "Why?"

"I have a message which could profit him. Is he here?"

She shook her head. "He's gone to the store. He's due back any moment, though. Won't you come in?"

I started in and something hit me from behind. I'll never know where the blow came from — maybe someone hiding under the stoop. But as I fell and the skyrockets flared out in my brain, I remembered where I'd seen the face of the bulky man.

I came to, smelling wet sawdust mixed with a faint odor of fish. Under me, I could feel the splintery planking of what seemed to be a thick floor. There was a bitter, bile–like taste in my mouth. My .38 was gone.

The room was completely black, but one guess as to my whereabouts seemed likely. I was probably in one of those lake icehouses, insulated by sawdust and imprisoned by heavy planking all around. Screaming wouldn't do me a damned bit of good. I moved, and a voice said, "You coming around, Puma?"

"I'm alive. Lenny, is it?"

"Right. They conned me; too."

"You went up to talk to Magnus then, after I left you?"

"Not right away. When I saw him with Dutch Schroeder I got nosey."

That was the big man, Dutch Schroeder. He was a reformed safe cracker, and he used to give lectures on his former art. I'd heard one of his lectures when I was still with the Department.

"You got nosey, Lenny," I guessed, "and tried to put the bite on them. And they took care of you."

"Now wasn't that a hell of a thing to say. You think I'm a crook, or some–thing?"

"Yup. Or you'd have gone to the police."

"Huh! Like you did? We're sharing this room, honor–bright. How come you didn't go to the police?"

"Well," I said, "I'll tell you how it was. Magnus came to me and said you were his former brother–in–law. And you were behind in your alimony payments and he knew you were shacked–up with the Widow Johnson up here. He paid me fifty dollars to send me up here to reason with you. I didn't believe a word of it, and I'm surprised to find you here, Lenny. You know, I'm beginning to think that kid was right."

Lenny said, "They've got both of us out of the way. They're going to knock off the Third Street Security Bank. Tonight or early tomorrow sometime."

"You're not as lousy a detective as I thought."

"You see, Magnus plans it. Schroeder tackles the safe. The little trigger–itchy punk handles the door, Schroeder's wife out there the car. Quick and easy and off to South America for the sun. Some life, huh, Joe? I heard them discuss it before they threw me in here."

"Lenny, is this an ice–house?"

"It sure as hell is."

"Aren't they usually air–tight?"

Lenny said too quietly, "The good ones are. I noticed I could breathe much easier right after they opened that door to throw you in here. It's a rented cottage, Joe. When they leave, the owner might not be around for weeks."

"Isn't there anything around we could use to batter a hole with?"

"Nothing," Lenny said. "One chance I thought I had — that latch handle pivot goes right through that planking door. But I've torn two fingers to hell trying to turn it."

I got slowly to my feet and inched toward the wall. I followed it by touch until I came to the door. The nut on this side of the pivot had been pinned to prevent the thread from turning. It was immovable.

I said, "You lived for over twelve hours in this air. Maybe the place isn't air–tight."

"Maybe it isn't. But Joe, it's food tight."

"And if we screamed and hollered and beat on the walls with our shoes?"

"Now? Or after they've gone?"

It was autumn; who'd be around after the quartette left? Who'd be around to hear what little noise that would emerge through those double planking walls filled with saw dust?

But now? Could we make them nervous with a racket now?

They would come with guns, undoubtedly. We were still alive, but would we be after they came with the guns?

Lenny said, "I figure they'll hole up here for a couple days after the job. This lake doesn't get much traffic in the fall. That Magnus is a cool operator."

"The door is our best bet," I said. "If we kept kicking away right under that latch ..."

Silence from Lenny.

I reached for a cigarette and then decided not to crumb up the air any more than necessary. My lighter was still in my pocket; I lighted it for a look around.

Planking walls, planking ceiling and floor. Meat hooks were set in rows along the ceiling. Lenny looked pale in the flickering light.

"And there are two walls like that," Lenny said, "with sawdust between."

"The door is only one thickness, though."

"That's right. Two by sixes bolted to the cross–pieces."

"How about the ceiling? That's usually single. The blocks of ice are put in the sawdust around the sides, aren't they?"

"So we can break through the ceiling if our heads are hard enough. Do you want to start?"

"Well, damn it," I said, "we can't just sit here! Which way is the lake?"

"Right behind here, about thirty feet."

"Lenny," I said, "I'm going to holler. And if they open that door, I'm going to make a break for it. It should be dark out there. How about you?"

"I'm alive," he said. "And I figure if I don't move and keep my mouth shut, I've got a small chance to stay that way. I figure you haven't got any chance your way?"

"Okay," I said. "But I don't want to spend the rest of *my* life in an ice house." I began to hammer on the door with a shoe. I had taken both of them off.

In only a little more than a minute, I heard the back door of the house slam and a few seconds after that, a man's voice asked, "What the hell's all the commotion about?"

"I got a broken arm," I said. "I want a doctor."

"You'll have worse than that if you don't shut up. We're not playing games, shamus."

"I want a doctor," I repeated, and began to hammer on the door again.

"Damn you," he said, and then I heard the rasp of the latch. I slammed into the door as it started opening.

There was a curse and I saw him on the ground as I burst through. He was the little man. He had an awful big gun in his hand and was swinging it right toward my belly. My kick got his hand.

I jumped sideways, raced for the lake. There was a pier leading out about twenty feet.

I heard a big boom and something flicked away the lobe of my ear. As I hit the water, another shot missed me by inches.

I didn't swim out. I stayed under and made the big turn, back under the protection of the pier. The water was clear and calm.

My ear burned like fury, my right foot throbbed from the kick. A post of the pier brushed my shoulder, and I came up for air, hidden by the boards overhead.

I heard the woman say, "Did he get away?"

"Nope. I know I hit him. See the blood?"

"But wouldn't he come up, if he was hit?"

The little man said. "Yeah, when he starts to bloat, he'll come up. But we'll be a long way from here then."

"I'm going to watch, anyway," the woman said. "He might just be injured."

My hand went to my ear and came away red. I heard footsteps above me, I went under again.

When my lungs began to burn and spots flared on my eyelids, I came up.

I heard the woman say, "How about the other one?"

"I guess he likes that ice house. We'll leave him there. How long can he live without food?"

"I see," the woman said thoughtfully. "You've got a point there, George."

"Come on. Will be late getting into town. That would throw everything out of schedule."

"Just one second. We gotta be sure. I want another look under this pier."

I grabbed a post to hang onto when I went down this time. I was starting to get weak. The bullet that had torn away my ear lobe had creased the side of my jaw and I was losing a lot of blood.

When it was a question of drowning in one more second, I came up for air again. And heard footsteps on the boards above and sent up a small prayer of deliverance.

My handkerchief was wet and cold in my jacket pocket. I put it to ear. Was there an artery running along the jaw line? I didn't know. I wondered if Lenny knew.

The way it turned out, I'm glad I didn't release Lenny first.

When I heard the car start I started for the house. I made it. I couldn't have gone a hundred yards more, but I made the phone.

Captain MacGill in town didn't waste any of my breath with foolish questions. He promised to send the nearest doctor.

Then I turned back toward Lenny. I got through the door and five steps into the front yard before I collapsed.

I came to this time in an amber room on a hard bed. A face came into focus and it was Johnny's face.

"You're going to be all right," he said.

"Johnny, you're in the Scouts. Is there an artery running along the jaw there?"

He nodded. "You almost didn't make it, Mr. Puma. Mr. Magnus didn't. He got killed when they staked out the bank. Guess that's not much loss, huh?"

"I'm no judge of that. How about Lenny Donovan, that hotel dick?"

"He's trying to cut himself in," Johnny said. "But I got that straightened out. He and those crooks used to huddle plenty. I told Mr. Donovan it would be best if he just kept his mouth shut."

"I'm not following you, Johnny."

"Like I said, he's trying to cut himself in. I mean he was. He isn't any more, since I told him how often I'd seen him with those crooks."

"On what, cut himself in on *what* Johnny?"

"On the ten grand reward. That's the Banker's Protective Alliance Security — you know, standard reward. I'm glad the cops didn't get to 'em before they made the try though, huh, Mr. Puma?"

I took a deep breath. "Who did you figure deserved the reward, Johnny?"

"Fifty–fifty, you and me. I was the finger, right? And you were the arm. We're not going to have any trouble about that, are we, Mr. Puma? We're not going to argue some more, are we?"

"No," I agreed. "You're too much for me, Johnny. Where am I?"

"At St. Mary's. I figured this was the best bet. I don't trust those small–town hospitals. I'll bet you don't know who's here?"

"I'll bet I do. I'll bet it's your beautiful sister."

He smiled. "Right. And she sure isn't mourning that Magnus slob. Well, I'll bring her in and she can apologise to you, but you'll have to take it from there, Mr. Puma. I can't handle everything."

"Okay, Johnny," I said humbly. "Shoo her in; I'll give it my best."

Deadly Beloved

1.

She was obviously past thirty, but I couldn't judge whether she'd reached forty. Her figure was firm, her face unlined, her hand–knit boucle suggesting she had enough money to keep her figure firm and her face unlined.

She was telling me about her husband and from her account I was gathering that the gentleman was a bum.

My office was hot and her voice petulant and I wondered why she wanted this man located if he was such a slob.

Which I suggested at the first break in her monologue. I said, "Maybe you're well rid of him."

She frowned, and her eyes grew faintly hostile.

"You say he married you for your money," I pointed out, "and that he's been unfaithful ever since. Is it a detective you wanted, or a divorce lawyer?"

Her face was stiff. "I want him back. So I'm a fool. But he's a pretty good man to have around, despite his faults." She colored slightly as she looked at me.

"Where would I begin to look for him?" I asked.

"Any one of a half dozen places. I'll give you a list."

"And if I find him, what do I tell him?"

Her smile was wry. "All is forgiven — and I'm waiting."

Some man, he must be. She wasn't young, but she was attractive. And rich. I said, "All right, Mrs. Engle, I'll get right to work on it."

She made out a check for the retainer and left me with the persistent fragrance of her perfume. I sat there for a few moments wondering if it was sheer loneliness that had made her seek my services or if this Alan Engle was some kind of superman. Why was it rich and attractive women were never attracted to *me?*

I took the check around to the bank and headed the flivver for Malibu. I had her list. Why hadn't she phoned these people to ask about her Alan? That might be embarrassing, but certainly not more embarrassing than sending a private operative to track him down.

On the Coast Highway, the bathers' cars were parked bumper to bumper on both sides of the road. To the north and east, the Santa Monica Mountains were dark green against the clear blue sky. If Alan Engle was out chasing quail, he'd picked a fine day for it.

The person I was on my way to see didn't live in the Colony; she lived in a beach shack south of there, out of the high tax area. I found her on a rock about fifteen feet from shore in front of her cottage.

She was wearing a simple black bathing suit without straps and there was a towel over her face.

I stood on the beach and called, "Miss Elizabeth Adams?"

She rose to a sitting position and nodded. "Who are you?"

"My name is Joseph Puma," I told her. "I'm — looking for Alan Engle."

She stood up and she was the kind of girl born to grace a swim suit. She just stood there looking at me curiously.

I said apologetically, "I rang your bell, but there was no answer, so I followed the path along the side of the house."

"That was shrewd of you," she said. "Are you a friend of Alan's?"

I hesitated, and said, "Not exactly."

"Did his wife send you?"

I nodded. "More or less."

Elizabeth Adams sighed. "Poor Alan —" She jumped down into the hip–high water and came wading toward me.

Her hair was dark and short, her eyes a dark blue. When she reached a quiet dialogue distance, she asked, "Do you know Jeff Roeder?"

Jeff was another private investigator, a lad who got a lot of the carriage trade. I nodded.

Miss Adams said, "You're another one of those, I suppose?"

I hesitated again and then nodded.

"Come in," she said wearily. "I'll brief you."

There were some steps leading up from the beach to the rear living room of the cottage. I followed her up those. At the door, she took a terry cloth robe from a hook and slipped into straw sandals.

The living room was mostly rattan and raffia, but warm and pleasant. The rear wall was all window, with a fine view of the shoreline.

Miss Adams indicated a rattan love seat and asked, "Beer? It's cold and it's Eastern."

"Thank you," I said. "It's been a dry day."

She brought a big copper mug full of beer and sat down nearby with a twin of it. She said, "I suppose Grace gave you a list?"

"Grace —?"

"Mrs. Engle. I suppose she gave you a list of people to annoy."

I didn't answer that. I sipped my beer.

Miss Adams was looking at the floor. "Alan's not a — bad gent. He — can be charming."

"How about Mrs. Engle?"

Elizabeth Adams looked at me. "She's fifteen years older, and it's *her* money. How would you like to be in a situation like Alan's?"

"Let's not be naive," I said. "It's the kind of situation I'm looking for. And so was Alan, probably."

She looked at me scornfully, saying nothing.

"Okay," I said. "So I never met him. But who twisted his arm? Did he *have* to marry this older woman with money? She bought him, didn't she? And now he doesn't want to stay bought. Well, that's a breach of contract, like any other."

"My," she said lightly, "aren't we indignant! Why, Mr. Puma?"

I drank my beer and smiled at her. "I'm sorry. I run into these cases now and then. This area is full of them. You don't know where Alan Engle is now, I suppose?"

She looked at me candidly. "I honestly don't. Jeff Roeder almost managed to locate the poor boy, though. So don't despair."

"I get paid either way," I said. "You know Jeff, do you?"

"I met him when he came looking for Alan, one time. We've gone out together a few times."

"Lately?"

She looked at me quizzically. "Within the past year. Why did you ask that, Mr. Puma?"

"Jeff's married," I said. "He's been married for six years. Did you know that?"

Color in her face. "Not that it's any of your damned business, but I didn't know that."

"It wasn't any of my damned business," I admitted, "but if I'd thought you had known it, I wouldn't have mentioned it. Does that clear me?"

A half smile. "Some."

"He's a very handsome guy," I said. "He married money, too. That's how he gets the carriage trade. I wonder why Mrs. Engle came to me, this time."

She shrugged, and sipped her beer. On the Highway, a big Diesel blasted by and the cottage windows rattled.

Miss Adams shook her head. "Those — monsters. But I suppose they keep the rent down."

"You've no idea," I said, "where Alan Engle is?"

Her voice was sharp. "I told you I didn't."

I stood up. "Well, thanks for the beer. Have you any idea why Alan does come back when he's finally located? Has Mrs. Engle some hold on him?"

Silence, except for the traffic noises from the Highway. A frown and then Elizabeth Adams said slowly, "I understand Alan was in some trouble with the law at one time. I'm not definitely sure about that, though."

"Okay. Sorry to have been a nuisance."

She smiled. "You weren't. And you *did* tell me about that bum, Jeff Roeder, didn't you?"

I nodded. "You're too good for him, Miss Adams."

Her glance was wry. "You certainly love to jump at a conclusion. You could be just as wrong about me as you are about Alan. Happy hunting, Mr. Puma."

She came to the door with me and watched me climb into the flivver. I thought she looked lonely, but it could have been just wishful thinking. There wasn't any reason for a girl like that to ever be lonely.

My next stop was also in Malibu but also not in the Colony. It was on the other side of the Highway, off a road that led up into the hills.

This was no cottage, but a large place of bright red barn siding and shake roof, on the bull–dozed top of a hill that overlooked the entire bay. A smock–encased thin man with paint on his nose was sitting on a redwood chaise longue on the front lawn. He had a drink in one hand and a magazine in his lap.

Somewhere a dog barked, as I stepped out of the car onto the blacktop of the parking area. I paused; I'm allergic to dogs.

The man called out, "It's all right. He's penned up in the back yard."

I came across a dichondra lawn to where he sat, and asked him, "Mr. Felix Sandow?"

He nodded. "You're not selling anything, I hope?"

"No, sir. I'm looking for a Mr. Alan Engle."

"Oh God! Somebody usually is. Does he owe money?"

"Not that I know of, sir." I looked out over the water. "Beautiful view you have here."

"It is. Are, you, by any chance, a detective?"

I looked back at him and nodded. "Have you seen Mr. Engle in the last three days?"

He shook his head and then frowned. "But I think my wife has." He turned his head to call, "Armine —"

A thin, short, dark woman in denim shorts and striped cotton jersey came around from the side of the house. She was wiping her hands on a paint–stained rag as she came over to us.

"This," Felix Sandow said, "is a detective who is looking for lover boy. Have you seen him lately?"

She nodded. "At Barge Shirvanian's party night before last." She looked at me concernedly. "Has something happened? Is Alan in trouble?" She looked at her husband. "You did mean Alan, didn't you?"

I answered for him. "Yes, he meant Mr. Engle. Do you know where he's staying?"

Her big, brown eyes rested on her husband for a moment before turning to me. "I don't. Is he in trouble?"

Felix Sandow said irritably, "Of course not, Armine. It's Grace on the trail again, no doubt. Please get that horribly maternal tone out of your voice."

Armine Sandow looked at me sorrowfully, saying nothing.

Sandow said, "Alan is the problem child of all the ladies in our snug little set. He gives them that lost little boy look and leads them tenderly to the bedroom. Let me prophesy that when you find him, *if* you find him, it will be in some simpering woman's arms."

"That's nice work if you can get it," I said, and turned again to Mrs. Sandow. "Did Mr. Engle come to the party alone?"

She nodded, glancing again at her husband.

"And leave alone?" I asked.

She took a breath. "He — brought me home. I don't know where he went after that."

"Didn't he mention where he was staying?"

She shook her head. Her husband sipped his drink, looking unconcernedly out at the bay.

I took out my list. "This party was at a Barge Shirvanian's? He lives in Bel Air, doesn't he?"

She nodded.

"Isn't he an agent?" I asked.

Felix Sandow said, "He's a purple–foot from Fresno, a peasant with literary pretensions."

Mrs. Sandow said calmly, "He's about the finest authors' agent in town. He handles some big names. Alan helped him finance his business when he first started. They're very good friends."

"Two of a kind," Sandow said. "They really belong together. The hairy purple–foot and lover boy, a stunning pair."

Mrs. Sandow looked at him quietly for a moment and then at me. "You mustn't mind my husband. He resents anyone with talent, even me. Sorry I couldn't be of more help, Mr. —?"

"Puma," I said, "Joseph Puma." I gave her one of my cards. "If you learn of Mr. Engle's whereabouts, I would be grateful for the information."

She took the card and nodded, saying nothing. Her husband sipped his drink and belched. She was already going back toward the house when I walked over to the flivver. He still sat on the front lawn as I made the last big turn below that cut him from view.

2.

Those two calls completed the Malibu end of town; I headed south on the Coast Highway, past Miss Adam's cottage and the endless lines of parked bathers' cars.

It was a clear and beautiful day, a day for loafing, but I didn't have a rich or talented wife. From the two feminine numbers I'd seen so far among Alan's friends, I would guess that Mrs. Engle certainly had her problems. Still, she was rich and that made up for a number of lacks.

Bel Air, like Brentwood, is only an attitude; it has no geographical reality. The Shirvanian home was on a knoll, surrounded by eucalyptus trees, overlooking the constant traffic of Sunset Boulevard.

It was a two–story home of gray stone and copper roof, looking out of place, looking midwestern and substantial above the glittering cars on Sunset a few hundred feet below.

A maid told me Mr. Shirvanian was still at the office. Mrs. Shirvanian was home, however, and would see me.

The living room was furnished in heavy mahogany, and thick, dark–red Oriental rugs covered the floor. The drapes were heavy maroon velvet. The purple–foot had made good.

Mrs. Shirvanian was dark and short and heavy, but not unattractive. I told her who I was and why I was there.

She shook her head sadly. "Poor Alan. That wife of his —" She shook her head again.

"He's married," I pointed out. "That's bound to limit a man's freedom. No–body's forcing him to stay married."

"Only his conscience," Mrs. Shirvanian said quietly. "If Alan should leave Grace, I wouldn't be surprised if she did something desperate."

I was getting awful damned sick of poor Alan and I hadn't even met him yet. I said, "How desperate? Do you mean something like cutting him out of her will?"

Mrs. Shirvanian stared at me reproachfully. "That was unkind. You don't even know him, do you?"

"Never met him," I agreed. "And it looks like I'm not going to. Do you know where he is?"

She shook her head. "But Barge, my husband, probably does. He should be home any second now. He phoned fifteen minutes ago that he was on his way."

The maid came in with a tray and silver coffee service.

Mrs. Shirvanian said, "Do you like Turkish coffee? My husband and I always have a cup when he comes home."

"I'd like some," I said. "Tell me what you know about Alan Engle. He's beginning to interest me."

He was just a boy, she told me. A blond boy of twenty–eight, who had had small parts in a few B pictures and had been a prominent local radio announcer at nineteen and was now trying to get into TV.

"As an announcer or actor?" I asked.

"As either. He has a fair singing voice, too."

"He was in some trouble with the law at one time, wasn't he?"

Mrs. Shirvanian was quiet for a moment. Then she said softly, "Yes, when he was twenty–two. The girl — was fifteen."

I said nothing.

Mrs. Shirvanian's quiet voice had some protest in it. "But she looked *much* older. One of those full bodied, brazen young girls this town is so full of."

"Fresno, too," I reminded her gently.

She smiled. "In Fresno, the parents have more interest in their children."

Then a wide man of medium height was coming toward us from the entry hall, and I rose.

He had a virile, dark face and flint–hard brown eyes and grip worthy of a man much heavier. After the introduction, he went over to kiss his wife.

"Good day?" she asked.

"Good enough," he said. "Sold Warwick to Metro for ten weeks. Warwick will come through yet, you mark my words."

"I'm sure he will," she said. "Mr. Puma is looking for Alan."

The hard brown eyes considered me. "Are you employed by Mrs. Engle?"

I nodded.

"I don't know where Alan is," he said curtly.

"Now, Barge —" Mrs. Shirvanian said softly.

He looked momentarily at her and back at me. Nobody said anything for seconds.

Then Mrs. Shirvanian said, "I've asked Mr. Puma to have some coffee with us."

He sighed. "My little peacemaker." He managed a smile for me. "She means Turkish coffee, Mr. Puma. Are you familiar with it?"

I said I was.

He sat on the davenport and leaned his head back. He covered his wife's hand with his, and closed his eyes, shutting out the world.

It was a pleasant domestic scene and uncommon in this area, but it wasn't getting me any closer to Alan Engle. I said, "Engle certainly can't solve any of his little problems by hiding from them, can he?"

Shirvanian kept his eyes closed. "He has only the one problem — Grace."

"He could divorce her."

Nothing from Shirvanian.

I asked, "Is Mrs. Sandow an Armenian?"

He opened his eyes. "Yes. Why?"

"Because of her first name — Armine. I knew an Armenian girl by that name at Stanford."

"Not Armine Dirkejian, by any chance?" Mrs. Shirvanian asked.

I nodded.

"Fresno girl," her husband said. "Beautiful girl." He closed his eyes again.

I stood up. "I don't think I'll have time for the coffee. Sorry I bothered you people."

Mrs. Shirvanian looked concerned; her husband couldn't have looked less so. She said, "Barge doesn't mean to be rude. He works too hard."

"Most of us do," I said. "I can find my way out."

Three calls and all I had was a character brochure. And a growing sense of frustration. The Fresno purple–foot hadn't meant to be rude; he was an executive now and no longer needed the friendship of inferiors.

Where now? I had nothing to report to Mrs. Engle and the remaining name on my list was way up in the Valley. I didn't intend to buck that Sepulveda traffic at this time of the day. I went back to the office.

I typed up the reports of my calls for the day and tried to find something in the printed versions that I'd missed in the actual. Nothing showed. Nothing, except an unusual sympathy for the plight of Alan Engle on the part of all his friends.

In my book, he had no tears coming. A pretty boy who had married money and now didn't have the guts to cut himself off from it. What was so pitiable about Alan Engle?

I was pondering that deep philosophical and psychological question when my phone rang.

It was Elizabeth Adams. "I've a lead for you."

"I'm glad," I said. "I knew you'd come through."

A momentary silence, and then, "Do you remember I told you Alan was once in trouble with the law?"

"I remember. And I've since learned it was because of a girl, a fifteen–year–old girl."

She sounded relieved. "Yes. I didn't want to tell you that. Well, she's not fifteen now, of course."

I did some rapid calculating. "No, she must be twenty–one."

"That's right." A pause. "And I heard less than an hour ago that Alan has gone back to her. You might not believe it, but Alan has a very deep sense of morality."

"I'll try to believe it," I said. "Do you have the girl's name and address?"

She did, and she gave it to me. A Gina Pastore and a West Los Angeles address. "An Italian girl," she added. "Very beautiful, I've heard."

"Thank you, Miss Adams," I said. "Do you want to tell me who gave you this information?"

A pause, and then, "I'd rather not. I don't think it's important. And there's no point in disturbing any more people than we have to, is there?"

"None," I agreed. "Thank you, again."

3.

The address was a four unit apartment building on National Boulevard, near the Santa Monica airport. The first floor apartment on the right was the home of Gina Pastore.

From behind her door, I thought I could hear the sound of a woman crying. I pressed the bell button and heard the chimes and the crying stopped.

A little later, the door opened. The girl who stood there was wiping her eyes with a handkerchief.

She was young and dark and attractive, but already showing a touch of the bulk she would grow into. A little too bosomy, a little too hippy.

"Miss Pastore?" I asked.

She nodded.

"I'm looking for Alan Engle," I told her.

Quick apprehension in her soft, brown eyes. "Why? Has something happened?"

"I don't know," I told her, "except that he's missing."

"Missing —? Missing from where?"

"From his home. Have you seen him lately?"

She said nothing for seconds, her gaze anxiously on my face. Then she nodded wordlessly.

"When did you see him last?" I asked.

She took a breath and faced me defiantly. "Last night. He stayed here last night. Make what you will of that."

"Do you know where he is now?"

She shook her head. "He left this morning. He was going to meet me for lunch. He didn't. He didn't phone. Do you know where he is, now?"

I shook my head. "That's why I'm here. He was supposed to meet you for lunch, you say, and he didn't?"

She nodded.

I asked gently, "Is that why you were crying?"

She looked at me quietly, saying nothing.

I asked less gently, "You thought he was running out on you again? You thought you had been conned, again?"

She put a hand on the doorknob, as though to close the door.

"Wait," I said. "I'm better prepared to look for him than you are. Did he stay here night before last, too?"

A pause, and she nodded. "Do you think something could have happened — I mean, maybe he did intend to meet me for lunch and something happened — something —" Her voice began to shake, and she stopped talking.

"It's possible," I said. "May I come in?"

She looked at me doubtfully. "Are you a policeman?"

I showed her the photostat of my license. "Private. I've been looking for Mr. Engle all day. Maybe you know something that would help me to find him."

"I doubt it," she said wearily. "But come in."

I learned that Alan Engle had not only spent the previous night here, but also the night before that. Which meant he must have come here after taking Armine Sandow home from the Shirvanian's party. He'd told Gina that he was finally leaving his wife. He'd also told Gina that they would be married as soon as his divorce would become final.

She'd believed him. Until he hadn't shown up for lunch today. Now, she didn't know what to believe.

I said, "You knew Mr. Engle years ago, didn't you? Have you been seeing him right along since you first met?"

She shook her head. "He drove, into *Baker's*, about a week ago. That's a drive–in on Olympic. That's where I work."

"And that's the first time you saw him since when?"

"That's the first time I saw him in almost six years," she said. "But that doesn't mean he — I mean — it was no cheap pick–up, you understand. He — told me he'd always regretted what happened six years ago."

But he'd made no effort to find her. A thought I didn't voice.

But she did. She said, "He told me he'd wanted to look me up a thousand times. But he thought I hated him."

"I see. And this morning he didn't tell you where he was going?"

She nodded. "He told me he was going home. He was going to tell his wife he wanted a divorce. He was going to tell her everything."

"And that's all he told you? That was the only place he was going?"

She nodded.

"And," I guessed aloud, "you thought his wife might have talked him out of it?"

She nodded more slowly. "Something — like that."

"You know it was his wife who hired me to find him."

Gina Pastore stared at me and the tears began to gather in her eyes again. Her voice was hoarse. "Where could he be?"

I shrugged.

She sniffed. "He's been — despondent. You don't think he might have —" The tears began to stream.

"No," I said. "I'm sure he's not the type for that. If you'd like, I'll phone you after I check back with Mrs. Engle. She might have some word of him by now."

"Thank you," she said. "That would be kind of you."

I thought of phoning Mrs. Engle, but I wasn't too far from Brentwood, so I drove over.

There was a Department car in front and I parked behind it. I was just getting out, when I saw Mrs. Engle coming down from the house. She was crying. Sergeant Dully was with her; he's a detective out of Homicide.

There was another detective I knew behind the wheel of the Department car, and I went over there. I asked, "What's happened?"

"Her husband's been killed. We think it's her husband. She's going down to make identification now. What are you doing here, Puma?"

"She hired me to look for him. Where was he killed?"

"We're not sure. But he was found in one of the canyons out in the Palisades." The man frowned. "You'd better come along, Puma."

Duffy and I weren't lodge brothers; we'd had words a few times. He didn't look happy to see me.

Mrs. Engle said softly, "Will you come along with us, Mr. Puma? I need — someone."

"He's coming along," Duffy said gruffly.

She and I got in back; Duffy rode in front with the other officer.

Her voice was choked. "And all the time I thought he was — I'm so ashamed of myself."

I looked out at the heavy traffic. I couldn't think of anything to say. I thought of Miss Adams and the Sandows and the Shirvanians and Gina Pastore. Gina would grieve, too; I wondered about the others.

"He was so attentive lately," Mrs. Engle whispered. "I should have known something had happened. I should have known he hadn't run off —"

There was mascara on her cheeks and her face was puffed. She looked more than forty now. I can bleed for the weak, but not for the maudlin; I felt un–comfortable.

"He was a good man," she whispered. "Misunderstood, but a good man, just a boy, really —" She began to sob.

In the rear view mirror, Sergeant Duffy's eyes met mine cynically. In the lane to our left, a big diesel went by, fouling the air with exhaust fumes.

The sound of it made me think of Elizabeth Adams and her cottage near the Highway. I would have to ask her who had told her about Alan going back to the Pastore girl. It was the only lead I could think of.

And if I told Duffy about the Pastore girl, about Alan's living there, who would benefit? Not Gina Pastore and not Mrs. Alan Engle. Justice might, but justice was only a word. The other two were people.

At the West Side Station, Duffy said to the other officer, "You accompany Mrs. Engle." Then he turned to me. "I'll get a stenographer to take your statement."

In a small, bright and airless room, a uniformed stenographer wrote the account of my day as I gave it to him. When I came to Gina Pastore, I mentioned only that she had been the last I know to see him. I didn't mention her story of Alan's staying there.

Duffy had come in before I'd finished dictating and he listened to my recounting of the last two calls of the day.

"You can sign it after it's typed," he said. "Tomorrow will be all right. Ready to go?"

I nodded and stood up. "How was Engle killed?"

"Bludgeoned to death." He studied me. "You're through with this case now, you understand? We don't like peepers messing around in murder cases."

"I understand," I said. "I was hired to find him. He's been found."

He nodded curtly. "Right. So keep your nose clean and stay in business."

"I'll stay in business," I told him. "And I can do without your insolence, Sergeant."

He considered me for a few seconds. He had the badge, but I had twenty pounds on him. He grunted something and nodded toward the door. He followed me out.

In the car, Mrs. Engle was no longer crying. Her body was rigid and her eyes blank in shock. Her hands trembled in her lap. Sergeant Duffy and his partner sat in front again.

It was after six; the traffic was a shade thinner. Mrs. Engle said hoarsely, "I want you to find the person who did this, Mr. Puma."

Duffy's eyes met mine in the mirror again. I said, "Trained men will be working on it, Mrs. Engle. Men with equipment and the personnel to work around the clock. I wouldn't add much."

"He's dead," she said. "If the police were that good, he wouldn't be dead. I want you to work for me."

Duffy said, "We're going to give it a lot of attention, Mrs. Engle."

Her eyes burned into the back of his head. "I was talking to Mr. Puma, Sergeant. It was a private conversation."

My eyes met Duffy's blandly. There was a warning in his.

In front of her house, Duffy got out to open the door for us. Mrs. Engle got out first and took a few steps toward the house.

Dully put a restraining hand on my arm. "Remember what I told you, peeper."

I looked at his hand until he took it away. "I've an excellent memory," I said. I followed Mrs. Engle to the front door.

There, a maid told us the doctor was waiting. And in the living room, the doctor told me that he was giving Mrs. Engle a sedative and wanted her to rest.

She gripped one of my hands in both of hers. "Stay on this. You're working for me. Don't spare any expense."

"All right," I said. "Listen to your doctor, Mrs. Engle. Try to find some peace."

She went out with the doctor and I got the maid's permission to use the phone. I called Elizabeth Adams.

"Have you eaten?" I asked her.

"No. Why?"

"I thought we could pick up a steak somewhere."

A pause, and then, "Are you single, Mr. Puma?"

"I am. And a gentleman."

"Well, then buy a couple," she said, "and I'll broil them here. I'm in jeans and I don't want to get dressed."

"How are you fixed for beer?" I asked.

"I've three cans."

I picked up some beer and a pair of steaks in the Palisades on the way out. I'd promised to phone Miss Pastore, but I was sure that Sergeant Duffy was already there with information about her beloved Alan.

The hills were turning purple, but the sea was still a deep and shining blue under the rays of the western sun. The fishing boats were heading in toward Malibu and the restaurant parking lots were beginning to fill up.

I had to wait a long time for a big enough break in the traffic to permit a U–turn. I pulled off on the sandy shoulder and walked down the steps to the cottage.

4.

Elizabeth Adams was wearing a flared cotton skirt and rawhide sandals and an embroidered peasant blouse.

"Where are the blue jeans?" I asked.

"Blue Jeans are for hamburger," she said. "You promised to bring steak."

I handed her the package of meat and took the beer over to the refrigerator. My back was to her when I said, "I've brought bad news."

"So —?"

I turned. "Alan Engle is dead."

She stared at me. "How — when —?"

"He was clubbed to death," I said, "some time today."

The package dropped from her hand and plopped softly on the floor. She seemed to waver, and I came close.

She shook her head. "I'll be all right. Who did it?"

"Nobody knows. Who phoned you to tell you about Gina Pastore?"

She stared silently for seconds. Then, "Did you come here to find out about Alan? Is that why you brought the steaks?"

I shook my head. "I wanted to get some place where I could look at the sea and eat a good steak across from a pretty girl. This seemed to offer the proper combination."

Her eyes probed my face. "You're not lying?"

"No. It's been a bad day. I get a lot of them in my business."

"All right," she said. "All right. Jeff Roeder told me about Alan going back to that Italian girl. He phoned, the snake."

I smiled. "Did you tell him off?"

She shook her head. "I told him I'd go out with him if his wife was going along."

"And how did Alan Engle get into the conversation?"

"That was before Jeff asked for the date. I told him you had been here, doing his old job."

I came over and picked up the steak. I handed her the package and patted her shoulder and said,

"Let's try not to think of Alan Engle. I've had nothing else all day."

"I can't get him out of my mind," she said. "You see, right from the beginning, he was in company too fast for him. He never had a chance."

"He did very well," I said. "He must have made a lot of money since he was nineteen."

"Money," she said scornfully. "Alan left it for his first love, didn't he?"

"I don't know. Neither do you. Shall I open a can of beer for you, too?"

Money ... I wondered how long Alan and his slightly over–ripe first love would have got along without it, if he'd been given the chance. Money is only unimportant when you have a bank full of it.

The wind came from the west and we could see Catalina. We could see the lights of the bay and all the stars and the lights of the big birds heading for International Airport.

Elizabeth Adams told me of the perils of modeling, exaggerating some of the stories, I'm sure. And I recounted the perils of my trade, exaggerating a few items, I'm doubly sure.

The steaks were exactly right and the salad exceptional and the beer soon gone. Around ten–thirty, I moved a little closer.

She stood up and went over to put some records on the record player — for my benefit.

"Don't be annoyed," I said. "I'm just naturally affectionate."

"So am I," she said calmly, "but aren't you crowding things? We only met today." She lighted a cigarette. "I'm not sure I trust you, Joe Puma." She stood next to the record player, appraising me.

I smiled and said nothing.

"You're still on the Alan Engle case, aren't you? I'll bet you're still working for Grace Engle."

"I could be. She wants me to. But that isn't why I'm here. You seem — so different from the other girls a gent runs into out here."

She closed her eyes. "Oh, no. Not that line out of antiquity."

"Seriously," I said. "You're like — Connecticut rain."

"Gawd," she said. "Man, you're reaching."

"So help me. You look New England and washed and in possession of all your faculties and —"

She put up a hand. "And I think it's time to say good night. I've an early call tomorrow."

"Okay," I said. "Do we shake hands or something?" I stood up.

"You may kiss me lightly," she answered. "It was a fine steak you brought."

I kissed her lightly. Her lips were soft and cool and her fragrance cool and clean. I trembled a little, fought the beast in me, and stepped back with a sad smile.

"Good night, Liz. Lot of luck tomorrow."

"You, too," she said. "You are single, aren't you?"

I nodded. "Good night."

I was halfway up the steps to the road, when she called, "Joe —?"

I turned, my pulse hammering, and my knees softening. "Yes?"

"Check that Roeder. I've a feeling he's been mixed in some shady business right along."

"I planned to," I told her. "Good night, Liz."

"Good night," she said, and closed the door.

Traffic was sparse on the highway, but moving fast. I pulled over in the right hand lane and just dawled along. There'd been a Chev Club parked across the road when I'd come out of the cottage; I'd assumed it was the car of some beach picnicker.

At the Topanga Canyon light, I saw it was behind me. In the reflections from oncoming headlights, I could make out only a single male passenger behind the wheel.

I drove along at twenty–five miles an hour, which is equivalent to parking on the Coast Highway. The Chev stayed behind me.

It was a beautiful night and maybe he was enjoying it as I was. At the Sunset intersection, I swung over to the extreme left lane, from which a motorist is permitted only to turn left. The Chev swung in behind me.

Traffic was light, and there were no cops in sight. I went straight ahead from that lane, breaking the law. The Chev followed.

I cut over to the right again, and ran the flivver up to fifty. The Chev stayed a few blocks behind, but lost no ground. I stopped three blocks this side of the Chautauqua light, and stepped out from the driver's side.

The Chev slowed, and I waved. It pulled in ahead of my car, and I went over.

The man behind the wheel was Dutch Hofmeister. He'd been a wrestler and a tackle for the Forty–niners. He'd been a private operative until he'd lost his license for acting as a go–between in the Sylvester kidnapping.

"What's my attraction, Dutch?" I asked him.

He grinned. "None for me. I was out for the air. That's illegal? I saw your car and thought I'd heckle you."

"You're a liar," I said.

"Easy," he cautioned me. "You're not big enough to talk like that to me."

"Step out and we'll see."

He shook his head and chuckled. "You Latins — so impetuous. How'd you make out at the cottage, Puma?"

"I'm reporting this to Sergeant Duffy when I go in to see him tomorrow," I said. "You can't stand any police attention you know, Dutch."

"Maybe not." He started his motor again. "The sixty–four thousand dollar question is whether you can, Puma. You've still got your license to lose." He gunned away, his tires throwing up sand from the blacktop.

At home, I stayed in the shower a long time. Then I put on a robe and sat next to the front window, watching the traffic on Wilshire. Dutch Hofmeister could be working for *anybody*, though a responsible citizen wouldn't be likely to hire a man who'd lost his license. Of course, Dutch could also be working for the man he'd always worked for, himself. Maybe he saw a dollar in this case somewhere.

The dry western wind moved through the open window, keeping the night bright, roughening the skin, clearing my sinuses. I went to bed and slept without dreams.

5.

In the small office, Duffy said, "The statement will be here in a minute. This Hofmeister we'll lean on a little." He looked at me levelly. "What were you doing at Miss Adams?"

"Eating steak and drinking beer and talking. What else?"

"Putting your big nose into this Engle kill, maybe?"

"Not last night. I told her Alan Engle was the last thing I wanted to talk about. What's new on that?"

He looked at me bleakly. "It's all in the morning papers. Pick up a copy."

"What's new, that isn't in the papers, Sergeant?"

"Nothing."

"Did you talk to Gina Pastore?"

He nodded. "She was working at the time Engle was killed."

"What time was that?"

"Between eleven and noon yesterday." He took a deep breath and frowned. "And before he was clubbed, he ate a hearty meal. That's what the autopsy showed." His frown deepened. "It's all in the papers."

Then a uniformed man came in with the report I'd dictated yesterday and I signed it. Duffy left while I was signing.

In the hall next to the squad room, Sergeant Hansen was drinking from the bubbler. I'd done him a favor once.

He straightened and smiled and said, "How's your golf, Joe?"

"Lousy. Got time for a cup of coffee, Arnie?"

His smile remained. "Nope. And I don't know anything about the Engle case. And if I did, I sure as hell wouldn't want to get on the wrong side of Duffy. That man's going places in the Department, Joe. He's a fire–ball."

"He's a Mick slant–head," I answered. "And you know it. You've got a short memory, Arnie."

He nodded and sighed. "And a steady job. Life *can* be beautiful."

I used a naughty word and went out into the dry, bright morning. The good men in my trade try to work with the law but the law persists in making that as difficult as possible. I suppose, if the law were perfect, I'd be out of business, though. On this current quest I was getting nowhere, but I had a feeling Duffy wasn't doing much better, despite the air of competence he had developed to impress his superiors.

I ate breakfast at *Zukie's* and drove over to the impressive suite of offices on Wilshire known as *The Roeder Agency*.

A lacquered blonde in the reception room informed me that Mr. Roeder would be free in a few minutes. I sat and leafed through a copy of *Fortune* while I waited.

Jeff had the front one needs to get the carriage trade. Before he'd married money, his office had been as crummy as mine.

In about five minutes, he came out of his office with his hand on Al Lederman's shoulder. He said, "Discretion on this one, you know, Al. The velvet glove. *These* are important people."

Al seemed a little uncomfortable. "I understand," he said. "I've handled this sort of thing before, boss."

I thought Al had put an ironic touch on that last word. He saw me and came over to shake my hand. Jeff said, "With you in a minute, Joe." He went back into his office and closed the door.

Al sighed. I said, "So big. So very, very big."

Al nodded. "And attractive to women, too. How's it going, Joe?"

"All right. I'm free and hungry."

"Couldn't use a partner with twelve hundred in cash, could you?"

I shook my head. "There isn't that much work. Our boy has really gone Hollywood, hasn't he?"

Al's eyebrows lifted. "Wait'll you get a whiff of his new cologne. See you around, Joe."

The lacquered blonde said, "Mr. Roeder will see you now, Mr. Puma."

Jeff's office was gray and silver, with a splash of brighter color here and there. Some Hopper reproductions were on the walls.

Jeff asked, "Business this morning, Joe?"

"You smell good enough to date," I said, "but alas, it's business." I paused. "The Engle business."

He frowned. "Unfortunate, that."

"Let's take it over from the top," I said. "The part doesn't call for an English accent."

Some malice in his gray eyes. "All right, Joe. What are you here for?"

"First, I'd like to know when Dutch Hofmeister went on your payroll."

"Never. What makes you think I'd hire a bum like that?

"Just a hunch. Second, how come Mrs. Engle didn't call you in again to find her husband this last time?"

"I've no idea. Any more questions you want to ask me?"

"One more. Why didn't you tell Elizabeth Adams you were married?"

He smiled. "Would you, if you were married? And why did you tell her I was?"

"Because she's too nice a girl to get mixed up with a phoney philanderer."

The gray eyes glinted. "Don't let my tailoring lead you astray, Joe. I'm not a boy you want to buck."

"Yes, you are. I'd like to do it for a living. Jeff, if you know something I should, it could be a good time to sell me. I'm staying with this case."

His smile was scornful. "Duffy will be pleased to hear that." He expelled his breath. "Well, I've a full morning. Good luck."

I nodded and went out past the blonde and the pretty prints and down in the self–service elevator to the ground floor. The morning traffic glittered along Wilshire and there was a Chev Club parked about four cars back of mine.

Jeff hadn't been much worse than a genial swindler before he'd married money. Now, he had no other loyalty. And Arnie Hansen's loyalty was to his job, which represented his kind of money. It was a bad town for loyalty to *people*.

Something stirred in my unconscious and evaporated. I sat in the flivver, waiting to see who would climb into the Chev Club behind. A matron in a Cadillac looking for a parking space came abreast of me and looked at me quizzically. I shook my head and she drove on, frowning.

In five minutes, a thin man carrying a brief case came out from a store and climbed into the Chev. This town is full of Chev Clubs.

At my office, my phone answering service reported no calls since I'd last checked it. I took out my reports of the day before and tried to think of any comments I'd missed putting down.

Nothing, nothing, nothing ... I typed up today's visit with Duffy and with Roeder in my efficient, two–fingered way.

I phoned Gina Pastore and waited while her phone rang five times. Her voice was blurred and thick.

"This is Joseph Puma," I said.

"The private detective? The police told me not to talk to you, Mr. Puma. They told me it will go a lot easier on me if I cooperate with them."

"I won't tell them. I thought there might have been something you neglected to tell me yesterday. I'm working on this case, too, Miss Pastore."

"I don't want any trouble," she said. "I might even lose my job because I stayed home today. I can't afford any trouble."

I started to say more, but the line went dead. I looked up Mrs. Engle's unlisted number in my card file and dialed that.

The maid told me Mrs. Engle was still sleeping. She had been given another sedative by the doctor late last night.

Well, where was a thread I might unravel? A husband seemed like a good bet if Alan's feminine conquests had been physical as well as spiritual.

I drove out to the Sandows. Felix wasn't on the front lawn today; Armine was pruning the lemon tree in the side yard.

"Hello, again," I said.

She put the clippers down and took off the heavy gloves she was wearing. "Let's go around to the patio. It's cooler on that side of the house."

The patio was red brick, framed in roses. She went over to a portable bar. "There's no ice, but I can get some from the house. Would you like a drink?"

"No, thanks," I said. "I suppose you were shocked by what happened."

She came back to sit on the end of a redwood bench. "We all were. Is there anything new on it this morning?"

"Not that I've been told about. You know, the logical suspect would be a husband, wouldn't it?"

Her thin body was still. Her dark eyes considered me gravely. "I hope you weren't thinking of Felix?"

"Just — husbands generally."

She looked past me. "Felix isn't — emotional. He's extremely civilized." She looked at me. "Were you thinking of Felix? The police didn't indicate that they were."

"The police aren't sensitive," I said. "Did you love Alan Engle?"

She shrugged. "Everybody loved Alan. I wouldn't say he had an unusual physical appeal, though."

"Your husband thinks he had."

"I meant for me," she said quietly. "I guess he had plenty of physical attraction for some — kind of women."

"What kind?"

"The physical kind. Are you sure you don't want a drink? I'd like an excuse for not working this morning."

"Anything to oblige a lady," I said. "Something with gin in it."

When she came back with a silver bucket of ice, I asked, "Do you know Jeff Roeder?"

"Only through his professional visits. I know that friend of his though, that Elizabeth Adams. A lovely girl."

"She certainly is," I agreed. "Is your husband around this morning?"

She shook her head. "He had to go into Hollywood on some scheme of his."
She came over to hand me a drink. "You're not seriously considering Felix as a
suspect, are you?"

"Not seriously. Was he here between eleven and noon yesterday?"

She nodded. "Right where you found him, on the front lawn, soaking in the sun
and alcohol." She sat down and sipped her drink. "Felix can now afford to be
merely ornamental; my pictures are beginning to bring fine prices."

Nothing from me.

She said, "I hope that didn't sound bitter. I'm quite content."

I asked, "Does your husband paint, too?"

She nodded. "Only when the mood moves him and never for the market. Please
don't misjudge him; he's an amusing and frequently gentle man and worth every
nickel he costs me."

I thought of Grace Engle and sipped my drink. I said, "Alan planned to marry
that Pastore girl. You knew he'd gone back to her, didn't you?"

Her eyes widened. "I didn't. I haven't seen a paper. How were they going to
live?"

"She had a job at a drive–in," I said. "I guess some of those girls make out
pretty well, what with tips and all."

Armine Sandow smiled, and then she laughed. Suddenly she stopped.

Her voice was tight. "I shouldn't laugh, should I? Not with Alan dead. But this
absurd, this monstrous trinity. I mean, Grace and Alan and Felix and me and then
Alan and this other girl. A matriarchate — that's where this civilization is heading."

"I'll vote for it," I said. "Why else would Alan die, if we eliminate husbands?"

"I've no idea," she said. "The Turks used to kill us just for the sport, but there
are no Turks in this, are there?"

"None. Do you know Grace Engle very well?"

She shook her head. "She didn't mix much with our gang. But speaking of
wealthy wives, didn't that Roeder person have one, too?"

"I've just come from his office," I said. "I feel he has a place in the picture,
somewhere, but it's mostly hunch. Did Alan ever have any trouble with anybody in
this — gang of yours?"

She looked thoughtful. "I can't remember any time. I think, though, that you
can eliminate husbands as suspects. I can't think of any husbands in the gang who
take that drastic a view, of adultery."

"And if we eliminate jealousy, we come to money. How does your gang feel
about that?"

She smiled. "Most of them take a very casual view of it. But — maybe this
Pastore girl had a new boy friend? It's quite possible she could have one with
middle class views on morality."

"It's possible," I agreed and looked at her levelly. "You've come a long way
from the grape–picking days, haven't you?"

She colored slightly. "I suppose I did sound a little pretentious. To answer your
question, yes, I'm a long way from Fresno." She paused, and met my glance
defiantly. "*Artistically*, too."

I stood up. "Okay. I guess I was rude. I apologize, if I was. There's absolutely nothing you can tell me that might help?"

"Nothing," she said wearily. "Alan was well–loved."

I went down the hill again thinking of her last words. Well–loved he apparently had been. But not well–heeled. Eliminating hate and greed, what was left for motive? A murder needs a motive. Lacking a motive, it's only manslaughter.

Well–loved, usually, also implies well–hated. The same quality in one person inspires love in some and hate in others. And there was no reason to limit my suspicion to Alan's closest friends.

6.

I drove over to the four unit apartment building near the Santa Monica Airport. A block away, I thought I saw a Chev Club parked and it looked as though someone was behind the wheel. But the car was in the shade of a huge eucalyptus tree, and I couldn't be sure from this distance.

After my fourth ring, Gina Pastore came to the door. Her face was puffed and her eyes red rimmed; she looked twenty years older.

"I'm not supposed to talk to you," she said, and started to close the door.

I put the palm of my hand against it. "I work for a living, like you do, Miss Pastore. I'm trying to earn my living. The police can give only a fraction of their time to investigating his death. It's my entire job and I need all the help I can get. Don't you want to help? Wasn't he important to you?"

"I want to help," she said sullenly. "But I don't want trouble. And how do I know Mrs. Engle didn't hire you to shut me up?"

"Mrs. Engle loved him," I told her gently. "She took a lot of abuse from him."

Her eyes flared. "She bought him. His body, that's what she wanted. Well, she's got it, now."

"You're being unkind," I said. "And foolish. You have to believe in *somebody*, Miss Pastore."

Her haggard eyes studied me listlessly. She took a deep breath, and finally said, "All right, come in, come in."

There was a musty, wine–tinged odor in the living room. All the shades were drawn and the room was dim. The morning papers were scattered all over the davenport. A girdle was draped over the arm of an occasional chair.

I pushed the papers to one side and sat on the davenport. I said, "When Alan left you yesterday morning, your understanding was that he was going directly to see Mrs. Engle?"

She nodded.

"He was going to ask for a divorce so he could marry you?"

She seemed suddenly frightened and whispered, "That's right."

"You were going to keep your job?"

She looked at me suspiciously. "What's that got to do with it?"

"I wondered how you were going to live. Alan had no income of his own, did he?"

Her face stiffened. "He always had money. Why, when he was only nineteen years old, he was making over two hundred dollars a week."

"In radio," I reminded her. "There have been some changes in radio, since then. He lived high, probably."

She shook her head. "He was no spendthrift. He watched his money. He didn't need to spend *his* money, after he married that old woman."

"This is a new angle," I said. "I had an idea, somehow, he was a high–flying bird."

"He wasn't cheap," she said. "But he wasn't foolish, either." Her body shook and she began to cry.

I asked, "Has another detective, a man named Jeff Roeder, come to see you?"

She shook her head without looking up. "There was a detective, but that wasn't his name. A big man. I don't remember his name. He — drove a Chevrolet, a gray one."

"Hofmeister?"

She shook her head. "Wait. It was Abbott, Lewis Abbott."

"Recently?"

"This morning. Do you know him?"

"I *knew* him. He's been dead for two years."

She lifted her head to stare at me. There was fright in her wet eyes.

I said, "It's probably a man named Hofmeister. He isn't licensed any more and he gave you a phoney name. Would you say he was heavier than two hundred pounds?"

She nodded. "He could have been fifty pounds heavier than that. Who is he? What does he want?"

"He's a crook," I answered. "I'm not sure what he wants. You should have told the police about him."

Her soft body was tense now. "You don't think — Could he have had some-thing to do with Alan's murder?"

"He could be working for the person who killed Alan. Or maybe he even did it himself."

"But why should he? What was he following us for?"

"What do you mean, following?" I said sharply. "You didn't mention that."

"I'm not really sure about it. It's just a feeling I have. There was a car like his parked outside the night — the night Alan came here. The next night, too. I never gave it any thought, until now that —"

"Wait a minute." I was thinking fast. "Maybe that's Hofmeister's angle. Blackmail."

She gasped, like someone dropped in cold water.

"It's exactly his kind of dodge. Maybe he thought there was a buck to be made, trailing Mrs. Engle's wandering boy. And when he saw him shack up here, maybe he put the arm on Alan for money. Could be Alan wouldn't give."

"Maybe they had an argument!" Gina's big eyes were bigger. "And then —"

"Look," I said, "could you recognize him if the police picked him up?"

She nodded. "I'm sure I could. Will you phone the police? Will you tell them about this man right now?"

I said, "There's a possibility he's only a block away from here this minute. Sit tight; I'll be right back."

I went to the door, intending to go out to the sidewalk, but there was no need to do that. The Chev Club was parked across the street and there was somebody behind the wheel. I beckoned him.

Gina Pastore came to the door, and she said, "That's the same kind of car. But there are a lot of them. We get them at the drive-in every day."

A man was getting out from the driver's side now, a big man. He waited for traffic to pass; and then came across the street.

Gina Pastore said doubtfully, "That could be him." And as he drew closer, "That's him, that's him."

I said, "Lock the door," and went down the walk to meet Dutch Hofmeister.

He was smiling.

"Need some help, buddy?"

I shook my head. "Lewis Abbott is dead, Dutch."

He continued to smile. "So?"

"You used his name."

"Like hell. Who said so?"

"Miss Pastore."

He was no longer smiling. "She lied."

I shook my head. "Who are you working for, Hofmeister?"

"For Douglas Aircraft, nights. Not that it's any of your damned business, Puma."

"The police will be interested to know you used Abbott's name and were bothering a material witness in a murder case."

"Huh," he said. "Are you trying to frighten me? You already told Duffy about last night, and here I am, free as a bird. Do me something, Dago."

"Easy, Dutch," I warned him. "You're not that big. Nobody is."

He smiled. "I'm scared. You and your paisan friend are cooking up a frame for little Dutch, huh?"

"I'm going in right now to phone the police," I said. "Do you want to wait for them?"

He stood without moving a muscle. "I ought to paste you one. I just might."

"Please do," I said. "Please?"

"I'd slaughter you," he said.

I nodded. "Maybe. One thing you want to remember, Dutch, your strength is all below the neck. If you're smart, you'll come clean before things start getting tough."

He looked at me scornfully. "To hell with you. Go ahead, phone the Department. And then try to explain what you were doing here."

He snorted and gave me his broad back to look at as he went back to his car. I watched him drive off.

In the apartment, I told Gina Pastore, "Phone Sergeant Dully and tell him a man named Hofmeister approached you under the name of Lewis Abbott and tried to question you about Alan's death."

She phoned the west side station and was told Sergeant Duffy was not in. She looked questioningly at me.

I said, "Ask if his partner is there. Tell them it's about the Engle murder case."

She did that. There was a pause. Then another man must have come on, and she repeated what I'd told her to tell them.

Another pause, and she looked at me. "He wants to know how I know the man's name is really Hofmeister."

"Tell him he used to be a customer at your drive–in."

She told the officer that and again looked at me. "He wants to know who is here now."

"Tell him the milkman."

She took a deep breath. "Nobody's here now. But I'm afraid that that man might come back and kill me, too. Don't I get any protection?" A pause. "All right. I'll wait. But tell whoever comes to park right in front; so I can see his car through the window."

She hung up and said, "They're sending a detective over."

"I'll go," I said. "He should be here in a few minutes. You won't be frightened, will you?"

She shook her head. "I'm not frightened. I'm just — tired." She looked to–wards the open door of the bedroom. For the first time, I noticed the cheap, imitation–alligator valise on the floor, with the pink look of a bra sticking out of the side. "I thought I'd go away for a week or so," she said. "To my sister in Frisco."

"Good idea. Only you don't pack so good, honey."

She looked at the valise and smiled. Then she was serious, and her brown eyes moved over my face. "Are you Italian?"

I nodded. "Paisan. Chin up, kid."

"I should have known I could trust you. I'm sorry I didn't."

"Don't fret," I said. "Most intelligent people don't. And you're still a young and very attractive girl, Gina. Keep that in mind. The world hasn't come to an end."

"I'm going to be a horse," she said. "A cow. My mother weighs almost two hundred pounds."

I patted her cheek. "A little less lasagna and little more massage. You're all, woman, honey, and that's the important thing."

She managed one small, sad smile before I left.

7.

I got out of there thinking about things like love and money, wondering which force would be stronger in getting somebody to commit murder. Thinking about money brought Armine Sandow's comment to mind. *"Our gang takes a very casual view of money ..."*

But Alan Engle's view wasn't casual. Neither was Dutch Hofmeister's. He sure wasn't running up mileage on that Chevy of his for fun.

On nothing but hunch, I steered the car back into the hills, on a repeat visit to the Sandows.

Armine must have gotten tired of pruning chores. She was stretched out on the slats of a redwood bench, and there was a glass beside her on the patio that looked like it had been emptied more than once. She looked up when the flivver took the driveway, shielding her eyes against a sun that was hanging fat and red over the bay.

"I knew you couldn't stay away." She laughed, a little shrilly I thought.

I got out of the car. "Mr. Sandow still in Hollywood?"

"Yes. It's an all day scheme he's working on. All night, too, most likely." She sat up and brushed back her hair. Then she reached for the glass, and frowned when she saw it was empty.

"All night?" I said.

"Listen, Mr. Puma." Her voice was testy. "I merely said Felix was civilized. I didn't say he was docile."

I thought about that for a few seconds. Then I said, "I just paid a call on Gina Pastore. You were right about her, Mrs. Sandow. She's a beautiful gal."

She snorted. "That's Alan for you. A great man for variety, Alan. A real democratic lover ..."

Whatever had once been in the glass had obviously loosened her tongue. I saw this as opportunity.

"I don't quite get you," I said.

"Bless 'em all," she giggled. "Bless 'em all. The short and the fat and the tall —"

"You mean Alan went for all types?"

"Types? Say, do you know what Alan's type was? Two legs, two arms, two eyes, two —" She completed a bawdy description.

I didn't say anything for a while after that and neither did she. Finally, she arose with a fatigued sigh and put her shoulders far back as part of stretching.

"Don't get Alan wrong," she said, speaking softly now, almost tenderly. "He had real sensitivity. He could talk about painting, and make sense. And he could be real sweet sometimes. Real sweet. You know how he was on radio? Yes, of course you do. He had a voice like —" She looked at the water, her eyes distant. "I don't know how to describe it. Oh, did you ever take a good thick lotion and just let it slide over your skin after a shower? That's what Alan's voice was like. Really."

I cleared my throat, but not to interrupt.

"Sometimes," she said dreamily, "we used to sit out here at night and just look at the moon. Sounds corny, doesn't it? But it didn't *feel* corny. Not when Alan was here. He'd talk, and I'd listen. God knows, I couldn't repeat a word he used to say. I'd never really listen to the words; just to his voice, pouring over me ..."

"And where was Felix during all this?"

I thought the remark would strike fire, but she just shrugged. Then I got an intuitive itch, and scratched it.

"And what about Gina?" I said. "Did he ever talk to you about her?"

That did it. Emotion flashed in her face, the like of which I'd never seen there before.

"That two–bit Lollobrigida!" she exclaimed. "That Italian whore! *She* couldn't have given him anything. Nothing more than a good —"

I played my trump. "You hated, Gina, didn't you? Even more than you hated Grace Engle. *She* was your real threat — not Alan's wife. Isn't that so? Am I right?"

"Get out of here!"

"You were the last person to see Alan before he went trouncing off to Gina's loving arms, weren't you? Maybe you knew where he was going. Maybe he passed up your own fourposter for hers and —"

"Get out!" It was a shriek.

"You could have followed Alan. And have built up enough steam to want to kill him. Right?"

She stood up. The spirit had gone out of her.

"Right?" I prodded.

"I *was* sore enough," she said. "Haven't *you* ever gotten that sore? Haven't *you* ever thought you could kill?"

"Did you follow Alan after he took you home that night?"

She nodded. "Yes. But I didn't —"

"What kind of a car do you drive?"

"What?"

"What kind of car?"

"A Buick."

"What color?"

"A two–tone. Tan and green."

"How close did you get to Gina Pastore's apartment house?"

"I just drove up and down in front of it. Then I parked across the street and just waited. God knows what for."

"Did anybody else drive up that night?" I asked her.

She shook her head.

"Be sure about this," I said. "Was any other car parked outside? With some–body in it?"

"No. All I could see was Alan's car. A Jaguar."

"How long were you there?"

"I don't know. Practically until dawn. It was almost four o'clock by the time Alan left me. The Shirvanians like late parties."

I started digging in my pocket for the car keys. "Okay, Mrs. Sandow. I better get going."

"Wait." She came over and her thin hand started kneading my coat sleeve. "It's getting late," she said. "Do you have dinner plans? I hate eating alone."

"Sorry. Got to see a man."

"Tomorrow's another day. And I cook, too. Believe it or not. With my own hands."

She was bending over me, and so close that you couldn't tell how thin she was. What do they say about gray cats?

"Really," I said. "I've got an errand. I'm still on Grace Engle's payroll, you know."

"You have a fine head." She was trailing her fingers over my hair. "Such good Latin bones. I'd like to do a portrait sometimes."

"Your price is too steep."

"I give discounts," she said, "for prompt payment."

I got out from under, and turned my back on her.

"Some other time," I said.

I climbed in the car, and spun the wheel until I was pointed down the hill. I could feel her eyes on me until I hit the highway.

8.

I had that *almost* feeling now. That nagging, nuisance–type feeling that the round pegs were almost in their round holes.

At least, I knew where to hit next.

Dutch Hofmeister's.

His crummy apartment wasn't more than half a mile away. I stopped off at *Bess Eiler's* and had some lunch. Then I drove over to the weather–beaten, rectangular stucco building of eight units, four to a floor. Dutch's Chev was sitting outside.

I went up the bare stairs and down the hall to his door. I rang the bell.

Silence for seconds, and then his gruff, "Who's there?"

"Puma," I said. "Don't cringe, Dutch."

He opened the door a crack. I could just see the end of his davenport–bed and the open suitcase on it.

"Leaving town?" I asked.

"Beat it," he said. "I got business in Phoenix."

"I think you'd better hang around. The law will be looking for you. Miss Pastore phoned them less than an hour ago."

He glared. "Puma, for your sake, you'd better be lying. Tell me straight now, you didn't have that wop girl friend of yours phone the law, did you?"

"I certainly did have her do it. And don't use the word 'wop' when I'm around, you crook."

"Why not?" he said, and opened the door wide.

He wasn't fast, but he had plenty of time to put one of his ham–like fists about three inches into my belly. Nausea swelled in me, and I tasted bile in my mouth. He'd sent me back against the opposite wall of the hall, and I bounced off that and into him again.

He hadn't expected me. His second punch whistled past my neck, and he went stumbling into his apartment.

I heard a door open down the hall and the excited voice of a woman, but I gave all my attention to the work at hand.

My right elbow was in front of his face; I swung it savagely into his nose. He grunted and pushed me off and started a haymaker from his hip. I hit him with a nice clean left hand going away and the swish of his haymaker only grazed my ear. I moved to my right, away from his big right hand. I was glad to see his nose bleeding from my elbow work; it proved he wasn't invulnerable.

He was not only vulnerable, but extremely clumsy. He drew back the right hand again. And I hit him three times in the face while his right was getting under way.

He went down with a thump and somebody squealed from the direction of the doorway.

I turned to face a thin, dark–haired woman in a soiled kimona. She stared at me, frightened, momentarily speechless.

I said very calmly though out of breath, "Will you kindly phone the police immediately? They're looking for this man and he was trying to leave town."

She nodded nervously and hurried away down the hall. I knelt beside the motionless slob and reached for his wallet. There was a thick pile of bills in it, and they all looked like twenties. I made a rapid count. It wasn't big money, not in the Bel Air sense, but it was two hundred and forty bucks, which was probably more than Dutch Hofmeister had been toting for a long, long time.

I went over to the bed and looked down at the open suitcase. It had really been packed in a hurry. There were a couple of fancy shirts, both with grimy collars with a monogrammed 'H' under the pockets. There was one suit, right out of a Fresno bargain emporium, with widely separated chalk stripes. Some underwear and stuff were rolled up Army style. And there was a tin box with faded lettering on all four sides.

I pulled out the box. Maybe it once held cookies. It was about eight inches high, and it weighed about a million pounds. I almost dropped it in surprise.

Then I pried off the lid and dumped the contents on the bed. I got a kick out of seeing the shining Niagara of halves and quarters and nickels and dimes, the kick a kid gets when he smashes his piggy bank. Only this was a big piggy. This was a rich piggy, with maybe a hundred and fifty bucks in small change.

I scratched my head as I looked down at this jackpot and then started shoveling the coins back into the tin box.

Then that *almost* feeling went away.

Because I had the whole thing pinned down now, with every little peg right where it belonged.

Now all I had to do was ask one more question.

9.

The sun was starting to dunk itself in the bay when I reached the apartment building near the Santa Monica Airport.

There was a black sedan parked outside, and it didn't have to be labeled "Cop" for anybody to identify it as "Cop." I didn't know the driver, so maybe he didn't know me.

I went inside, pausing at the entrance to scrap some imaginary crud off my shoe, to allow Gina's "protection" to get a real good look at me. What the hell, I can cooperate with the law sometimes.

Gina was wearing something called a traveling suit. It was a shame, too, because her soft curves weren't displayed to best effect. But I hadn't come to pick her wardrobe.

"Mr. Puma!" she said, looking big–eyed.

"Paisan," I grinned. "How's it going?"

"All right, I suppose. What's happened? Have they picked up that man yet?"

"Somebody's picking him up all right," I said. "Literally."

"Do they — do they think he killed Alan?"

"That's hard to say." I took a seat, and glanced towards the bed room. The valise was still there, with its pink loop between the crack. "You still pack a lousy suit case," I said.

"Oh, oh I didn't get around to —"

"I saw another suitcase today. It was packed lousy, too. So you're not the only one, Gina." I lit a cigarette, and offered her one. She shook her head.

"For one thing," I said lightly, "this lousy packer really carries money around in a strange way. Like this." I brought the tin box out from behind my back, and jiggled it.

Her whole face got alarmed when she saw the box, and she whispered something like *"Dios!"* Then she was after it, her red–tipped fingers coming for the box like the claws of a predatory bird; I pulled it away just in time.

"Uh–uh," I said. "This is somebody else's dough, baby. A fellow named Hofmeister —"

"Give it to me!"

"Sorry, paisan. This little piggy goes to the cops."

"It's mine!" she shouted, her eyes burning.

"I know it is. It's all the tips you've been getting at Baker's. Right? It's plain you've been saving your dough like a nice girl. Only you shouldn't have given it away, Gina. Not to a creep like Dutch Hofmeister."

"He stole it! He stole it from me!"

I shook my head. "No, Gina. You gave it to him. And you gave him more dough than this, the folding kind. You gave him every nickel and dime you could. There must have been a reason, Gina."

"He — he was blackmailing Alan. I told you that. I — I wanted to help."

"Uh–uh. That won't wash. You couldn't care less if Alan's wife knew about you. That's what you wanted. You wanted Alan to tell her."

She sagged against the back of the davenport.

"No, paisan," I said. "You were paying Hofmeister. Now, why? What for? To kill Alan?"

"No!"

"Then why?"

"To find out!" she said. "Only to find out for me!" I put on a puzzled look, until she went on. "He told me he was a private detective. I used to see him around the drive–in. He told me he was a private detective named Abbott. Then — when I met Alan again, and he swore that he would divorce his wife and marry me —"

"That's a switch," I said. "You hire a private eye to trail the husband — to see if he's faithful to his wife."

She didn't think it was funny. "I had to know! I couldn't stand it if he was lying to me again — just like the last time —" She began to sob, but I didn't have time to get sympathetic. The cop outside would have reported my description to head quarters by now, and Duffy would soon be descending on the apartment house.

"Go on," I said softly, "get it off your chest, Gina."

"He — he began to follow Alan. But he wasn't here the night after the party. I just made that up."

I said, "I know. I already found that out."

"Then he came here once, and —" She stopped, and the sobs took over again.

"Come on," I said. "Cut that out."

"He told me Alan was lying. That all Alan wanted was just to have a little more — a little more fun with me. That he didn't really intend to marry me."

"How much did you pay this creep for his services?"

"Fifty dollars."

"Then how did he get the rest?" She compressed her lips as though she'd never speak again. "Answer my question," I told her and, incidentally, let her see my doubled–up fist.

"Well, after he told me that about Alan — he went away. But he didn't stop following us. The other day, I asked Alan to take me out on a picnic, to the canyon. Him and me, just the two of us. I said I'd get the morning off. I had one of my girl friends fill in for me at the drive–in. In those fancy uniforms, it's hard to tell us apart."

"And your girl friend never told the police?"

"She didn't know what it was all about. No, she didn't tell them. She just thought the boss was checking up on me — trying to get me fired."

"So you went on your picnic?"

"We went all right. I — still didn't want to believe Alan was just — using me." She lowered her eyes, her mouth turned down at the corners, and let out a long sigh. "He made love to me, up there. Turned away afterwards and — and went to sleep. Just like I was some animal ..." Her hand tightened on the arm of the davenport. "I picked up a rock then and —"

She stopped talking right there, and didn't resume for what seemed like an awfully long time.

Then she said, her voice a despairing monotone, "Hofmeister had followed us. And he saw what happened. When I got home, he was waiting for me. He took every cent I had — even the tip money I'd been saving for a trip I wanted to take to Frisco. But he still wasn't satisfied. He made me say I'd go away with him. Today." She shivered. "He's like a — a — Oh, God, what difference does anything make? Nothing matters. Not now. Nothing —"

I gave her a cigarette, and she puffed away hard at it and sobbed. Finally, Duffy's big fists were making noises on the door.

Duffy was sore as hell, just on general principles, for the first five minutes. Then Gina talked some more, dry–eyed now, without emotion. By the time she was through, Duffy was shaking his head and thinking thoughts obviously not fit for the record.

Arnie Hansen had accompanied Duffy from the station. He took Gina down to the official car parked out front, but not before he had dropped me a congratulatory wink.

"I suppose you're proud of yourself," Duffy grunted, when the room was cleared.

"Hell, no," I said, and I meant it. "There's a lot of guys ought to be hit with rocks. It's just too bad a nice bambino like this one had to do it."

"We picked up Hofmeister," the Sergeant said. "I don't think we'll have any trouble with him."

"Good."

We went down the stairs together, and when we hit the street, the sun was making one last splash before dropping behind the watery horizon. It was a beautiful sight, and I began to feel philosophical.

"You know, Duffy," I said. "It wasn't love or money, after all. There are other motives for murder, apparently. This time it was pride — just plain, old–fashioned, eternal womanly pride."

"Hell hath no fury," he growled as he climbed into the car, "Like a woman scorned."

"Why, Sergeant!" I said, laughing. "You're a goddamn poet!"

He told me to do something that was biologically impossible. Then the car drove off, and I could swear I caught a glimpse of the big Irish man grinning.

I got into my own flivver, and I knew what came next. I was going to see Elizabeth Adams. I'd pick up some beer on the way. And this time, I hoped I might stay a little longer.

Death of a Big Wheel

It had been a hot and trying day and I'd come in for a quiet drink. I'd had the first and was contemplating the advisability of another, when the man took the stool next to mine.

His face was familiar, a worn face, sensitive and still virile. His clothes were a bit frayed, but he wore them well; his voice was a trained voice. He ordered a Scotch on the rocks.

I knew him now. He'd played in my favorite picture before the war. He'd starred in it, and registered a very fine performance.

The bartender said, "Palm Springs, Mr. Haskell? I see you've been getting the sun."

"I've been getting the sun," the man said mildly, "but not at Palm Springs. How is every little thing with you, Charles?"

"Fine, Mr. Haskell. I had Needles, yesterday."

John Haskell smiled. "I didn't even know you were on the stuff, Charles."

The bartender grinned and shook his head. "The horse, I mean, Mr. Haskell. Ain't you betting any more?"

John Haskell shook his head and sipped his drink. "Not betting the horses or taking blondes to Palm Springs. It's a monastic life I lead."

"I'll bet," the bartender said genially. He looked at me, "Another of the same, Mr. Puma?"

I nodded.

John Haskell turned. "Joseph Puma, the private detective?"

I nodded again. "The same, Mr. Haskell. Where have you heard of me?"

"In the *Examiner*, on the Engle murder. I'm addicted to murder stories, *true* murder stories. You did a beautiful job on that case."

"Thank you," I said. "And you did a beautiful job in *Man in the Street*. I think that's my all–time favorite picture and yours was my all–time favorite performance."

He looked at me without expression. "That was a long time ago. That was before the war."

I said nothing.

He said quietly, "I was very big before the war. I was so big I thought it would be smart to be independent. I turned down four duration contracts before I went into the service."

Here it comes, I thought. *The detailed and lengthy story of John Haskell's fall. And all I meant to have was one drink.*

I shook my head sympathetically, but said nothing.

John Haskell said, "The studios put all the boys to work who had signed pre–service duration contracts. They had to pay the lads anyway, so they put them to work. What keeps an actor alive is work."

I nodded and sipped my drink.

John Haskell chuckled. "Don't look so bored. I only told you all that to forestall the tedious question too many people ask me. They continually ask me, 'What happened to you?' Well, that's what happened to me."

"I wasn't going to ask you," I said with a smile. "I'm not a tourist, Mr. Haskell."

"Of course you're not," he said. "I should have realized. Now, tell me about the Engle case. What put you on the trail of the Pastore woman?"

The man was drunk, I realized now. He spoke carefully and held himself primly erect, but he was almost blind drunk and only a supreme effort of will was keeping him off the floor.

I said, "Why don't I buy you a dinner while I tell you about the Engle case? I'd like to tell my grandchildren, some day, that I bought a dinner for John Haskell."

His voice was very steady. "I don't need your charity, Mr. Puma."

"One dinner is hardly charity, Mr. Haskell."

Silence, while he stared at me. "Italian, are you?"

"That's right."

"My first wife was Italian. Very compassionate people, Italians. You were undoubtedly thinking that if I had some food in me, the alcohol would have something to work on besides the walls of my stomach."

"You're discerning," I said.

"And so are you. But of course, that's your business, isn't it?"

"Part of it," I admitted. "My size and my hunger help, too."

He looked at the bartender and talked to me. "Now, Charles, here, serves drinkers day and night. But he didn't know I was drunk. Charles is not discerning."

Charles smiled and said nothing, as good bartenders do.

"A steak," I said, "and some coffee, Mr. Haskell, and the story of Gina Pastore. There's a quiet booth over there in the corner."

He turned slowly to look at the booth and then swung back slowly to look at me. Finally, he said, "Fair enough. And you may call me John."

The bartender looked at me and shrugged. I ignored him.

Haskell swung around on his stool, his drink held steadily in his hand. I stood close to him, waiting for him to fall. He didn't. I walked alongside him all the way to the booth and he never wavered.

The waiter came, and I ordered a pair of steaks. Then I told Haskell the story of Gina Pastore who had asked Alan Engle to go on a picnic with her and had, during the course of the picnic, bashed in Engle's head with a rock,

It was a story even uglier than my resume, but it didn't affect the appetite of John Haskell. He ate the steak and all the rolls they brought and all the butter — everything, in fact, but the dishes.

Then he leaned back and looked at me contentedly. "A fascinating story. I knew Alan Engle in high school. He was always in trouble."

There had been some satisfaction in his voice. I said, "You sound as though you've had an opinion vindicated."

"A pattern," he said. "We're all victims of a pattern, don't you think?"

"No," I said. "That's defeatism."

He smiled. "A big muscular Italian like you would no doubt be a hedonist."

"Partially. I guess almost everybody is, partially. If I'd had a talent, though, nothing would have stopped me. And certainly not booze."

He looked at me curiously. "You're speaking of me, now, I suppose? You think I have a talent?"

I nodded. "And so did all the critics. How many actors can please all the critics? Name me five."

He smiled sadly and patronizingly. "Critics — They won't even pay to get in; that's what they think of the theatre. Joe, I hit my peak at the age of twenty–seven. Then I had four years in the service, three years of it overseas, two of them in combat."

"You enlisted, if I remember right," I pointed out. "Where was the pattern there? That was an act of your will."

He shook his head. "It was an act of my youth. Of emotional thinking, my enlisting." He gestured to the waiter and ordered a pair of drinks.

At a table on the other side of the room, we were getting a lot of attention. A blonde in a pale green cashmere sweater was pointing us out to her escort.

The escort was sitting, so I couldn't judge his height, but his shoulders were impressively broad.

Our drinks came, and Haskell lifted his. "To luck."

"You don't believe in it," I told him, "but I'll drink to it."

We drank, and I said, "Don't look now, but do you know that blonde across the room who's giving us the eye?"

Haskell swung his gaze that way and said, "I know her. Her name is Lira McCrea and she hates my guts."

"Who's the muscle with her?" I asked.

Haskell shrugged. "Never saw him before. He looks — malignant, doesn't he?" He sipped his drink. "I met her at a party. I was drunk and she was ready. I was too drunk to take advantage of that. At any rate, that's my memory of the thing. About a week later, at *Ciro's* she walked over to my table and really told me off. It was very vulgar."

I said, "I think you're due for an encore. She's on the way over right now. And the muscle is trailing her."

Haskell smiled. "I'll take her. You can have the big guy." He didn't look their way.

The blonde seemed younger than I had first imagined her. And the big man was not tall, only broad. He had the kind of a face that looks naked without a number under it. I was sure I had seen it before, if only on a poster in the post office.

The blonde said nastily, "Well, well, if it isn't drunken John Haskell. Have I told you what I think of you lately, John?"

He smiled and shook his head. Behind Lira McCrea, the muscle looked at us impassively.

I said, "Lady, we were having a serious conversation. Would you mind running along?"

Her gaze swung to me. "Don't get flip, big boy. I've got all the man I need behind me."

"Not quite," I said. "And I'll tell you something else. If I have to get up to pop him, I may also hand you one for luck. Beat it."

John Haskell's eyes were bright with interest. The muscle growled something I didn't catch and the blonde reached forward to slap at Haskell's face.

I put a hand out that pushed her off balance, and she stumbled against the edge of the booth.

Her escort came charging in, then, to join the fray. I came up out of the booth and brought the good left hand along.

It was a lucky punch. My body was in it and it caught him just exactly where it was supposed to. He went stumbling backward until a table got in his way. Luckily, it was an empty table. He took it over with him.

The blonde screamed and a waiter and the bartender started our way and John Haskell said, "Now might be the intelligent time to leave."

We stood up and I put some money on the table and we were out of the place before the resistance could get properly organized.

On the parking lot, John Haskell said, "Well, Puma, it's been a pleasure. We must do this again."

"You're not driving, are you?" I asked. "You're not in condition to drive."

"I'm not driving," he said. "I sold my car. I'll get a cab down at the corner."

"All right," I said. "Take care of yourself. If you ever crawl out of the bottle, you might make a comeback, you know."

He smiled. "Don't worry about me, Puma. I'm not that important. Nobody is."

I watched him as he made his way steadily and leisurely toward the corner. He certainly didn't look drunk from the back.

I went to a movie that night and the next day I put in on a hotel skip. I couldn't get Haskell out of my mind. He was faintly arrogant and soft on mysticism, but I'd liked him and I'd always thought of him as one of this town's really good actors.

Friday morning, his picture was on the front page of the *Times*. He had been bludgeoned to death. By a person or persons unknown.

2.

What was Haskell's death to me? Nothing. I'd enjoyed him as an actor and talked to him for an hour and now he was dead. There were ten thousand police officers in this town. So what was it to me?

According to the *Times*, there was very little that the police had to go on. John Haskell had no known enemies. Most of his old friends had lost track of him; he was living in a cheap motel in Santa Monica. The most logical theory seemed to be that he had been the victim of a prowler. That, of course, could have been the reporter's theory, not the Department's.

It was a bright and sunny morning and I had nothing to do. I could have run over to the Department and told them about the blonde, Lira McCrea, and her pugnacious boy friend. But that might be unfair to the blonde.

I phoned an agent I knew and asked him if Miss McCrea was an actress, and if he knew where she lived. He'd heard the name, he told me, but very little more. He would check and call back.

He phoned back in ten minutes and told me Lira McCrea was a starlet under contract to *Verital Films* and he gave me her address.

Verital was a small outfit, specializing in low budget pictures, and there was a strong rumor around town that Arnie Roman had a big piece of the firm. Arnie had come up through pandering, dope and gambling to Las Vegas and the big time. He was a highly respected citizen of that Nevada rat's nest now, and active in Los Angeles real estate speculation.

If a man can afford it, buying a small studio is a fine way to keep supplied with dames. The blonde could be one of those.

Not that any of it was my business, but I had liked John Haskell. And I wasn't busy at the moment.

I climbed into the flivver and drove over to Beverly Hills.

The apartment house was on the edge of that gilded village, a rambling, two–story stucco building filled with small units. The directory in the lobby informed me Lira McCrea had a second floor apartment.

She was without make–up this morning, wearing a lounging robe of brocaded red satin, and the natural brown of her hair was showing at the roots.

"What the hell do you want?" she asked.

I studied her. Her toughness was not inherent and it seemed recently acquired; she obviously wasn't thoroughly at home in the gutter yet. I said, "Information. I'm looking for enemies of John Haskell."

"Look somewhere else," she said. "You're not the law; you're a private man."

"How did you know that?"

"My friends know you."

"How well do you know them?" I asked. "Well enough to expect them to rush to your rescue if I tell the police about you?"

Her face was momentarily vulnerable and she looked at me doubtfully. I said quietly, "How long ago did you decide *Verital* was the studio for you? How long ago did you learn there were short–cuts in this acting game?"

Her young face showed scorn. "What are you, a minister? Crummy, angle–shooting private eye —"

"You've been watching television too much," I said. "I'm a respectable member of a dignified profession. You could probably use an ally like me."

"I've got friends," she said, "who could buy you with their cigar money."

"The man was never born who can buy me," I told her. "But it's your decision. I'll let you argue with the boys from the Department."

I turned, took two steps, and she said, "Wait."

I waited, looking at her quietly.

"I don't want any trouble," she said. "I don't know anything about John's enemies. My friends aren't his enemies."

"You looked like an enemy two evenings ago."

"That was — personal." She hesitated. "Come on in."

I went into a one bedroom apartment furnished in just–under–first–class modern. She said, "I'm making some coffee. Want a cup?"

"Yes, thank you."

I followed her to a small dinette.

"Maybe some toast, too?" she asked. "I've got some really special marmalade from England."

I chuckled. "Why the Dale Carnegie touch for a crummy, angle–shooting private eye?"

She looked at me bleakly. "Maybe you're not one. Maybe you're what you claim to be."

"Maybe. All is not lost, anyway, if you can still think like that. Why did you hate John Haskell?"

"Didn't he tell you? Weren't you a friend of his?"

"I met him only that evening in that bar. He told me you had made a play for him at a party and he hadn't been interested. He seemed to think your vanity was inflamed."

She stared at me blankly. "The lying son–of–a–bitch —"

"Easy, now. Let's hear your story."

She said quietly, "My best friend committed suicide because of John Haskell."

A pause, and I asked, "Unrequited love?"

"Yeah. If that means unreturned love." She went to the small stove to get the percolator. "After an abortion."

"John Haskell's child?"

"He claimed it wasn't. She claimed it was and I believed her. I knew her since we were seven and she *never* lied to me."

"Why didn't she get a lawyer?"

"Because she loved him and he could talk fast. He was a great talker, that bastard."

I asked softly, "Why do you use those ugly words? It's not really natural for you."

She put some toast into the toaster and sat down across from me. "It's an ugly world, isn't it? If anybody should know that, you should."

"I should. But you shouldn't. Not yet." I sipped my coffee. "Did Haskell know you were a friend of this girl's?"

"Of course he knew it. We used to double–date."

"Was she an actress, too?"

Lira nodded. "Only she had more talent than I have. And she was prettier."

"Did she consider Haskell a step in the right direction?"

Lira McCrea looked at me steadily and angrily. I said, "I don't want an emotional answer. *Think*, now, and be honest."

She took a deep breath. "She loved him very much. She knew knowing him would help her career, but I honestly think she would have given up her career for him."

"I'll buy all of that," I said, "but now let's think of it from his viewpoint. He had probably met dozens of girls as pretty and talented as your friend. And many of them were undoubtedly — available. A gent in — oh, say Cedar Rapids might consider himself very lucky to marry a girl like your friend. To John Haskell, there were too many of them; she was only one of many. We're all victims of our environment to a degree, you know. He simply had more chances to be immoral than his less fortunate brothers."

"Man thinking," she said. "You're all alike."

"That could be. But some of us are worse. How long have you been hanging around with the hoodlum element in this town?"

"Is there another element in this town?"

I didn't answer. I spread some toast with marmalade and took a bite. "It is good marmalade," I said.

She didn't look at me. "If you only met him two evenings ago, why are you here now? Did somebody hire you?"

"Nobody. I liked him. I hate murder and I wasn't busy."

Doubt was on her face.

"Nobody is paying me," I repeated, "and nobody is required to tell me anything. What was your girlfriend's name?"

"Jean Morley. I've a picture of her, if you'd like to see it."

I said I would and she went into the bedroom to get some snapshots. Some of them were of the girl alone, a thin and attractive dark–haired girl. Two of the snaps showed her with John Haskell's arm around her. In one of these, she was wearing a bathing suit, and she wasn't thin any place it would hurt her.

I said, "Are her parents living?"

"No. The only living relative she has is a brother."

"Does he live out here?"

"He —" She paused. "Why do you want to know?"

"I'm looking for a killer, Miss McCrae."

"Well, it wasn't Jean's brother. He lives in New Jersey."

She looked at me candidly as she said this, but I knew she was lying. Lying, like her toughness, was too new for her to handle skillfully. I'd believed what she'd said about Jean Morley, but perhaps Jean Morley had lied to her.

And then I remembered Haskell's preoccupation with a pattern in lives and wondered if that was the way he was trying to absolve his conscience from the guilt of Miss Morley's death.

"Why so quiet?" Lira asked.

"I've been thinking about Haskell. It's hard to get a picture of a man from the newspapers, isn't it?"

"It is, if he has a good press agent. And John could be very charming when he wanted to make the effort."

"So can you," I said. I stood up. "Move warily among your new playmates, won't you? Keep your guard up."

"I'll get by," she said. "Are you still going to look for the man who killed John?"

I nodded.

"He wasn't fit to live."

"We can't decide that. Good luck, Miss McCrea."

The sun was still shining and there was a slight breeze from the east. I drove over to my office and phoned the agent again.

I asked him, "Do you remember a Jean Morley?"

"Sure do. She committed suicide. Great young talent."

"Do you know anything about her brother?"

"Didn't even know she had one."

"Could you find out about him?"

"For how much?"

"For nothing," I said. "It's a charity case; I'm working for the public. Don't you ever do public service work?"

"Not unless there's a promotion angle."

"All right," I said. "Good day. To hell with you."

"Wait," he said. "Don't let your wop temper get the best of you. Some day I may need a little free investigating. I'll tell you what I'll do. I'll ask around among a few of Jean's friends. Okay?"

"Fair enough," I agreed. "Is Arnie Roman really the big man at *Verital*?"

"Right. I hope you don't plan to tangle with him. He's got too many strings to too many places, Joe."

"I'm shivering," I told him. "You let me know about Jean's brother. I'll be here at the office."

I was going over some statements when the phone rang. I thought it was my friend calling back, but it wasn't.

A feminine voice said, "This is Arnold Roman's secretary, Mr. Puma. Would it be possible for him to talk with you this afternoon?"

"I'm sure I can squeeze him in," I said. "Where does he want to talk to me and about what?"

"Here, at his office, at two o'clock?"

"I can make it. Is it business?"

"I — I imagine so, Mr. Puma. He only instructed me to arrange an appointment for this afternoon." She gave me the address.

"I'll be there," I assured her. "Thank you for calling."

I went back to the statements, and had addressed and sealed the hopelessly past due ones when my agent friend called back.

Jean Morley's brother, he informed me, worked at an auto body repair shop on Lincoln Boulevard and lived in Venice, in an apartment over a four car garage. He had both addresses for me.

"You're a noble man," I told him. "I hope I can repay you in kind, some day."

"We both do," he said. "What are you hounding this kid for?"

"I'm not. How do you know he's a kid?"

"One of my — informants told me he was on the sunny side of thirty. That's a kid to me. He also told me he served with John Haskell in the army. And with Haskell murdered and all, I thought you might have something I can sell to *Confidential*."

"Who served with John Haskell, Morley or your informant?"

"Morley. My informant served under Teddy Roosevelt. Is there a column item in this business, Joe?"

"Not yet," I said. "If there turns out to be, you'll be the first to know, of course."

"Good boy. Got to feed the dirt, you understand, if I expect to get plugs."

"I understand," I said. "Carry on."

On the sunny side of thirty? How could he be and still have fought in a war that had ended eleven years ago? If he had been only nineteen when that war had ended, he would be thirty now. Of course, there had been some young ones who had lied about their ages. And for combat, the powers that decide had preferred the young ones. John Haskell had had two years of combat.

One of John Haskell's patterns was forming.

3.

The fat bald man in the office said, "He's out on a call right now. He's due back soon, though, if you want to wait."

I said I'd wait. I sat on a bench in the bare office, listening to the pounding of the lead mallets on body steel from the shop and studying the three identical Monroe calendars that hung on the wall. Cigar smoke from the office mixed with the smell of acetylene from the shop and I thought about the war.

So you're a kid from nowhere and you meet a wheel from Hollywood in the service and get to be buddies and when the killing is over, you move out here and look up your old friend and even introduce him to your sister. And your sister falls for the big wheel and he is no longer the nice guy you knew. And your sister commits suicide, so you take one of those leaden hammers and look up your old, big wheel service buddy.

On the phone, the fat man was saying, "Sure, that's wholesale. What the hell did you think it was?

So, go to Acme. I'm crying for your business? Yeh? Well, I didn't get fat off you. I got fat off my wife's cooking, and she can stretch a buck from here to Topanga." He banged the receiver down, looked at me and shook his head.

"Another lost account," I said.

"Him? Hell, I've been talking worse than that to him for eighteen years. He'd think I was sick if I talked any other way."

I lighted a cigarette to combat his cigar. I said easily, "Has Arthur Morley been working for you long?"

"Five years. Good man. Real good man. He's not in any trouble, is he?"

"Not to my knowledge. How old is he?"

"Around thirty. He looks a lot younger, though. Before his sister died, he looked about eighteen. You a cop?"

"Private investigator," I answered. "I — do a lot of insurance work."

"Oh? The suicide clause, eh?"

"Not exactly," I said. "Arthur's sister was a lot younger than he was?"

"Five, six years, I'd guess. Pretty girl, if you like 'em skinny." He looked out toward the shop. "Morley just came in. You want to talk to him in here?"

"No need. I'll see him in the shop."

Arthur Morley was thin, like his sister had been. But he was taller and had light hair in a crew cut. I told him who I was and that I was investigating the death of John Haskell.

"For who?" he asked. "Who'd pay to find that out? He didn't have any friends."

"Weren't you a friend of his?"

"Not since my sister died. I didn't kill him, if that's why you're here. I thought of it, but what would it prove? I had all the killing I wanted in New Guinea."

"You served with Haskell there?"

"Under him. He was a first looie, a platoon leader. He was one hell of a fine soldier, too, I've got to admit. He lost some men, but never foolishly."

"That's the first nice thing I've heard about him today," I said. "When was the last time you saw him?"

"Four months ago, in a bar on Wilshire."

"I see. Where were you last night?"

"Bowling and then out for beers. I got a raft of guys that'll swear to that."

"Better get them alerted," I said. "There's a line the police can follow from a bartender to John Haskell to me to Miss McCrea and then to you. She told me you were in New Jersey, but I didn't believe her and I'm sure the police will check it."

"I'm not worried," he said.

"Miss McCrea has some strange new playmates, hasn't she? You ought to give her a serious talking to."

Arthur Morley shrugged. "She's old enough to know what she's doing. And nobody would call me a first–rate judge of character, not any more."

I could have asked him who his alibi friends were, but I wasn't too sure I was going to continue the search for Haskell's killer. When I did charity work, I had to have my heart in it. Haskell's death seemed less important than it had that morning.

It was past noon now and I was hungry. I drove over to the Santa Monica Pier for some sea food.

Actually, if that bartender had read the morning paper, the police should be almost on the same trail I had followed, but it would have started with me. Unless the bartender knew Lira McCrea. In which case, they would have started where I had started, with her.

I ate sea bass and thought back on my morning and ahead to my appointment with Arnie Roman. In the yacht basin, sails bellied and the fishing boats went out loaded. On the pier, the old men sat in the sun only half watching the bobbing floats on their lines.

The imitation red–head in the reception room told me that Mr. Roman would be free in a few minutes. I sat on a plastic upholstered chair and leafed through a copy of *Nugget*. There were some fine pictures in there; some were up to the trio on that body shop office wall.

In a few minutes a fat and expensively dressed man left Roman's office and the red–head smiled and told me I could go in now.

I went into a gray–carpeted office with dull gray walls and brightly colored drapes and upholstered furniture. It was more like a living room than an office. Above the desk, there was an expensively framed reproduction of Shahn's "Miners' Wives." Beneath the picture, Arnold Roman was rising to greet me.

He was a big man with blue–black jowls and gray–streaked black hair, beautifully tailored and well barbered. He had come a long way from the two dollar girls.

His brown eyes looked at me warmly. "Mr. Puma. I know you by reputation."

"And I you," I said.

His grip was firm and strong. Black hair curled on his wrists below the French cuffs.

He indicated a chair and I sat in it. He sat down and said, "You've been busy this morning, haven't you?"

"I try to keep busy. I suppose Miss McCrea phoned you?"

He nodded. "And that's why you're here."

I looked past him to the picture above his head. I asked, "Did you ever work in the mines, Mr. Roman?"

"For seven years," he said. "I started when I was thirteen. How did you know that?"

"I just couldn't figure any other way you'd be a Shahn collector. A picture like that can keep a man driving, can't it?"

He looked at me quizzically. "I didn't make the appointment to discuss art, Mr. Puma."

I said nothing more, meeting his gaze and waiting.

He leaned back in his chair and gave me the executive look. "A few evenings ago, you had some trouble with an employee of mine. This trouble centered around a man who was murdered this morning. I don't like my employees to get into trouble."

I said nothing.

"Certain officials in this town are looking for an excuse to persecute me."

"Persecute or prosecute?"

His face stiffened. "Are you trying to be funny, Mr. Puma?"

I nodded. "I guess I missed, huh? Mr. Arnold, there's a bartender who knows me and knew Haskell who will undoubtedly tell the police about your employee with the glass jaw. The police will eventually come to me and I'll have to send them to Miss McCrea and she will lead them to my opponent, if she has any sense left. So why am I here?"

Roman carefully straightened an ebony ink well on his desk. He said casually, "The bartender won't tell the police anything. And I would like to hire you to investigate Haskell's death."

"Why?"

"To clear my employee, if that's the way the chips fall. To pin the murder on him, if that happens to be the way it is. I don't like my men to — engage in outside — activities."

"I see. And why should he want to kill Haskell?"

"I've no idea. I doubt if he did. But he is in love with Miss McCrea and there is a remote possibility he may have gone over to work Haskell over a little and —" Roman shrugged.

I asked, "Did you know Haskell?"

"Not really. Miss McCrea told me she brought him to a party at my house one time, but I don't remember meeting him."

"A famous man like that — you'd remember, wouldn't you?"

Roman smiled. "The last movie I saw starred Tom Mix. I was twelve years old."

I sat and he sat. Neither of us said a word for seconds.

Then he said, "Business must be good, Mr. Puma. Don't you want my account?"

"Yes. Two things bother me. First of all, the police don't like private men investigating murder cases. I've done it before and got away with it, but I've never done it for a man the police don't like. That's the second thing that bothers me."

"Five hundred dollars minimum," he said, "And your regular rate."

"You're talking my language. And if I learn something, I take it to the police?"

"If you learn who killed John Haskell you take it to the police. If you learn anything that might damage me, you had better not."

"There's the bind," I said.

He said nothing, sitting quietly in his chair, staring at me without expression.

Finally, I said, "All right."

He must have known how I would answer. Because the check was all made out. He smiled, and slid it across the desk toward me. "Miss McCrea assured me you couldn't be bought."

"But I can be rented," I said. "I'll get right to work on it."

The name of Roman's employee was Krup. This information plus Krup's address and three separate small photographs of him and his fingerprint card were in the sealed envelope the red–head handed me when I stopped at her desk. Krup, Eddie Krup, age thirty–four, weight a hundred and ninety–six, height five feet nine, complexion ruddy. Kenmore Apartments, Hollywood.

What an efficient man was Arnie Roman. And what did he have against Eddie Krup? There was still time to make the bank with the check, but I decided against cashing it. If things started to smell, I might be glad I still had the chance to return that check.

Was I being conned? Was I being paid off? If I spent a couple of days on a wild goose chase, it would be kind of late for me to run to the police with my story of the saloon fight.

I knew a couple of detectives in the Santa Monica Department; one of them might throw me a bone. I caught one off duty and at home, out in the front yard seeding his lawn with dichondra. He wasn't on the case, but he knew about it. The police had very little, so far. It was the work of a man they were certain and he had used a hammer, but there had been no motive established. Two fingerprints, one of them bloody, were still unidentified.

I thought of telling him about Arthur Morley, but decided that could wait.

He said, "What's your interest in this, Joe?"

"I knew Haskell. I admired him very much before the war."

His smile was skeptical.

"How about the fingerprints?" I asked, "the unidentified ones? You couldn't have checked with Washington yet."

"Not yet. That bloody one should be the clincher if Washington has a record of it."

And if the bloody one was Arthur Morley's, I thought, Washington would have a record of it. All the boys in the service had been fingerprinted.

4.

The *Kenmore Plaza Apartments* in Hollywood was an old building in good repair, located half a block north of Sunset. I was nosing along, looking for a parking space, when I saw Lira McCrea stepping from a Chev Bel Air parked on the other side of the street. She was heading for the apartment building.

I slowed and let her get by before driving on to find a space half a block past the building. From here, I could watch the entrance in my rear vision mirror. It was possible that she was going up to see her monster for an afternoon tryst.

But it was also possible that she was coming here to tell him about me. I waited.

I didn't wait long. The girl came out again less than ten minutes later, and Krup was with her. They climbed into her car.

In my mirror, I saw the Chev swing into a driveway for a U-turn, which would bring them past me. I ducked low in the seat. They turned west at the corner and I followed in the flivver.

They were taking the trip I had taken this morning, to Lincoln Boulevard in Venice. Had Arthur Morley phoned her after my visit to him? I doubted it. She could be coming to warn him about me, or, more likely, she and Krup could be visiting him in order to determine the possibility of Arthur's guilt. Krup had his own neck to consider.

It was an easy car to follow; I gave them a constant three block lead. At the body shop, the Chev turned into the parking lot. I drove past and parked at the curb half a block down.

I walked back on the far side of the street. Through the show window of the shop office, I could see Lira talking to the fat proprietor. Krup still sat in the car.

And now Arthur Morley came out with Lira and they walked over to the car. It seemed like a good time for me to make my entrance; I walked across the street.

I came at the right time. Their voices were rising when I reached the curb and Krup had stepped from the car by the time I got to the lot.

He looked menacing, but I couldn't be sure he was threatening Morley. Possibly, I might have irritated him.

In a few seconds, Morley and Lira turned to look at me, too. I smiled as I came closer.

Eddie Krup said something to Lira, then more loudly to me, "It's a private conference, peeper."

"I'll wait," I said. "I want to talk with Morley." I looked at Lira. "I thought he was in New Jersey."

Her eyes were scornful. "I don't have to tell you anything, Mr. Puma."

"It would have been better if you had," I said. "Because now you'll have to tell it to the police."

Krup said, "Beat it. I know who you're working for and you won't be going to the police."

"Don't make book on it," I said. "I'll wait until you've finished talking with Morley."

Arthur Morley said, "They're through right now, whether they know it or not. What did you want, Mr. Puma?"

"I want to know why they're here," I said. "And I want to know anything else you know about Haskell's death."

He looked at me defiantly. "I don't know anything about Haskell's death. I told you that before and I just finished telling them that. Now I'm going back to work and I don't want to see any of you again."

Krup said, "Take it easy, Morley. We haven't finished."

Arthur Morley turned his back on them and started for the office. Krup took two steps and reached a heavy hand out to spin the kid around.

Here I was, fighting Krup for somebody else again. I moved in, reached my own hand out for his shoulder — and he turned very neatly while I was off balance.

He hooked a clean left into my gut and caught me high on the cheek with a right. I brought over the big right hand from hip level, but it never got home. He tagged me like a professional, smack on the button, and I went down.

Well, you can't win 'em all.

I was drowning. The wave had been too high and the surf board too narrow. I took a deep gulp of the salt water and discovered it wasn't salty.

There was parking lot gravel in my hair and a numbness from my temple to the point of my chin. The sun was out again and I was propped in a sitting position up against the front bumper of a car. The fat proprietor stood in front of me, an empty bucket of water in his hand.

"You could have waited," I said. "There wasn't any time–keeper. I'd have come out of it without the water."

He said apologetically, "In the movies, they always use a bucket of water. What the hell, I'm not the Red Cross."

My shirt, jacket and the upper part of my trousers were soaked. To the left of the fat man, Arthur Morley looked down at me without expression.

"Did they leave?" I asked him.

He nodded. "You've been out for almost three minutes."

I climbed shakily to my feet and rubbed the back of my neck. "Last time we met, he was easy. I guess I was overconfident."

Morley's voice was quiet. "You know who he works for? For Arnold Roman. Man, you're on borrowed time, right now."

The fat man said, "Well, somebody has to work around here. Make it as quick as you can, Art; we're way behind." He left.

I said, "You can't think of me as a friend, I suppose? But I could have thrown your name to the law. Really, I tried to play ball with you, boy."

He said evenly, "I can't tell you what I don't know. And I don't know who killed John Haskell. If you want the names of the guys I bowled with, I'll give 'em to you."

"Give 'em to me," I said.

In the office, he wrote down the names of three men and copied their addresses out of the phone book. As he handed me the slip, he asked, "Are you going to tell the police about me?"

"Not yet. Maybe never." I didn't tell him that if his fingerprint was the bloody one, I wouldn't have to tell the police. They'd have him.

I went home and changed my clothes and then phoned Arnold Roman. I told him, "Your boy Krup just won a return engagement. And he seems to be investigating this murder himself. Are those your orders?"

"No."

"And he says he knows who hired me. How could he know that?"

"Did he say he knew it was me?"

"No, he just said he knew."

"He was lying. It was a tactical lie. Stay with it, Puma."

"Right." I hung up.

I wondered if Arnold Roman had lied to me. He, like all the hoodlums who owned Las Vegas, had an air of semi–respectability now. The so–called solid citizens had accepted the legality of Las Vegas and thus by implication accepted the hoodlums who were getting fat off the town. And this trash was coming into Los Angeles and buying into legitimate businesses, adding to their stature.

They were still hoodlums and Roman could right this minute be playing me for a patsy. He might have hired me for that reason. There was a strong possibility that I had made a bad decision.

So what was preventing me from giving him his money back and taking the whole sorry mess to the police?

Nothing was preventing me, really, nothing but my avarice.

I was hanging my wet jacket on a hanger in the kitchen, having decided to have dinner at home, when somebody rang my doorbell. A number of innocent people often ring my doorbell, but I took the .38 from the dresser drawer before going to the door. I kept it in a pocket, my hand on it.

A youth of about twenty stood there. He wore cotton gabardine trousers of a dirty tan and a checked gingham sport shirt.

"Mr. Joe Puma?" he asked.

I nodded.

"My name is Duane Putnam. Can I come in?"

Duane Putnam, indeed. He must have lifted it from an old theatre program. I held the door open wider and he came in, warily, like a cat in a new neighborhood, and stood not far from the doorway.

"What's on your mind, Duane?" I asked.

"Murder," he said.

They get that from TV, these cryptic, monosyllabic answers.

"Whose murder?" I asked.

He took a breath and said, "John Haskell's."

I said nothing, waiting for him to go on.

He took another breath. "I couldn't go to the police. I've had a — a little trouble myself, so I couldn't go to them. But I saw this guy, see, and I had to tell somebody —"

"What guy?"

"The guy that killed Haskell. I mean, I saw a guy leave there, last night, and he was carrying a thing that looked like a hammer, and he was sneaking along the empty lot next to the motel, and —"

"Hold it a second," I said. "Who sent you to me?"

He stared, discomfited. He looked toward the door. Finally, he said, "I was walking along Lincoln Boulevard a little while ago and I saw the guy, the same guy that came out of the motel last night."

"Where did you see him?"

"At that auto glass shop there, in the parking lot. He was with that blonde in the Chev Bel Air. I saw him hit you, so when you left, I followed. The way those guys in the shop talked to you, I figured you were a cop, so I asked them, and they told me who you were."

"You asked them and still picked up my trail? Duane, do you want to start over and make it reasonable this time?"

"Phone 'em," he said. "Right now, go ahead. Ask 'em." His face was grim. "Phone the glass shop, go ahead."

"It wasn't a glass shop; it was a body shop," I corrected him. "Sit down. I'll phone them."

I phoned them and Arthur Morley answered. I asked him if Duane Putnam had talked to him about me.

"I don't know what the guy's name is," Morley told me, "but some young fellow came over right after you left and asked if you were a cop. I told him you were a private detective."

"Okay, Arthur, thank you," I said.

I hung up and studied Duane Putnam. I said, "I guess that part of it wasn't a lie. But the rest sure as hell was and you're making a serious mistake, lying about anything as important as murder. Duane, what kind of trouble did you have with the law?"

"That's not important."

"Yes, it is. Are you running from the law now?"

He shook his head.

"All right, then," I said, "I want you to tell the police what you told me."

He shook his head again.

"Be reasonable," I said patiently. "If we hope to convict the man, you'll have to go into court and point a finger. Otherwise, why did you bring me this information? Don't you want the man punished for his crime?"

He nodded. "I already pointed a finger. Aren't you a good enough detective to get the rest?"

"No, and neither are the police. There isn't any kind of police grilling that can break down a man like Eddie Krup. He's undoubtedly been through it all before, time and again. Duane, I insist that you go to the police with me, right now."

For the third time, he shook his head. And this time, he said, "No!"

"Yes," I said, and took out the .38.

His eyes went from the gun to my eyes and he smiled. "You wouldn't shoot me."

"If you try to leave, I will."

Again he looked warily at the door and then at me. His gaze dropped to the gun and he smiled once more. Maybe he wanted to get shot.

In any event, he broke for the door. He'd pegged me right; I didn't even aim the gun. I tried to intercept him before he got through the door, but he was too fast for me. He was nearly out the front door when I got to the head of the steps.

By the time I got to the door, a chopped and channeled '34 Ford coupe was gunning away from the curb in front. I didn't have anything that would catch that, nor could I read the license number from where I stood.

5.

I went back to my apartment and got the dossier on Eddie Krup that Roman had given me. I took the fingerprint card out of the envelope and drove back to the house of my Santa Monica Department friend.

He was still planting dichondra.

There was no name on the card. I gave it to him and said, "Check that against the bloody fingerprint you found. If it matches, phone me, and I'll give you the man's name."

"Why not give it to me, now?" he asked.

"I'm private, remember? P–r–i–v–a–t–e."

"You're also a citizen," he said. "I hope."

"A better citizen than you imagine."

I left him glowering and drove back to the poor man's edge of Beverly Hills. The Chev Bel Aire was at the curb; I wondered if Eddie Krup was also there.

Eddie was there all right. Lira McCrea came to the door and beyond her I could see Eddie sitting on a studio couch.

"Now, what?" she asked.

"I came back for the rubber match with your fat boy friend," I told her. "I don't think he's that good."

"Get out of here," she said, "before I call the police."

"You'd better check with Eddie before you phone," I said. "He doesn't want any law here, I'll bet you."

From behind her, Krup said, "Let the slob come in. He doesn't scare me."

She opened the door wider and I came in. Krup didn't move from the studio couch.

"Do either of you know a Duane Putnam?" I asked.

Lira shook her head.

Krup said, "I've seen him play with the Rams. What the hell has he got to do with this mess?"

That's where I'd heard the name. The kid had picked it up from the sport pages. I said, "I don't mean that Putnam. I guess the man who approached me used a pseudonym."

Krup laughed and shook his head. "Dick Tracy. Oh, man, you are a cute one."

"Easy, shorty," I said. "Don't let that lucky punch give you delusions of grandeur. This man claims he saw you leave John Haskell's motel after Haskell was murdered. You were carrying a hammer and sneaking through that empty lot next to the motel."

Lira looked at Krup meaningfully.

Krup was sitting erectly now, interest in his face. "A man or a kid?" he asked.

"Never mind that. Eddie, if you did kill Haskell, you won't get any protection from where you might expect it. And if you didn't, but know something, you'd be very wise to tell me."

"Drop dead," he said. "What'd this Putnam look like?"

I took a card from my pocket. I read off a telephone number and said, "Phone that number and ask if you should cooperate with me."

"That's Roman's number," he said quietly.

"You should know it."

Krup looked at Lira and then back at me. "It's not a private number," he said. "Anybody can look up a phone number. When I get orders to cooperate with you, I will. So long, peeper."

"It's your decision," I said. "You wouldn't want to come outside for a title fight, would you? My vanity is suffering."

"I've got more important things to do," he told me. "Look, if this kid saw me, why didn't he take it to the police? Chew on that and see what you come up with."

"I didn't say he was a kid."

"So long," he said. "Don't lead with your chin."

I didn't bother to answer. I went out quietly.

So, Krup knew he was a kid. So, Lira had taken Krup in her car over to see Arthur Morley. That would indicate the death of John Haskell came from the Morley side of her life, not the Roman side. They were worried, no doubt, and that could mean Eddie was guilty. It could also mean Eddie would get dumped by Roman if enough suspicion for Haskell's death should be centered on Eddie.

For a man in Eddie's line of work, being dumped by Arnold Roman certainly wouldn't enhance his employment chances with other employers in Roman's field. So it could be the loss of Eddie's job that was bothering him, not the loss of his neck.

Duane Putnam … In my mind, I heard Eddie's laugh again and I could feel myself blushing. Duane Putnam had seen Eddie Krup leave the motel with a hammer in his hand. With a hammer in his hand … Had there been anything in the papers about a hammer? I couldn't remember.

An item like that might very well be kept from the papers, because it could be a valuable item to use in a lie detector test and its value would be lost if it was an item of common knowledge.

I phoned my Santa Monica detective friend. He asked me to phone back in ten minutes; he'd find out what I wanted to know.

I phoned back in ten minutes and he told me the hammer item hadn't been given to the papers and it had been withheld from them deliberately, just as I had guessed. And it was still a secret and had better remain so or I might wind up working on a parking lot.

"You might, too," I said. "None of us are really versatile, are we?"

"No, but some of us are bright," he said.

I hung up and went out to the flivver. What did I have? This much: the man who called himself Putnam knew a hammer had been used. He didn't want to go to the police. He did want to pin the crime on Eddie Krup.

Now why would he want to do that? Either he had seen someone leave with a hammer or he had left with the hammer himself. But if he was the killer, why had he come to me? His bright move would be to get out of town, as far from this town as possible — unless he had relatives here, or friends who might be suspicious of his leaving. Maybe he was still living at home. Why had I thought he wasn't?

Back now. Why would he want to pin the crime on Eddie Krup?

Two reasons came quickly to my mind, to divert suspicion from himself or from a friend.

And who could his friend be? Elementary, Watson. I only had two real suspects. I drove back to Venice, to an apartment over a four–car garage, the home address the agent had given me.

I went up the outside steps and knocked on the door. I could hear music inside, and it sounded like it was coming from some very expensive hi–fi equipment. It was George Shearing's music.

Arthur Morley came to the door and looked at me wearily. "God," he said. "You, again. Look, Mr. Puma, I've had a hell of a day at the shop and I came home to relax. Can't you give me a break?"

"A man's been killed," I said.

"A lot of men have been killed. I killed over nineteen myself. And got a medal for it. Over half of my platoon was killed and all of them were better men than John Haskell."

"Maybe," I said. "But not better soldiers, I'll bet."

"The war's over," he said. "It's been over for eleven years."

"I'll bet he was a disciplinarian," I said. "I'll bet a lot of you guys hated his guts."

"Whose guts?"

"John Haskell's. *Lieutenant* John Haskell's."

Arthur Morley looked at me doubtfully. "So?"

"Let's go inside," I suggested, "where we can talk."

He shrugged and stepped aside and I came in. It was a roomy and comfortable apartment and I could see the ocean from the western windows of the room I was in. Roomy and comfortable and cheap; that's the kind of place you can get in Venice if you're not class conscious.

Shearing changed to Wallen. This man must love the piano, I thought. I asked, "Got any Tatum?"

"I got all the Tatum there is. Sit down, I'll bring you a beer."

He brought me a frosted can of eastern beer and I sat down in a comfortable canvas and wrought iron chair. He stretched out on what looked like a home–made couch, wide and long and low. To a man who had killed nineteen, the death of John Haskell was probably not very important. Otherwise, I was sure he wasn't completely dispassionate.

"Some life," I said. "I'll bet you have fun, single and handsome and right next to the beach."

"I'm not kicking. What's on your mind, Mr. Puma?"

"A kid," I said. "A kid who calls himself Duane Putnam."

"Never heard of him."

"Not under that name, I'm sure. He probably just gave it to me on the spur of the moment. It's the name of a football player."

"Oh. Why did he give you a phony name?"

"To protect himself. He also told me he saw me in front of an auto glass shop. He meant the place you work."

"We're not a glass shop; we're a body shop."

"I know that, and so did the kid. But he figured, in his story book detective way, that if he made a mistake like that, I wouldn't be inclined to guess he knew you."

Silence, and then, "What makes you think it was a *deliberate* mistake?"

"Any kid that can chop and channel and soup a '34 flivver knows a body shop from a glass shop. This kid also knew what kind of weapon Haskell was killed with."

Arthur Morley stretched and his voice was tired. "What kind was it?"

"I'm not permitted to tell you that. Do you know the boy, Arthur?"

"No."

"Then why should he want to protect you?"

"I don't need protection. I don't know him."

"And I don't think he even saw me in front of the shop," I went on. "I think he found out from you what had happened. Did you phone him after I left? I could ask your boss if the kid was a witness to my knockout. I can do it now."

"You think I'm lying? Why should I lie?"

"To protect him. To protect him from a conviction of murder, just as he tried to protect you from the suspicion of murder. He's a buddy of yours, isn't he?"

"I don't hang around with nineteen year old kids," he said. And then he was suddenly silent and I could hear him breathe.

"I didn't mention his age," I said. "Where is he, Arthur?"

"Finish your beer and beat it. Go to the police with your crazy story. I don't give a damn. I'm clean, *clean* ..."

I sipped my beer. "The kid must have been eight years old when the war ended. So that couldn't be the reason. He sure as hell wasn't in the war."

Arthur Morley closed his eyes and said nothing.

"The police have a fingerprint," I said. "A *bloody* fingerprint. It's just a question of time. What is the kid, psychopathic or something? Is he your brother?"

Morley's voice was soft. "Did Haskell ever get to you with that pattern kick of his, that pre–determination jag he was on?"

"A little."

Morley sat up. "I need a beer. Then I'll give you a silly pattern to chew on, an eleven year pattern."

He got himself a beer and came back to sit on the edge of the low, wide couch.

He told me the story of Patsy Lankowski, private in the platoon commanded by Lieutenant John Haskell. Patsy was a sorehead and a grumbler, but quite possibly the best combat scout in the 32nd Division and John Haskell knew it. Patsy got all the dirty assignments, but never a rating beyond PFC.

And home in Waukesha, Wisconsin, Patsy's mother got his growling letters, complaining of the persecution his Lieutenant was inflicting on him, and swearing that if he ever came out of this thing alive, he would look up the good lieutenant and give him the pasting of his life.

And more than once, he had added that if he didn't come out of this thing alive, Lieutenant John Haskell would be to blame, and he wanted the world to know it.

"And Patsy didn't come out of it alive?" I asked.

Arthur Morley smiled. "Sure he did. He's selling insurance in Iowa, right this minute. I just used that name, another member of our sad platoon. The guy who really hated Haskell and really wrote the letters home, his name wasn't Lankowski and he didn't live in Waukesha, Wisconsin. But he had a brother, and the brother reads the letters that had been written to his mother."

"And held a grudge for eleven years? He *must* be psychopathic." I finished the beer. "This man, of course, didn't come out of the war alive."

Morley said, "He died on a patrol. He hadn't volunteered for the patrol. The mother didn't show her other son the letters. But when she died, a month ago, the brother found them."

"And he came out here," I guessed, "looking up the men from his big brother's platoon. And from you, he got the story of the further adventures of Lieutenant John Haskell. And from comic books, he got some distorted ideas of justice and vengeance. Where is he now, Arthur?"

He smiled and shook his head.

"My God," I said, "John Haskell was murdered. What kind of man are you?"

"A 32nd Division kind," he said. "Murder is nothing new to us. Where were you when all that was going on?"

"In the 7th Division," I said. "Maybe you've heard of them?"

"I've heard of them," he admitted quietly, "and I apologise."

"And you're a citizen now," I reminded him. "You're not a soldier or a professional veteran or a judge or the swift arm of vengeance. You're a citizen, quite possibly the most important thing a man can ever be."

He shook his head. *"The most important thing a man can be is a friend.* I learned that the hard way. And there aren't enough cops in this world to ever make me anything less than that." He stood up. "I told you this to get you off the kid's neck. I figured you weren't the law and would listen to reason."

"I'm the law," I said. "Sit down; I want to check your closets."

"Why?"

"To see if the kid's clothes are here. He's been staying with you, hasn't he?"

"I don't know what you're talking about," he said. "If you want to look around, come back with a warrant."

"Don't mess with me, Arthur," I said. I started for the bedroom.

He came over to stand in front of the open bedroom doorway. "You're going to have to fight your way in here."

"Don't be ridiculous," I said.

"You've forgotten my sister," he said. "What about her?"

"I'm sorry about her. But a man's been killed. If that isn't important to you, you never learned anything, in New Guinea or any place else. Stand aside. This is the last warning."

"Start swinging," he said, and lifted his hands.

He'd killed nineteen men, but that had been with a rifle. I could have hit him five times while he drew back his right hand. I only hit him once, clean and neat and on the button and I caught him as he fell, lowered him gently to the floor.

I have a lot of respect for 32nd Division men. And I saw the shadow in the bedroom and then the fury hit me as I came through the door. And this one bit and clawed and used his knees and grunted and used words no nineteen year old should know.

But I subdued him, finally, and dragged him with me to hold while I phoned the Santa Monica Police.

In the neat office of the Chief, Sergeant Koski glowered and chewed his lower lip and the Mayor frowned and the Chief looked at all of us blandly. He was the bland type, fat and smug.

Koski said, "The fingerprint matches. The kid's ready to confess, anyway."

"What's his name?" I asked.

"Lestre Burkholtz. German kid. He's from Eau Claire, Wisconsin."

"And what've you got against Arthur Morley, Chief?" I asked with a sneer.

The Mayor said, "Don't be insolent, Joe. Chief Roeder is simply trying to do his duty."

"That's all I want from him is his duty," I said. "I did mine. I came in with a killer, didn't I? I could have turned him over to the Los Angeles Police; I picked him up in Venice, and that would make him their baby. I brought him here because I thought maybe Arthur Morley would get a break. And I'm staying until he does."

Chief Roeder smiled his smug smile. "Mr. Puma, I run the police department here. And in Santa Monica, we don't toy with accessories to murder. In Santa Monica, we like everything tied up neat and clean."

I looked at him pityingly. I said, "And I'm going to sit in Santa Monica until you change your mind or your district attorney is going to look awful silly in court when I tell the jury Morley wasn't even home when I picked up Burkholtz."

The Mayor said, "You'd perjure yourself? Joe, I thought you were a citizen?"

"I am," I said. "But I'm something almost as important, too. I'm a friend. God forbid I should have to explain that word to a politician."

There was a lot of hemming and hawing and political double talk after that, but it was meaningless and we all knew it. At seven–thirty, Arthur and I stood on the front steps of that big, new municipal building, looking out toward the ocean.

The ocean made me think of eternity which, in turn, brought the late John Haskell to mind. In spite of all that I had recently learned about the man, my feeling at the moment wasn't harsher than pleasant reminiscence.

"Patterns," I said. "What do you think, Arthur? You think the individual can get away from a pattern?"

Arthur shrugged. "Don't know if I get what you mean."

"Skip it," I told him.

"After what you just did for me, I'll go along with anything you say."

I smiled and we went down the steps together, arm in arm.

Don't Crowd Your Luck

He looked like an honest man. His tailoring didn't match his face; the tailoring looked expensive. His face matched one I'd seen in the public prints quite often, I was sure, but my memory wouldn't bring up the name.

He said, "What am I? A fair–to–middling mechanic and first–rate lube man and all right on the drive, too. But this new life, frankly, has me beat, Mr. Puma."

"New life?" I asked.

"That's right. Don't you know who I am?"

"Your face is familiar," I admitted, "but I've been trying to remember why, Mr. Hogue. Do you have another name?"

He shook his head. "The face should be familiar; it's the same face Randall Crowther had forty years ago."

"That's it," I said. "Hell yes." And then it hit me. Hogue, Hogue ... I said, "You married his widow."

"Crowther left her eighty–two million. Wouldn't you marry her?"

I smiled. "You beat me to it, Mr. Hogue. Now tell me what can trouble a man who has just married an attractive widow with eighty–two million dollars."

"Her friends," he said. "And she's not as attractive as she was in the old days."

In the old days she'd been a child star. She would be about 40 now, and Crowther had been 76 when he died. Hogue had run a service station near one of their mountain retreats, I now remembered. The papers hadn't played up the resemblance; this new marriage was supposed to have been love, love, love ...

I said, "You're not considering divorce, Mr. Hogue? I don't handle divorce work."

He looked at me bleakly. "Divorce? Seventeen years I pumped gas and salted away twelve hundred bucks. Now I marry a woman with millions. Divorce?"

"I guess I wasn't very bright. Why are you here?"

"Because I heard you were an honest man. That's not a real standard thing in your trade, is it?"

"Not at my level. But the big agencies are fairly honest."

"I tried one," he said. "They looked too smooth and slick for me. I'm a plain man, Mr. Puma."

"I see. Who recommended me?"

"Art Morley. He works in that auto–body shop on Lincoln Boulevard."

"Oh, yes. And why do you need a private investigator?"

He looked at the top of my desk. "Maybe I don't. Some things have happened, but they could be just gags. Maybe it's just a — well, a feeling I have."

"Mmm–hmm. Could it be a feeling of insecurity? I mean, you never had quite this much to lose before, did you?"

"I never had anything to lose. No, it's got nothing to do with that. Matter of fact, here's a sample of what's been happening." He reached into an inner jacket pocket and brought out an envelope. He threw it on my desk.

It was a Beverly Hills postmark four days old. There was a typed note inside. I read:

Rube:
> *Why don't you get out while you're still in one piece? Don't crowd your luck.*

The note was unsigned. I said, "Have you shown this to the police?"

He shook his head. "I don't want no publicity. We've had too much already."

"At your new level," I suggested, "the police can be very discreet."

He shook his head and said nothing.

I asked, "Does anyone you know call you 'Rube'?"

"Not to my face. And here's something else: we got a post office box and an unlisted phone number. How'd this character know where to send that letter?"

"There are people," I told him, "who specialize in unlisted phone numbers and addresses. Did you get any threats by phone?"

"Two. Sounded like a man's voice, but I couldn't even be sure of that."

"And you want me to investigate?"

"How could you? A one–man office — where would you begin? No, I figured you ought to move in with us. Not as a private eye, of course. You could be an old buddy, a guy I went to high school with back in Eau Claire."

"I see," I said, though I didn't. "Would your wife approve of that, do you think?"

He looked at me steadily. "I wear the pants in the house."

Well, a bodyguard ... Behind me, a shade flapped gently in the afternoon breeze from the ocean. A service station operator who'd looked like a former husband and the widow had fallen for him. Luckily, she was a *rich* widow. But I liked this George Hogue; he was a plain man, like I am.

"What are you thinking about?" he asked. "You afraid my credit's no good?" He smiled.

I smiled, too. "No, I was trying to look honest, as though I was trying to arrive at a fair price. But I'll probably soak you."

"No, you won't," he said. "Art told me you were a straight guy. He thinks a lot of you, Mr. Puma."

"I kept him out of jail. Well, all right, Mr. Hogue. Seventy–two dollars a day should handle it."

"That's a pretty good hourly rate," he said.

"Not for twenty–four hours. And not in Beverly Hills."

He chuckled. "I guess you're right at that. They sure put it on around here, don't they?"

"Without even knowing it," I said. "I'll go home and get some clothes."

It wasn't too big a house for this little village — about five or six bathrooms and as many bedrooms, and a living–room not much larger than the Coliseum. George had introduced me under my real name as his old deer–hunting buddy from Eau Claire and the maid had shown me to my room, which flanked the bridal chambers.

Linda Hogue was obviously beyond her child–star days, but a very attractive woman for all that. The late and apparently unlamented Randall Crowther had been from Texas and in oil. There was a possibility he had been as rough a diamond as her current master and that might explain the warmth of her reception for that old deer–hunting buddy, Joe Puma.

I have never been to Eau Claire, but a hell of a lot of rubes come out of Texas.

I was sitting near the window, estimating the acreage below, when there was a knock at the door.

I said, "Come in," and Linda Hogue came in.

She was smiling as she said, "You're not from Eau Claire."

"I could easily be."

She nodded. "But you're not. You've done some work for Anthony Ellers, haven't you?"

Anthony Ellers was a lawyer who got a lot of the carriage trade. I said nothing.

Linda Hogue came over to sit in a chair nearby, "What's bothering George?"

"I'm not sure. It could be the eighty–two million dollars."

She sighed. "That was a newspaper figure, a *Los Angeles* newspaper figure. There's about three million in the whole estate — if it's properly disposed of."

I still said nothing.

She said, "I love him. I love him very much. He's a sincere and honest man. Why are you here?"

"I'd prefer that you asked your husband that."

"I will. I suppose, to maintain the illusion, I had better call you 'Joe'."

"I suppose," I said. "That's the name on my birth certificate."

A silence, and then she said, "You don't really tell much, do you?"

"I'm lost in the magic of your calling me 'Joe'," I told her. "Very few people who make more than eighty a week would be that democratic."

She rose. "Insolent, too, aren't you?" She looked down at me patronizingly. "Puma — is that, an Italian name?"

"Yes'm," I said. "There are three Italian families in Eau Claire. We were the wealthiest."

She continued to stare at me and then the smile came back. "We can be friends, can't we, Joe?"

I nodded and returned her smile. "Any friend of George's is a friend of mine, Ma'am."

She stalked out.

I sat where I was and finally estimated the lawns and patio and tennis courts and swimming pool should add up to about seven and a half acres. That's a good–sized lot, even in Beverly Hills.

In a few minutes George came in and said, "How about a session in the pool? Got lots of trunks, all sizes."

"I brought a pair," I told him. "I'll meet you down there."

It wasn't a bad way to earn seventy–two dollars a day. It was a hundred–foot pool with both high and low boards. But George confessed to me it wasn't up to the stone quarry where he had learned to swim.

Around five o'clock some of Linda's friends came for cocktails. Unless they were new friends, her former husband must have favored younger people. Because most of this gang seemed to be in their middle thirties.

George had always worked for a living; it was hard to tell how old he was. But he was no butterfly and this kind of people was alien to him.

We showered, dressed, then joined them. A few martinis made us all brothers and sisters. Gin is the stuff for eroding veneer. By dinner time we were one big happy family.

After dinner some more people drifted in and one of them was Anthony Ellers. He was the attorney Mrs. Hogue had mentioned, the one I'd done some work for.

He cornered me at the bar next to the patio about an hour after he'd arrived. He asked, "What's going on, Joe?"

"A party. What do you mean?"

"What are you doing here?"

"Eating and drinking. I wish somebody would suggest dancing — I've got a yen for that imitation red–head."

He looked insufferably patient. "You're being cute, Joe. You're here pro–fessionally, aren't you?"

I lied with a shake of the head. "I'm a friend of George's. We're both from Eau Claire."

He took an audible breath. "You can trust me, Joe. I'm a confidant of the family."

I smiled at him. "That's good. Then they can tell you what I'm doing here."

His face became stiff with controlled annoyance. He said carefully, "I wouldn't want to think that George Hogue might be planning something tricky. Mrs. Crowther married him against my advice, you understand? Through some trick of her emotions, she believed marrying a man who resembled Randall Crowther might bring back the happiness she knew with Crowther. I intend to protect her even against her emotions."

"She looks happy," I remarked. "And one question, Tony —"

He glared. "Ask it."

"Would you worry just as much about her if she were poor?"

He sipped his drink. "I wouldn't have had any reason to meet her if she'd been poor." He turned his back on me.

Well, well ... The man could be emotionally involved himself, and I didn't blame him. I remembered George telling me in my office that his wife wasn't as attractive as she had been in her younger days. He was wrong about that; it was the one thing I was sure both Ellers and I would agree on.

George might not be enough of a connoisseur to appreciate the superior flavor of ripe fruit.

Twenty minutes later somebody suggested dancing and I forgot George and Ellers and Mrs. Hogue. I danced with the red–head and learned there was nothing imitation about her. She showed me how the red ran true to the scalp line and explained that her hair was the kind of red the imitation red–heads favored. That's why my snap judgment had been wrong.

Her name was Mary Brennan and she worked for a custom furniture wholesaler and she was a friend of Linda Crowther Hogue's. She was single.

"Who brought you here?" I asked.

She had come with a married couple, the Pattersons.

We made a complete and graceful circuit of the patio, and she asked, "Who did you come with?"

"Alone," I said. "Somehow I sensed you'd be here."

We made another half–circuit, and she said, "That should have been 'whom', shouldn't it? I should have asked with *whom* you came?"

"I guess." Her fragrance was clean and cool.

"I'm illiterate, more or less," she went on musingly. "And poor. Are you poor, too?"

"Does it matter on a night like this? We don't get many nights like this."

She sighed. "The poor ones always favor me. Linda and Beth always attracted the wealthy boys."

"Who's Beth?" I asked.

"Linda's sister, her younger sister. Beth and I were friends at school."

"What school?"

"North Hollywood High. Why did you have to ask that? Couldn't you have assumed it meant college, and preferably some swank eastern female college? Won't you leave me even my implied superiority?"

"I will. Tonight we will maintain an illusion. You went to some swank eastern school and I just bought the controlling interest in General Motors. Did you know Mr. Crowther very well?"

"Fairly well. He looked like an older edition of George."

"This was his first marriage, was it?"

"That's right. He used to tell Linda he'd been waiting all his life for her. He was past fifty when they met. Why do you want to talk about him?"

"He intrigues me. He had a reputation for being a very interesting character. Linda must have loved him, to marry his twin."

"She must have. Are you pumping me?"

"Not intentionally. Would you like another drink?"

She said she would, and I went over to the bar for a pair of them. The Hogues were there, talking to Ellers, and George winked at me.

"Making out all right, buddy?" he asked.

"Fine. It's a wonderful party, George. We never had it like this in Eau Claire, did we?"

He laughed. "Never."

Mrs. Hogue and Ellers didn't seem to think that was very funny. Their smiles were no more than polite.

It wasn't too important; Mary Brennan was waiting for her drink, and *her* smile was warm.

At two o'clock there was a general exodus. At two thirty George came into the living–room where I was having a final end–of–the–day jolt of his expensive booze.

He plopped down on the sofa next to me and sighed happily. He yawned and said, "People are mostly okay if you get some liquor into 'em, aren't they?"

"Some people. How long did you live in Eau Claire, George?"

"About ten years. My ten happy years. Why?"

"I just wondered. Where were you born?"

"Phoenix. My mother died there. My dad died there, in a mine cave–in two months before I was born. When my mother died, I was eight. My aunt in Eau Claire sent for me then. Wonderful woman." He stretched. "What's on your mind, Joe?"

"A pattern," I said. "I wondered why my life didn't lead me to a home like this."

He chuckled. "You got to get married, first. And not to that red–head. She's a working girl."

He rose, stretched again. "Well, I'll see you in the morning. How about a dip before breakfast?"

"If breakfast is late enough," I told him.

I went to bed thinking about George Hogue and fell asleep to dream about Mary Brennan.

Breakfast was pool–side, as they say, in the morning. Neither of the Hogues looked as hungover as I felt; Mrs. Hogue looked particularly bright–eyed and healthy. She told us she had planned some shopping for today; we would have to entertain ourselves.

George asked, "How about some golf, Joe? You play it?"

"Not well, but often," I assured him. "Could we rest for a few hours, first?"

"You can rest on the course," he said. "We'll get one of those electric carts."

We went to the Canyon Country Club, which is no place for dubs. The entire course is within the confines of the canyon and there is a barranca threading through it at the most inopportune places.

I do love to belt them off the tees, and on the public courses I usually played this was no handicap. At Canyon the straight shot was the sane shot.

We had a combination bet of a dollar Nassau and two bits a hole on top of that. At the twelfth tee George was already into me for two dollars and a half. On the wages he was paying me I figured I could afford that much.

The twelfth is a straightaway fairway with the barranca just in front of the green. I figured it for a good belt off the tee and perhaps a number eight iron over the barranca. With only seven holes left, I thought it was time to play a little more strategically.

"Take the honors," he said. "Maybe it will change your luck."

I went to the back of the cart for my driver — and suddenly bark and splinters stung my face from a eucalyptus tree near the cart. George yelped and reached for his shoulder as the sound of the shot came from the rim of the canyon above.

Silence, as George stared at me, and then he said, "It's just a nick. He missed."

"Duck behind the cart," I said. "I'm going up there."

"You're not armed. Don't be crazy —"

"It's my job," I said. "Damn it, George, get behind that cart!"

He ducked as I started up the slope through the chaparral. Above me I could see a man running out from behind some brush, a rifle in his hand. He was heading for an empty lot between two houses.

He wasn't in sight when I reached the rim. From the street beyond, I heard the sound of a motor starting and I ran that way. I got to the curb just in time to see a green and white car turn out of sight at the next intersection.

On the front lawn next door a girl about seven had set up a lemonade stand. I asked her, "Did you see that man who got into the car?"

She nodded. "He was carrying a gun." Her blue eyes were wide.

"What'd he look like, honey?"

"Mean," she said. "Would you like a five cent glass or a two cent glass?"

George was now coming through the empty lot. I said, "I'd like a five cent glass. Do you think your mommy would let me use the phone?"

She nodded. "Aren't you going to buy a glass for your friend?"

I gave her a dime and went up to the house. From the phone there, I told Sergeant Pascal that we'd meet him at the Canyon clubhouse. He's from the west side station and this would be his baby.

The bullet had scarcely broken the skin as it nicked George and gone on into the tree. But the lady of the house insisted on putting a Band–Aid on it.

She said, "One of those boys with a .22 rifle, I'll bet. It's not the first time they've shot down into that canyon." She shook her head sadly. "Today's children —"

This had been no .22; they don't make as much noise as I'd heard from the canyon top. George and I went down again to the twelfth tee and then back to the clubhouse.

Pascal was already there. His thin and sour bloodhound face showed nothing as I related the entire story, including the anonymous threatening letter and the phone calls.

When I'd finished, he looked at George. "You've told the Beverly Hills police about these threats, of course."

George shook his head. "I figured I had enough publicity already. Linda and I don't need any more ink."

"I see. You assumed a private operative would be better than professional men, is that it?"

"Not necessarily better," George answered. "Quieter."

Pascal looked between us in his impersonal way and then said, "We're digging out the bullet now. Then I'm going up to see that little girl who was selling lemonade. I'll be back and we'll go to the station together. Wait here."

He went out toward the first tee.

George sighed. "Cops — aren't they the big ones?"

"He was right, George. You should have gone to the Beverly Hills police after the first threat."

"Maybe. Look, he said to wait, but he didn't say we had to wait dry. Let's have a drink."

"Fine," I said. "You don't seem very nervous, George."

"Maybe I don't show it, but I'm nervous all right. Who the hell do you think it could be, Joe?"

I shrugged and asked, "Is there something you should have told me and didn't when you came looking for a bodyguard? Is there someone you've wronged, somewhere? Or even someone who might think you wronged them?"

He frowned. "I sure as hell can't think of anybody — at least, anybody I made mad enough to want to murder me."

I said softly, "George, this is a community property state."

He stared at me.

I plowed on. "Do you own half of your wife's property?"

He shook his head. "Dead or alive, I don't own a nickel of Crowther's money. And if Linda wanted to get rid of me, all she'd have to do is divorce me."

"She'd need cause."

He shook his head again. "We agreed that both of us are free as birds." The waiter brought our drinks and George waited until he was out of hearing. Then he said smilingly, "Don't misjudge my wife. If she wanted to get rid of me, she'd do it openly and with witnesses."

"*Somebody*," I said, "shot at you. It was a man, but he could have been hired."

"He wasn't hired by my wife — I'll guarantee you that." He lifted his drink. "C'mon, relax."

We were on our second drink when Pascal came back. He said, "No need to go to the station. We'll get a statement from you boys here if you want, and then Puma can come in and see me tomorrow."

They let us use the office of the pro shop for the statements we dictated to one of the uniformed men. And before he left, Sergeant Pascal told us, "It was a 30–30 slug. Could have been a deer rifle. You got any deer–hunting enemies, Mr. Hogue?"

George smiled. "Not in this state, Sergeant. And none that would miss from that distance."

Pascal nodded solemnly. "Of course, we can't be sure the man was shooting at you, Mr. Hogue." He looked at me. "You got any feuds going on with your hoodlum friends?"

"I haven't any hoodlum friends, Sergeant," I said evenly. And added, "Outside of the Department."

His smile was humorless. "Well, I'll see you tomorrow, Puma. About ten."

He left and George made a face. "Cops —"

"They're overworked and underpaid and generally disliked," I said. "They haven't much reason to be happy."

"Maybe. One more and then we'll go home and have a swim. You owe me two and a half bucks."

We didn't talk much on the drive home. I had a feeling George wasn't telling me all he knew. Murder needs a motive, and that had looked like premeditated murder back there in the canyon. Well, he wasn't hiring me to find a killer, only to prevent him from getting killed. And he was paying me well for that.

The vagrant thought came that the whole incident could have been staged, that George could be playing me for a patsy. But why? The remark of the sergeant's came back to me, the suggestion that the man might have been shooting at me.

What if George had been playing with his wife? And she'd been shot? He could claim the killer had been aiming at him and had killed her by mistake. He'd have the letter and the phone calls to document his theory.

And now he'd have an official record of having been shot at.

George didn't take his eyes from the traffic as he asked, "Why so quiet? The man wasn't shooting at you.'

"I was thinking," I said, "that when a man gets too cute in planning a murder, he usually winds up making a serious mistake. The complicated capers are the easiest kind to solve."

We went the rest of the way without further dialogue. At home the maid told us there had been a call from Sergeant Pascal and he wanted me to call back.

He told me, "A green and white four–door hardtop didn't quite make the curve at the top of Chautauqua. It was a stolen car. It rolled to the bottom, and the driver was killed. There was a 30–30 rifle in the rear seat."

"Has the driver been identified?" I asked.

"Not positively. One of the officers out there is sure it's a St. Louis hood named Frankie Lewt, but that's unofficial yet. Do you know Frankie, Puma?"

"I never heard of him until this minute, Sergeant."

"Does Hogue know him?"

"I'll put him on," I said, "and you can ask him."

I handed George the receiver, and he said "No" twice, and handed the phone back to me.

Pascal said, "This Lewt, if it's him, is just a gun for hire. He was probably brought here for the job and has no other connection with the planner. Has Hogue told you anything you haven't told us?"

"Not a thing, Sergeant."

"Well, you know you're working with us or you're out of business, don't you?"

"Yes."

"Keep it in mind." He rang off.

George asked, "Who is this Lewt? Is he somebody they picked up?"

I told him about the car accident and the rifle.

"So now," George said, "they find out who hired this Lewt and we know who's out for me and they put him in jail and you can go back to working for a living, right?"

"I'm working now," I said. "Let's get our swimming trunks on."

As we went through the entry hall toward the stairs, George walked over to pick up the mail that was on the floor near the door. He rifled through it casually and then stopped to hold one letter aloft. "I haven't heard from her in a longtime."

"Girl friend?"

"No, an old girl who knew my mother, back in Phoenix. She used to write to me once a month. But this is the first letter since I've been married." He turned it over. "It's been forwarded from my old address."

The maid came in then and I thought she looked startled. "The mail's early today, Mr. Hogue."

George frowned and I stared at the maid. I thought she blushed. An idea flickered briefly in my thick skull, then went out again. I said to the maid, "Is it illegal for the mail to be early?"

"Of course not, sir."

"Is it embarrassing?"

"I don't understand you, sir."

"I don't even understand myself," I told her. "Did you know your employer was shot at this morning?"

She stared between us. "Mrs. Hogue was shot at?"

"Mr. Hogue."

"*Mrs.* Hogue is my employer, sir. Would there be anything else?"

George asked, "What in hell is going on around here?"

"I'm not sure," I told him. "If I was, you'd never get me at these coolie wages."

"C'mon," he said impatiently. "You don't have to put on the Sherlock Holmes act to stay employed. It's too hot."

We went up the stairs. Something was wrong, something that required the attention of one of these English–type detectives who could go poking around after clues. Something was as wrong as a three–dollar bill and unfortunately I was more physical than mental. Well, I could stay with him and try to see that he stayed alive. That was really all he was paying me for.

But just the same, I called a hoodlum friend of mine as soon as I got to my room. I caught him at home and asked, "Have you ever heard of a gent named Frankie Lewt?"

"Real sharpshooter, Joe. Why do you ask?"

"Who would be his connection out here?"

"Anybody who wants a job done. Frankie has no permanent connection. He calls St. Louis home. Is he out here now?"

"He's out here, on a slab at the morgue."

"You're kidding. Who could get to Frankie?"

"A curve on Chautauqua. Could you find out who brought him here?"

"Not for free, I couldn't. What have you ever done for me?"

"I kept your sister out of jail."

"That was no favor. Now, I've got to support her. Try again, Joe."

"To hell with you," I said. "I've got a memory."

"Fifty," he suggested. "What's fifty to you, the kind of clients you get?"

There was a knock at the door and I said "Come in," and George came in. I asked him, "Would you spend fifty dollars to find out who hired Frankie Lewt to shoot you?"

"Natch," he said.

I told my friend, "Okay. Fifty dollars." I gave him the phone number of my office–answering service and told him to leave the message there.

I hung up, and said, "Where are your trunks?"

He shook his head, "I have to go somewhere."

"I or *we*?"

"I'd better go alone," George said. "She said it was personal."

"You mean you're going to Phoenix?"

He nodded.

I said, "The police won't want you to leave town right now. Tell me about it, George."

"There's nothing to tell. This woman, this Mrs. Rydell, says there is something she should have told me a long time ago, but she never realized it was important until lately. She said I had better come to see her."

"I'm going along," I said.

He shook his head. "Why? You take care of this end. Maybe, between us, we'll get a story that'll clear everything up. Nobody knows I'm going — I'll be safe."

"Don't be foolish, George. Unless you give me a direct order not to, I'm going with you to Phoenix."

He smiled and said clearly, "I'm giving you a direct order to work for me at this end. I'll be back tomorrow, Joe. I'm taking the Jag."

"All right. Keep it under a hundred. And be sure you don't tell anybody where you're going."

"I won't. Will you be staying here?"

I shook my head. "I think I'll sleep at home tonight. Let me know as soon as you get back."

He promised he would.

I was going down Sunset, toward my office, when his Jaguar went drumming past. He waved cheerfully and I wondered again if he was playing me for a patsy. He should have been more scared.

At the office there were some bills and a few ads, but no checks. I opened a window to air the place out and then sat in front of my desk, thinking.

My phone rang, and it was the hoodlum. He said, "Couldn't learn anything except that Lewt rented an apartment for a month over on San Vicente. That would mean he wasn't brought to town just for one kill, wouldn't it?"

"Not necessarily. You don't figure that's worth fifty dollars, do you? I could have got that from the police."

"I figured it was worth something. But I guess not. You get the address from the police, then. So long, Joe."

"Wait," I said. "Maybe they won't want to give it to me."

"Maybe not. They wouldn't give it to the reporters."

"All right," I said. "Five bucks."

"Ten."

"Okay, ten."

He gave me the address and I wrote it down. I put a ten spot in an envelope, addressed it to him, and went out to the jalopy.

It was a three-story apartment building of redwood and maroon stucco, set back on a beautifully manicured lawn. Bougainvillea ran wild along the fence bordering the San Vicente side. There was a Police Department car in front.

As I parked, I saw Officer Mayo, a side-kick of Pascal's, come out from the entrance and walk toward the car. I waited until he had pulled away.

The first door off the lobby had a sign on it and the sign held a gilded *Manager*. I rang the bell.

A bleached blonde with skin like leather opened the door, looked at me suspiciously, and said, "Well —?"

"I was supposed to meet Officer Mayo here," I explained. "Has he arrived yet?"

"He's come and gone," she said, and started to close the door.

"One moment, please," I said, in my best official voice. "There are a few questions I'd like to ask."

"Ask him," she said. "I didn't have any answers for him, either. I'm not running a credit bureau. They pay their rent and keep quiet, I don't bother 'em. Get your foot out of the doorway."

"Maybe you'd rather come down to the station and answer the questions," I threatened.

A moment's silence, then she said, "Okay, let's see the badge."

"I have a photostat of my license here," I explained, "and I'd certainly appreci-ate —"

Scorn came to her leather face. "License —? A *private* peeper? And im-personating an officer, too, weren't you? Oh, wait until they hear about this."

"I am an officer," I said, "licensed by the State."

"Beat it," she said. "Run, before I get some law here to take you away."

I took my foot out of the doorway just before she slammed the door. I went over to the board which held the names of the tenants and saw no *Frankie Lewt*. But of course he wouldn't have rented the place under his real name.

Then the name *Mary Brennan* popped out at me from the board. It couldn't be; there were a lot of Mary Brennans in this town. It couldn't be my Mary, not that sweet and candid red–head.

But maybe it could. Although she had assured me she was poor, this was no apartment for the poor. Maybe she had meant she was poor by the standards of her friend, Linda Crowther Hogue.

She probably wouldn't be home for another hour, so I went over to Santa Monica to eat. While I ate I thought back on everything that had happened from the moment George Hogue had walked into my office. A pattern was trying to break through, but I couldn't force it into the light. Something obvious, obvious ...

What was obvious? The motivation was, but why couldn't I grasp it?

I lingered over my coffee and then drove slowly back to San Vicente. Her apartment was in the rear, on the second floor, and I heard footsteps almost immediately after my ring.

Would it be my Mary Brennan?

It was. She wore a linen suit in pale green and her gray–green eyes considered me speculatively. "The oversize Gower Champion — What brings you to my humble door?"

"Love. Am I welcome?"

"You are. Come in but leave the love outside. I'm just about to broil a steak."

It was a well–furnished apartment, overlooking the pool. It wasn't the apartment of a poor girl. I said, "You were conning me, eh?"

She was putting on an apron. "About what?"

"About being poor. I wish I was poor enough to afford an igloo like this."

The gray–green eyes were mocking. "Maybe I'm not paying for it. I'd have to stretch the steak to make it do for two. Could I fix you an egg?"

"No, thanks. I just finished dinner. Did you know that one of your neighbors died this afternoon?"

She paused on the way to the kitchen. "I don't know the neighbors very well. Is that why you're here — was he a friend of yours?" She paused. "Or *she*?"

"He was no friend of mine," I said. "His name was Frankie Lewt."

"Never heard of him." She continued toward the kitchen, and I followed.

It was a good–sized kitchen for an apartment, with an upholstered breakfast nook at the far end. Between the breakfast nook and the kitchen's working space there was a small counter.

Mary Brennan pointed toward the shelves under the counter and said, "The booze is there. Mix us a pair of martinis."

I took out the gin and the vermouth and asked, "How dry?"

"Five to one for me," she said. "Olives and onions in the refrigerator. Tell me, Puma, is this purely a social call?"

"So far," I answered. "Until I've had the free martini."

She sighed. "I might have known. I thought some romantic whimsy had brought you, but it's business, no doubt. Well, I don't know the neighbors very well."

Light touch, but it couldn't be coincidence that a friend of George Hogue's wife just happened to live in the same building with the hood who'd shot at George.

As I stirred the drink, I said, "This Frankie Lewt may have been registered under another name. He's a professional killer from St. Louis."

"Ouch! Living here? Say, why are you interested? Are you a policeman?"

"Not quite. Though I'm professionally interested in Frankie Lewt." I poured the drinks. "He tried to kill George Hogue this afternoon."

I turned with the drinks to find her staring at me, her poise unmistakably shaken. "Joe, what did he look like?"

"I don't know. I only saw him from a distance. He took a shot at George over at the Canyon Country Club and then in getting away he rolled the car he was driving over the cliff on Chautauqua."

I held her drink out to her and she took it with a trembling hand. She went over to sit in the breakfast nook. I sat down across from her.

I sipped my drink and waited for her to sip hers. She did, nodding in approbation. Her voice was low. "As soon as I finish this, I'm going down to see the manager."

"Why?"

"For reasons of my own. Don't ask me any questions until I get back."

"All right, Mary. What kind of day was today?"

"Hungover. We certainly drank enough last night, didn't we?" She put the cool glass to her forehead. "Are you a policeman, Joe?"

"I'm a private investigator. By the looks of this place I should have got into the custom furniture business."

"'Was that a crack?'"

"An envious remark. How long have you known George Hogue?"

"Only since he married Linda. She came back from a vacation in the mountains and brought him with her, as a husband. I am — not exactly a George Hogue fan, if you're interested."

"Why not?"

"He seems a — well, a little too calculating for my taste. Every time he looks around the room I get a feeling that he's making an inventory."

"He has nothing but his allowance," I said. "They signed one of those prenuptial agreements. You know, like the movie stars."

"I've heard of them," she said. "Who do you think would want to kill George?"

"I've no idea. What do you want to talk to the manager about?"

"About a tenant. I want to find out if a certain man was this gun man."

"A tenant you brought here?"

"A tenant who came here right after I told another man there was a vacancy."

"And who was this other man?"

"I may tell you when I come back from the manager's apartment, and I may not. Could I have a little more of this?"

There was more and I gave it to her. I wondered if the man whose name she was withholding was paying the rent for this place. That wasn't a nice thought and I tried to drive it from my mind.

"Moody," she said, "aren't you? I noticed that last night."

"I'm easily confused," I said, "and when I am I've got to shut up until I get my bearings. Was that a joke about your not paying for this apartment?"

"Why? Are you interested in my — character, Joe Puma?"

"I guess. That's silly, isn't it?"

"It's comforting," she said. "Well, I'll go down and see old straw–hair now, though it's nothing I look forward to."

Her poise had returned. In her crowd, a poor girl with rich friends, poise was probably very important. She left and I went over to see if there was a dribble of alcohol in the melted ice.

I sat there and finally the obvious broke through. The resemblance, that was the key. *The resemblance ...*

Mary Brennan came back looking pale. She said, "The man who was killed rented the apartment under the name of Alan Frank. He was the man who moved in after my friend asked about the vacancy. That doesn't mean there's a connection, does it?"

"I guess not. Why don't you want to tell me the name of your friend? Is it a name I know?"

She hesitated, studying me doubtfully. Then she said, "My friend's name is Nicholas Allis. Is that a name you know?"

"Big Nick? Hell, yes. Dope and women, and originally from St. Louis, isn't he?"

"I don't know. Are you sure about the dope and the women? Are you sure he isn't a legitimate business man?"

"He could be now," I said. "A lot of them end up that way. Where did you meet him?"

"His decorator brought him in for some furniture. He seemed very nice, and he's always been gentle and thoughtful around me."

"Honey," I explained, "you can take one of those big boys and give him a haircut and a shave. You can put him in a three–hundred–dollar suit and douse him with the right kind of toilet water and he can almost pass for a human being. But underneath, he is still a murdering slob, and never forget it."

She walked shakily back to the breakfast nook to sit down again. She said softly, "I — had no idea — I mean — Oh, God, what do I mean?"

I said, "It's always tough to be poor. But it's toughest when you have rich friends, isn't it?"

She flushed.

I asked quietly, "Is Big Nick paying for all this?"

She glared at me as her flush deepened.

I said, "Who is Nick's lawyer?"

"Anthony Ellers. As a matter of fact, I introduced Tony to Linda when she was still married to Crowther."

"Did you get a commission for that from Ellers?"

"That's enough," she said. "You've gone too far, Puma. Get out."

"May I use your phone first? I want to call Ellers."

She glared, then put her head down on the breakfast nook table. She began to sob.

I used her phone to call Ellers' office. His secretary told me he was unavailable and wouldn't be back until tomorrow.

"Where'd he go?" I asked. "Out of town?"

"I am not in possession of that information," she said coolly.

"Like hell you aren't," I said. "Did he leave right after Mrs. Hogue phoned him?"

"I have no record here of a call from Mrs. Hogue," she said, even more coolly.

"Sister," I said, "you are forgetting there are jails for women, too." I hung up sharply.

Then I dialed long distance. The second Mrs. Rydell I reached was the right one.

I told her, "If you value your life, you had better phone the police for protection right now or hop the quickest plane to Los Angeles."

"Who is this talking?" she asked. "One of George Hogue's few friends," I said. "If you had told him in the letter what you planned to tell him when he gets there, he wouldn't be on his way to see you right now. He'd be safe. You had better alert the Arizona police that he's on the way now. I'll try to take care of this end. Believe me, Mrs. Rydell, this is no joke — George was shot at by a hired hoodlum this morning."

"I believe you," she said. "I'll get right to work here and then take the first plane."

I gave her my office and home addresses and my phone numbers and then called Pascal. I told him, "Pick up Nick Allis and send a man over to keep an eye on Mrs. Hogue. Or maybe the Beverly Hills boys could watch her. Big Nick could be the

boy who brought Frankie Lewt to town. And I'm sure he brought him in to work for
Anthony Ellers. Ellers is probably on his way to Arizona right now."

"We can't pick up Allis on some whim of yours, Puma. This man is no longer a
hoodlum; he's got connections.

"Damn it, Sergeant, this is no whim. And I want the State Police alerted to pick
up George Hogue, who is driving to Arizona. He's driving a Jaguar — you can get
the license number from Mrs. Hogue."

"Slow down," he said. "Who the hell do you think you are, handing out
orders?"

"Sergeant," I said evenly, "you've been warned. If George Hogue dies, his
blood will be on your hands."

"Where are you?" he asked.

I gave him the address and asked, "What difference does it make?"

"I want to see if you're sober."

There was the sound of door chimes, and Mary Brennan came through the
doorway from the kitchen. She looked at the door and at me. She said, "That's
probably Mr. Allis now."

From the phone Pascal said, "Puma, you still there? What's going on?"

"A hundred things you're too stupid to understand, Sergeant," I told him gently.
And I hung up. Mary Brennan still stood indecisively.

I said, "Open the door."

I was sitting on the sofa, leafing through a copy of *Life* when she opened the
door to Nicholas Allis.

He was big and broad and meticulously tailored. He had curly silver–gray hair
and his virile, masculine face was burnished in a Florida tan.

His voice was resonant, but with just a faint rasp in it. He said easily, "Well,
well, Joseph Puma. The last time I saw you was in Las Vegas."

I nodded. "You looked more at home there, Nick. How are all the little rackets
running?"

His face stiffened, and he looked at Mary. He said, "You've been crying.
Why?"

She didn't answer. She gazed doubtfully between us, then started toward the
kitchen.

Nick said, "Wait, Mary. I want to know what the trouble is. Why is this man
here?"

"I don't know," she whispered. She began to cry again.

He looked at me and his eyes were stone. "You had better explain yourself and
fast. Or you'll be in more trouble than you can handle."

"Sit down, Nick," I said. "Don't threaten me. You haven't enough friends or
enough pounds to frighten me. I came here to check on that hoodlum buddy of
yours, Frank Lewt. I ran into Mary while I was here and dropped in for a drink. I'm
not in nearly as much trouble as you are."

He stood there like a rock.

I asked, "Did you know Randall Crowther very well, Nick?"

He shook his head. "I've heard of him, that's all."

"Did his wife ever tell you that he lived in Arizona as a young man?"

He shook his head.

I said, "You know Frankie's dead, don't you? Died in a stolen car on a curve he didn't quite make. Were you going to pay him for the kill or was that Ellers' idea?"

"I don't know what you're talking about," he said. "I'll give you ten seconds to leave quietly, Puma. Or I'll throw you out."

From the kitchen came Mary's sobs again. I said, "You can't force me to leave. It's *her* apartment."

"Is it? I can force you to leave if I'm big enough. And I'm big enough."

I smiled at him and shook my head. "Not big enough or strong enough or fast enough or gutsy enough." I stood up.

We stood quietly, eyeing each other. I was sure he hated me at the moment, but not nearly as much as I hated him. Because of Mary Brennan. Because of all the Mary Brennans who take cultivated tastes and small purses out into a man's world.

I was praying that he would have guts enough to come for me. I wanted him to give me an excuse to do to him physically what he had done to her spiritually. And to how many others?

My trouble is I'm Italian, and more emotional than intellectual. I wanted him to come for me emotionally, though the rational speck still operating in my brain assured me he might be more than I could handle. He had grown up among tough boys. But I too had grown up among tough boys.

I said, "Come on, gutless, you can't be *all* yellow."

He came for me. Not like a hoodlum, clawing and kneeing. He came for me like a man with experience, feinting a left, a right — and throwing the left.

And a very good one, catching me in the neck below the chin and numbing the whole right side of my face. He had just missed the button.

Then I also missed the button, but broke a canine on the right side of his face. I tried one for his belly where I figured he should be soft, these days.

He wasn't. When they leave their hard and scrambling days behind, they have handball and tennis and golf and masseurs and stuff like that. My fist bounced off his belly and his forehead came into my nose.

Blood spurted from my nose and ran down my throat inside and I forgot all the things Slugger Donovan had tried so patiently to teach me and became just a tough kid fighting his neighborhood enemies in the hot sun of a Fresno summer.

He caught me on the temple and the floor began to swing and tilt. He got a thumb in my eye and I brought a knee up sharply and it jackknifed him enough to bring his nose into the top of my waiting head.

Then I had his throat in my big left hand, and I swung and swung my right hand into his face.

He went down and I was on top, his soft throat still in my left hand and my right beginning to bleed as all the skin left the knuckles. He began to moan.

And I was still hitting him, unconscious though he was, thinking of Mary Brennan, thinking of all the Mary Brennans ...

They told me later I was still hitting him and cursing like a maniac when Pascal and Mayo came in to drag me off of him. That's my trouble; I'm too damned emotional.

In the drab office, Pascal said, "Who the hell do you think you are, the avenger? He may live — just may."

"Does it matter?" I asked. "Better men die every day."

"Don't get smart, Puma."

"Smart, huh? Does the obvious still escape that lamebrain of yours?"

His jaw was a sharp, tight line. "I'd listen to your version of it."

"All right," I said. "George Hogue is the living image of a dead man. Is that maybe half of a clue?"

"You tell me."

"Many sons look like their fathers," I said. "Even sons who are products of common law marriages."

He stared. "You think Hogue is Crowther's son by a previous marriage?"

"By a previous common law marriage. How else could George be a threat to the Crowther estate, *except by inheritance?* They wanted him where they could keep an eye on him and possibly put him away when the opportunity seemed ripe."

"You're crazy," he said. "Common law marriages aren't recognized in this state. And that would eliminate any claim of Hogue's."

"Sergeant," I asked smugly, "have you ever heard the legal term 'comity'?"

"So?"

"It means this state respects the legal status of citizens who were partners in a common law marriage in states where common law marriage *is* recognized. Arizona is one of those states."

"So?"

"So Randall Crowther had no legal right to marry Linda. He wasn't a free man. And she is not, therefore, his legal wife."

"This is all from left field," Pascal said. "You're guessing at all this. We haven't heard from that Mrs. Rydell yet. You don't *know* this is true."

"Look," I said patiently. "Add it up. When I walk into the Hogue home, why does Mrs. Hogue tell me Ellers has mentioned my name? Why would he mention my name unless he knew George had gone to me and it worried him? They must be working together, Mrs. Hogue and Ellers, right?"

"Possibly. What does that prove?"

"That there's a *legal* reason, or she wouldn't need Ellers — a legal reason why George mustn't get too nosey. And then he tells me he hasn't heard from Mrs. Rydell since he's been married. Why not?"

"You tell me — you've got all the answers."

"Because his wife or the maid intercepted the letters. I could get that from the maid's embarrassment when George got to the mail first. And then Ellers leaves town. Who told him George had gone to Arizona?"

"Maybe nobody. We don't even know that Ellers left for Arizona. We've got a man checking the airport reservations right now, and we'll see how true that part of your story is. What makes you think it was a common law marriage?"

"Sergeant, if your mother told you your dad had died in a mine cave–in before you were born, wouldn't you be suspicious?"

"No. I believe my mother."

"Look. I'll bet you'll find that Hogue was her maiden name or the name of a previous husband."

"Puma, do you realize what you're saying? What if it's all hogwash? Nick Allis making a fight for his life over at St. John's — the Beverly Hills boys holding one of their biggest citizens — the State Police trying to find her husband and one of this town's most influential attorneys. Do you realize where you'll be sitting if it's as crazy as it sounds?"

I smiled at him. "You listened to me on the phone. You took my advice."

"Keep talking," he said. "It might be your last chance, before you get into the gas chamber."

"So," I went on placidly, "we will dwell on Anthony Ellers, that influential attorney. It is possible he is back–dooring George, but even if he isn't, Ellers can be worth enough to Mrs. Hogue to make him a desirable third husband. But he doesn't know enough local hoods to get a local killer, and they're not too reliable anyway. So he goes to a client, Big Nick Allis, and asks casually if there are any St. Louis boys reliable enough to earn a king–size fee. And Nick gives him a name, though that wouldn't implicate him, would it?"

Pascal frowned. "Why should you worry if Nick's implicated? Maybe you had another reason for beating him up, huh? Maybe he's got something on you."

I shook my head. "And you're the man who tried to tell me you believed in people."

"I didn't say people. I said my mother."

"I don't give a tinker's damn what you do to Nick Allis."

"Oh?" He grinned. "The red–head, maybe?"

"She's the one who put me wise to Big Nick and his association with Ellers. If you try to implicate her, I'll tell the Commission you refused to give George Hogue protection."

He grinned again. "Tell 'em what you damned well please. I'd like to point out that George Hogue lived in Beverly Hills, and that is *not* Los Angeles."

"Okay. I'll think of something else."

His stare held more wonder than belligerence. "Take it easy, man. What is she to you?"

"A symbol," I said. "One of the errant lambs, and they are my particular charge."

He shook his head. "You sloppy bleeding heart. Puma, you fool —"

A detective came in and said, "Ellers didn't go by commercial airline. He flies his own plane, and he took that. I've sent out the call to the CAP."

Pascal nodded, and the man left. Pascal looked at me and there was some fear in his eyes.

I said, "Those Jags are fast, but not as fast as a plane."

"It's crazy," he said. "It's right out of one of those old Pearl White serials."

"It's from hunger, from desperation," I said. "Since Lewt missed that shot, time became very important. And when George got the letter, there just wasn't any time left. And we're dealing in million–dollar thinking, don't forget that."

Pascal wiped his brow, then wiped his hand on a handkerchief. He went over to look out the window.

I said, "On the desert that Jag will stand out. There can't be too many of them. Ellers can land at any of a dozen towns in front of the Jaguar and wait for it to come tearing along. He can flag George down —"

Pascal turned from the window. "Shut up, damn you!"

The phone rang and he picked up the receiver. He said, "Hell, yes, I'll talk to Arizona. It's about time."

I didn't get any of it except Sergeant Pascal's occasional grunts and mono-syllabic answers. I waited patiently, a vision in my mind of a Jaguar and a light plane racing across that bleak desert in the dusk.

Pascal hung up finally, and said, "So after all these years this Phoenix dame reveals she knew all along Hogue was Crowther's son. So why does she keep it a secret?"

"For George's sake. It would be better for him to pump gas and think his father was an honorable man than to be a rich and illegitimate son, wouldn't it?"

"Those were almost her words. How did you know?"

"Logic. But once she realized from reading the papers that George had married Crowther's widow, she began to worry. So she wrote him."

Pascal nodded. "And the letters were intercepted. So where the hell are Hogue and Ellers now?"

It was another hour before we got the news. Hogue was found in the Jaguar, two miles south of Wickenberg, most of his head blown off by a shotgun.

And Ellers didn't quite have the gas to get back. His plane crashed into a peak near Prescott, as he tried to glide down. They found a shotgun in the plane — the right shotgun.

"What the hell is it?" Pascal said. "I mean — Lewt tries to shoot Hogue, and dies. Ellers makes it, and he dies. What the hell is it?"

"Your guess is as good as mine," I said. "Mary Brennan is in the clear, isn't she? Let me know now — I want to phone her."

"She's in the clear," he said wearily. "I guess I owe you something."

"Thanks," I told him, and went to phone her. Maybe we could stretch that steak, now.

No Client of Mine

They came in around dusk, a well–tailored, nondescript pair of men smaller than I am, but not small. My office had all of the doubtful benefit of the afternoon sun and I was hot and irritable.

"Puma?" one of them said. "Joe Puma?"

I nodded and answered, "At your service, gentlemen." I turned my back on them and went over to open a window. Traffic sounds came up from the street one story below.

I was still looking down at the traffic when one of the men said, "Why should Don Abrams need a private eye? He got troubles or something?"

I turned to face them. "None that he told me about. I didn't know he'd hired an investigator."

One man looked at the other and back at me. "Oh —? You were with him last night, right?"

I nodded. "As a friend; he's no client of mine." I added, "Not that it's any of your damned business, whoever you are."

They both looked at me blandly. The one on the right said, "How is he a friend of yours?"

I sat down behind my desk and smiled at them. "Do you have some authority you can show me? I don't like your questions."

The one on the right moved a hand smoothly under his jacket and it came out holding a short–barreled .38. He said easily, "Is this authority enough?"

I looked at both of them again and at the gun which was pointed in the general direction of my left lung. I said, "I knew Don in the army. He was an instrument corporal in my mortar platoon. When he came out here to visit his sister, he looked me up. Last night we kind of hung one on. That's it. He didn't tell me about any trouble he was in."

The man with the gun looked at the other man and that one shrugged.

I yawned. "Do you boys plan to cause Don any trouble?"

The gunless one asked, "Why should we?"

"Don't," I said. "Just a warning. Now, either shoot me or beat it because I'm going to make a move if you don't."

"He's close to you, huh?" the gunless man asked.

"He's close. He saved my life a long time ago in a war that probably made you slobs rich in black marketing."

In the man's hand, the gun raised. His face stiffened and his voice grated. "I've got some shrapnel scars on my belly that make a liar out of you, Puma. Go ahead, tough guy, make your big move."

The other man said, "Relax, Sam; the war's over." He looked at me coolly. "I served with the Third Army, myself."

I smiled. "So, okay, Old Home Week. So there's a new bottle of Canadian whiskey in the file over there and I've got three glasses and the dentist next door has ice. Why talk about Don Abrams?"

The gunless man grinned; the other looked doubtfully at me.

I said, "Even from here, I can see the cylinder's empty. Have you got a shell in the chamber, or is that a water pistol?"

The gunless one said, "He couldn't shoot anybody. Not since the war. That's why they threw him off the cops; he just can't pull a trigger any more. Come on, Sam, let's drink the man's whiskey and talk about Don Abrams. That's why we're here, you know."

Sam put the gun away. I went over to bring a couple of straight–backed chairs closer to the desk. I said to Gunless, "Go next door and tell Doctor Graves' office girl I want a tray of ice cubes. I'll get the bottle open."

The man left. I got the bottle and came back to the desk. Sam sat there, staring bleakly at the wall, his face pale. "Nice guy, your friend," I said gently. "What's his name?"

"His name's Leo," Sam said, "Leo Kranski. My name's Sam Minash. We work for Paul Fairchild. Do you know who he is?"

"A lawyer," I said. "Also a rich man. Owns some fair fighters and a starlet here and there. A promoter, I suppose he'd be called. Though there are probably people around town who'd have some harsher names for him."

His belligerence didn't go away. "Yeh? He's an ace, that's what he is. You couldn't meet a nicer guy. So he gambles. So what?"

"How did you land with Fairchild? Did you go right to him after the Department released you?"

His jawline stiffened. He said nothing.

Leo Kranski came in with a tray of ice cubes. "Some office girl that doc's got. Jeez, what a pair!"

He glanced at Sam and sighed. "Stop sulking, will you? The guy's buying. Forget the cops; you never had it this good."

I poured three drinks and added ice and water. I lifted mine and said, "To better understanding."

We all drank. And then I asked, "What's Fairchild's interest in Don Abrams?"

They smiled at me.

I said, "Jean Adair's name was Jean Abrams. Did you boys know that?"

They both nodded.

"Jean's doing all right," I said. "Has Paul Fairchild got a piece of her?"

They smiled.

"All right," I said. "So if he has, that shouldn't make him worry about Don Abrams. Don's not the kind who would interfere in Jean's love life."

"That's fine," Leo said. "That's what we were sent to find out — if Abrams was trying to climb onto the gravy train. You see, when Mr. Fairchild promotes a starlet, he doesn't relish any interference by greedy relatives."

"So he sent you here?"

Leo nodded.

"Armed —?" I asked.

Leo's smile was shame–faced. "Aw, that wasn't Mr. Fairchild's idea. If he knew Sam was carrying that, we'd both go back to wearing fifty–dollar suits. Sam reads too much Mike Hammer."

Sam glared at his friend and then reached over to pour himself another drink.

I asked, "Just what do you boys do for Paul Fairchild?"

Leo shrugged and licked at an ice cube. "Oh, we squire some of his potential stars around and fill in at parties and keep our ears open."

"Sort of — procurers?" I asked mildly.

Sam Minash said, "Easy, Wop."

"Don't call me that," I said evenly.

Leo said, "That's right, Sam; you and I both live in a glass house." He shook his head. "Jeez — we're sitting on top of the world and this Minash acts like a man with an ulcerated tooth. Some guys just can't be happy, right?"

"Some guys don't have any reason to be," I said. "Maybe Sam's got too much conscience to like this world the way it is."

Leo nodded sadly, looked at his empty glass, and poured himself another drink while Sam stared at me in dull anger.

I said, "I'll bet you won a lot of medals."

Sam colored and said nothing. Leo said, "And how! And he'd have got a Congressional too, if we hadn't had a big, fat, stupid, bigoted Mick for a battalion commander."

Sam said quietly, "Leo, you talk too much."

Leo smiled. "I have to talk for two. You don't talk enough. And when you do, you say the wrong things. You should practice talking more, Sam."

Sam's color remained high but he said nothing. I asked, "Is Fairchild paying Jean Adair's rent?"

"Shut up!" Sam said.

Leo smiled and shrugged.

I said, "I'm having dinner with Don Abrams tonight. Why don't you come along and meet him?"

For the first time there was something besides sullen anger on the face of Sam Minash. He looked at Leo hopefully.

Leo shook his head. "Mr. Fairchild might not like it." He stood up. "Well, if this Abrams is a friend of yours, he must be all right. We'll tell Mr. Fairchild that. Thanks for the booze."

I waved. "Glad you dropped in."

Sam stood up and looked at me doubtfully. "Where do you plan to eat?"

"At *Cini's*," I said. "Right off Beverly Drive."

"I know where it is," he said. "Maybe I can make it."

"I hope so," I said. And added quietly, "Stick with that Leo, Sam. You've got a real friend there."

He nodded. "I know it. He's lippy, but my best friend."

They left and I sat at the desk for a few minutes thinking back on their visit. Then I thought back to last night. Don had talked very little about his sister, except to say her future looked bright as any in the shaky industry. She was living in a

Sunset Strip apartment and Don wasn't staying there, for some reason, but with friends out in the Valley.

She was a slim, dark girl in the elfish pattern that seemed to be in vogue these days, complete with Italian haircut and Carnegie clothes. Properly promoted and with a modicum of talent, her type was currently as sound as diamonds or A.T. & T.

Paul Fairchild's reputation as an insatiable stud was as wide as the audience for this kind of information and I wondered if he was making out with Jean Adair.

Not that she was anything to me; I had never even met her. But why wasn't Don staying at her place? It bothered me for Don's sake.

I wasn't due to meet Don until eight o'clock; on the way home I stopped off to see a girl I once made music with, a blonde who had gone from me to a small part in a big picture. The rumor I'd heard was that Paul Fairchild had got her the part. And, quite possibly, for value received.

She was in the sheltered court of her Westwood apartment, relaxing on a redwood chaise longue with a fashion magazine. "Ye Gods!" she said, "my old Latin Lover. Where *have* you been, Puma?"

"Places I was wanted. How are things, Ruth?"

"Which things?" She considered me speculatively. "You're looking fit. Still on that Dick Tracy kick?"

"I'm still a bonded and licensed private investigator, if that's what you mean."

"That's what I mean. Making your steady forty bucks every week and driving the '52 Chev. Man, I was on a dead–end street with you, wasn't I?"

"I've got a new Plymouth," I said. "I mean new to me, only twenty–six thousand miles on it. You seem to be making out all right, Ruth."

She stretched. "Why not? If you had my figure, you'd make out, too."

"Mmmm–hmmm. Like a cigarette?"

She looked at me suspiciously. "Why are you here, Joe?"

"Auld lang syne," I said lightly. "I woke up this morning full of nostalgia and last night's whiskey. I've been thinking of you all day."

"I'll bet," she said. She blew some more smoke my way. "Checking on Lenny?"

I looked at her blankly. "I don't know who you're talking about," I said. "To be completely honest, I came to ask some questions about Paul Fairchild. And a couple of his stooges, Sam Minash and Leo Kranski."

"I never heard of those last two," she said. "What did you want to know about Paul?"

"How crooked is he?"

She stared. "Not at all, so far as I know. He's rough and arrogant and clever and I suppose he bends the law here and there. But nobody I know ever thought of him as a crook."

"And who's his favorite girlfriend now?"

She shrugged. "Someone young and probably virgin. Paul takes a romantic view of his lust–life."

"Mmmm–hmmm. Have you heard of a girl named Jean Adair?"

"Who hasn't? On the way up, that one. Is that Paul's current favorite?"

"I don't know," I said. "I don't know her. But I hope not. Maybe it's just the camera work, but she looks sweet and innocent to me."

Ruth smiled cynically. "Don't they all? God, Puma, you're still a rube, aren't you?"

"I guess," I admitted. I rose. "Well, it was nice to find you healthy and prospering, Ruth. Think of me once in a while, won't you?"

She stretched again. "If I do, I'll phone. But let's hope things never get that rough, right?"

I said good–bye and went out to the waiting Plymouth. Ruth had more or less confirmed what I'd always believed about Paul Fairchild; he wasn't heavy. A man can study law in order to support it or to prepare him to circumvent it. Fairchild was a lawyer and there were many doubtful ways for the knowing to make money without carrying a gun. Those two lads had been sent over to check on Don Abrams, not on me. And the gun hadn't been Fairchild's idea. That had been Sam's idea because of his reading, the empty gun.

So what business was it of mine? Well, none. Except that I sort of owed it to Don to keep an eye out for him.

Don was waiting for me in the bar, at *Cini's*, and he seemed faintly worried. I didn't know whether to tell him about the visit I'd had or not. I decided not to, not right away.

I never got a chance to. We had finished our drinks and were on the way to the dining room when Lieutenant Grierson came in. We knew each other by sight, but weren't friends and I was surprised to see him headed my way.

It wasn't me he was interested in. He said, "I was told you were having dinner with a Mr. Don Abrams. Is this him?"

I nodded and Don looked at the lieutenant puzzledly.

"Come along," Grierson said curtly, "down to the station."

Don looked at me and back at Grierson. "Why? Am I parked in the wrong place or something?"

Grierson said, "Paul Fairchild's been killed. Come along."

Don frowned, "Who's Paul Fairchild?"

Grierson said. "Come on. Your sister's at the station. Maybe she can tell you."

"May I go along, Lieutenant?" I asked.

He looked at me casually. "If you've anything to contribute."

"I might have."

"Come along, then," he said.

Sergeant Riddle was at the wheel of the Department car outside. I knew him better than Grierson but neither of them were known as friendly to the private man. He nodded to me as Don and I climbed into the back. Grierson sat up in front.

Don said quietly, "Who is this Fairchild?"

"A lawyer and promoter," I said, loud enough for the two in front to hear. "Anybody could have bumped him; he's got more enemies than Molotov."

"But why is Jean down there at the station?" he asked. "What is her connection with him?

"I'm not sure," I said.

From the front seat, Grierson turned around, looked at me musingly, and turned back again.

I asked, "How was Fairchild killed, Lieutenant?"

"He was shot twice right through the neck." He paused. "With a thirty–eight."

"Where?"

"Ask Abrams."

"When?"

Grierson turned around again. "Are you a reporter? Are you working for some newspaper?"

I didn't answer him. We rode in silence the rest of the way to the station.

In an office, off the head of the hall, I met Jean Adair in person for the first time. Her eyes were red from crying and her careful make–up was smeared, but she was still a beauty. Don held out his arms and she came to him, sobbing.

At the other end of the room, Leo Kranski sat staring at the floor. Grierson went over to him, sat down on a chair next to him. The lieutenant began to talk and Leo kept shaking his head as though denying everything Grierson was saying.

Sergeant Riddle said, "Come in here with me, Puma."

I went into a smaller room off this large one, and Riddle pointed toward a chair. I sat in it and he brought another over next to it for himself.

"That fellow Lieutenant Grier son's talking to — know him?" he asked too casually.

"Leo Kranski," I said. "Third Army."

"When did you last see this Kranski?"

"This afternoon."

"Where?"

"In my office."

"Alone?"

"Who else was there?"

"A man named Sam Minash."

"He was going to meet you for dinner, wasn't he, you and Abrams?"

"If he could make it."

"Why was he going to meet you?"

"I don't know, Sergeant. Maybe he likes the food at *Cini's*."

He stared at me a few seconds. "Don't you think it would be smart to cooperate? You need us a hell of a lot more than we need you."

"I don't need you at all, Sergeant," I said. "I came along with you at *my own* suggestion," I pointed out. "I asked some questions that weren't answered. Then, when we get here, you bring me away from the others and start to grill me as though I were a suspect."

His breath came a little faster, but his voice was calm. "All right, Puma, one question — where's Sam Minash now?"

"I haven't the faintest damned idea," I said. "I saw him once in my life, this afternoon in my office."

He looked at me thoughtfully. "That's the gospel?"

"So help me, that's the word. Now, what should I know?"

He looked doubtfully at the floor and then at the closed door that led to the other room. Finally, he said, "Just because I trust you — Minash is missing. Kranski says that doesn't mean anything; that Minash couldn't have killed Fairchild because he couldn't kill anybody. He claims he couldn't pull a trigger and the Department knows that — they've got a record of it. A psychic block, Kranski said it was and the Department psychiatrist will back him up."

"That jibes with what Leo told me this afternoon," I said. "But I'll do you a favor and tell you this without your asking me — Minash was carrying a .38 this afternoon, an *unloaded* .38."

He shook his head. "Boy, you are one, aren't you? What's your beef with officers, Puma?"

"Their four–hundred–dollar–a–month self–importance," I said. "I've always hated bullies and phonies."

Grierson came in and said, "We got the psychiatrist's report, Sergeant. It checks with what Kranski said."

The sergeant shrugged. "In anger, a man will do anything. Especially a psycho. That doesn't change a thing in my opinion."

Grierson smiled. "Mine either. I guess we don't need a medical degree to know *anyone* can kill, huh Sergeant?"

I said, "What made you two think Abrams might be guilty?"

Grierson paused, and then said, "Kranski. He pointed out a lot of people who could be guilty instead of his buddy and Abrams was one of the names he handed us. And why not? If he knew Fairchild was trying to make hay with his little sister?"

"Do *you* know that?" I asked.

Grierson didn't answer me. He said, "You can let Puma go any time you're through with him, Sergeant. I guess he's probably clean, don't you think?"

"I think so," Sergeant Riddle said.

I stood up. "And so do I, and that makes three. But couldn't I wait around for my friend, Don Abrams?"

"If you don't get in the way," Grierson said. "Just keep your mouth shut and stay out of the traffic lanes, and you can wait."

"Thank you, sir," I said.

He looked at me suspiciously, but my gaze was earnest. He sniffed, and went away.

"Why do you have to be such a wise guy?" Riddle asked.

"It keeps me from remembering how truly impotent I am," I answered. "You know, it's like the punk's sneer and the whore's perfume."

He said wearily, "Wait out in the hall." He nodded toward another door.

"One question first, if I may, Sergeant. Why should Minash kill Fairchild?"

"Because Minash was in love with Jean Adair. Why else?"

"And Jean was in love with Fairchild?"

He smiled cynically. "If that's what you want to call it. For a man who gets around, you act awful damned naive at times, Puma ..."

He started to say more, but then Jean and Don came out through another doorway to the larger room and he hurried up that way. Flash bulbs flared and reporters crowded around them. Lieutenant Grierson and a uniformed man pushed through the crowd ahead of Don and his sister, making a path for them as they headed for another office.

In a minute, Leo Kranski came through the deserted doorway with Sergeant Riddle. Riddle nodded toward the hallway and Kranski came over to stand next to me.

He grinned hollowly. "Well, I guess this means we're not suspects any more, huh?"

"I guess," I said. "Sam didn't hate Fairchild, did he? He called him an 'ace' this afternoon, I remember."

"Sam's poor," he said. "If the law wants a conviction, they drag in somebody poor."

"That's cynical," I said. "You two are out of a job now, I suppose."

Leo nodded sadly. "Back to reading gas meters. Well, it was great while it lasted." He looked at me wonderingly. "Who could have bumped him?"

I shrugged. "A number of people. He wasn't the most popular man in town."

"You going to try to find out?"

"Why should I? Nobody hired me."

"You come high, I suppose."

"Save your money," I said. "If Sam wasn't guilty, why did he disappear?"

He shook his head stubbornly and avoided answering, "Sam couldn't kill. Sam had all of that he could handle. He couldn't even step on an ant any more. They could maybe railroad him, but I know he's innocent, and I'd bet my right arm on it."

"Why should they want to railroad him?" I asked gently.

"Politics," he said. "The Department wants a conviction, when anybody as important as Fairchild is bumped."

"That's not the way it is," I said. "Believe me, Leo, I know better." I put a hand on his arm. "Do you know where Sam is?"

His stare was innocent. "Hell, no! If I knew where he was, I'd have him here. And I'd *swear* he'd been with me ever since we left your office. They'd never break me down."

"Maybe not. Did Sam love this Jean Adair?"

Leo expelled his breath. "Jeez, he had it bad. He thought she was some kind of angel. Man, he was dumb about her." He looked up suddenly. "Why are we using the past tense? Hell, Sam ain't dead."

"When did you see him last?"

"Right after we left your office. I said I was going over to report to Fairchild and he said he wanted to shave and clean up and then he was going to meet you for dinner."

"And you saw Fairchild?"

Leo shook his head. "He wasn't at the office, so I went to our apartment, but Sam had already left."

"And where was Fairchild shot?"

"In his living room. He's got a house up there in the Hollywood Hills section. He doesn't spend much time there, with all the quiff he's got stashed around town, but he was there tonight, and somebody must have known it."

I said, "I want an honest answer, Leo. Did Sam have reason to be jealous of Paul Fairchild?"

He nodded somberly. "Jean was goofy for Fairchild. She planned to marry him."

"I hope she's got an alibi, too," I said.

"She says she was shopping at the time," Leo said. "And why would she want to kill him? She was his favorite."

The door to the office opened, and Don came out alone. He looked harried and sick. He said, "Joe, I want you to work on this. They're not looking for a killer, they're looking for a stooge."

"No, they're not, Don," I said. "They're looking for a killer, and that's all. Their methods make you think the other way, because at the moment they don't know who the killer is."

He stared at me doubtfully. "You should have been in there." He lighted a cigarette nervously. "I still want you to work on it." He looked at Kranski. "Where's your pal?"

Kranski glared at him without answering.

Then Jean came out with Lieutenant Grierson. Grierson was smiling at her, but Jean looked as troubled as she had when they entered the room.

They both came over to us and Grierson said, "Well, it's your buddy, all right, Kranski. His gun was registered here and that's the gun that killed Fairchild. Now, do you want to tell us where he is?"

Kranski said steadily, "Even if I knew, I wouldn't tell you, Lieutenant. Grill me all you want; you'll be wasting your time."

"I've got a lot of time," Grierson said. "Come along."

Kranski reached into an inner pocket and took out a wallet. He handed it to me. "Work as long as that will carry you. And get me a lawyer, will you?"

Grierson said, "Keep your nose out of this, Puma."

I handed Kranski his wallet. "You heard him. I'll tell you what I will do, though. I'll look up Sam for you." I patted his shoulder, and headed for the door.

Grierson said, "Just a minute, Puma." I turned.

"If you find Minash," he said quietly, "you bring him right to me."

"Naturally, Lieutenant," I said easily. "What else?"

Then Don said, "We still haven't had our dinner, Joe. Can't the three of us go back to *Cini's*?"

"Why not?" I answered. "I can't think of pleasanter company."

As we walked to her car, Jean told us, "Luckily, I saw Lois Ogren at *Bullock's* when I was out shopping this afternoon. Otherwise no one would have seen me, and I'll bet the police would have been satisfied. They never would have checked Sam's gun, would they?"

"They would have as a matter of routine," I said. "Sam's been their number–one suspect all along."

"I don't believe it," Don said. "Not after the way they grilled me."

It was a new role for me, defending the Department against indignant citizens — particularly against the man to whom I owed my life.

Don and I did most of the talking at dinner, and we parted at *Cini's*. Jean said she would drop Don off in the Valley; I phoned Grierson to learn if they had released Kranski.

"Not yet," he said, "but soon. We're getting nowhere."

"I suppose you'll keep a man on him?"

"That would be Department business, Puma."

"Sorry. Has he got transportation home?"

"No. We brought him down."

"Tell him to wait," I said. "I'll pick him up."

"If you know something, Puma —"

I said politely, "I don't know anything you shouldn't, Lieutenant. Both of us know Sam Minash couldn't pull a trigger."

"No, we don't," he said. "I don't believe that about anybody in the world, under all conditions."

"All right. Then you shouldn't kick if I try to find Minash for you."

"Not if you find him for *us*. But what's your interest? Who is going to pay you?"

"I've a hunch, Lieutenant," I said wryly, "that nobody will want to pay me, if I'm successful. My interest is — well, in *justice,* maybe?"

"Huh!" he said. "That'll be the day. Keep in touch, Puma."

"Yes, sir," I said. "Tell Kranski I'm on the way."

Leo was standing out in the cool night air in front of the station when I pulled up there fifteen minutes later. He climbed in wearily and leaned back in the seat.

"Got any beer at your place?" I asked him.

"Plenty," he said. "I never thought a guy could be beat to death with words."

"That's because you're not married," I said. Behind, I couldn't see any Department car following. "Sam could have killed him," I said, "couldn't he?"

"No. And especially, he couldn't kill somebody he loved. For anybody he liked, Sam would do anything and take anything."

Suddenly he said, "I can't figure you. I just can't figure a private eye doing *anything* for nothing."

"Don't you believe in justice?"

"It's a word," he said. "I've been drowned in words all evening. Tell me why you picked me up, Puma,"

"For information," I said. "If it was money I was after, you've got to remember I could be holding your wallet right this minute. You gave it to me. What changed your mind about me?"

"I'm sorry," he said. "Let's get to my joint for that beer. Turn right at the second light from here.

It was a nice apartment. With a pool and a view of town, complete with hi–fi and bar.

"This," Leo said bitterly, "is the kind of deal Sam has to louse up. It's back to grubbing for both of us."

"Not Sam," I said. "Not unless we can clear him."

He looked up from punching holes in the tops of the beer cans. "You want to clear him? Is that why you want to find him?"

"Why else?"

He shrugged. "To nail him, to get yourself in good with the Department." He brought me a can of beer. "What makes you think we have to find him to clear him?"

"Think," I said. "Sit down and have a sip of beer and think. I'm sure the obvious will occur to you. Think of Sam and the kind of guy he is and the obvious will slap you in the face."

He sat down and sipped the beer and wrinkled his brow. "I'm kind of dumb," he said.

In a few minutes, he said, "Damn it, maybe you got something. It's just the kind of dumb thing Sam would do if he was conned right."

I nodded.

"Well," he said, "where do we start?"

"With Sam. Where is he?"

"I don't know. So help me. He promised to phone me at a certain bar at mid–night." He looked at his watch. "That's an hour and a half away. What do we do until then?"

"We could look up somebody who must have been lying," I said, "and find out why."

He nodded, staring at me. Then, "Puma, you wouldn't cross me, would you? Sam's a hot–head, but the best friend I got in the world."

I returned his stare. "Do you know who my best friend is?"

"Abrams?"

I nodded.

"Jeez," he said. "You are something. Maybe that justice isn't only a word with you —"

We found out about the lie and it was eleven–twenty. We came out to my Plymouth and Leo said, "How do we know we're not being followed? We go to that bar and the cops might put a tap on the wire when I get the call, and that'll nail Sam for sure. I hate to take the chance, Joe."

"Where's your car?" I asked him.

"At the apartment house. They got a basement garage there."

"With only one exit?"

"No, there's one that opens onto the alley, too."

"Okay," I said, "we go to your place, park my heap in front as though we're going upstairs to wait for Sam. But instead we pile into your car and go out the alley. That ought to work."

That's the way we did it, and when we got to the bar out in Santa Monica, I would have given odds that we were in the clear.

It was a quarter to twelve when we got there, a quiet place, famous for its steaks and almost completely masculine clientele. *Really* masculine, I mean, not what you're thinking.

I made a call and then we waited for Sam's.

Leo said, "If it works and he comes, he's going to be damned mad to learn we double–crossed him. He can be unreasonable — and violent."

"He could get killed, resisting arrest, too," I pointed out. "And Sam's the boy who'd resist it."

At ten to twelve, the phone rang in the booth and Leo waved at the bartender, "I'm expecting it." He went into the booth and closed the door behind him.

When he came out again, in a few minutes, he was sweating. He said quietly, "That's the first time I ever lied to him. Jeez, he's going to hate me."

"Is he coming?"

"In a couple minutes. He must be close."

He came through the doorway not three minutes later. We were in a booth, protected from the rest of the barroom by an el, and he came directly there.

He sat down and Leo shoved his untouched drink over toward him. Sam took a deep swallow and asked, "Why'd she confess, the poor kid?"

"She hasn't, yet," I said.

Sam's shocked gaze turned toward Leo. "You lied to me —"

Leo nodded. "But she's going to confess, Sam. She couldn't leave it the way it was. She had to bring in a girlfriend to swear she'd seen her at *Bullock's* this afternoon. The girlfriend is bound to crack; too many people know *she* wasn't at *Bullock's* today. The cops haven't got to her yet, because they think you're the answer to all their problems, and they've neglected the others."

"You lied to me," Sam said again, and glowered at both of us.

"This girl friend," I said, "this Lois Ogren got very talkative after she warmed up. You knew Jean was in love with Fairchild, didn't you?"

"That's a lie," Sam said, "A dirty lie."

I shook my head.

He finished the drink and glared at me. "I'll tell you how much she loved him — she borrowed my gun to protect herself against him. She had to go up to his house to see him about something and she asked if she could borrow it, because he'd been making too damned many advances lately and he was getting impossible to handle. That's how much she loved him — she didn't want any part of him."

"Sam," I said gently, "you've been conned but good. And then you took off to make it look like you were the killer? Why? If she killed in self defense, why?"

"To give her time to get organized. I didn't want her railroaded. And I knew I'd never get the gas chamber, not with that medical discharge the lawyer could use to prove me incompetent."

"She conned you, Sam. Lois told us about the abortion Jean had and Fairchild paid for. Would he pay for an abortion if it wasn't his kid?" His face whitened and his hand tightened on the glass in front of him. "Damn you, Puma —"

I said, "She killed Fairchild because he had a new favorite. He'd promised to marry her and now she was just another one of his discarded dames. Well, I don't blame her for killing him, but I do despise her for using you as a patsy. These are all things we intend to prove, Sam."

"You can't," he said. "It's all out of your filthy mind. You're trying to trap me. I don't believe you," he said. "I don't —"

"Here she comes now," I interrupted. "Ask her."

Her eyes were hard, as she came around the el. She was wearing a green cashmere coat and carrying a saddle–leather handbag. Her voice was husky. "Sam, for heaven's sake, get out of town. Don't you realize the risk you're taking?"

"They told me you'd confessed," he said. "They trapped me."

The eyes were even harder. "*I'd* confessed? To what? Are you out of your mind again, Sam? You told me you were cured. You told me you were all right."

He stared at her, unbelieving.

I said, "Save it, Jean." And added the lie. "We've already talked to Doctor Retesack. He's admitted the abortion."

Her face was rigid. "I don't believe you. And even if he did, what has that to do with murder?"

"It's a reason, it's a motive?"

She looked at me coolly. "Is it? Nobody can prove it was Paul's baby. That's all beyond proving."

"We can prove he paid for it."

For a moment there was a silence as she glared at us.

And then Sam said, "Nobody will have to prove anything. I've heard it from her own mouth, now. I've got the story and she's probably still got the gun."

Another moment of silence, of motionless waiting and she said, "I certainly have," and she started to open her handbag.

She only had the gun halfway out when Leo clipped her on the chin.

Grierson said, "All right, I guess that's good enough." He glanced casually through my typed statement. "She's starting to crack. And that Ogren girl is giving us enough, anyway. And then her having the gun and all, well —" He shrugged.

"Well, *thanks*, is that what you meant to say, Lieutenant?"

His smile was weary. "Okay — thanks. If you weren't such a lippy bastard, we'd all probably like you a lot better, Puma." He stretched. "Abrams is out in the hall. Do you want to go out by another door?"

"Hell, yes," I said, and stood up. "Do you think he would have saved my life, thirteen years ago, if he knew some day I'd send his sister to the gas chamber?"

Grierson shrugged again. "Who knows? A man does what he has to, I guess. How about Minash and Kranski? They're out there in the hall, too."

"Could you tell them I'll meet them in the car, Lieutenant? We're going out to hang one on. Don't let Don Abrams hear you tell them though."

He stood up, too. "Okay, I guess I can do that much for you." He paused. "Be careful, though, if you pick up any dames, won't you? I'd kind of miss you around here, Puma."

I promised him I'd be careful.

Stolen Star

I got into the mess late and not by choice. The local papers were giving it more ink than the Japanese surrender and I can imagine it was front page news from coast to coast.

Laura Spain had been kidnapped. Laura wasn't the youngest star in the business but she still had her figure and enough looks to pull all the men over thirty into any theatre showing one of her pictures.

The thing had a bad odor right from the first ransom note. The local police are skeptical about publicity shenanigans; a jewel robbery out here is almost certain to be no more than that. But kidnapping?

It didn't seem logical that a sane citizen would go to that extreme for free ink, but then a sane citizen wouldn't fill a swimming pool with champagne for a party, either. And Laura had done that a few years back.

So the F.B.I. wasn't called in, but on the other hand, the local gendarmes didn't treat it as a gag, either. And woe to Laura, the D.A. was quoted as saying, if she had dreamed it up. She would be prosecuted to the limit.

The thing that made it seem fishy was the modest ransom the kidnappers were asking — twenty–five thousand — and the fact that Laura had been snatched right at her house and had evidently taken a rather complete wardrobe along for the trip. There were three dogs in that house, Dobermans, and two servants, one of them an ex–pug.

Well, it made good bar talk and there were as many opinions as there were people to voice them and nobody was shy about voicing them. It became a farce, almost, and kidnapping is nothing that should ever seem humorous. There are too many crack–pots who get ideas from the kind of spread this thing was getting.

Forty–eight hours after the first news break on the story, Hal Slotkin came to see me. Hal is a divorce and criminal lawyer, about as rich a barrister as this town knows and we had never done business before. And he didn't *send* for me; he *came*. He must have been worried.

"Mr. Puma," he said, "I have known of you for some time, by reputation."

"And I you, sir," I said. "Won't you sit down?"

He took a good look around my inexpensive office before sitting down, as though he'd been searching all the places that might hold a tape recorder.

He sat down and sighed. "Your ethics, I've been told, are unassailable and your courage immense." He was a short, fat man, and his language seemed a little pompous. But I was impressed, nevertheless. In a jungle, he had become king of his tribe.

"My ethics have been stretched from time to time," I told him, "and my courage ebbs with the years." Gawd, now he had me doing it.

He rubbed his fat neck with a pudgy hand and stared wearily at the bamboo shades behind me. Match–stick bamboo, Sears–Roebuck, five bucks a panel. He said, "It's been a hectic two days, hasn't it?"

"Not for me, sir," I said, "but as Miss Spain's attorney, I imagine you've had a busy time of it."

He nodded. "If I had it to do over, I'd have gone in for corporation law." He sighed. "Or probate work. I might have made a few dollars less, but I wouldn't be pampering my ulcers."

I didn't comment. I can never find the proper comment for the wailings of the wealthy. I tried to put some sympathy into my smile.

2.

He said suddenly, "How would you like to earn a thousand dollars for two hours work?"

"It would depend upon the work, Mr. Slotkin," I answered.

"Can you guess?" he asked.

"Delivering the ransom money? I thought you'd lost contact with Miss Spain's abductors."

"We had. Until half an hour ago."

"Have you informed the police?"

He shook his head. "I was expressly warned not to."

I said, "Mr. Slotkin, acting as an intermediary in a kidnapping case would not only lose me my license, it could put me in jail."

"Not if you're employed by Hal Slotkin," he said, "not in this town. I could include the Chief in our confidence, if you want me to."

"That puts a different light on it," I said, "but not the whole light. How do I know I don't get bumped? If Miss Spain is dead, the boys who killed her aren't going to hesitate about wiping out one poor private investigator. I might be able to finger them later, they'll realize."

"All right," he said, "I'll make it two thousand dollars." He shrugged. "It's not my money."

I chuckled. "You figure I wouldn't commit suicide for one thousand, but I might for two?"

"Somebody has to deliver the money," he said matter of factly. "If you don't want the job, I'll go elsewhere. If I'm forced to, by your refusal, I'm sure you'll keep this a secret until Miss Spain is safely home again."

"Of course," I said. "Give me a moment to think."

He nodded, and leaned his head back in the chair and closed his eyes. His face was pale and his neck flabby. He didn't look at all like the courtroom tiger of his legend.

I thought about the brake job I needed and the new tires, about the five hundred I owed the bank and the new suit I should have.

"Well?" Slotkin asked.

"Okay," I said. "What's the deal?"

"It's in the desert," he said, "near Canyon Springs. Flat country and they can see if they're being crossed, I suppose. By the way, don't get cute with this, will you? Just deliver the money and pick up Miss Spain."

"Of course," I said. "Why would I get cute with it?"

"I don't know. Maybe to grab a headline. That seems to be a disease in this town." He handed me a slip of paper. "Here's the address." He paused. "Don't deliver the money until you see Miss Spain, *alive*."

"And if she's not in sight, I still get paid."

"You get paid right now," he said, and took out a checkbook.

He must have been sure they were going to deliver the girl or he never would have paid in advance. Which smelled a little, but it also led me to think I wasn't likely to run into any violence. And yet, I couldn't believe if the whole thing was a hoax that a man of Hal Slotkin's eminence would be a party to it. He had a reputation as a tricky operator but all his tricks were well within the law.

Any reservations still in my mind were quieted by the slip of paper he handed me next. *Pay to Joseph Puma, two thousand and no/hundredths.*

He told me I was to pick up the ransom money at his office in an hour. It would be a fairly bulky package as they were all small, old bills.

The bank was still open; I went over immediately and deposited the check. And then I phoned Tommy Verch. Slotkin hadn't stipulated I was to go alone, and Tommy could use the business. His office is in Venice and he doesn't get the carriage trade I do.

I said, "How much would you charge me to ride along on a little job tonight?"

"What kind of job?"

"I hate to say over the phone, but it includes delivering some money."

A pause, and then, "A headline story, Joe?"

"That's right."

Another pause, and he said, "You know my rate."

"Yes, but I'm getting two thousand dollars for the job."

"I'll up my rate then. Two hundred all right?"

"That's more than fair."

"You want me armed, Joe."

"Absolutely," I said.

"I'm on the way over," he said.

When he got there, I said, "Maybe you'd better eat, first. I'm going over to pick up the money. When I get back, I'll park in the small lot behind the building here. You climb into the back while I go over to eat. That way, if I'm being watched, nobody will see you get into the back of my car. Once out in the desert, you can sit up again. Clear?"

He nodded. "You looking forward to trouble, Joe?"

I shrugged.

He said, "I'll go and eat." He went out, a stocky man of medium height with a flat and broken nose looking out of place in his thin face.

3.

Slotkin wasn't at his office when I got there; I was handed a package by one of his young associates. I'd brought a small grip and I carried the money with me when I went to eat.

The afternoon *Mirror–News* informed me that there were no new developments in the Laura Spain kidnapping. The earlier police skepticism, according to this piece, had disappeared and anxiety about Miss Spain's safety was growing. If nothing new developed by tomorrow morning, the F.B.I. would be called in.

One of Laura's former husbands was quoted as saying he still thought it was a gag. But that could be just the bitter words of a poor loser.

When I got back to the car, I could see that the blanket had been pulled down from the back seat. I got in, started the engine, and asked, "All safe, Tommy?"

"Roll her," he said. "It's the first job I've had in a month."

I rolled her, heading for the Hollywood Freeway which would take me to Highway 99, which would take me to the desert and Canyon Springs. The place I was supposed to make rendezvous was on this end of town. The road leading to it would be visible for miles, and I was supposed to arrive before dusk, just before dusk.

Delivery would be made as close to dark as possible, so they could use its cover to get away. But light was necessary for them to be able to watch all the roads. It would require good timing, and I hoped my tires would hold up. A flat would throw the time–table off.

Once off the freeway, I watched to see if any cars persisted in following, slowing and speeding in turn. When I was sure we were unwatched, I told Tommy, "You can sit up now, boy, for a while."

He grunted and came up off the floor, relaxing in the back seat. He said, "Where's the pick–up?"

"Right outside of Canyon Springs."

"Good pick for a desert spot," he commented. "They can go four directions from there. How do you figure it, Joe, a gag?"

I shrugged.

He leaned back. "Well, as long as I'm getting only ten percent of the money, I hope I only get ten percent of the lead they throw."

"It was your price, Tommy," I reminded him.

"I know, I know — and very welcome. So starving to death is no easier than being shot. Onward, moneybags."

I looked into the rear–view mirror to see if his comment had meaning, but he looked content and peaceful, his eyes closed. Well, if things went right, I could slip him an extra fifty.

I was doing a steady sixty–five, but traffic went blasting past me. The safest driving in the world should be in the desert, with its unlimited vision, but it had a horrible safety record.

I hit Beaumont at about the proper time and turned south a few miles beyond, down a less traveled road. Nobody followed. To the west and north, the mountains were beginning to show shadows, beginning to take the glare out of the sun.

In the back seat, Tommy stirred, took his .38 from its shoulder holster and spun the cylinder. He replaced it and said, "Maybe I'd better get out of sight again; this road is kind of deserted."

I nodded agreement.

He said, "If you want, you can give me a signal when you see the girl. I guess I could show after that, couldn't I?"

"Why antagonize them?" I asked. "If I need you to come up gunning, I'll holler."

A silence, and then he said, "You nervous, Joe?"

I nodded.

"Me, too," he said, and went down below the blanket on the floor.

We were coming to a crossroad now, a two lane asphalt strip that led east to Canyon Springs. A State Patrol car was parked here and I was glad Slotkin had paid me in advance. Because it could easily be a stake–out or a road block. And if it was, the kidnappers would certainly be alerted.

The car was off the road, over on the sand, and both troopers were sitting in the front seat. I slowed, waiting for a signal from them, but none came. I turned east on the crossroad, keeping a careful eye on them in the mirror.

Their car didn't move. I said to Tommy, "Just passed a parked State Patrol car. It might be a coincidence."

"I get my dough either way, remember," he said.

I didn't answer him. Ahead, the first buildings of Canyon Springs were coming into view. Far behind, the police car was still immobile. The purple dusk of the desert was shrouding the harshness of the landscape and one early star was visible in the east. We went over a culvert spanning a dry arroyo and ahead I could see a solitary cactus with a sign pointing toward some buildings to the right. Air–conditioned cabins, the sign read.

4.

There was a man standing next to the sign and he wore the red jockey cap I was to look for. I slowed, stopped and opened the door on the right side.

"I've brought the money," I called.

He was a thin man, fairly tall, with a long, narrow face and grayish stubble in the black of his week–old beard. He came over and climbed into the seat beside me.

"Up past the cabins," he said.

"There's a State Patrol car back at the turn off," I told him. "What gives? I don't want to get into trouble."

"It's okay," he said. "Past those cabins, to the end of this road."

The cabins looked deserted as we went by, old–fashioned adobe buildings that probably couldn't compete today. Up the road, now, I could see a solitary, larger cabin, with two cars parked around in back of it. I couldn't read the license plates from here and by the time I got to the cabin, the cars would be out of sight behind it. Well, I wasn't being paid to learn anything.

I said, "I see Miss Spain before you see a nickel. I see her alive."

"Hell, yes." He chuckled. "But what if I told you to go to hell. What could you do?"

"I couldn't tell you right now. I'd have to decide about that when the situation came up."

"You armed, shamus?"

"Always," I told him. "Even on a publicity romp like this, I figured a gun wouldn't hurt."

"I'll take the gun," he said.

"No, you won't. The money's right there, all in small and dirty bills, like you wanted it. When Miss Spain comes with me, that goes with you, and everybody wins."

"The broad isn't here," he said. "Do you think we're crazy? When you hand over the money, we send out the signal and she'll be released. How crazy do you think we are, sitting here in the middle of nowhere with a broad that hot?"

"All right, then, I'll wait until I get word from her attorney that she's safe. Then you get your money. Okay?"

"Hand over your gun," he said, "and stop yacking, or I'll put a hole in you. Get to it, man."

"Okay, Tommy," I said clearly. "Now would be the time."

The man next to me whirled around — just in time for Tommy to press the barrel of his .38 in the middle of the man's forehead. Tommy said lightly, "Don't even blink, skinny. Don't even breathe heavy. I'm nervous."

The man stared and some obscene muttering came from his thin throat. I had my gun out, now, and I relieved him of the one in his hand. It was an army .45.

I asked, "Is Miss Spain here, or isn't she?"

"No," he said hoarsely. "Look, maybe I talked too rough. She's going to be all right, believe me. And there are plenty of guns in that house; so don't think you can get away with anything."

"I came to deliver the money," I said. "I came in good faith. Now listen care-fully — I'm going to let you go up to the house. One of your men can come with me to Canyon Springs, one unarmed man. I'll phone Slotkin from there. The second he hears Miss Spain is released, I'll hand this man this satchel containing twenty-five grand. I'll even give him your gun back. My job was to deliver the money, not you hoodlums, and I'll go through with it. Is that clear?"

His eyes went from me to Tommy and back. "There's Tommy guns in that house; there's sawed offs."

"And there's you," I pointed out, "sitting here courting a hole in your head. It's a hell of a situation, isn't it? Just because there's no honor among thieves."

Silence all around for a few moments.

Then I said, "I'm going to turn around so we're headed the way we came. I'm going to let you go — unarmed — up to the house and deliver my message. If you're not back in three minutes, with your hands well away from your body and empty, I'm going to go into town and get a lot of law out here." I nodded toward the door on his side. "Get out and go to the house, *now*."

He got out and went trotting toward the house as I turned around and pulled a couple hundred feet down the road from the place. Tommy stayed in the back, watching everything through the rear window.

Without turning around, he said, "Gutty, aren't you? Do you believe him about the fire–power they're holding?"

"No. The rube sees too many movies. Old ones, on TV. Tommy guns, cripes!"

"Maybe, maybe," Tommy said doubtfully. "I still don't like it; Joe."

"It's rougher than I figured," I admitted. "I think I'll give you an extra fifty, Tommy."

"That's white of you," he said. "I wish that bastard would come out again."

"Maybe they'll send somebody else."

"Hell, no. We've already seen *him*; the fewer we can identify later, the better for them."

Tommy was right; in another minute, the same thin and grizzled gent came down the road toward the car, his hands well out from his body. I could see no sign of life from the cabin behind him.

He got in as I opened the door. He said, "I'll go with you. If you try to cross us, those guys will kill you, sure as you're alive this second. They've got your license number and they can find out who you are."

"I'll save them the trouble," I said. "My name's Joe Puma and my office is in Beverly Hills. If everything is okay, the money in that satchel is yours. You can take it out and check it right now."

"Don't worry," he said. "It's there. Or Slotkin will get what I promised you."

"It's my satchel," I said. "When I get the word, you'll get the money, but not the satchel."

He shook his head. "A cheap private eye, worrying about his crummy suitcase. What are you getting for the job, Sherlock, twenty bucks?"

"Fifteen and the gas," I said, "and twenty cents for every shell I have to use."

Tommy said, "Keep a civil tongue in your head, skinny. I don't like lippy hoodlums."

"Go easy on him, Tommy," I said. "The old gent's scared. He's lost his moxie and he's scared."

5.

Next to me, the thin man smiled and I thought there was some anticipation in it. I was back on the two lane asphalt road that led into Canyon Springs and to our right was a modern motel and restaurant with a mammoth parking lot.

I said, "You stay in the car with skinny, Tommy. I'll take the money inside until I get in touch with Slotkin."

"Right," he said. "Park out of view of the highway, though."

I pulled around behind the el the motel office made and took the ignition keys. It was almost dark now, and all the motel lights were on. I didn't want to bring skinny into that bright office; just seeing him would make any desk clerk in the country phone for the police.

I had the unlisted number Slotkin had given me and I phoned him collect. He must have been sitting on the phone; he answered immediately.

"Puma," I said. What's the word?"

"Give them the money," he said. "She phoned me two minutes ago from a drugstore in Hollywood."

I told him okay and hung up. I went out to the car wondering how the police would like this; she had been free and in a public place *before* her abductors had taken delivery of the ransom.

I had an urge to keep the money and turn Skinny over to the local law, but I'd been paid to do a job, not act like a citizen. I wasn't proud of myself as I opened the door of the car.

"Well?" Skinny said.

"The money's yours, boy. Should I leave you here with it, or do you want me to take you back to the house?"

He smiled in the reflected light from the motel office. "Leave me here; you've been followed all the way."

I gave him the money, keeping the grip. He tucked the package under his arm and said, "Drive careful, shamus. There's a lot of desert ahead of you." He climbed out of the car and headed across the parking lot toward the road.

We watched him approach a three–year–old Mercury on the other side of the street. Tommy said, "Ornery bastard, isn't he? I don't think he likes me."

"We'll never see him again, probably," I said. "Want to climb up in front now?"

He shook his head. "I think I'll try to get some shut–eye. I'll curl up on the back seat."

The Merc was still parked at the curb when we headed out of town. It was dark now, and traffic would be light until we got back on 99. The state patrol car was no longer at the corner.

Easy money, I thought. *But if the police swallowed this as a legitimate snatch, I'd have to believe that Slotkin owned the Department. It smelled every way but right. So, what was all that to me? I was paid.*

It continued to bother me.

A half mile past the cut–off, I saw the lights beginning to move up from behind. For no reason at all, I said to Tommy, "What do you think Skinny meant about all that desert ahead of us?"

"Just words," Tommy said drowsily. "He had to sound tough."

"A car turned off back there from the Canyon Springs road," I told him, "and he's catching up. Be careful."

He sat up. "Why? Look, we paid, didn't we?"

"Sure. But both of us could put the finger on Skinny. I don't think he meant it that way. You were along, which he didn't expect. And he's one of those pro–fessional tough guys, remember."

Behind, the car's headlights grew closer. Another car was coming from the opposite direction, and I told Tommy, "See if you can get a look at that car behind in the headlights of this one coming. See if it's the Merc."

A few seconds after the car went past, Tommy said, "It's the Merc, all right, Joe. I'm going to lower this back window."

"Don't," I said. "If they shoot at us, it's better to have the windows closed. And don't you do a thing, Tommy, unless they shoot at us."

"I won't shoot unless they do," he said. "But I'm going to lower this window."

"As they start to go by," I said, "I'll hit the brakes. Be ready for that."

The lights grew and now they darted back at me from the rear–vision mirror. I waited until they began to swing out to pass before taking my foot off the accelerator.

I misjudged the speed of the car behind; it was next to us before I could touch the brake. I heard the blast of the sawed–off, and then another shot, but heard no answering shot from the rear seat before the third shot hit my shoulder.

The shock of it made me twist the wheel and the Plymouth went screaming to the right. I almost caught it in time. I would have caught it in time if the arroyo hadn't been there, and the thick concrete wall of the culvert.

The right front wheel caught that wall and we went careening end for end across the road and into the ditch on the other side. The last thing I remember was flying through the air, free of the car, my shoes lost from the impact. *The sand could be soft*, I thought; *the softness of the sand could keep me alive.*

6.

I didn't regain consciousness for two days. When I did, I was in a Los Angeles hospital and one of Hal Slotkin's associates was sitting in a chair next to the bed.

He smiled at me. "Feeling better?"

"I don't know. I don't know how I felt before. Where am I?"

He told me.

I said, "How about Tommy?"

"Tommy? Do you mean Mr. Verch?"

"That's right."

"He's — dead. He died before the car turned over."

I closed my eyes.

The young lawyer said, "Don't worry about a thing, now. All your bills here will be taken care of, and your car's almost all rebuilt by now. That'll be taken care of, too."

"Why?" I asked.

He smiled at me. "Why not?"

"I've a lot of regard from Mr. Slotkin," I said, "but I never for a second confused him with Santa Claus."

The young man smiled knowingly. "Maybe it's not his money. That needn't concern you. Your concern is to get well. Don't worry, now."

It concerned me. Tommy Verch was dead and that had to concern me. But I didn't argue with the young man. I never argue with anyone *before* they pick up the tab.

I'd been brought here from the hospital in Riverside, and I could guess I'd been brought here so it would be convenient for one of the Slotkin young men to remain at my bedside. I relaxed and tried to regain my strength and forget Tommy Verch.

The nurse brought me all the papers; that was another expense somebody was shouldering, a private nurse. I had good coverage in all the papers.

And then, as frosting for this expensive cake, I was honored with a visit from Laura Spain. Complete with five photographers, seven reporters, two publicity men and a Slotkin representative. If she was coming to my bedroom as reward, you'd think the least she could have done would be to come alone.

She was certainly a beauty, and her advertised charm was not over–rated. If she had come alone, I think I might have forgotten Tommy Verch.

The morning after her visit, I walked out of the hospital with a Slotkin man, and my car, looking better than ever, was ready for me on the hospital parking lot.

There, the Slotkin man said, "If we can be of any further service, don't hesitate to call on us, will you?"

"I won't," I promised. "Maybe you could give me the West Side Station, huh, for my very own?"

He frowned. "I don't understand, Mr. Puma."

"Yes, you do," I said. "We all understand each other. Take care of yourself, young fellow." I patted his shoulder and got into my car.

He was still standing there, watching me, when I turned into the traffic heading west.

At my office, I checked the week's accumulation of mail and wrote checks for a couple of bills I'd owed for some time. I was writing a letter to my aunt when the phone rang.

It was Hal Slotkin. He said, "I've heard that you're not happy. Would you mind telling me why?"

"This phoney kidnapping rankles in my small soul, I guess, Mr. Slotkin."

"What makes you think it was phoney?"

I gave him all the reasons. The too early release of Miss Spain, Skinny not counting the ransom money and not being worried about the State Police and his not even looking in the back of my car before climbing into it.

"So, maybe he was an amateur."

"Maybe. An *armed* amateur, and a real tough, cool one. I don't think he was an amateur thug, though this may have been his first snatch."

Silence, and then, "Well, I only represented a client. I'm not involved personally. You believe that, don't you?"

"I think I do, Mr. Slotkin."

"So what difference does it make? You got paid and you're not the police."

"In a way, I'm a policeman. I'm licensed by the state. But that isn't important. Mr. Slotkin, the important thing is that a man is dead."

"And that's important to you?"

"Yes. Isn't it to you?"

"It used to be," he said. "I suppose it should be." He sighed. "Well, I guess we have nothing else to say to each other, Mr. Puma."

"I guess not," I said. "Thanks for the business, anyway."

I hung up and sat there, angry for no reason I could isolate, burning. I was no knight; I didn't even have a horse. Why should I burn?

I phoned Slotkin again, intending to ask for Miss Spain's unlisted phone number. His office girl said Mr. Slotkin was not in and Miss Spain's phone number was never given out to anybody.

Well, I knew where she lived; I went down and climbed into the rebuilt Plymouth.

7.

The house was low and probably the architect had tried to give the impression of a sprawling, western ranch house. What emerged from the drawing board was a low, red, shake–roofed home for a Hollywood star who entertains informally.

The maid asked, "Did you have an appointment, Mr. Puma?"

"No, I didn't. I'm just returning Miss Spain's recent visit to me. She didn't have an appointment that day, either."

The maid frowned. "Are you the — the —"

I nodded.

"One moment, please," she said.

In a few minutes, she came back to say, "This way, please."

It was a sunny day; Laura Spain was pool–side in a Bikini. Her body belonged to a younger woman, her face was slick with oil.

"Mr. Puma," she said, smiling. "How pleasant."

I stood at the pool's edge and looked down. "Is this where you had the champagne?"

"That's right. Though the story was exaggerated. We only filled it to a depth of three feet."

She was sprawled on a pad; I sat down next to her and said, "I've been thinking about this kidnapping, Miss Spain. The whole business smells of fraudulence."

Her young–old face stiffened. "Really? And why?"

I gave her the same reasons I'd given Slotkin.

She reached out and took a package of cigarettes from a low stand nearby. I lighted one for her. She looked at the water, and said, "I've no idea what the standard operating procedure for kidnappers is. You might be right about their lack of experience. But even if it was a monstrous publicity stunt, why are you concerned?"

I said wearily, "It's a sad civilization that makes me keep explaining that *a man is dead.*"

"Millions are," she said reasonably. "Thousands of men die every day, I imagine."

"Not violently in my car, working for me," I answered. "Don't you feel *any* responsibility for his death?"

She nodded. "Some. What can I do about it?"

"You could tell me who the men were you hired. I'm sure you didn't expect them to extend their services to murder."

Her face was stone. "I didn't hire any men. It was not a publicity stunt, Mr. Puma. And even if it were, would you actually expect me to implicate myself publicly?"

I took a deep breath. "No. But I had to take the chance." I stood up. "Well, I'll know the man if I ever see him again. And when I do, I'll know how to work the rest of it out of him."

She shook her head. "You sound absurd. You sound like Dick Tracy. This is 1957, Mr. Puma."

"Of course," I said. "I wasn't thinking of violence. I was thinking of a deal with him."

Her eyes were blank. "You were thinking of violence. That's your kind of operation, I would bet."

I said, "If you're still in touch with them, warn them to stay out of my way."

"I don't know them," she said lightly, "but from what I've seen of them, I can imagine you don't frighten them much. Good day, Mr. Puma. Don't hurry back."

I went out, fully aware that I had learned nothing, but I *had* left a message. And if she were involved and did forward the message, I wouldn't have to look for her abductors. They would find me.

Which was emotional thinking, adolescent thinking, but I wanted to meet Skinny again so bad I could taste it. And Miss Spain had set a wave of violence into motion with her fraudulent stunt; she couldn't escape the responsibility of that. Which absolved me from any concern for what justice might do to her career.

I had a pair of names and two addresses still to check. The first one I went to was a four unit apartment building on Olympic in Santa Monica. This was the address of Laura Spain's second husband. He was an assembler at Douglas Aircraft now, and the manager of the apartment told me he wouldn't be home until 4:30.

Her first husband was undoubtedly also working, but the place he worked wasn't far from here. He was a car salesman for a Venice Ford agency.

He was a big man, almost as big as I am. He wore an Italian silk suit and a hand–painted tie and an air of complete disillusionment. His face was florid, the face of a heavy drinker, but still handsome in a completely virile way. He was on the used–car lot when I drove up.

He said, "I'm due for a coffee break in five minutes. Hang around and we'll go across the street."

Five minutes later, in a crummy greasy spoon on the busiest street in Venice, Jack Dugan, Laura Spain's first husband, gave me the story of that early romance.

She was nineteen when he met her, a refugee from Oklahoma, a thin, tough, very attractive girl whose innocence was at least five years behind her even then.

I said, "I never got that picture from the fan magazines; I had the feeling she came out here clean as new snow and won a beauty contest."

He smiled. "Sure. Not that I'm rapping Laura, understand. She still sends me a buck now and then for auld lang syne and she's bailed me out of some monumental drunks. There's nothing cheap about the girl. It's just that she has this damned driving urge to stay way up there on top."

"We built a civilization on it," I said. "Knowing her, would she have the guts to pull a phoney kidnapping for ink?"

"For publicity," he said, "Laura would arrange to have Eisenhower kidnapped." He shook his head musingly. "And you know, she might get away with it, at that?"

"What was her family like? Did you ever meet them?"

He had. And he told me about them and I wondered why a man who still got a "buck now and then" should go into such detail to hand a private operative a case against his benefactor.

And because I wondered, I asked him. "Why give me all this? How can you benefit from giving me all this?"

"Benefit?" he said. "Look, I'm a drunk and a pitch man and a lot of things that aren't exactly admirable. But I'm still a human being, right?"

"Right," I agreed. "So —?"

"So a man is dead, isn't he? Isn't it important that a man is dead?"

"It always has been to me," I assured him, "but I was beginning to think I was old–fashioned." I smiled at him. "I'll pay for the coffee. And when I need a new car, I'll head this way."

"Do that," he said. "I might even rob you less than the others. Who knows?"

I left him, and went back to the office. I didn't think there was any need to look up Laura's second husband. She'd been young when she had married her first; he had her true story, the story she'd told him before she realized that in Hollywood, backgrounds are invented, not lived. He could be quite possibly the only man in the town who had her true story. Until now.

8.

I sat in the quiet office and nothing happened. I went out for lunch and came back and the place was still quiet. I had a hunch now who the skinny man was, and maybe if I sent the hunch out on the grapevine, it would stir up some action. But if I sent it out on the grapevine in this town, the damage would be done but Tommy Verch's killer might still be free.

That blast from the sawed–off had been meant for both of us. He hadn't shot out of pique; he was a pro. He had hoped to kill us both because either of us could identify him.

And if he was a pro, would he come here, into this best–policed town in America, Beverly Hills? There were a number of areas in the county where the police protection is not exceptional; this town would be dangerous hunting grounds. Of course, he didn't lack guts. He had a number of lacks, undoubtedly, but I was sure guts wasn't one.

Why should I sit there burning; solvent, fat and alive? What was Tommy Verch to me? A colleague, a brave and humorous man who lived as honestly as he could in a trade where that wasn't always good business. A man who had been forced to risk his life for two hundred dollars and lose. Tommy Verch was important.

I hadn't put my car on the lot; I'd left it parked right in front of this building so anyone who was interested could see I was in the office. I could have gone home and waited, but I had carpeting on the floor at home and that's harder to clean than the asphalt tile of the office.

The door opened and the hand in my lap stirred. It was Doctor Graves, the young dentist from the office next door. He said, "How about some golf tomorrow afternoon?"

"Maybe. I'll let you know tonight."

"What's the matter?" he asked. "You look nervous."

"I'm still not right. Had a concussion, you know. And a badly strained back."

"Maybe we'd better forget the golf, huh? The back —"

"I'll let you know tonight," I repeated. "How's everything otherwise?"

He yawned. "All right. I'm solvent. I sure get sick of looking into people's dirty mouths, though."

"I get sick of looking into their dirty souls," I said.

He chuckled. "Oi, a philosopher. Two hundred and twenty pounds of thought. You look like you're waiting for Armageddon." He winked. "Call me at home, Joe. Good luck, kid."

I waved my left hand. My right was still in my lap.

My mom had always insisted I had prescience, but my mom had a lot of peasant superstitions. I knew I was more certain than I had a reasonable right to that I'd see Skinny again. I thought I knew who he might be, and if I didn't see him, I would go to the police for help in looking up a picture of the man.

But analyzing what Jack Dugan had told me, it seemed logical that Skinny could be the man I thought he was.

In the windows behind me, the sun was now low and soon the mountains to the west would cut it from view. On the street below, the going–home traffic was noisy.

I heard footsteps in the hall going past; soon the offices on this second floor would all be vacant, all but this one. I lighted a cigarette and turned on the light. I stood by the window a few seconds, looking down at the traffic, and then came back to sit behind the desk again.

How much did Slotkin know? He was no dummy. Of course, in his business, it wasn't always wise to know too much. His job was leading people through the intricacies of the law, not writing biographies of them. He did his job well and was satisfied to stay within the limits of it.

If Tommy Verch hadn't died, I would have been happy to stay within the limits of my job, which had been to deliver some money.

It was dark now and the light overhead wasn't very bright. From the direction of Wilshire, I heard a siren and a clang of a fire truck.

From the hall outside, I thought I heard a pair of footsteps coming up the stairs. They grew louder, and they were very deliberate footsteps and now they were coming down the hall. I sat where I was.

The door opened slowly and quietly. If I hadn't been facing it, I wouldn't have heard it.

Skinny stood there. Shaved and wearing a cheap dark suit and no longer sporting the red jockey cap. His hair was black, not sprinkled with gray as his beard had been. He had one hand in his jacket pocket.

He came in and closed the door quietly behind him. "You made it, eh?" he said. "Tough guy. The way that heap went end for end, I figured you for a goner."

"I'm tough," I said. "Peasant stock. Where's your brother, waiting in the lot behind here, with the engine running?"

His face showed a momentary bewilderment. "Brother —? How'd you guess —" The face went blank again. "You don't know nothing."

"I know there was an Okie named Lorna Spangler who had a couple of no–good brothers," I said evenly. "A couple of punks who thought Dillinger and Nelson and that breed were the greatest Americans of their generation. The girl grew up to become Laura Spain. What happened to the boys? We could find out, I suppose. We could check."

He said nothing, studying me carefully.

"And when Lorna, or Laura, wanted somebody she could trust to pull a cheap publicity stunt, what better pair than these no–good brothers? Man, you've aged a hell of a lot more than she did, haven't you? You didn't take care of yourself like she did, bumming around, knocking off the kind of cheap jobs you're big enough for."

"You're trying to make me hate you, eh?" He looked at me with his head cocked to one side. "Why, shamus? What's your beef? You got paid."

"I'm sick of explaining it," I answered. "Why are you here now?"

"Unfinished business," he said. "You're not much, but you're still a finger."

"I was hoping you'd come," I said. "This thing was getting too personal. It was building into an obsession."

He smiled. "And here I am." In his pocket, his hand moved and came out holding the big .45.

In my lap, my hand moved and my .38 came up swiftly and I just kept pulling the trigger, even though the first shot caught him in the neck.

It's an asphalt tile floor.

His brother was waiting, the engine running, when the local gendarmes put the arm on him. They'd been watching the office, but not looking for a '57 Olds. When they heard the shots, soon after Skinny had come up, they realized the man in the Olds could be their man.

If Skinny hadn't shaved, he would have been picked up downstairs because then they would have seen the gray in his beard. His hair was so black, it didn't seem logical to the men below that his beard could have any gray in it. His hair was touched up, we learned later.

I was glad Skinny had shaved. Because though he was guilty of murder and would have been eligible for the gas chamber, there was a possibility he might have avoided that.

There are an awful lot of smart criminal lawyers in this town.

Just look in the phone book.

My Father, Bill Gault

My dad was born in Milwaukee, and though he spent the last 48 years of his life in California, he never really left the Midwest behind. He maintained a blunt, populist, quintessentially Midwestern approach to the world throughout his life. The protagonists of his work mostly share that approach. They think and talk like he did.

Growing up in the 1920s, Bill Gault — according to his own stories — was a slightly irresponsible young man who took seven years to complete high school, a fact he blamed on the Wisconsin winters. Each year when the snow started to pile up he would ditch school and make his way to Florida, where his mother owned several boarding houses. One December he and three friends drove non–stop from Mil–waukee to Tallahassee, arriving in the 80–degree heat still dressed in raccoon coats and mufflers.

In Milwaukee in the '30s dad worked as an iceman, a hotel manager, and a sole–cutter for Weyenberg shoes. It was while working in the shoe factory in 1936 that he sold his first story, a short–short with a surprise ending, winning a contest put on by a newspaper syndicate. He began selling stories to the pulps. He married briefly, had a son (William Barry), divorced, and in 1942 was married again to my mother, Virginia Kaprelian, daughter of Armenian immigrants. His stories and novels were full of Armenian characters and food, which he loved.

After being drafted and before shipping out to Hawaii with the 166th Infantry in 1944, dad trained at Fort Ord on the Monterey Peninsula, and fell in love with California on the spot. He came west to Pacific Palisades in 1950 with Virginia and one–year–old me, swearing he would never endure another Midwestern winter. He got a job as a mailman, and built a makeshift office in the garage of the house, where in six weeks in 1952 he wrote his first novel, the Edgar–winning *Don't Cry for Me*. Making the leap then to full–time writer, he quit his Post Office job and made his living as a writer for the rest of his life. He never lost the sense that he was a very lucky man to support his family doing what he loved. Countless times I heard him say, "I can't believe they pay me to do this." It was a matter of great pride to him that until the early eighties he sold everything he ever wrote.

When they decided to install parking meters on the streets of Pacific Palisades, dad decided it had become too urban. At meetings of the Fictioneers (an informal writer's group) in LA he had become friends with Willard Temple, who lived 90 miles north in Santa Barbara. After a few visits to the Temples, dad moved the family to Santa Barbara in 1958, convinced it was the most beautiful town on earth. He never changed his mind.

Pop had begun writing juvenile sports novels in the '50s, and as the market for mysteries dried up in the '60's he began writing juveniles exclusively. He thought of his juvenile novels as books for "nonreaders" and loved it when he heard that his titles were among the most stolen from school libraries. If we could just get people to read, he believed, there was hope for the world. He answered every letter he got from his young fans, encouraging them to keep reading.

After we moved to Santa Barbara, dad became a regular at the bi–weekly writers' lunches there, organized by Ken Millar (Ross Macdonald), another Santa Barbaran. He attended just about every session from the late fifties into the eighties. When there was heated discussion in the '70's about inviting women to join the all–male group, pop came down squarely on their side. Generally in a room full of people, daddy would gravitate to the women. Except in the case of writers, where he had no gender preferences, he thought women were more interesting to talk with than men. And he loved to talk — specifically, to argue. Nothing pleased him more than to be in a room with people — preferably other writers — who he could argue with. He loved the give and take, and often blithely switched sides mid–argument if the talk was in danger of turning tepid. Caught in a contradiction, he would tell people cantankerously, "Consistency is the jewel of little minds."

When I was four years old my dad came into my bedroom before I went to sleep, and carefully closed the closet doors. He explained to me that otherwise I might wake up in the night and think my clothes were monsters — an idea that had never occurred to me until that moment. Forty years later, as he entered his eighties, the real monster in daddy's closet turned out to be dementia. The wit and spark that had stimulated, entertained, and irritated everyone who knew him for so long gradually faded. But even as his mental function failed, there were flashes of imagination, and he never forgot he was a writer. He would love it that these stories from his prime are seeing the light again.

Shelley Gault
June 2002